Praise for Lexi Blake and Masters and Mercenaries...

"I can always trust Lexi Blake's Dominants to leave me breathless...and in love. If you want sensual, exciting BDSM wrapped in an awesome love story, then look for a Lexi Blake book."
~Cherise Sinclair USA Today Bestselling author

"Lexi Blake's MASTERS AND MERCENARIES series is beautifully written and deliciously hot. She's got a real way with both action and sex. I also love the way Blake writes her gorgeous Dom heroes--they make me want to do bad, bad things. Her heroines are intelligent and gutsy ladies whose taste for submission definitely does not make them dish rags. Can't wait for the next book!"
~Angela Knight, New York Times Bestselling author

"A Dom is Forever is action packed, both in the bedroom and out. Expect agents, spies, guns, killing and lots of kink as Liam goes after the mysterious Mr. Black and finds his past and his future… The action and espionage keep this story moving along quickly while the sex and kink provides a totally different type of interest. Everything is very well balanced and flows together wonderfully."
~A Night Owl "Top Pick", Terri, Night Owl Erotica

"A Dom Is Forever is everything that is good in erotic romance. The story was fast-paced and suspenseful, the characters were flawed but made me root for them every step of the way, and the hotness factor was off the charts mostly due to a bad boy Dom with a penchant for dirty talk."
~Rho, The Romance Reviews

"A good read that kept me on my toes, guessing until the big reveal, and thinking survival skills should be a must for all men."
~Chris, Night Owl Reviews

"I can't get enough of the Masters and Mercenaries Series! Love and Let Die is Lexi Blake at her best! She writes erotic romantic suspense like no other, and I am always extremely excited when she has something new for us! Intense, heart pounding, and erotically fulfilling, I could not put this book down."

~ Shayna Renee, Shayna Renee's Spicy Reads

"Certain authors and series are on my auto-buy list. Lexi Blake and her Masters & Mercenaries series is at the top of that list... this book offered everything I love about a Masters & Mercenaries book – alpha men, hot sex and sweet loving... As long as Ms. Blake continues to offer such high quality books, I'll be right there, ready to read."

~ Robin, Sizzling Hot Books

"I have absolutely fallen in love with this series. Spies, espionage, and intrigue all packaged up in a hot dominant male package. All the men at McKay-Taggart are smoking hot and the women are amazingly strong sexy submissives."

~Kelley, Smut Book Junkie Book Reviews

Lost and Found

Other Books by Lexi Blake

ROMANTIC SUSPENSE

Masters and Mercenaries
The Dom Who Loved Me
The Men With The Golden Cuffs
A Dom is Forever
On Her Master's Secret Service
Sanctum: A Masters and Mercenaries Novella
Love and Let Die
Unconditional: A Masters and Mercenaries Novella
Dungeon Royale
Dungeon Games: A Masters and Mercenaries Novella
A View to a Thrill
Cherished: A Masters and Mercenaries Novella
You Only Love Twice
Luscious: Masters and Mercenaries~Topped
Adored: A Masters and Mercenaries Novella
Master No
Just One Taste: Masters and Mercenaries~Topped 2
From Sanctum with Love
Devoted: A Masters and Mercenaries Novella
Dominance Never Dies
Submission is Not Enough
Master Bits and Mercenary Bites~The Secret Recipes of Topped
Perfectly Paired: Masters and Mercenaries~Topped 3
For His Eyes Only
Arranged: A Masters and Mercenaries Novella
Love Another Day
At Your Service: Masters and Mercenaries~Topped 4
Master Bits and Mercenary Bites~Girls Night
Nobody Does It Better
Close Cover
Protected: A Masters and Mercenaries Novella
Enchanted: A Masters and Mercenaries Novella
Charmed: A Masters and Mercenaries Novella
Treasured: A Masters and Mercenaries Novella, Coming June 29, 2021

Smoke and Sin
At the Pleasure of the President

URBAN FANTASY

Thieves
Steal the Light
Steal the Day
Steal the Moon
Steal the Sun
Steal the Night
Ripper
Addict
Sleeper
Outcast
Stealing Summer

LEXI BLAKE WRITING AS SOPHIE OAK

Texas Sirens
Small Town Siren
Siren in the City
Siren Enslaved
Siren Beloved
Siren in Waiting
Siren in Bloom
Siren Unleashed
Siren Reborn

Nights in Bliss, Colorado
Three to Ride
Two to Love
One to Keep
Lost in Bliss
Found in Bliss
Pure Bliss
Chasing Bliss
Once Upon a Time in Bliss
Back in Bliss
Sirens in Bliss
Happily Ever After in Bliss
Far From Bliss, Coming 2021

Lost and Found

Masters and Mercenaries:
The Forgotten, Book 2

Lexi Blake

Lost and Found
Masters and Mercenaries: The Forgotten, Book 2
Lexi Blake

Published by DLZ Entertainment LLC
Copyright 2019 DLZ Entertainment LLC
Edited by Chloe Vale
ISBN: 978-1-942297-01-7

This is a work of fiction. Names, places, characters and incidents are the product of the author's imagination and are fictitious. Any resemblance to actual persons, living or dead, events or establishments is solely coincidental.

Acknowledgments

I wrote this book at a difficult time in my life. Someone once told me that mourning takes at least a full year. I worry that all the stories I tell during this first year after losing my mother will have a hint of the grief I feel. But I hope that each one also has a thread of what I've learned in this time. Mourning is a time to reflect, but if you open yourself to the full experience, it can be a time when you discover that love is all around you. My husband has been a rock and my children supportive. My friends drew me close. But someone else showed up, standing at my side and promising to be there for me. When I lost my mom, I found my mother-in-law. We started out rocky, but then sometimes strong females butt heads. She gave birth to the best man I've ever known and she loves my kids with a passion. And I realized she loves me, too.

For what I lost.
For what I found.

For Esta.

Sign up for Lexi Blake's newsletter
and be entered to win a $25 gift certificate
to the bookseller of your choice.

Join us for news, fun, and exclusive content
including free short stories.

There's a new contest every month!

Go to www.LexiBlake.net to subscribe.

Prologue

Sixteen years before
Boston, MA

Becca stared through the window of the hospital room at the woman who'd been her rock all of her life and couldn't quite get her brain to comprehend what was happening. "I don't understand."

Her father's hands were shaking slightly as he put them on her shoulders. "I'm sure you understand far better than anyone else your age could. Sweetie, your mom is sick. Have you noticed how she's been forgetting things? Right before you went to camp there was that day when she couldn't find her keys. She was panicked, remember? You found them in the freezer. Disturbance in cognitive ability is one of the signs of the disease your mom has."

Her mom had laughed it off. She'd also laughed off the incident when she'd completely forgotten where the library was. She'd winked Becca's way and said she needed more caffeine.

Now that she looked back, she could see a hundred small signs.

She hadn't read anything about degenerative mental diseases. She'd spent her summer studying emerging viruses with students five years older than she was. Most of them completely ignored her. Some of the girls were nice though. None of them could really be considered friends.

She wanted her mother's arms around her. How could this be

happening? Tears threatened.

Her father looked down at her and he stopped. "Becca, I'm sorry. I'm not handling this well." He seemed to get choked up for a moment. "I...I don't know if I should be honest with you or protect you for as long as I can."

At least he was feeling something. "Is that why you didn't tell me?"

A woman with dark hair walked up, her eyes wide. Melissa. She'd been with the department for as long as Becca could remember. Melissa babysat when her parents would go out on dates. Her mom would get all dressed up and she would be smiling and happy and her father would promise he wouldn't even look at his phone. Melissa would watch Disney movies with her and tell her to not do her homework for five freaking minutes.

"You told her here?" Melissa hissed the question. "We talked about this, Leland."

Her father flushed and moved them toward the on-call room. "She came on her own. I didn't expect her home until tomorrow. She was supposed to go to her grandmother's for the night but she showed up here."

"I took the subway." She hadn't wanted to go to her grandmother's. She'd been away all summer and she'd wanted to see her mom. It had been easy to change her flight to an earlier one because she'd had cash and a sob story and sounded far older than her years. She'd discovered as long as she talked the talk, most people were ready to believe she was at least sixteen. So much of life, she'd learned, was about walking in like she owned the place.

Her mother had taught her that. Her college professor momma had told her nothing could hold her back.

If you get to the end of the road, my love, build a new one. It will be hard and many people will try to block you, but you build it so the women who come after you have an easier time. I built part of that road and it will be your time to add to it soon. If we all do it, if we're brave enough, we can build one to take us all the way home.

How could she be in a hospital bed?

Melissa frowned at her dad. "Still, you don't tell her like that." She looked back to Becca. "First off, what you did was insanely dangerous. I know you're crazy smart for your age, but you can't do that. Anything could have happened to you."

It seemed like something horrible had happened and it had nothing to do with the fact that she'd managed to navigate the public transit system. It was easy. There was a map and everything. All she'd had to do was buy a ticket and she'd gotten home. When she'd realized no one was there, she'd walked to the hospital her dad worked at. It was only four blocks away and after having spent an entire summer locked in a classroom, it had felt good to be in the sunshine for a while.

Now she wished she was still outside, still in that moment before she realized how everything was crashing around her.

Her father had practically gone white. "God, I hadn't even thought about that."

"She's not an adult, Leland," Melissa said, though not unkindly. "I know it's easy to forget because of how smart she is, but to the world outside she's a kid, and that big brain of hers won't protect her. And you can't protect her from this, but you could have eased the blow."

She tapped on the on-call room door before entering and leaving them out in the hallway. The door closed behind her and she was alone with her father again.

Her dad looked hollow. "I didn't mean to tell you like this. I wanted you to have fun this summer."

He knew her well. Most parents wouldn't think sending her to a university summer camp to learn about emerging viruses would be fun, but her dad got her. So did her mom. They supported her. They gave her what she needed. "How long have you known?"

His steel gray eyes met hers and she could see the guilt there. "Five years. When she first started to show cognitive decline, I ran a DNA test. She tested positive for the markers and we knew her diagnosis. Melissa has been helping us out at home."

The door came open again and a bleary-eyed intern stumbled out, pulling on his shirt. "But my pager didn't go off."

Melissa wasn't taking no for an answer. "You're needed in the ER. Better run, buddy." She reached out and took Becca's hand. "Come in here. We don't need an audience."

The door closed and the three of them were alone.

His eyes were steady as he looked down at her. "I didn't want to interrupt your studies. Neither did your mother. Rebecca, this shouldn't derail you. God, how can it not derail you? It's derailing me. I love your mom. I love you, baby. I don't know how to say it. I want to tell you that she's sick and she's going to get better."

"But you can't. She's got Alzheimer's. She's young for it." She might not have spent much time studying neurological conditions, but she knew this one. She knew the name of the disease that would kill her mother.

"It's early onset," Melissa agreed. "Only about five percent of patients get it this early. Your mom asked me to get some books for you to read. And there are a couple of classes you can take."

She would feel better with a book in her hand. Things might make sense if she could understand what was happening in her mom's head.

Becca went back over the last few years. How could she have missed it? Melissa would come over and stay the night sometimes when her father was on call. She would explain that she didn't have anything better to do, and wasn't it fun to have girl time?

She'd been making sure her mom didn't hurt herself.

"Why is she in the hospital?" It was obvious they'd done a lot to keep this quiet.

"She took a hard fall down the stairs," her father explained. "I think she forgot what she was doing and missed a step. They have to replace her hip. The disease has progressed to the dementia stage. It's not bad yet, but I don't know what to do. She'll have to be in assisted living while she's recovering."

Bile threatened to boil over, the taste sickening in her throat. "You want to put her in a nursing home? I'll take care of her. I'll come home and do it. I've had enough training. What I don't know, I can learn."

She was a prodigy, after all. Oh, her father didn't use that word around her. He claimed it wasn't technically what she was. A genius-level IQ didn't necessarily mean a prodigy. A prodigy was one who excelled in a certain area. Medicine wasn't normally one of those areas, but she knew she could do it. She could certainly take care of her mother.

Her father once told her she was like a superhero, that she could be Super Doc if she tried hard enough. Saving lives in a single bound. She had no idea what a single bound had to do with anything, but her dad had been so happy as he'd said it, she'd pretended to understand his aged pop culture references.

He shook his head. "Absolutely not. You're scheduled for a second summer session. You'll be studying neurology. I thought that was apropos, and perhaps maybe it will help you understand what your mother is going through. You leave in two days."

"No." She couldn't leave.

His jaw clenched. "I'm going to bring your mother home as soon as I can, but you shouldn't see her like that."

"She's my mom. I love her. I should see her every way I can." She stood up to him. They rarely fought, almost never because her father was a softy, but this was one fight she couldn't lose. "I'll take the classes here, but I'm staying home. I can help."

Melissa was suddenly beside her. "And I'm taking a sabbatical."

"We talked about this," her dad began.

"Yes, we did. Sonja and I talked about this," she admitted. "She doesn't want me to give up my life, but taking care of people is my life. Now I have the chance to take care of one of the finest women I've ever met. Do you know the strength she's given me? She got me through my divorce. She helped me walk away from an abusive bastard and find my strength. Now I'm going to give some of it back to her."

Tears rolled down Becca's cheeks and she took Melissa's hand. "Me, too. If you send me away, I'll come back and I'll be by my mom's side. I can do everything I need to do from home. You said I could be anything I wanted to be. I want to be a doctor. I want to help people. I'm going to start with my mother because you always said the best medicine is love."

Her dad lost it. His clipboard dropped and he hit his knees, no longer able to control his grief.

Becca moved in, wrapping her arms around him, and oddly found comfort in knowing she could help.

Thirty minutes later, Melissa guided her to the door of her mom's room. "You sure you don't want me to go in with you?"

"I think Dad needs you more." He was currently in the bathroom washing his face and trying to look professional. "Convince him to bring someone else in. He's too emotional to be on call right now."

Melissa nodded. "I will. I'll order dinner for the two of you and I'll stay here and watch your mom. Pizza okay?"

Anything would taste like cardboard. "Sure. Pepperoni and

mushrooms, please. And thank you. Thanks for helping me convince him to let me stay."

"We'll get through this." Her voice had broken but she cleared her throat. "Don't stay too long. She's on a lot of pain meds."

Becca opened the door and her mother looked up, a smile plastered on her face.

"Hello," she said. "You're young to be a nurse. Are you lost, honey?"

"Mom?"

A cloud crossed her mother's pretty face. "I have a daughter. Her name is Becca but she's only three. Are you lost? We can call someone to help find your mother."

It was already starting. She wanted to run, but she couldn't. This was her mom. She'd never run from anything in her life. It was time to pay her back.

"I came to sit with you for a while." She wasn't sure how to handle the situation. Should she remind her mother that she was Sonja Walsh? Should she go along with her mom's memory lapses?

She would start reading tonight. For now, she would simply sit.

"That's lovely," her mom said with a whisper of a smile. "I'm feeling lonely. I seem to have broken something. The doctors are nice though. I miss my daughter."

Becca reached for her hand, emotion choking her. "She misses you, too."

"I want her to be happy." Her mother was staring as though she could see something Becca couldn't, but her hand clutched hers. "I want her to be so happy. I want her to choose to be happy."

"She will," Becca promised.

She held on to her mother as she shifted and started talking about a dance she was going to with a boy named Leland. She was excited about it because he was awfully handsome.

Becca sat and listened as her mother's life played out in bits and pieces in her fragmented brain.

But she would never forget the promise she'd made. Never forget what she owed her mother.

A happy life.

* * * *

Fourteen years later
London, England

The dark-haired man stared down at him. "Owen? Owen, do you remember anything?"

He remembered that his whole body ached. His head was foggy with the drugs they'd given him. Good drugs. He knew that much. The drugs held back the agony of having his skin flayed open. They'd bandaged him up and his skin was healing, but it still felt like he'd been set on fire from the inside. "I don't...where am I?"

He wasn't going to ask the real question. Who am I? He was fairly certain that he didn't want to know. Anyone who felt this much pain had to be cursed.

He couldn't remember anything. He knew he was in a hospital, knew that the woman who'd come in wearing a white coat had been a doctor, was certain the thing in his arm was an IV.

Why couldn't he remember his bloody name? He was supposed to have a name, right? The black-haired man had said a word. Owen. Was that a name?

"We've taken you back to London," the black-haired man said. He had some kind of an accent. It was heavy, though his English was perfect. Yes, the man was speaking English, but his accent was Russian.

Panic welled because a lot of things were coming back to him. He could describe the world around him, understood what to call the body parts that ached despite the drugs, but his name, who he was, eluded him.

"Am I from London?" The man had used the word back. Did that mean he lived here?

A deep frown creased the man's face. "You're originally from Edinburgh, but you've lived in London for years. You work for a company called McKay-Taggart and Knight."

"He doesn't remember?" a new voice asked.

"Ian, I think it would be best if you give his team time to figure out what's going on with him."

He turned and two large blond men were standing close to the door. One was slightly smaller than the other, but they were both extremely large and muscular. Military men. Or something like it.

The black-haired man put his body between the hospital bed and the men in the doorway. "Now is not the time. Theo, I know what he did to you…"

"But he doesn't, does he?" The one named Ian came stalking in and Owen suddenly wasn't so sure his pain was over for the day.

Pure instinct made him force his body up. Where was his gun? He carried a gun.

There was no gun here. Why did he carry a gun?

"Nick, I'm not going to murder him," Ian said.

"No, he's going to walk away now." Theo put a hand on Ian's arm. "She dosed him with the new drug, Ian. He's not the same person he was before. I know you're angry. I am, too. He betrayed me and Erin."

"Dr. McDonald was holding his mother and his sister," Nick said and Owen could hear the anger in the Russian's voice.

Were they talking about him? He tried to get up, but his limbs wouldn't move. What was wrong with his legs? They wouldn't move at all.

"And he worked at a place where we fucking specialize in saving people." The words spat out of the big guy's mouth with the force of a machine gun. "It never occurred to him to mention that he was in trouble? His first reaction was to sentence my brother and Erin to hell?"

"They're all he has," Nick replied. "Had. Could you please remember that he's suffered for what he did?"

What had he done? God, he didn't understand a damn thing. "What are you talking about? I don't understand. I don't know who you are or why I'm here. If you're going to kill me, get it the hell over with."

There was a hollow feeling in the pit of his stomach. That anger had been focused on him. White-hot rage had come off the big guy in waves. The Russian had been trying to protect him. Were they friends? The man he thought was called Nick acted like they were supposed to know each other.

Someone had taken his mother and sister? His head ached as he tried to remember. A mother and a sister? He should know them. Their faces should be right there, but his mind was a blank slate.

Pain flared through his brain.

"Let it go." Theo stood in front of him. "You're trying to remember, and it won't work. All you'll do is give yourself a massive headache."

"And the fucker deserves one," Ian said.

Theo turned on the man named Ian. "Brother, I understand that you're angry, but walk out right now because I'm not going to let you beat the shit out of a man who has no idea who he is or what he's done."

Ian's eyes narrowed. "You're a better man than me."

"Everyone knows that," Theo said, but there was a chuckle to his tone. He sobered quickly. "I know where he is. I've been there, and I assure you there is no revenge like what he's going through. If I could have spared him this, I would have."

"And I might have pushed the plunger." Ian turned on his heels. "I'm going to go find Charlie. I suppose you're going to make me keep him around."

"Where else are we supposed to send him?" Nick asked. "He's got nothing."

"I have a mother and a sister." They'd said so. Nick had said they were all he had in the world. Where were they? Were they coming to get him? He couldn't remember his mother's face or her name, but a mum took care of her children. A sister would show him kindness. If they were here, maybe they would help him remember what had gone so wrong with his life. "Where are they?"

The room seemed to go completely still, as if the air itself wasn't moving.

"You said I had a mother and a sister." He looked to the friendliest guy in the room. The big Russian had a grim look on his face. "Are they here?"

He hesitated. "Owen, I..."

Ian's jaw squared as though he'd made a decision and he took over. "Your name is Owen Shaw. You work for me and a man named Damon Knight. You are former SAS and for the last several years have served as an operative on many intelligence missions. Nikolai Markovic was your partner. We've been working on a case where we were attempting to track down a rogue doctor. Her name was Hope McDonald and she was performing memory experiments on men she then turned into her own personal army. A few days ago, your mother and sister were kidnapped by the doctor in an attempt to get you to turn over my brother, Theo."

His head hurt worse than ever. "Why would she want him?"

"He was her favorite subject," Ian continued in his matter-of-fact way. Owen found he preferred it to Nick's sympathetic hesitancy. "You turned over my brother and his fiancée, a woman named Erin Argent."

"I betrayed my team?" Even in the fog of pain and panic he was in, he knew that wasn't a good thing.

"You did," Ian explained without an ounce of emotion.

"He had his reasons," Theo argued.

"And Dr. McDonald killed your relatives anyway. She murdered them and dosed you with the same memory-wipe drugs she used on my brother. You had an allergic reaction and the doctors weren't sure you would pull through. It'll be a miracle if you come out of this only losing your memory." Ian's eyes softened marginally. "I'm sorry. Everyone will say I'm an ass but there's no other way to tell you. She very likely killed them before she even figured out that you refused to turn over my nephew."

There had been a kid involved? He felt his head shaking. None of this made a lick of sense. "Why should I believe you? You might have been the person who did this to me. Why can't I feel my bloody legs?"

"I'll update Damon," Ian said with a sigh. "You're right. He's a moron, not evil, and I'm still too pissed to make decisions. I'll let them know you'll be coming back to The Garden. Keep me updated."

Theo looked down at him. "I know how scared you are and how angry and confused. I'll explain everything and Nick here can tell you about your life before today."

Nick sank down into the chair beside his bed. "I'm your friend, Owen. I'm here for you."

Theo started to talk, but the words didn't make sense. Owen closed his eyes and let the desolation wash over him.

He had no family, no home, no past.

No matter what they said, he was alone.

Chapter One

"When I look at him, all I see is unharvested organs," a sarcastic voice said.

"Could you be serious for two minutes?" another voice asked.

"Oh, oh, oh, I know the answer to that question. I totally know this one." His brother, Tucker, was likely holding his hand up and waving it, but Owen kept his eyes on the screen.

Same shit. Different day. Now Tucker would say no, Big Tag couldn't be serious. Sasha would start snoring because he'd been up far too late drinking. Dante would keep quiet as a mouse until he absolutely had to say something. Jax would be texting his wife and completely out of the current loop. He wouldn't look up from his phone until he heard something that involved him. Ezra and Big Tag would bicker like an old married couple for a few moments and then Robert would try to get them all back on task.

This was the way the last several months of his life had gone. They'd been ready to start the op months before but key elements had fallen through, only coming together in the last few days. They'd scattered around the country, each working a different angle to set this op up, but it was now go time. He wished he could be more excited about it.

"No," Tucker said and Owen was certain there was a triumphant smile on his face. "Big Tag can't be serious at all."

"I assure you I'm entirely serious about carving up Levi Green for parts," Big Tag replied. "Think about it. All that skin. He's wasting it and there are lots of people out there who need some. Burn victims totally deserve that skin more than he does, and I bet his liver could go into like three different people."

"It depends on how big the liver is," Tucker mused. "But honestly, you can do living liver donations. Of course, it might be way more fun to take the whole thing. I hate that man."

"And we could do a test to see if Tucker here really was a surgeon," Tag mused. "This is a win-win."

Owen let the conversation fade into the background as Sasha started to snore lightly.

Sometimes he was absolutely certain that he'd had no life at all before this one. His days started with some form of slide presentation complete with his boss's never-ending snark, at some point he sat in front of a computer gathering data, or sat in a car taking pictures, and that was really more like gathering data than it sounded, spent an hour in the gym because the aforementioned boss said he would get pudgy if he didn't, and then he microwaved something terrible, listened to Tucker bemoan his fate, and finally drank enough whiskey to pass out.

Yet he knew he'd had another life. There was evidence of it, pictures of him smiling with two women he obviously loved—his mum and sister. There were videos of him laughing and talking with them at Christmas. He'd seen photos of himself with Nikolai Markovic, read the emails and joking texts between himself and his one-time partner.

He'd been that partner. Owen Shaw had been in those messages. The man in those texts to Nick had been funny, seemingly loyal, and yet that same man had also betrayed a nice couple, had been willing to send another person into hell to save his own family.

His mother and sister were gone. They were nothing but photographs now, smiling ghosts who tripped through his brain like wispy butterflies he couldn't quite catch.

"I'm only saying we could do some good in the world," Big Tag argued. "I'll scoop his eyeballs out myself. I've been practicing. Corneas are in short supply."

A long-suffering sigh came from Ezra. "Shouldn't you go back to Dallas? Doesn't your plane leave soon? You should head to the airport."

"I'm flying private, man," Tag shot back. "Billionaire sister-in-law, remember? Who would have guessed Case would end up being the smartest one of us all? I've got plenty of time."

A collective groan went through the room.

Owen sat back and closed his eyes as Robert started talking about the actual op and what they still needed to do. Make contact with the target. Make friends with the target. Bug the target's mobile. Bug the target's condo.

Yadda, yadda, yadda.

Turned out Toronto wasn't so different from Dallas. He'd only been here a few days, but he'd spent his time looking through records and prepping the documents they would need to begin the mission. Robert's job was logistics, and Owen was his partner for this op.

In the beginning he'd been the lead. Ezra had put him in charge when they'd been worried that the target might recognize them. There was still a risk, and they had less data on a couple of members of the team, but they were almost certain there was no way Walsh had met any of them. When they had been sure they would go through with it, Big Tag had handed the op over to Robert, shoving Owen to the sidelines.

Turned out he was mostly muscle. Until the bullets started flying, there wasn't much for him to do.

He hadn't always been muscle. At one point in time, he'd been a bloody good operative. He'd been SAS for years. Or so the files told him. Of course, back then he'd had his memory and a body that hadn't been ravaged by an experimental drug.

Sometimes he wondered why he was here at all. Guilt, perhaps. They dragged him along because he had nowhere else to go.

He felt a hand nudging him from his right side and he looked up, realizing all eyes were on him.

Big Tag stared at him, his body relaxed, but there was tension in those icy eyes of his. "Sorry, you don't snore like Sasha there. I couldn't tell if you were awake or asleep. I asked if you had anything to add since until a few days ago you've been the one following Green."

Yes, he'd been the one sitting in a car outside of numerous bars because the fucker liked to party. "If the bugger works at all, I can't tell. He spent a total of ten hours at his office in Langley. Not that I could get all that close to it. They tend to not like you spying on the spies."

Another set of blue eyes was on him. Ezra Fain's always seemed warmer than Big Tag's. Tag's could have come from the arctic, the kind of blue lit by ice. Fain's were more like a Caribbean sea, the kind that was so clear he could see his feet even when the water hit his chest.

"I have my own people on the inside," Ezra explained. "He met with groups over the course of a couple of days. My person thinks he met with a senator and a general as well, but we don't have proof of it. He's getting all his ducks in line to make his big play. I believe he's going to use the intelligence he intercepted from us at The Ranch to move up in the organization."

"Is your person Kimberly Soloman?" He had to ask the question because he had something else to tell his boss, and Fain wasn't going to like what he'd found.

At the sound of his ex-wife's name, the former CIA operative paled. Owen could see it even in the dim light. Fain's smile faded. "No. I haven't heard from Solo since the day Jax walked into the woods."

He waited for a moment. No one was watching him now. They were all set on the boss. Well, except Sasha, who was still sleeping. Even Jax had looked up from his phone.

Robert shook his head. "You're seriously not even going to ask? The last time anyone saw her she'd been shot."

"She was dying the last time I saw her," Jax said. Of course he would know. Jax had been dying, too.

Luckily the drug that had taken his memory hadn't taken his skills. Owen had been the one to fly the helicopter that day. He'd helped the doctor to load Jax in and gotten him to a hospital. It had been one of the brief times he could remember that he'd felt like he meant something.

Ezra's stare had gone stubborn. "There's nothing to ask. I assume she's alive. You can't kill her. She's like a cockroach."

He took exception to that since Kimberly Soloman seemed like a nice lady to him. She'd given them valuable intel, and according to Jax she'd been at the site in the woods in Colorado to help them. But then what did he know? "It's all in my report. Now can we move on to Dr. Walsh? I signed the lease on the condo yesterday. I've got movers for tomorrow."

At least they'd trusted him enough to let him call the movers in.

"Seriously, you don't care if she even lived?" Tucker ignored him, preferring to gift Fain with a judgmental stare.

"I told you. I know she lived. You don't take out Solo with a single gut shot. Though I noticed he didn't go for her heart. She would have been much safer if he had since she doesn't exactly have one." He'd been wrong about Ezra's eyes. They could go incredibly cold when he wanted them to.

Big Tag slapped Ezra on the back. "Good one, man. That's some serious denial right there. And she totally lived. I've already read the report and talked to her on the phone. She had a rough couple of weeks, but she's on the mend."

Here was the bad part, the part Big Tag hadn't read. Owen opened the folder in front of him and slid the photo on top Ezra's way. "She's back at work from what I can tell. She met with him for roughly ten minutes at a café outside Langley before she went to her office. I wasn't close enough to get audio."

Ezra's smile held not an ounce of amusement as he stared down at the photo of his ex-wife sitting across from the man who'd burned him and tried to kill him. "I don't need audio. She's plotting with her boyfriend."

Intel on Dr. McDonald's experiments and the other doctors she'd worked with hadn't been the only thing they'd learned from their time in Bliss, Colorado. They'd also learned far too much about the boss's marriage. From what they'd pieced together, Ezra had been married to Kim Soloman, also known as Solo. She'd been responsible for the mission Ezra's half-brother had died during. He'd blamed her and they'd divorced. She'd had something brief with Levi that had given the bugger crazy-stalker vibes about her, and Ezra wasn't even close to being over her.

He hadn't needed audio either. "She was angry with him. There was a lot of tension on both sides, but she was the truly angry one. I know she had security keep him out of her hospital room. She was alone in there the whole time. Not a single visitor."

He'd thought about sneaking in to see her but decided not to try his luck. He was already the group fuck-up. It would be worse if he also became the one who got his arse hauled to jail.

He'd learned a bit about his boss's ex-wife. She was alone in the world. She was an heiress who'd chosen to turn her back on the life of privilege that could have been hers.

The door opened and he watched two figures moving through the shadows toward the conference table. He would bet a lot those two were women, and that Robert was about to lose his shit.

"I don't want to talk about Solo. Now that we're here in Canada, someone else will take over the surveillance of Levi Green. I want to know where that asshole is at all times. He's the one who sent us here, and I'm sure at some point he'll show up." Ezra slid the photo back to him and clicked the remote, changing the image on the wall of their borrowed office. "Now that our subject matter experts are here, we can get down to real business. Ladies, welcome."

Ariel Adisa walked in wearing a perfectly tailored suit that managed to be both modest and ridiculously sexy since the woman wearing it couldn't be anything but sexy. Her dark hair was in gorgeous curls that seemed to form a halo around her. The stark white of her suit showed off how beautifully dark her skin was. She was an utterly fascinating woman, but he'd always known she had a thing for Robert. The second woman he'd met only briefly. She was a new hire to the McKay-Taggart and Knight team in London.

"Ariel?" Robert stood up and despite his obvious shock, moved to pull her chair out.

She nodded cooly his way. "Robert, it's good to see you again."

"It's surprising to see you," Robert said, stepping back. "You're supposed to be in London."

"You weren't kidding, were you?" Nina Blunt sank into the chair beside Ariel with a shake of her head.

Ariel sighed. "I mentioned to Nina that you wouldn't be happy to see me."

"It's not that I'm not happy. It's that it's dangerous," Robert replied.

Ariel waved that off. "It's Canada. Nothing bad ever happens in Canada. Now that Bliss place, I steered clear of. Do you know what the per capita murder rate is? You're lucky any of you came out of there alive at all. Hello, Tag. Thanks for flying me over. It was lovely."

Big Tag grinned. "That was my personal plane, of course. Only the best for my London team."

Tucker groaned. "He just admitted he steals his sister-in-law's planes. Case's brother-in-law is a billionaire, and he must really love his sister to put up with Big Tag."

Tag shrugged. "That's fair. Now how about we shelve the romantic drama for now, though I fully expect to get regular updates from one of you."

Robert frowned the boss's way. "There's no drama. Let's move on to Dr. Walsh. I'm sure that's why Dr. Adisa is here."

The picture changed from that asshole Green to a woman in a white jacket, her brown and gold hair in a slightly messy bun. She wore a pair of tortoise shell glasses and a plain black dress. She smiled at the camera, the restrained expression of a professional.

Thirty. Rebecca Walsh was thirty years old and running her own department at one of the world's most elite research facilities.

Had Rebecca Walsh been the one to help Hope McDonald erase his mind? Was he looking at the woman who'd helped rid him of his past?

"She's pretty," Tucker murmured.

She was, but in an oddly bland way. There was nothing that stood out about her. Her skin was blemish free, her face nicely symmetrical. He couldn't tell a thing about her body. The only thing that stood out to him was the look in her eyes. Those eyes were big and brown and soulful.

This was the woman he would live close to for the next however many weeks or months it would take for them to do what they needed to do. Robert would be the one to befriend her. Jax and River were already living on the same floor, keeping an eye on things. Nina was her brand-new daily barista.

He and Robert were the last pieces to slide into place. They were going in as a couple. A newly married couple. He was not looking forward to it. If Owen had his way they would be the least affectionate newlyweds in history.

"Dr. Adisa has been studying our target." Fain was all business again. "And Ms. Blunt has been setting herself up to be a part of the target's daily life."

Tag leaned in. "For those of you who haven't met her, Nina Blunt joined the London team a few months ago. She used to work for Interpol. She's an expert analyst, and we've brought her in to help us deal with Dr. Walsh. You've all met Ariel."

Ariel knew him well. She'd been his therapist while he'd lived in The Garden. She'd helped them all.

31

Nina was a pretty woman with auburn hair. She was exactly the type of woman he would usually hit on, but since he'd seen Jax lying there on the floor of the underground research facility known only as The Ranch, he'd drawn in on himself.

This was serious. Jax had almost died. This wasn't about a good time or finding as much pleasure as he could. He could die and he had zero idea who he was. He could die before he'd ever lived.

Before he'd had a chance to be more than the man in that file, the one who'd betrayed his friends. The one he was almost certain none of them truly trusted. It was precisely why he took the background jobs. He was with them, but not. Never quite one of the lads.

"I've written a report on her with the aid of Nina," Ariel explained. "I've sent it to your emails for your perusal. Most of my observations are based on research. I haven't met Dr. Walsh, but she's been written about quite a bit. I relied on Nina for more personal observations. She's an odd one. Quite complex and intriguing."

Nina leaned forward. "I've been here for a couple of weeks. I'm working at the coffee shop at the bottom of the building Dr. Walsh lives in. One of the things that stands out about our target is her devotion to schedule. I would say she's got a mild form of OCD because that happens often with genius-level intelligence. But it also might be a simple habit she's gotten into because she's quite busy. It should make her easy to monitor. I've included that schedule in the report. The third week of every month is a bit different because that's when she works on her second job."

From what he understood she was involved in some kind of volunteer effort to teach kids science. He was certain she was a good teacher, but how did a woman who hadn't had a childhood, from what he could tell, truly connect to kids?

"I agree with Nina," Ariel said. "Dr. Walsh has gotten into a routine, but I also think she craves something to take her out of it from time to time. Her volunteer work proves she's got a sense of humor and fun."

He wasn't sure how much fun the kids had listening to lectures on science. She didn't look like the kind who would teach kids how to blow up soda bottles. She would likely read from a prepared report and then wonder why the kids had fallen asleep.

"Which is precisely why I think finding a new friend could be the perfect way to get close to her," Nina admitted. "In her previous jobs, she usually had a close group of friends, but most doctors her age are finishing up internships or finding fellowships. What I basically mean is they move around a lot. Because of her youth, she struggled to find close friends, but she's certainly had a healthy social life up until recently. Do you want to go over the salient facts before we get into specifics?"

He opened the attachment and glanced through it as Ariel spoke.

"Dr. Walsh began showing signs of genius when she read at the age of three. By the time she was five years old she was working complex math and her father brought in a tutor."

"Her father is Leland Walsh?" Tucker whistled.

"You say that like it means something." Owen flipped back, trying to figure out who the bloke was.

"Leland Walsh invented a surgical technique that revolutionized the way we deal with brain tumors." Tucker always sounded different when he talked about medicine. More competent. And then more scared because they were all almost certain he'd worked with Dr. Hope McDonald, evil mistress of the mind. Dead but not forgotten. Except by him, since she'd died after she'd dosed him but before he'd woken up.

"So she comes from a family of doctors?" Robert asked.

"Her father, grandfather, and two uncles were renowned surgeons," Ariel explained. "Not that her mother's side of the family wasn't full of brainiacs. Her mother was a professor. She taught psychology and ran a women's shelter. Rebecca chose to go into research, specifically into researching the brain and memory and how degenerative neurological diseases affect memory."

His eyes lit on a specific fact. It was listed in the middle of the bio Nina had prepared, but it stuck out to him. "Her mother was diagnosed with Alzheimer's."

Nina nodded, but her eyes held a certain sympathy. "Yes, when Rebecca was nine, but from her accounts, she wasn't told about the diagnosis until later, roughly nine months before her mother died. She spoke about it at a conference. It was a quite moving speech. She and her future stepmother cared for her mother at home until she passed."

"Her future stepmother?" Robert asked.

"So her family life is rough, I take it." He couldn't imagine how the girl had taken that. Mum dies and dad marries her nurse?

"She's quite close to her family," Nina corrected. "She was the maid of honor at their wedding three years after her mom died. She's close to her young sister, and from all accounts enjoys spending time with her father."

"Must not have been close to her mum." Owen didn't get it. Not at all.

Ariel was frowning his way. "She was a teenaged girl who put aside her needs to keep her mother out of a nursing home. I would say she proved her love for her mother. As for being close to her stepmother, well, funny things happen to survivors. Sometimes they cling together. Until you've lost someone, you can't judge how others react. Honestly, even when you have, you know damn well you shouldn't. Grief is different for everyone."

Tucker leaned over. "I think you should be quiet now. She looks pissed."

She looked annoyed, but then he could do that to a woman.

He'd lost two someones, but he didn't understand grief. How did he cry and ache for two people he couldn't remember? "I'm sorry. I was surprised. Of course I don't know anything at all. Please continue."

"She doesn't seem to have a large social circle here in Toronto. I'm surprised she has many friends at all since when she would normally have been forming her social identity, she was thrown in with much older students. She was much younger than the average student at the schools she attended. She would have been an outsider at best, a target at worst," Ariel said.

"A target?" Robert asked. "What do you mean? I understand she's our target, but why would her school friends want to investigate her?"

Ariel's lips tugged up slightly. "It's always odd to be reminded of how your memories break. You know so much about the world, so many facts, but often normal experiences are gone and with them the street-like knowledge that's second nature to the rest of us."

"That's shrink talk for you're a shiny new baby," Big Tag explained.

"What she's saying is Rebecca Walsh was so young she couldn't relate to the other students," Ezra explained. "Even though she was certainly smart enough to be in a class with them, emotionally she wasn't ready to run in their circles."

Sometimes he still felt like that. "You're saying that even though she's bridged that gap now, she still isn't comfortable in social situations? Has trouble making friends?"

Ariel nodded. "She might be awkward at times. You're going to have to be patient with her."

"I don't know about that," Nina mused. "I've talked to her and I was surprised at how nice she seems. She ordered a vanilla latte instead of her normal plain latte. I mentioned it and she told me she's on a quest to expand her horizons. She seemed enthusiastic about it. I know it's only a shot of vanilla, but it's outside her routine. I think she might welcome some new friends."

"She loves animals," Ariel pointed out. "She doesn't have a pet right now, but I think that's because of her long hours. She spends her breaks at a dog park, though she doesn't own one."

Jax gave her a thumbs-up. "Buster to the rescue. No one can resist his manly smell. No, seriously, River's at the groomer's right now. We're getting rid of his stink. He thought a skunk would be a good playmate. It was really terrible."

"Preach, brother," Tag said. "Bud is not smart about the fuckers. They get him every time. I swear there's a family of them living on our property and they've got a bet on how many times they can spray my dog. They only got Kala once. We had to go to family therapy after that."

"What's her financial situation like?" Fain asked, clearly ready to get the meeting back on track.

"The family is wealthy, but it was earned through white-collar jobs, not generational money," Nina replied. "She received scholarships to pay for her schooling. Her education was unconventional, to say the least. She graduated from high school at the age of twelve. College by the time she was fifteen. She went to medical school from there."

He glanced back at the photo. How hard had it been to always be the youngest person in class? To stand out in such a way? "What about her relationships with men? The basic info says she was married at some point."

"Yes, but it didn't last three years. He was a doctor, too," Nina explained.

Dante uncharacteristically showed some interest. He was staring down at his folder like he gave a damn for once. "Why did they divorce?"

"I believe he left because he couldn't handle her success," Ariel explained. "She won her first Wolf Foundation Prize and when she accepted a prestigious position with the Huisman Foundation, they divorced. Her research is funded by the Huisman Foundation primarily and various pharmaceutical companies who have an interest. The Huismans are an old, venerable family here in Canada. From what I can tell, they fund everything she asks them to. She works closely with the son, Paul. He's a neurologist as well."

"She worked with McDonald before she joined the foundation?" Owen asked.

Big Tag nodded. "Dr. Walsh worked closely with McDonald at Kronberg Pharmaceuticals. She was brought in to assist with a project. The nature of their true relationship is unclear. It's something I'm interested in learning more about. But I'm also interested in Walsh's other job. How the hell does that fit into her profile?"

Ariel grinned. "Like I said, it proves she's got a sense of humor."

Fain hit a key on his computer and the picture of Walsh changed from a sedate doctor to…a woman in spandex and a cape. Gone were the glasses and professional bun. In its place was a superhero costume that clung to her every curve. Yep, the white jacket had hidden a nice set of breasts, and that smile on her face, so controlled before, was now wide and warm and inviting.

"Meet Captain Neuro," Nina said with a chuckle. "She goes into elementary schools and teaches kids about brain health. She's been doing it for about a year now, and every school in Toronto wants her to come in. There's talk of her doing a local kid's show about science."

He'd sat up in his chair because he hadn't expected that. He'd only read about her many accolades, all her intellectual awards. Somehow on paper she'd seemed cold, probably aloof, but this woman had a glint in her eyes. This woman practically glowed with something he didn't understand.

She was beautiful. Which woman was she in real life?

Big Tag sighed. "Don't tell my girls we're going after a female superhero. They're all about Wonder Woman right now. Do we think her side project offers us a way into her work world?"

Ariel flipped it back to the first picture, and Owen was surprised at how disappointed he was. "No, I just thought it was fun. And we should remember that she's the kind of woman who spends her time helping kids. She's not merely ambitious. She's kind, too."

"Or it's good cover." He couldn't help himself. It didn't make sense, that smile of hers. She'd lost so much, grown up far too fast. The smile had to be the cover. The smile hid the real woman underneath.

"Cynical," Tag said with a nod. "I like it. Keep that healthy suspicion up, Shaw, and you'll do fine. Still, it doesn't hurt to know how she spends her time. Does she have a foundation she works through, or is her volunteer work done through Huisman?"

Nina glanced down at her notes. "She set up one in her mother's name. The Sonja Project. Her father helped her but she runs it."

Fain nodded Taggart's way. "Jax will start looking into the financials. His cover is he's working for an investment firm anyway. Hopefully we can get her talking if everything goes our way. I don't know how much Dr. Walsh knew about what McDonald was really working on. That's something I'm hoping Tucker can uncover. He's interning with the foundation. He won't be working directly with Dr. Walsh, but I'm hoping he can get close enough to some of the employees that he's a part of the rumor mill."

"I've already met a nice doctor lady," Tucker assured them all.

"And by met her, he means he slept with her," Jax added helpfully.

"I'm not cleaning that up," Dante huffed as he sat back. "Next time you will all be janitors. I hate this job. Sasha is not good at it at all. He will get us fired."

Tucker's eyes widened and he held up his hands as though surrendering as he looked Big Tag's way. "I double wrapped. I promise."

"See that you continue to do so," Big Tag said sagely. "Condoms for everyone. Well, except Robert and Owen. Unless you're planning on experimenting. Or really getting into your role as a couple." He leaned forward. "I know you can't get pregnant, you two, but I still advise wearing condoms until you're absolutely certain you're willing to commit to each other."

Robert sighed and rolled his eyes. "Sure, boss. We'll do that."

Big Tag frowned. "You're no fun."

He'd learned how to handle Taggart. He gave the boss a smile he didn't truly feel. "Robert wishes he could get into all this. And might I add, as husbands go, Robert makes a handsome one."

Robert's lips quirked up slightly. "Thank you, Owen. I agree. I

37

think we'll be a lovely couple."

Big Tag's laughter boomed as he stood up. "Well played, gentlemen. Don't ever tell Adam though. Guy's known me most of his life and still can't resist taking the bait. I'm going to get home. I feel the sudden need to prank his ass. I'll figure out something. You're dismissed. I need to talk to Fain before I leave. Ariel, if you'll join us in the office, I would appreciate it. Don't fuck up, boys."

The words weren't for him. They were meant for Robert and the rest of them. He couldn't fuck up. His only job was to back up the better operatives. As long as he stayed awake when he was supposed to, he could do his part.

How long before he could open the bottle of whiskey he had back in his motel room? Five o'clock? Would four be too soon? He'd gotten good at looking perfectly sober even when he damn well wasn't.

He knew he should stop, but he didn't dream when he drank himself to sleep.

How had he known about the blue of the Caribbean? It struck him suddenly that he hadn't read about it. When he'd thought about Ezra's eyes, he'd seen that blue in his head, had known he could see his feet, practically felt the heat of the sun and heard the surf.

He'd been to England, Dallas, Colorado, DC, and now Toronto. None of those places had a warm beach. The closest he'd gotten to a beach was his screensaver.

"You okay?" Robert was standing in front of him. The rest of the group was starting to shuffle out with the exception of Sasha, who was still sleeping.

He shook his head. It must have been from a dream. Sometimes he dreamed he'd gone places he hadn't. Typically the dreams ended with some form of brutality, some terrible death that turned out to be his fault. "I'm fine. I've got the movers ready for tomorrow. Nina helped decorate. She picked stuff out of a catalog. Turns out I'm crap at it."

Nina shrugged. "You've got a guy's guy taste, meaning none whatsoever. He was way more interested in a big telly than anything else. And he was planning on skipping the couch and buying two loungers."

Robert stared at her. "And that's bad, why? I don't get the point of decorative pillows."

"No one is ever going to buy that you're a couple if the place looks like a frat house," she pointed out. "And I know perfectly well that gay couples can have bad taste, too, but it's rare that both men in a couple are clueless. Trust me. I've done right by you both. I don't suspect Becca will care about your furnishings, but she is very observant when she wants to be. Don't forget that."

"You've spent time with her?" He couldn't help but look back at the wall. Her picture was still there. He wasn't sure why, but he couldn't not look at her. Perhaps it was mere curiosity. Her life was so different from what he knew of his own.

Or maybe it was the fact that there was something in her eyes, something that threatened to pull him in.

He was glad now that they'd changed the picture. He could handle this Rebecca Walsh better than he had the glowy, smiling one.

"I've talked to her, but it's busy in the mornings," Nina said with a thoughtful look on her face. "I'm working the later shift a few times this week. She stops in after work and usually picks up dinner at eight p.m. She calls it in at seven thirty and walks over before she heads up to her place. That's when you'll have your best shot at running into her. I've got to warn you though, from Ariel's profile she's standoffish with men. I think it's a smart idea to go the friendly route."

Because the other route would have been the romantic one. "If she's not friendly, I'm not sure how Robert's supposed to work his way in."

"I didn't say she wasn't friendly. She's quite nice." Nina gestured to the tablet on the table. "Read Ariel's report. She's got some ideas about how to get close to the target. I think she's obsessed with her research, but she's not cold. She seems worried about something to me."

"Do you think she's capable of working with Dr. McDonald?" Tucker leaned against the desk.

"He means work with her knowing what she was doing." Jax had slid his phone into his pocket. "Do you think Dr. Walsh would have helped McDonald torture us?"

Nina seemed to think about it for a moment. "Dr. Walsh is consumed with her work, and Ariel and I believe she's motivated by losing her mother as a young woman. From what we've dug up, it's obvious to both of us that she's trying to find a cure because she watched her mother die. I don't think she would actively harm someone, but if the damage had been done, she would likely use the research. She would justify it by thinking the pain and suffering could bring about something good."

"The ends justify the means," he murmured. Unfortunately, in this case, he'd been the means. His life, his health, his past—those had been the currency that bought the research.

Except when he thought about it, they hadn't. How terrible was it to know that his pain had been about revenge? At least the others had a reason to have gone through what they did. He'd been a loose end she'd needed to clean up.

He looked back at the woman on the screen. Who was she? Villain or innocent player in a game she couldn't imagine?

It wasn't his place to find out.

He sat back as Robert began talking about the mission. It was time to fade into the background.

Chapter Two

Becca Walsh stared at the man in front of her. Jimmy was only two years younger than she was, but there were times when it felt like there were decades between them. He stood there in his perfectly pressed slacks, his button-down, and hair he'd likely spent hours getting to look like the wind had swept it back. He was young and single and obviously ready to mingle.

And he was obviously insane.

"Go over the side effects again, please," she said. Had he really thought she wouldn't read that sucker?

He flushed as though he'd actually thought he might get away with it. "Mild headaches, upset stomach, diarrhea, hair growth, drowsiness…"

She held up a hand to stop him. "That is not what you said the first time."

The man sitting beside her chuckled. "You know she has ears, Jim. You were never going to get that past her."

Paul Huisman had a slight French accent, having been born and raised in Quebec. In the beginning she'd found it magical. She'd considered the idea that they might be good friends, the type who talked in bed and stuff. But she'd been on a sexual sabbatical. She'd promised to give herself two years after her divorce to get her head on straight, and that had proven to be a godsend. Sleeping with Paul would have been disastrous. He was fastidious and fussy, everything she didn't want in a man. He'd also been angry when his father had passed him over in favor of her when he'd named a new lead in Neurological Research. They were friendly, but she knew he'd sent a report to his father detailing all the ways she wasn't right for the job. Still, so far he'd backed her up when she needed him.

She glanced down at the preliminary reports on the new drug they were testing. It had been a long shot in the first place, but Jimmy Lao, while young and shiny, was also incredibly smart and one day might revolutionize drug therapy for stroke survivors.

But this was only his first try, and it wasn't going to work.

"Extreme hair growth in female patients," she pointed out. "According to this, some of them actually grew beards."

"Don't forget the chest hair." Paul was shaking his head. "And why on earth would it cause the urine to turn pink?"

"Some of them were hairy to start with, and it was really more of a magenta color. At least it was according to the women in the group. They were very precise about the color. I thought pink covered it. I think it was a side effect of the high beet content in the supporting meds." Jimmy bit back a frustrated groan. "Sorry. It seemed to work well in the rats. I'll be honest, it's not as effective in humans. It's not doing anything I hypothesized. The results were roughly the same as the drug therapies we use now."

She stood up and moved around to the young man. She knew how it felt to fail. Sometimes she thought it was her primary job. But it was important to pull yourself up off the floor, shake off the dust, and try a-freaking-gain, as she often told her kids. "This is your first try. It never works the first time. This, my friend, is the start of many, many failures. I want you to think of them as another brick in the yellow brick road. You get me?"

He stared at her like he wasn't exactly sure how to respond. Not a big *Wizard of Oz* fan, then. "So I'm not getting fired? Because you read the part about the homicidal thoughts, right?"

"I'm fairly certain if I'd started growing hair between my toes, I would have homicidal thoughts, too." She'd discounted those. It had only been two subjects, and all the murderous intent had been aimed toward Jimmy. Totally understandable. "Go back to the drawing board. And check and make sure all your patients go back on normal therapies. Follow up with their primary doctors and ask them to continue to check in with us so we're certain there are no long-term effects."

His shoulders came down from around his ears. "Thank you, Dr. Walsh. I'll do that. And I'll get my team back to the drawing board. We learned a couple of things this time around. I wrote it all up for you and would welcome any notes or ideas. Thanks, Dr. Huisman."

He practically bounced out of the room.

"Was I ever that young?" Paul asked with a long sigh.

"I think I am that young and I'm asking myself the same question," she admitted. She glanced up at the clock. Almost time to go home. She would sign all the paperwork she needed to sign, say the same things she always said—have a great evening, lots of plans, don't party too hard—then she would get on the subway and go three whole stops to Spadina, get off the subway, walk exactly eight hundred forty-two steps to her building. She would get her normal Wednesday dinner order of a chicken salad sandwich and chips. She would ignore the bar next to the bistro with its too loud music and boisterous university students. She wouldn't think about the fact that they were in there eating poutine— which sounded disgusting and gross, and god she wanted some because it was delicious—and she would go up to her lonely apartment. She would turn on the news and eat her dinner and tell herself that this weekend she would do something fun.

She would end up right back here. She would work all weekend.

It was time. It was time to stop worrying about making another terrible decision and...probably make another terrible decision. Anything was better than standing still.

"Have you thought about the fact if you weren't in charge of a whole department, you might have more time for a life?" Paul asked.

They were back to this? "I have more control over my research this way." She shoved the paperwork into her briefcase. It was time to start her sad schedule. She certainly wasn't going to break it so Paul could try to talk her into giving up her position. Again. "I'll see you tomorrow. I might be a little late."

Maybe she would stop and have breakfast. There was a place down the street that had an all crepe menu she'd been meaning to try.

He leaned back in his chair. He was an attractive man in his late thirties with chestnut-colored hair and intelligent eyes. "You'll be here by seven o'clock tomorrow."

"Probably. I do need to check on Mickey and Minnie." She shouldn't even try to fool herself. She wouldn't go sit down for breakfast. She wouldn't spend her weekend sight-seeing. She'd been living in Toronto for two years and she'd barely gotten out of The Annex. For a wild day, she would head over to the University of Toronto and give a guest lecture.

The days were starting to seem endless. And bland. At first her "sabbatical" had been good for her. She'd healed from her divorce and gotten into the swing of her new work. She'd concentrated on her research and the charity she and Melissa and Dad had started. But now it was wearing on her...and that was good, too. It was good to want something.

"You have interns to do that," he pointed out, standing up and preparing to go as well. "We just brought on four more. I hired them myself. Two women and two men. One of the guys is interesting, a bit older than our usual. Tucker is a second-year medical student. He's not a moron, so I'm sure he can make sure your rats are still alive overnight. He could even check on them over the weekend."

It was precisely why they had student interns. "Let's see how it goes."

"All right, I know a no when I hear it. Well, I've got to get to Emmanuel's school. There's been another incident with that boy. I swear that Parker kid is a terrible influence on my son."

She kind of thought it was nice Emmanuel had found a friend. He was a weird kid, but then she'd been one, too. Something about him though...there was an odd darkness in the kid even though he was barely seven years old. "Don't be too hard on him. It's rough being the smartest kid in class. He's younger than the rest of them, right?"

"Only by a year," Paul replied. "He's bored. He should have been promoted to a proper grade for his intelligence, but his mother...well, she's against it. I barely managed to get her to agree to let him move forward a single class. You were lucky you and Gary didn't have children when you divorced."

Yes, lucky. Not that Gary had wanted children with her. He'd wanted her help in getting his career off the ground, and then he'd left her for his intern.

She wondered if this Tucker kid was handsome. After all, it wasn't like she was looking to get married again. A good time though…

They walked toward the doors and she shook off the ridiculous thought. She was not dating another doctor.

"Have a good evening, Rebecca," Paul said with a nod as he took himself down the opposite hall.

She trudged toward her office, a weariness invading her bones.

"I called your order in," her assistant said. Cathy was packing up for the day, shoving her planner into the big bag she carried. Sometimes Becca was utterly fascinated with that bag of hers. It seemed never ending. She could pull almost anything out of it. Need nail clippers? Ask Cathy. Forgot your pen? Cathy had fifteen, and in every color imaginable.

She also had something else in that bag. A long list of eligible bachelors. Cathy was something of a matchmaker.

"Why don't you come home with me? I've got a roast that's been cooking all day," Cathy said. "I know having dinner with my kids, and Bob regaling you with stories of his latest policy sale isn't what a young woman would consider fun, but at least you won't be alone."

No, she would be surrounded by a happy, functional family, and that would depress her even more. "Thank you, but I'm truly fine. I have a bottle of wine and some movies I've been meaning to watch. I'll talk to my dad and maybe hop on the computer and Facetime with my baby sis. I'm good with my plans, but maybe not this weekend. Maybe this weekend I should make other plans."

Cathy stared at her for a moment as though she knew what she would say next. "Please tell me you're letting me off the leash."

Becca had to laugh. For two solid years, Cathy had been trying to set her on a new love path. She didn't really want a love path, but a friendship with benefits path might be nice. "Find me a decent guy who isn't intimidated by female success and doesn't want to immediately impregnate me. Don't you laugh. Men get desperate at this age. They know they're losing their looks and they're getting a little paunchy in the middle. The old bio clock is ticking."

It was precisely why she wouldn't let Melissa set her up. Melissa only knew doctors, and she wasn't going there again. It wasn't that Gary had been an out-and-out asshole. He'd simply needed to be the one who shined in the relationship. He'd been hyper competitive, and having his wife beat him out for a fellowship had been the last straw.

He should have had a backbone and divorced her before he started sleeping with his intern, but he had impulse control issues. He'd already married the intern, gotten her pregnant and, if rumors were true, was cheating on her with a nurse.

And she'd thought he was Prince Charming. Yes, she'd needed these two years to figure out what she wanted, and it wasn't Prince Charming. Prince Knows Where the Clitoris Is would be welcome. Or maybe SuperOrgasm Man was a better name.

Cathy's hands fluttered, her excitement evident. "I have the perfect man. He's a lawyer and divorced but not bitter divorced. Well, not anymore. He's a nice man, and I think he's as lonely as you are."

"He sounds terrible." He sounded like a lonely sad sack, but then she was, too. She'd eaten the same damn chicken sandwich every Wednesday night for two years. "I don't suppose you know any hot geek boys who just want to have sex." She should be more specific. Her people could be slow on the social uptake. "Who knows how to have sex."

Comic Con was coming up. Maybe she should show some cleavage and see what she could drag out of a *Walking Dead* panel.

Or she could pray Cathy knew what she was doing.

Cathy's eyes widened. "No. No. No. And if you're thinking about breaking your self-imposed celibacy at Comic Con with some guy dressed up as Khal Drogo, unless he is actually Jason Momoa, I forbid it. And I control your schedule and your lunch orders and your whole life. You'll be picking anchovies off your pizza for a year."

"Well played," she admitted. "I was only thinking about it because it was easy. No real names exchanged. No whiny man clinging to me. I wouldn't have to ever see the inside of his apartment."

Cathy's brows rose. "What does that have to do with it?"

Cathy had married her high school sweetheart. She hadn't had to play the dating game. "I've found these things go one of two ways. Either I walk into his place and it's what you would think a frat house would look like after a kegger, or it's incredibly neat. The first one tells me dude doesn't care what I think. The second lets me know he's smart and he's weaving a web of organization and cleanliness around me. He's baiting the trap with Lysol, but it's false. That trap is going to close and I'll be stuck in there with his dirty socks that he leaves wherever he takes them off or worse, he never actually takes them off at all and I get his stinky, trapped-in-a-pair-of-socks feet forever."

"Should I point out the current hypocrisy coming out of your mouth?" Cathy asked with a kind of shocked disbelief. "I clean your office, you know. I've been to your apartment."

She knew where stuff was. And she probably needed to hire a cleaning service for something more than when her family was coming into town. "See, I know all the tricks. So all I need is a hot geek who's super good at sex, wants to clean my apartment, and he can cook, and he mostly just wants to support me."

"You understand that you're looking for a wife, right?"

"Bingo." She pointed Cathy's way. "Except I'm not. I'm looking for a good time. I'm looking for a reason to not spend my weekends and late nights here. The program is up and running. Paul has somewhat settled down. My own research is going well. What I am lacking is a booty call." Maybe she didn't have to go about it the normal way. She was thinking like a chick. "Do you know any escort services?"

She could pay for it. It might be simpler.

Cathy gasped and shook her head. "Absolutely not. You are not hiring a hooker. I'll look through my friends and set something up for you." She was still shaking her head as she walked toward the door. "You're incorrigible, you know."

"You are preaching to the choir, sister." She strode to her office door.

"And you didn't say no. I'm going to take that as a win," Cathy said, settling her bag over her shoulder. "Have a lovely night. Call me if you need anything. And I'm sending you a surprise. I think you'll like it."

Cathy ran out like any minute Becca would change her mind and the world would go back to the way it had been.

She probably *would* change her mind. The lawyer would only be interested in her until he realized she was as married to her job as he was, and she wouldn't change her mind and become a good housewife. When she wouldn't drop everything to pick up his dry cleaning, he would find some woman who would.

The hooker would be easier. The hooker might actually be cool with picking up her dry cleaning if she left him a big enough tip.

Was a dude who took money for sex called a hooker?

She stopped at the door to her office.

Dr. Rebecca Walsh

Head of Neurology Research

God, she hoped one day it would say Dr. Rebecca Walsh, chick who cured Alzheimer's and dementia.

Tears welled hard and fast and she forced herself to remember her mother as she'd been. Graceful, happy, intelligent. She closed her eyes and saw her mother sitting at her desk, a lone light illuminating the book she was reading. She always took notes for her lectures. In her mind's eye, she saw her mother turn to her and smile, welcoming her even though she was working. Her mom looked like an angel.

And then another image struck, one of her mother being held down as she tried to get out of bed. She'd screamed and fought and looked at Becca, hatred in her eyes.

She shook off the image. That hadn't been her mom. It hadn't. It had been a disease. She'd said she wasn't angry, but she'd lied. She was violently angry at the disease that had robbed her mother of her mind, her memories, her dignity.

She took a deep breath and pushed through. That was her life. Pushing through. She'd been born for this, born to fight this fight.

But even gladiators took the night off every now and then.

She glanced down at the reports on her desk. Cathy had done exactly what she'd asked. She had the accounting reports for the last few quarters. Now there was a mystery she wanted to solve.

Something was up with the accounting. Perhaps it was nothing more than a mathematical error or the misapplication of funds to one account or another, but there was a million dollars missing. It had been taken out in small figures. A hundred here, nine hundred there. There was a requisition for a seventy-five-thousand-dollar piece of medical equipment, but she couldn't find the delivery receipt. It all added up to one big suspicion. Becca intended to figure out where it had gone.

She gathered up the files. She'd had them printed out because she didn't want anyone to know she was looking into it.

Her cell rang and she sighed in relief. She didn't have to think about it for another couple of minutes. Her dad. He called as she was finishing up work every day he wasn't in surgery. She put her earbuds in and answered the call.

"Hey, Pops. What's going on?" She grabbed her tote bag and

shoved the paperwork in.

"Hi, Peanut." His warm voice came over the line. "Are you on your way to the subway?"

"I'm walking out now," she replied, doing exactly that. "We've got a good ten minutes. How was your day?"

He started to talk and she locked her office, ready to head home.

* * * *

Paul Huisman strode down the steps of the building that bore his name. Not his truly, as his father and grandfather would remind him, but rather of his family. He himself hadn't proven that he was worthy of the name yet. As though a medical degree from Harvard wasn't good enough, there was some other elusive thing he needed to find in order to make his family proud.

He'd done everything they'd asked of him. He'd gone to the right schools, done his residency at the best hospital, married the woman they'd asked him to, and produced a genius-level child, and they'd still given the position he'd worked for all his life to a woman ten years younger than him.

He hated Rebecca Walsh with a passion, and he was going to finally do something about it.

Perhaps what his family had been waiting for was a show of ruthless will. They were about to get it.

A limo pulled up in front of the building and he sighed. Hopefully it would move along quickly because this was the best place to catch a cab. He couldn't stand the thought of getting on the subway. Being stuck in traffic would be far better than sharing space with the riffraff.

He would hire a car and driver, but his fucking father had cut him off after Miranda divorced him. One more failure in his family's eyes. He couldn't help it that the bitch hadn't been able to handle his work schedule and needed some desperate, clingy man to make her feel alive.

He was going to ensure that the woman didn't emasculate his son. He wasn't sure how to do it, but he couldn't stand the way Emmanuel whined and cried and was scared of his own shadow.

The door to the limo came open as a perfectly good cab drove by, ignoring Paul's outstretched hand.

The driver of the limo was a big man whose tailored black suit looked barely large enough to encase his muscular body. He wore a black hat and hustled to move around the car. "Dr. Huisman?"

He pulled his hand back down. "That's me."

"My employer would like to have a moment of your time." The driver wasn't Canadian. Not at all. That accent was pure Boston, and not the educated kind. He'd spent years in Massachusetts studying, and he knew a Southie when he heard one.

"Your employer is?" If his father had sent a lawyer, then he'd likely discovered the plot against Rebecca Walsh and his whole life might end here and now. Nausea threatened. He had no idea what his father would do if he figured out how he'd planned on getting rid of his golden girl.

Still, he managed to remain calm. Perhaps his father had somehow discovered the missing money and tied it back to Walsh and wanted to discuss how to fire her. If he could get the bitch thrown in jail, it would be all the better.

The driver opened the door and he glimpsed a man he'd never met before. Definitely not a lawyer. Lawyers wore suits, not skinny jeans, short-sleeved button-downs with bow ties and suspenders. The man in the limo looked like he'd walked straight out of a hipster modeling session right down to the IPA he held in his right hand.

"Hello, Dr. Huisman. Why don't you let me give you a ride," the man with the dark hair said. "We can talk along the way. I believe we have some mutual interests, and you'll find we can help each other out. You're interested in eliminating Rebecca Walsh so you can take her place, correct?"

Fuck. This might be a trap, but he was going to have to find out where it led. Someone definitely knew about his plans. He had to get into that limo if only to find out how much this stranger knew. Besides, he wasn't sure the massive driver would take no for an answer. He glanced around to see if anyone was watching.

"Dr. Huisman, we're totally safe. I assure you I know exactly where Dr. Walsh is, and she won't be a problem. If you're worried about your father, I can tell you exactly how to handle him. Did you know he's got a mistress in Montreal?" the man asked.

He eased into the limo, the nausea more than a mere possibility now. Bile rose hard and fast, and he only barely managed to swallow it down. "My father always has a mistress. My mother doesn't care. No one does. Don't you think if I could unseat the man, I would? But no one prioritizes morals anymore as long as the foundation brings in money and continues to be respected. The cancer team won a Nobel Prize last year. Do you honestly believe the fact that my father cheats will overshadow his recruiting abilities?"

The door closed behind him. He didn't see a weapon on the man, but the very fact that he knew about his plot to regain his position was far more frightening than any weapon that could be used against him.

The mystery man offered him a beer. "It's a little hoppy, but I like the way it finishes."

"I don't drink." Ever. He wouldn't allow himself to be out of control. He'd watched his own brother drink his life away.

The man simply put the second beer down and took a swallow of the first. "Your loss, man. They only offer this sucker once a year. I find the seasonal nature enhances the experience. Anyway, I'm sure your father's other mistresses were lovely women, and anyone could understand how a powerful man needs his indulgences, but they usually become less willing to overlook an affair when a powerful man has one with a Chinese operative who's known for specializing in corporate espionage."

He felt his body still in utter shock even as the limo pulled away. "What?"

The man across from him looked thoughtful. "Is it corporate espionage? I think so. I mean I know it's a research group and it's supposed to be nonprofit, but the very word nonprofit is an oxymoron. I like that word. I always have. I genuinely look forward to using it in sentences. As I was saying, you're all funded by corporations. They give you money so they can have early access to the data and research. It's like that everywhere now, even here in Canada. I won't even get into the States. We're kind of the Corporate States of America when you think about it, and that's a problem for me."

"I'm sorry, you're American?" The words weren't quite penetrating his brain. His father's latest mistress was a spy?

Could he prove that?

"Oh, I'm one hundred percent red, white, and blue," he said. "I work for a division of our government interested in some of Dr. Walsh's former colleagues. You remember a woman named Hope McDonald?"

The name sent a chill down his spine. He'd met her at a few conferences, but one night he'd talked to her at the bar. She'd flirted with him and he'd been under no illusions that the woman was interested in anything but the Huisman Foundation and his access to it. After a few whiskeys, she'd told him the strangest tale. All nonsense, of course.

No one could steal a person's memories. No one could erase minds and make slaves of soldiers.

Could they?

"I know her. Knew her. She died a couple of years ago." Under somewhat mysterious circumstances. He hadn't looked too deeply into it, had merely been relieved he wouldn't have to deal with her again.

"Did you know Dr. Walsh worked with her when she was fresh out of med school? She'd written a paper while she was at Johns Hopkins about possibilities for breaking down the plaques in the brain that strangle healthy nerve cells."

"I'm well aware of how the disease works," he shot back. "I am also researching new drugs and therapies for dealing with Alzheimer's."

"But she's further along than you are, isn't she? So much further." The man's voice had taken on an oddly sympathetic tone, soothing almost. "You can't help it. Everyone listens to her. Her ideas aren't really new."

"They're derivative." He'd always said it. She was standing on the backs of the truly brilliant. Just because she'd solved a few problems shouldn't make her the darling of the neuro world, but she'd been exactly that for years. She was the shiny new thing they all followed.

"Who would take over her research if she, say, was found to have stolen a million dollars from the foundation? From what I understand, the foundation itself owns the research done here. If she went to jail, Huisman would retain the intellectual property, I assume."

That was precisely how it would work. "I would take it over."

He would take it over, and no one had to know they hadn't been his ideas in the first place. Everyone knew they worked together. He could easily slip into her role, and by the time he was ready to publish, no one would remember she'd ever existed.

"Yes, you would, my friend, and from what I understand, she's close," he said as the limo stopped at a red light. "But she knows something is going on and you're about to get found out. Did you know she asked accounting for the bank statements on the account you took the million out of? I assume it was you. If it wasn't, please accept my apologies and I'll drop you off."

"What do you want from me?"

The man finished off his beer and sat back. "Like I said, we have a mutual interest in Dr. Walsh and her research. She believes she's found a way to reverse the effects of the proteins that cause Alzheimer's. Dr. McDonald used many of Walsh's techniques in her own research, though in a very different way. I believe between Dr. Walsh's current research and getting my hands on McDonald's old research, I can find that cure and then I'll be in a position to help my country in a way no one can imagine."

The man knew how to ask for the world. Paul was in a corner and he wasn't sure he could find his way out. "I have no idea where Dr. McDonald's research is. She's dead."

A slow smile crossed the man's lips, a Cheshire Cat-like grin. "Yes and a few weeks before she died, she sent a box to Rebecca Walsh. Unfortunately, she was getting a divorce at the time and the package went to her husband's house. By the time I tracked it down, she'd settled in here and it had been delivered to her. It got caught up in customs for a while, but I have every reason to believe she has it. I had someone recently search her apartment and it wasn't there. I need you to figure out where she would have put it and get it and all of her current research to me. I had another plan in place, but then you fell into my lap. You're a godsend, Paul. If you can get me what I need, I won't have to deal with some unsavory characters, if you know what I mean."

Perhaps the corner wouldn't be so hard to maneuver out of. He could search her office. He knew the building like the back of his hand. Maybe this didn't have to be the end. "And I get?"

"You get my aid in achieving your goal," his own personal Mephistopheles explained. "You're going about it all wrong and it's time to up your game, my man. The players have recently changed and you're going to have to move quickly because there's nothing these guys love more than riding in like white knights when a lady is concerned. You need help or you're going to be the one going to jail. It's your choice. I can help you or find someone else who's willing to help me."

"I want proof that my father is sleeping with a spy." He might come out of this with far more than a department head job. He might come out of it with the whole foundation in his hands.

All he had to do was crush a couple of people.

"You'll have it," his new partner said, satisfaction dripping from his tone. "Now let's talk about how we strengthen the case against Walsh. We have to be careful. She's made some new friends, and while they're idealistic morons, they can be deadly when they want to be. The key is to make the narrative work for us."

"What the hell does that mean?"

"It means it's time for the real game to begin, Dr. Huisman." He sat back. "And you should call me Mr. Green."

The limo rolled on as Mr. Green began to talk.

* * * *

An hour later, Becca stopped outside the bistro on the ground floor of her building. There was a couch sitting in front of the windows where patrons watched the street as they drank their coffees and teas. The couch was a new addition, and if the moving van was any indication, it wouldn't be permanent.

Across the street, the pub was already filling up, and in another hour or so, it would be rocking for the rest of the night as university students and the young professionals who lived in the neighborhood blew off steam.

She would be up in her two-bedroom apartment, in the room she'd meant to be a guest room but had somehow morphed into a second office. Even when she wasn't at work, she was still there somehow.

Should she start early? Talking to her father today hadn't calmed her the way it normally would. He'd talked about her sister, Emma, and how she was giving the kindergarten teacher fits because she corrected her grammar.

Maybe she should grab a beer and see what the college set looked like these days. She hadn't partied a ton in college. She'd been far too young. By the time she was old enough to drink she'd been done with medical school, and then she'd married and been very serious about her career.

She was sick of being serious.

A massive white and brown ball of fur sat on a couch in front of the entrance to the bistro and a pretty woman with long brown hair held the leash. She was frowning down at her cell phone. The new chick in 7E. She and her husband had moved in two weeks before.

She'd met the new residents a couple of times. Jax seemed quiet and more interested in his wife than anything else. River was one of those women who glowed in a way Becca didn't quite understand. They were a mystery to her, but one thing wasn't. There was one thing about the new couple she totally got.

Becca dropped to one knee and petted that gorgeous dog. "Hey, Buster. How are you, boy?"

The adorable mutt thumped his tail and practically vibrated with excitement. God, she loved dogs. No muss. No fuss. Just unconditional love. Maybe she should skip the dude and get a dog.

Of course, the dog couldn't take care of her other needs. Maybe she could have both. A dog and a nice male escort on speed dial.

"Hey, Becca." River glanced down, sliding her phone into her purse. "How are you doing?"

"I'm good. It was a long day, but I think I managed to save a lot of women from some serious waxing in the future. Side effects. They get us every time." She gave River a grin. It was fun to scare the general public. "How about you?"

The smile River returned was slightly scared. "I'm so glad you could do that for the rest of us. I think I'm going totally hippie. I have some friends who swear they can cure everything with beets."

"Hey, there were beets in this formulary. If you like magenta urine, you should have at it," she offered, managing to duck a hardcore dog kiss. Buster tended to go for the mouth. "You off for your nightly run?"

River nodded. "Yep. I hope the boys can keep up with me. Just waiting on Jax. He ran upstairs to grab the bags. It does not pay to forget the bags because Buster here likes to poop. Don't you, boy?"

Buster got up and did a doggy dance, as though anything River said was the best thing in the world and he agreed.

No one looked at her like that, with total unconditional love. They either obsequiously kissed her ass because she could get their research funded or hated her because she hadn't funded their research. The dog thing could work. Not that she had a ton of time to take said beloved dog on walks.

Maybe the escort on speed dial could also be a dog walker.

"Hey, babe," a deep voice said. "Got 'em. You ready for a run?"

Of course no one had ever looked at her the way Jax looked at River either. Like she was the sun in the sky. Like the world had been dark before he'd met her.

She probably wouldn't get that from her fantasy escort.

"I am." River held her face up so her incredibly tall husband could drop a kiss on her lips.

He looked over as Becca got to her feet again. "Hey, how's it going? Looks like we're getting some new neighbors. Someone's moving in down the hall."

The rental agency had been quick. Only two days before, the Holders had moved out. From what she'd heard, the wife was pregnant and they were buying a place in the suburbs so they had more room.

She hoped the new guys weren't partiers. "University kids?"

Jax shrugged. "Nah, they're actual adults. Seem nice. Buster, get off that couch. They'll love us though since we've already given them the gift of dog hair."

River grinned and leaned in. "It gets everywhere. You get used to it. Hey, I meant to come by and see you. We're having a party Saturday night with a couple of friends of ours. A housewarming thing. This is our first real place since we got married. We were living in Jax's sarcastic uncle's basement for a couple of months before he got the job up here."

Jax shook his head, his relief apparent. "My uncle has three kids and is working on a fourth. Those kids are seriously going to be the reason for the next world war. I swear."

"That's why they're building an army," River agreed. "I love it here. It's so quiet, and no one has tried to burn the place down or practiced archery in a crazy, dangerous way. It's peaceful. We're never having kids. Only dogs. Lots of dogs."

"I would argue but I saw Kenzie modify a Nerf gun, and I'm pretty sure it's lethal now," Jax replied. "Buster can't make weapons. Well, he sometimes gets gas, and that's pretty powerful."

River lightly slapped her husband across his abs. "Whose fault is that? You're the one who sneaks him treats all the time. Dogs aren't supposed to eat Twinkies. For that matter, humans shouldn't either."

Jax laughed, but River glanced back at Becca. "Like I said, we're having a party and we would love for you to come."

A party? With people? And food she didn't order from a restaurant or microwave? "I'm totally in. I'm starting this new thing where I have a life outside of work. It's weird. There's this whole world and it's not in the Huisman building. I've heard there are people out here who don't care about neuroscience."

Jax chuckled at that one. "Yes, and if you come over Saturday, you'll meet a couple of them."

River shoved the small container of bags in her jacket. "It starts at six and we're having dinner. I say it's a party but it's only about six people. You would be seven. I'm making an insane amount of lasagna, so even if you only stop by for a bite, you would be more than welcome. We had a great group of friends back in Texas. We would love to have that here, too."

A group of friends. She had a group of coworkers, most of whom thought she was intimidating. Or awkward. The good news was she'd heard weird was the new chic. She'd seen it in a magazine on Cathy's desk and everything. Melissa kept telling her that one day she would find a man who could appreciate her unique sense of humor.

She hadn't found him yet. Not even close.

"I'll be there." It would be an excellent way to begin this new phase of her life. She would probably be the only singleton there, and that was fairly safe. Then she would go out with Cathy's lawyer friend, and hopefully he was superhot and watched Marvel movies and was good at no-commitment sex.

She waved good-bye to her new friends and walked into the bistro without looking back. Her dinner was in a bag and already paid for. All she had to do was pick it up and sign the bill, leaving a nice tip because they always had dinner waiting for her. Like clockwork. Everything running smoothly. Nothing out of place.

Her whole evening was spread out in front of her. The rest of her life, when she thought about it. She got up, showered, ate oatmeal and drank one cup of coffee, went to work, ate lunch when Cathy put it in front of her, came home, picked up her daily dinner and stared at a screen until she passed out.

Would going to the party Saturday night make a difference? She was stuck. It had been a good idea to put her head down and give herself some space, but she was caught in a routine, utterly stuck in a place she'd sworn she wouldn't be again.

She'd promised her mother that she would be happy. She wasn't.

It was far past time to work on herself.

She walked through the bistro to the street and around to her building, putting in her code to open the door. At least the new people had decent taste, if that couch was any indication.

She would wait until they had time to settle in and then she would introduce herself. She was going to be a good neighbor. And maybe she could make some friends. Maybe it would be a couple of fun-loving career women she could drink wine with after a long hard day of busting the glass ceiling.

Maybe they would know some nice male hookers.

She needed to get her mind off sex.

She glanced back at the entryway. A tall man with dark hair was talking to the movers. He frowned down at the couch and reached over, coming back with a pile of dog hair.

She covered her mouth before she could laugh.

He glanced up and his eyes widened.

Nope. She wasn't taking the fall for this one. She turned back and hurried toward the old elevator that always creaked and moaned as though it would give out at any moment. It was "vintage," as the homeowners' association would say. She caught sight of a man in a leather jacket entering the elevator and then the doors started their slow slide closed.

"Could you hold the elevator, please?"

A big hand came out and the doors opened again. She rushed in and turned to press the button for seven, but it was already lit. She looked up and into the bluest eyes she'd ever seen. She literally had to catch her breath. She'd heard the expression, and it was meaningful when it came to running hard or walking up a flight of steps, but she wasn't out of breath because of anything physical. He was the single most gorgeous man she'd ever seen in her life.

She turned her head to look at the metal doors.

"What floor do you need?"

And he was Scottish. That accent was sexy as hell and straight out of her every *Outlander* fantasy. She'd only read it because it had a surprising amount of medical knowledge in it. Herbs. She'd learned a lot about herbs. And that she thought Scottish men were sexy. She'd worked with a doctor a couple of years ago, much older than she was, and it hadn't mattered because that accent had sent her heart skittering every time he opened his mouth.

"Do you just like to ride up and down the lifts, lass?"

She glanced up. They were already at three. "I'm going to seven, too."

"Lucky me. I was worried this thing wouldn't make it to two different floors," he said with a chuckle. "We've got much better odds this way."

Where the hell had he come from? Obviously Scotland, but that wasn't the point. The dude belonged on a movie screen. Whoa. There was another possible reason. "You wouldn't happen to be a stripper?"

Cathy had said she'd sent a surprise. He would be a total surprise.

"Excuse me?" The hot guy with the gold and red hair turned to her, his full lips easing down into a frown that should have intimidated her but kind of made her hot. "Did you ask if I'm a stripper?"

Her big mouth got her in trouble. She'd never learned to moderate. She often said whatever came into her head when she was flustered. Her father told her it was charming, but then she'd never asked her dad if he was planning on taking his clothes off for cash. "Sorry. I haven't seen you around here before and my friend told me she was sending me a surprise. She's a little on the perverse side, so a stripper could have been in the mix." She looked up at the glowing light that indicated what floor they were on. The elevator was moving slower than usual. Four. Three more to go. "You're insanely attractive so I thought movie star or stripper."

"Am I now?" His deep voice had gone from irritated to amused.

"Oh, I think you know you're insanely attractive." She'd stroked his ego enough.

Only another thirty seconds or so and she could run off the elevator and be in her apartment, and maybe instead of going over those accounting reports while listening to the news and eating her chicken sandwich, she would binge watch some *Outlander*. That might be fun.

"A man likes to hear it, you know," he replied, standing right beside her. If he moved a little, his arm would brush against hers. Not his shoulder. He had a good half a foot on her. And she bet he worked out. A lot.

"Well, you're very nice to look at. If you wanted to make it as a stripper, I think you could," she said primly.

One more floor and she could stop making an idiot of herself.

"Nah, I'm shite at dancing," he admitted. "I'll stick to what I'm good at."

"And what's that?" She couldn't seem to stop talking.

"Shooting things. I'm an assassin."

She turned to him, her eyes open wide, and that was the moment the elevator shook and came to a stop. Right between floors six and seven.

And she was left stuck with a criminal.

Chapter Three

Oh, he liked the fact that he'd put that look on her face. She was far too flirty, but he got the idea she viewed him as amusing and nothing else. A pretty face. It oddly rankled. Odd because he'd never minded that before. A woman wanted a good time, he was her man. Something about the lovely doctor treating him like he was a lightweight bothered him.

Thought he was a stripper, did she?

"I think the elevator stopped." Her voice sounded breathless. "Did you do that?"

And she was naïve, or he was a far better actor than he gave himself credit for. It made him wonder though why she immediately thought he'd set this up. She was suspicious? That was interesting. "I work security, love. I was joking about being an assassin." He held his hands up, letting his shoulders fall back so his jacket opened. "See, no guns."

He wouldn't actually need a gun to take a person out. He might have forgotten everything about his past, but his body remembered how to kill.

It might be the only thing he was good at.

Besides, his Glock was in his bag, but she didn't need to know that. She didn't need to know that the messenger bag he was carrying held a Glock, extra ammo, two knives, and a taser unit. It also held a file on one Dr. Rebecca Walsh that would likely have her clawing her way out of this lift.

Her face had gone the sweetest pink. "It's because I thought you might be a stripper, isn't it?"

He shrugged and looked at the lift's panel. Seven was lit up, but it was obvious they were stuck. Oddly, he didn't mind. It might be the longest he got alone with the target, and he was going to use it to get to know her a bit. After this, Robert would be the one trying to befriend her and he would stay to the background. "A man likes to be known for his brain. Eyes up here, lass."

She'd gone even pinker because sure enough, he caught her staring at his chest. "Sorry. I work with a bunch of doctors and medical techs. Despite what you see on TV, they are not all stunningly gorgeous. They know what abs are but not how to work 'em, if you know what I mean."

"You look quite fit." She was different in person, more vibrant than any photo could convey. At first, he hadn't actually recognized her. She'd slipped into the lift and all he'd thought about was how luscious her ass was in that skirt she was wearing.

"Oh, I have to be. I wear a lot of spandex," she said and then winced. "That came out wrong."

"Who's the stripper now?" She was actually quite adorable, but in a surprisingly sexy way.

He couldn't help but think that if Robert hadn't been such a bloody picky bastard, he would be the one standing out at the street, directing the movers. He wouldn't be stuck briefly in here with the most intriguing woman he'd seen in forever. Well, in roughly two years, since he'd woken up with no knowledge of who he was.

"I'm a doctor," she shot back, but her lips had curled up as though she enjoyed the flirtatious air they'd found.

He was supposed to be Robert's husband. He didn't want to be Robert's husband.

It didn't matter. They would be out of here in a few moments and he would fade into the background. Hell, he could be bi for all she knew. It could help the op because he could be Robert's cheating bisexual husband and they could commiserate because he was fairly certain she'd divorced her husband for similar reasons.

The small phone on the panel rang and he picked it up. They

needed to get out of here as quickly as possible. He wasn't good at this part. Hell, he'd already announced to the target that he was a bloody assassin. This was Robert's job. He was the one who would break into her apartment while Robert distracted her. That was what he was good at. "Is there a problem?"

"Oh, eh, I was hoping no one was there. Sorry. The elevator seems to be broken," a tinny voice said. "I got an alert on my phone."

"No shite, mate," he replied. "And it's definitely not empty. There's two of us in here."

The doc was getting into his space. "If that's Colin, you tell him he can't just slap an out-of-order sign on the doors this time. I'm not living here for a week, damn it."

"Is that Doctor Walsh? Crap." Colin sounded slightly terrified. "Uhm, look, I have a call in to someone who can fix it, but I have to get my dad to okay the cost."

"Your dad? How the bloody hell old are you?" Owen asked.

"He's barely twenty-two, but his father owns the building and wanted to retire," Becca pointed out.

"I don't care how old you are, lad. You get someone to get us out of this bloody box." He couldn't be in here for hours.

"Sorry. I'll get you out of there as fast as I can," Colin promised and the line went dead.

Owen hung up and sighed. "Does this happen a lot?"

She backed away quickly, as if she realized she was far too close for comfort. "Not too often, but the last time it happened it was several hours before they managed to get that sucker working. It depends on where we are. If we're close to seven, they can pry the doors open and we can wiggle out. If we're solidly in between, they'll ask us to stay inside as long as there's no danger. Are you claustrophobic?"

She picked a corner and slid down to the floor, somehow managing to make the move graceful. She wore a black skirt, white blouse, and a prim pink cardigan. It made her look like a sweet little schoolteacher. The bottle in her hand was a contradiction. She'd reached inside her brown-and-white striped tote bag. He noticed she had a bunch of files in there, too.

That was interesting. He wouldn't mind looking through a few of those, but she would probably not like him making a grab for her bag.

He watched as she unscrewed the top of the bottle of wine. "Not really."

She tipped the bottle his way. "I am. A little. Don't worry. I won't flip my shit on you or anything, but I'm going to start on this bad boy before it gets warm." She looked at the green bottle in her hands. "Thank you, New Zealand, for your grapes and your rejection of pretentious corks in your wines. I would be seriously fucked if I drank red."

She tipped that sucker up and drank a surprising amount of Sauvignon Blanc.

She was not what he'd expected.

He glanced down at her. What *had* he expected? Certainly not a woman who looked like a sweet librarian and talked like a bloody sailor. Who had an MD and drank like a fish and talked about male strippers like she knew a couple or wanted to know a couple.

She was a walking contradiction. Well, a sitting one.

He put his back to the opposite wall from her and let his body slide down. He pulled the strap of the messenger bag over his head and settled it into the corner before reaching into his jacket. She was speaking his language now. He pulled out his flask and opened it, holding it up because a Scotsman knew how to toast even a clusterfuck of a situation. "Cheers, lass."

Robert wouldn't be able to drink with her. The man was far too in control. He didn't carry around his whiskey. He was all proper like and drank in bars out of posh glasses and not a flask.

Was Robert the right man to get close to this woman? He was starting to think they'd read her wrong. She might not need a serious, intellectual friend.

She might need a bad boy.

Her lips tugged up and she held up her bottle. "I bet you get a lot of women with that accent alone. Cheers."

They clinked beverage containers. "Less than you would expect." A lie, but he didn't want her to think he was a complete manwhore. There were bad boys and then there were walking venereal diseases. He certainly wasn't going to tell her about the women he'd gone through during his recent stay in Dallas. He'd run through the single subs at Sanctum in quick order. "So you live here?"

Small talk. They needed some small talk. Maybe he could find out a thing or two, prove he wasn't a complete moron.

She wasn't some file or a picture on the wall. She wasn't a bunch of degrees or the sum of her education and her job. She was a woman.

They forgot that at their own peril.

She nodded, taking another drink. "Yep. I've been living here for about two years and this stupid elevator is broken more than it works. Apparently it's an antique and the historical society doesn't want it to change. The historical society doesn't have to hoof it up seven flights of stairs." She frowned. "There's a more modern elevator at the back of the building, but I'm too lazy to walk to it. My laziness foils me again. I could be watching *Doctor Who* right now."

And she was a geek, though he shouldn't be so surprised since he knew about her secondary job. He had to pretend like he didn't, of course. "Is that why you wear spandex? You like science fiction and comic books?"

He took a swig of his whiskey and felt the familiar burn down his throat. Normally it would relax him, make him look forward to the next drink, but this time, he was focused on her.

"I love them," she said, her eyes lighting up. "When I was growing up, all I read were comic books and medical texts. I'm still a Marvel girl. I suppose you could say I didn't have a ton of friends. I was always the youngest person in my class. And the oddest. I was the weird kid who fell madly in love with viruses at a young age."

He could feel his brows rise. "Viruses?"

She nodded. "They're the true supervillains of the world. Snakes only kill fifty thousand people a year. Influenza? Over six hundred thousand in the world every year. We're scared of sharks and shit? They got nothing on a good VHF."

He was getting his flu shot. Tucker had been pestering him about it and he'd viewed the kid as a mother hen, but perhaps he knew what he was talking about. "VHF?"

"Sorry, uhm viral hemorrhagic fever," she explained, pushing her glasses up her nose. "VHFs come from one of six virus families, all nasty. I'm a particular fan of filoviridae. Filovirus virions are pleomorphic. That means they can come in different shapes. Some are like a six or a U. They have these long filaments. I remember the first time I saw one under a microscope. Zaire ebolavirus. I stared at it. So small and so destructive. We still aren't certain exactly how the fuckers replicate."

He had no idea what she was talking about. "And you were a child studying this?"

"Yep. My dad was a doctor. My mom was a college professor. I got a bunch of brains," she admitted. "I used to follow my dad around on rounds. The patients thought it was sweet at first, and then they would get disconcerted when I would offer a second opinion. Having a kid in pigtails arguing diagnoses is apparently scary. I was hell on teachers. Now I kind of wish I'd studied engineering and mechanics. I don't suppose you know how to fix an elevator."

"I could shoot it if I had my guns," he admitted, not bothered at all with his slight lie. She wouldn't be as comfortable with him if she knew how well armed he was. "I'm quite good at close combat, but it doesn't have a throat I can go for or balls I can kick."

She winced. "I thought balls were sacred to men."

"Not in a fight they aren't." He was comfortable around her. Way more than he would normally be. There was a reason he didn't date. He seemed to have lost most of his charm when he'd lost his memory. "In a fight all that matters is winning. I'm not talking about some posh MMA fight. I'm talking down and dirty, someone's dying fight."

She chuckled. "I don't know how many people would call a cage fight posh. You sound like you were in the military."

He rather thought he still was. Oh, they didn't call themselves that and they served no country, but they ran like a unit most of the time. "I was SAS for years. That's British military. I might not know how to fix a lift, but I can fly a helicopter. I can use almost any weapon known to man and I'm skilled at martial arts. Best thing I do now is step in front of bullets. I'm a bodyguard. I'm working for a firm here, providing security for celebrities and politicians, and rich people who need to feel like they're celebrities."

This was the part where he explained that his husband, Robert, had taken a job with a bank here in Toronto and they'd moved from DC. Robert had worked for the bank for years and when he'd had the opportunity to transfer, they'd taken it. He should explain that they'd been together for a couple of years and recently married in an intimate but lovely ceremony.

The words stuck in his throat and wouldn't come out. He took another drag off the flask.

Friendly wasn't the way to play this woman. She wanted to flirt.

She was attracted to him and from what he understood, she didn't have a lover.

Then there was the fact that he was attracted to her, too. He didn't want to cut off that possibility. Not if he didn't have to, not if he thought this was the better way to go. He was alone in here. He needed to follow his instincts.

Or you could follow the bloody plan, take a step back, and if it all fails, it's not your fault because you followed the bloody plan.

"I'm a doctor."

"No shite." He chuckled. "You're either a doctor or some kind of evil genius who's going to set a virus on the world."

"Well, if I was an evil genius, that's exactly what I would do," she admitted. "But I'm not. I work research. Neuro."

He sighed and decided to play it the way a bodyguard who didn't work intelligence would. "You're going to have to use layman's terms. Remember? I take bullets, not classes."

"I research the brain, more specifically degenerative brain diseases. I'm hoping to find new therapies, even a cure for dementia and Alzheimer's."

For the first time she spoke softly, almost shyly.

He'd found something to poke and prod. "The way you talk I would think you would have studied viruses."

"I thought I would when I was a kid," she admitted. "Things changed as I got older."

Because of her mother? He didn't like how that thought made him soften toward her. That was the funny thing about getting to know the target. It often made them human. "What sent you into...neuro?"

She was quiet for a moment. "My mom died of Alzheimer's, well, complications from it. I started studying the brain so I could understand what was happening to her. And then I kind of wanted to beat it, you know. It took her from me. I wanted to destroy it. I still do."

"I lost my mum." He wasn't sure why he'd said that but she had a hollow look on her face that made him want to connect to her. It felt right to talk to her. Hell, he'd never talked about this with anyone but Ariel, and only because she wouldn't clear him for play in The Garden or Sanctum until she felt like he'd faced it. He'd never faced it. How did a man face the loss of someone he couldn't remember?

"Did she get sick?"

They hadn't covered this in his briefing. Probably because he wasn't supposed to go this deep with the target. He wasn't supposed to be stuck in a lift with her. "She was killed in a break-in." He swallowed hard, the emotion welling up hard and fast. "She and my sister. The men who…well, they were caught."

Her eyes had widened. "That's terrible. I'm so sorry to hear that." She was silent for a moment and they both took long drinks. "Now you protect people."

"And you try to save them," he acknowledged. "Maybe it's tragedy that sets us on a path. Maybe it's the way we get fucked up that leads us to where we're supposed to be."

She held up her bottle again. "To fucked-up lives."

He could drink to that.

She set her bottle down. "I've got a sandwich. You want half? I've got some chips, too. Now I wished I'd given in and gotten those cookies I wanted."

Damn but she was pretty. "I've got a chocolate bar in my bag and a couple of protein bars, but they taste like shite. We should ration them. I'll share it all with you if you'll tell me why you wear spandex and just how tight it is."

A glorious grin transformed her face. There was the glowy girl he'd seen, the one who utterly fascinated him. "Deal. Let me tell you all about the magnificent Captain Neuro."

She passed him half the sandwich as she began to talk, and Owen got the idea that he was in trouble.

Chapter Four

Hour One

"This is pretty good, but it needs apples. Chicken salad needs some fruit in it," Owen said.

"Who hurt you?" Becca clutched her half of the sandwich and wondered what kind of a crazy person she'd been stuck with.

Hour Two

"No one says Sassenach," he insisted. "And you know I don't eat haggis with every bloody meal. Nor do I play the bagpipes."

"What kind of Scot are you?" She'd moved closer to him sometime after Colin had called to let them know it would be at least another three hours. The amount of times the kid had said the word *sorry* should be made into a drinking game.

Not that he needed one. He was out and he'd taken to helping her finish off the bottle of wine. She'd passed it back and forth, seeming not to mind that she was sharing germs with a stranger.

It made him wonder what else she might like to share with him.

Fuck, but she was sexy.

"A modern one," he replied.

She wrinkled her nose sweetly. "How about a kilt?"

"Don't even own one." There was a reason for that. He'd seen pictures of himself in a kilt, but he'd left everything behind. His house in Edinburgh had been closed up and he hadn't been back. "And yes, I wear underwear."

"Such a disappointment," she said with a shake of her head.

How disappointed would she be if she knew that while she'd closed her eyes and tried to find her calm a few moments before, he'd slipped one of the folders out of her bag and into his?

He suddenly didn't want to be the one who disappointed her.

Hour Three

"Sometimes when the towel dispenser in the bathroom, you know the motion activated ones…when they don't give me a towel, I wonder if I died and I don't know it and this is how I find out. Same thing with the soap dispenser."

She was bloody insane. It kind of did something for him. "I can see that public loos are difficult for you. Have you considered you might have watched too many movies?"

"Never," she swore. "Not even once."

Hour Four

She paced the length of the elevator. Two steps to the left, pivot and turn. Two steps to the right.

Fucking elevator. Meditation wasn't working and she was pretty sure her superhot elevator co-hostage thought she was a weirdo for sitting there and trying to breathe. He'd been polite about it, but he probably was questioning whether or not she would lose her shit.

Did they even have enough oxygen left?

"Tell me about your ex." Owen Shaw didn't look like he was ready to come out of his skin. He wasn't worried about the amount of oxygen left in the tiny box they were currently stuck in. He was cool and calm and it rankled.

How much longer? She'd kept it at bay for a while, but after Colin had explained they were waiting on a part someone had to drive in from freaking Burlington, she'd nearly lost her shit.

They were trapped and their cell phones didn't work. The only contact they had with the outside world was freaking Colin. This was a nightmare.

And her partner in the cage didn't look like it bothered him at all. She should have bought more wine. She knew what he was doing. He was trying to distract her. "He was an asshole."

"Obviously," he shot back. "Since you divorced him."

God, that man was far too gorgeous. She should concentrate on him. If she was staring at his glorious eyes and thinking about running her hands through his thick red and gold hair, she might not remember that they were suspended in a steel box six and a half floors up from the ground.

She took a deep breath. "He liked to cheat. The grass is always greener for some men. I think he thought when we got married that I would settle down and be his good wife or something."

"You were a doctor, too," Owen pointed out. "Did the bugger expect you to give up your career to make his dinner?"

"Not exactly, though there was a part of that in there. I think he expected me to help him shine more than I was willing to do," she admitted. "I was pretty smart and good at writing research papers."

"Ah, he wanted you to coauthor with him."

"Mostly he wanted to put his name on my stuff." The worst fight they'd ever had was over a paper for the *New England Journal of Medicine*. He'd claimed he should be in the byline because he'd supported her while she'd written it. "Anyway, he found someone who made him feel more like a man and I divorced his ass. The trouble with a guy like that is he's never going to feel like a 'real' man in a marriage. Marriage is about compromise, and there will always be fighting and nagging and struggle, and in the end what he really wants is that first glow of attraction. You can get addicted to it, think it's love. It's not. It's lust and it serves a purpose."

"That's not an incredibly romantic view."

"I'm not an incredibly romantic woman." Though she'd grown up around a couple who loved each other, they'd also been pragmatic and practical. "I think things through. After I got divorced, I decided to take a sabbatical."

His brows rose. Damn, he even looked sexy when he was surprised. "A sabbatical? It couldn't have lasted long. You said you started at the research center around the same time you divorced."

"Not from work. From…relationships."

He stared at her for a moment. "Relationships?"

"Yep. I realized I needed some time to think about what I want. I fell into the relationship with Gary, but I think what I was honestly looking for was stress relief."

"You married a man for stress relief?"

Put like that it sounded dumb, but it was the conclusion she'd come to. "We also had a lot in common. It kind of made sense. We spent a lot of time together. We seemed to like each other. It saved us some money to live together. I should have left it there, but he asked and it seemed rude to tell him no. I don't know. I was chasing something."

"Chasing?"

"Something my mom wanted for me. Before she died, in one of her lucid moments, she said the only thing she wanted was for me to be happy. I thought part of that was getting married. You go to school, have a career, get married, have two point five kids and live the American dream. I didn't consider the fact that not only was my American dream maybe different than other's, but that it would lead me to Canada."

"You needed two years and no boyfriends to figure that out?"

She shrugged. The walls were starting to close in again. "I'm slow on the uptake, but I know what I want now. I have a plan. I'm going to start dating. Or hire a male escort who also dog walks and picks up my dry cleaning. It's one of the two."

When she turned again, he was on his feet. For a big man, he moved quickly and quietly. She'd thought she could feel every movement of this damn elevator that really was held six and a half floors above the ground by a bunch of wires that were probably antiques, too.

"Hey, it's going to be okay, Rebecca." He was close to her, staring down at her with soulful eyes.

"Becca," she corrected, not thinking about the elevator now. She was too busy staring at his perfectly straight jawline. There was a hint of scruff coming in and she wondered how often he had to shave. Did he get all smooth every morning and by evening, his raw masculinity was reasserting itself? "My friends call me Becca."

"Becca," he replied, his voice low. "Concentrate on me, on our conversation. You've done incredibly well. You've been able to hold it off, but this has gone on far longer than you ever should have been expected to handle it. This elevator is tight. I feel it, too, but we can hold off the anxiety together."

She doubted the man in front of her was anxious. He looked solid, like the kind of man who took whatever came his way and simply dealt with it. He wouldn't have needed two freaking years to figure out what he wanted. He would have signed his divorce papers and moved on, not hiding in his work.

It struck her forcibly that she might never have met a man like Owen Shaw. Her childhood had been fairly sheltered. She'd constantly been surrounded by intellectuals, men and women who were far more concerned with their work than anything else.

The ground beneath her shifted and the elevator dropped what felt like ten feet, but she knew in her head it was mere inches. Her heart rate tripled, and she grabbed on to the closest thing she could—him.

His arms went around her, holding her up, and she heard it. He was so tall that her head naturally rested on his chest, and she could hear his heart beating in rapid time.

He was nervous.

The phone rang and Owen cursed, reaching out to grab it. The shaft was so small, he didn't have to let her go to grasp the handle.

"What the bloody hell is happening, Colin?"

She could hear his voice over the line. "Sorry. So sorry. We had to lower the car the tiniest bit. I should have warned you. It's not going to fall. Just needed to reposition to get to the problem. Not long now. Another half an hour or so and I'll have you right out of there."

"If you do that again, do you know what I'm going to do to you, Colin?" Owen asked.

There was a pause over the line and she could practically hear Colin's gulp. "Write my father a tersely worded letter of complaint?"

"No, I'm going to pull your heart out through your throat and then I'll shove it back up your arse."

Colin's breath hitched. "You sound very much like Liam Neeson in that movie."

"Liam Neeson is Irish. I'm a Scot. I assure you what I'll do to you will make you run into Liam Neeson's arms and beg him to save you." He reached back and hung up the phone with a resounding clang.

His arm went back around her. "It's going to be all right. They'll move faster now. So you've taken a sabbatical from men."

She breathed him in, loving how he smelled. Were men supposed to smell this good?

She could feel herself relax as he held her. She'd known him for three hours. She shouldn't let him hold her like this.

And why the fuck not? Because it wasn't smart? Because he might think she wanted something she shouldn't?

She was human. Why shouldn't she want him? Because society told her that good girls didn't make out with guys they'd recently met in an elevator?

Society sucked, and she wasn't a good girl. When her husband had tried to put his name on her work, she'd told him to fuck off and write his own paper. When he'd cheated on her, she'd walked away.

She was single.

God, was he single?

She stepped back.

"What's wrong?" Owen asked.

"Do you have a girlfriend?"

His lips curled up in the sweetest grin, as though he knew exactly why she was asking that question. "No, love. I don't have a girlfriend and I don't have a wife."

He was single. She was single.

The moment lengthened between them.

He stepped back. "I'm sorry. I'm coming on way too strong."

He wasn't. He'd been gentlemanly, friendly. Up until the last couple of moments, he hadn't put a hand on her or leered. She could feel his attraction. It was there in the warm way he looked at her, in the set of his shoulders, relaxed earlier and tense now that he'd touched her. He was thinking about the same thing she was.

"I'm very nervous, Owen. My logical mind knows that it's far more likely for me to die getting hit by lightning than in an elevator, even one that's stuck." Unfortunately, her logical mind was slowly losing control of her dumbass lizard brain.

"Will talking help?" Owen asked. "Because I'm willing to do that. Or whatever you need to take your mind off things."

There was a wealth of promise in those words. Dirty and sweet at the same time. They'd shared her wine, passing it back and forth between them, her lips touching the same place his had been moments before. When she'd drank after him, she'd thought about kissing him.

It had been too long. Two years was way too long to go without sex.

They had a half an hour or so. At least that's what Colin—who might be murdered soon by Owen Shaw—said. She even thought his name was sexy.

What exactly would it hurt if she did kiss him? If she touched him and let him touch her? Hell, what would it hurt if she fucked him? They were both single, both a little needy. They had some time to kill. They'd done everything else.

"I would like to kiss you." If he didn't want her to, he could say no and they could find something else to do. She wasn't going to be embarrassed because some guy didn't want her. Some stunningly gorgeous guy. Some funny, sexy guy. After all, she wouldn't see him after this. She'd never seen him before. He'd told her he was moving in, but she went into work early and came home late. He was a bodyguard, so he likely worked odd hours and traveled a lot.

He was safe. She could open that door, enjoy herself, and then close it again. Owen Shaw could be her first good memory in a long time, the start of many because it was time to get serious about finding some joy and balance in her life.

But only if he wanted some joy, too.

He moved, placing his back against the elevator wall, the sweetest smile lighting up his face. "You have no idea how much I want you to kiss me. I'm right here, love. Do your worst."

He was letting her make the first move. And probably the second. And the third. He was obviously a careful man. It would be easier if he took over, but he was right. This needed to be her choice, and she had to make the move.

She'd been the girl who'd told her parents at the age of five that kindergarten was boring and she wanted to move through the grades until she found something challenging. When they'd told her they wanted her to slow down and enjoy her childhood, she'd gone on strike until the teachers at her school begged her parents to let them move her up.

She was the girl who'd put it all on hold to take care of her mother, too.

Now she was the woman who took what she wanted, and she wanted Owen Shaw.

"It's been a long time since I did this." But her body was already heating up. Her body remembered. Her marriage might have sucked, but the sex had been fairly good. It had been the reason she'd married him. She'd gotten used to regular, good sex.

She'd get used to it again, just on her terms this time.

"Somehow, I think you'll remember," he said. "You play all you like. Stop when you want to."

She'd been right about him. He was a careful man. "And if I don't want to stop?"

"Then you should be happy I'm a man who believes in being prepared," he said, his voice huskier since she'd gotten closer. "The minute you know what you want, you let me know and I'll make it happen. I promise you won't be sorry and you won't be thinking about anything but how good I can make you feel."

He was making her feel alive, and it had been so long since she'd felt like anything but a brain.

Though she knew her brain was a part of this. Her limbic system had been triggered, had been slowly churning for a while now.

She touched him, finally getting her hands on him, and she could feel her respiration rate tick up. The decision made, she gave up on feeling self-conscious. Maybe it wouldn't be as good as she thought it could be. Maybe she was only nervous and killing time in a situation that made her want to pull her own hair out. It didn't matter. He was an indulgence and she'd earned it.

She went up on her toes and brushed her lips against his. Soft and warm and somehow still masculine. His scent washed over her, piney and clean. She could see him in the shower, soaping up his muscular body and oh, yes, it was very muscular. Her hands found his waist and ran up his torso. He was solid and fit.

He stayed still, seemingly willing to let her explore. He kissed her gently, as though he was afraid to scare her off. He obviously did not understand how much it would take to scare her off. Her body, so long denied, was pretty damn determined to have its way at this point.

His hands moved to her waist and he leaned over, deepening the kiss. This was what she'd needed for weeks.

She let her tongue play at his bottom lip and a thrill went through her as she felt his big body shudder, his hips moving against her as if he couldn't help himself.

He was already hard. He seemed to realize what he was doing and while he didn't stop kissing her, he tried to move his hips back.

Nope. She didn't want that at all. She pressed herself against him, trying to let him know she loved the feel of that hard cock against her belly. She leaned into him and his mouth opened, tongue touching hers.

"Tell me I can take over," he whispered between kisses. "Let me off the leash, love. It's killing me not to touch you the way I want to."

How did he want to touch her? Would he be gentle, or would he let his harder side out? She had no doubt this man had a hardass side, and she was curious about it. "Show me how you want to touch me."

A long sigh went through him and his hands came up to her shoulders, drifting over the cardigan that suddenly seemed way too confining. She didn't need it, right? His hands moved up to her neck while he kissed her and then he tangled his fingers in her hair and the kiss seemed to go wild.

His tongue invaded, stroking against hers. He held her still while he plundered her mouth. A wave of insane lust threatened to shake her to the core. Her body seemed to melt against his. All that mattered was his next kiss, the next touch. Her fingers found his shirt, pulling it free from his jeans.

"God, yes, Becca," he groaned against her mouth. "Touch me."

She ran her hands under his shirt, her palms finding his smooth, warm skin, and yes, all those muscles.

He reached down and dragged the shirt over his head, tossing it away before he kissed her again. "I know I shouldn't do this, but I can't help myself. This is going to come back to bite me in the arse, but I can't make myself care. Do you feel what you do to me? Do you know how long it's been since I felt like this?"

She wasn't sure she'd ever felt this out of control before, and it was glorious. She let go of any thought beyond him. She'd kicked off her shoes long before, but now it was time to dump more of her clothes.

She wanted to be skin to skin with him. It couldn't happen here, but she needed to at least feel his hands on her, and she couldn't do that with the cardigan between them. At least the thin camisole she wore underneath would offer him access.

The idea of his hands on her breasts, cupping her and running his

77

fingertips over her nipples, lit up her libido.

She slipped the cardigan off her shoulders and let it slide to the floor.

His hands immediately smoothed down her arms, as though he couldn't wait to touch her. A low, sexy growl came from the back of his throat and he turned her around in one powerful move, shifting her so her back was against his chest, his mouth against her ear.

"Do you have any idea what I want to do to you, girl? I want to eat you up. I'm the big bad wolf and you're going to let me in, aren't ya?"

That accent pierced through her. Fuck yeah, she was going to let him in. "Yes, Owen."

One big hand cupped her breast over her shirt and she leaned back against him. The sex had been good with her husband, but she'd been the aggressor. This was new. He was taking over, and it did something for her. She'd always thought she wanted to be in charge, but now she was reconsidering her position.

He'd told her she could stop him at any time, and she believed him. What if she could cede power and control for a single encounter, enjoy herself without having to think and strategize?

His left hand shifted from her breasts to her skirt, dragging it up. "I want my hands on you, my mouth on you. I want to make a meal of you, love. Do you understand what I mean? I want to bloody well lay you out right here and shove my tongue up your pussy. I bet you taste like honey."

Every word shot through her. "I want to taste you, too."

She wanted her mouth on his cock. She wanted to suck him until he was dry. She'd missed this, missed sex and intimacy. Why had she waited so damn long?

Maybe she'd waited for him.

She let the thought float away because there were more pressing matters. His hand was dangerously close to her underwear. Her breath held as he teased his way in.

"I think I should make sure you're satisfied. I'm not sure how long I'll last," he said against her ear. He nipped her lobe, the tiny sting shooting straight to her pussy. "I bet you're going to be hot around me. You're already wet for me, aren't you? Tell me you're wet and wanting because I promise you, I'm hard as hell and desperate to get inside of you."

Her hips seemed to move of their own accord. They shifted against his hand, trying to get him to touch her where she needed it the most. "I don't think I've ever gotten so wet so fast. I usually need way more foreplay."

But now that she thought about it, the last four hours had been a long kind of foreplay. She'd been attracted to him the moment she'd seen him, and she rather thought he'd felt the same. They'd been thrown together. Wasn't it natural that they should follow the path nature had set for them?

A single finger caressed her clitoris and she had to force herself to breathe.

She'd thought about lightning earlier. This was definitely a storm. Need rolled through her, quick and hard.

"You're luscious," he whispered, and she could feel his tongue running along the shell of her ear. "You're ripe and ready. Relax and let me take you there. Come for me and then I'll do the same for you."

He pressed on her clitoris, his free hand cupping her breast and holding her hard against his body. She was trapped and it felt like heaven. There was nothing at all to do except take the pleasure he was offering her.

Her whole body bowed as he pressed down and rotated that single finger. Pleasure swamped her senses and she rode the wave, pumping her hips against his finger, taking every single second of decadent sensation he gave her.

Her whole body felt languorous as she came down from the high of her orgasm. She was soft and deliciously malleable when Owen turned her around.

"Tell me I can have you." His handsome face was tight as he stared down at her.

Did he think now that she'd had her fun, she would turn him away? She wasn't even thinking about it. She wanted him. She wouldn't likely see much of him after this single encounter. They would go their separate ways and he would become a wild, crazy happy memory she could hold onto when the days got long. She wanted as much of him as she could have, and that definitely included his cock. Even in her dopamine-induced languor, she knew she would regret it for the rest of her life if she didn't have the memory of that hard cock pressing inside her.

"I want you, Owen." She reached for him even though her legs felt like Jell-O. "You said you were prepared."

"Fuck all, I am. You have no idea how prepared I am." He leaned over and kissed her, his tongue tangling with hers, and then he was reaching into his back pocket. His hands were shaking as he opened his wallet and pulled out a condom. The leather wallet fell to the ground, but he didn't seem to care. He was far too busy tearing open the fly of his jeans and releasing his cock.

She had the briefest glimpse of a truly beautiful cock. Long and thick, it was uncut and jutted out of his jeans. He quickly sheathed it and then her back was up against the elevator wall. He drugged her with kisses, tugging her skirt back up.

"I should get out of my panties," she managed to whisper.

"No time," he said as he pressed her against the wall and his free hand simply shoved the sucker aside.

His cock pushed against her pussy and she looked up into his eyes. They were ocean blue and they pulled her in like nothing else could. Not even the sensation of him fucking up into her body had the same effect as those eyes staring down at her. There was some unnamed emotion in his eyes that made her reach up and wrap her arms around him, not for balance or to let him get a better angle. She hugged him to show him her affection, to let him know she was here with him.

Then the desolation she'd seen there was gone, and he warmed up again.

"God, you're beautiful, Becca," he said before his mouth lowered to hers and he pressed up inside her. "I knew you'd feel like heaven."

She was crushed between him and the wall, and she clutched him for all she was worth. She wrapped her legs around his lean hips as his hands found the cheeks of her ass and he physically moved her, sliding her up and down on his cock. Her nails dug into his skin, but he didn't seem to mind. He nipped at her neck, gentle bites that sent her higher and higher.

She hadn't thought she could possibly come again. She'd always been a one and done woman, but she felt the delicious pressure build once more. He was big inside her, perfectly stoking the fire. His pelvis rubbed her exactly the right way, and it didn't take long before she went careening over the edge again, calling out his name.

Owen. Owen. Owen.

God, she would remember that name for the rest of her damn life.

He shoved inside her one last time, his body quaking as he came, and then he was simply holding her.

"I did not expect that." The words were shaky and deep, rumbling from his mouth across her skin.

She hadn't expected it either, and that was a good thing. Two years had gone past in a bland fashion, the days flying by without making any real memories.

Owen Shaw was a revelation.

He took a deep breath and lowered her to the floor, her feet finding purchase. She managed to lean against the wall but couldn't quite work up the will to shove her skirt down.

"Becca, I..." he began, his eyes soft on her.

The phone rang and Owen cursed, turning away. He grabbed it with his right hand as his left managed to tug at his jeans, tucking himself back in. "This better be good, Colin, because I'm thinking about murdering you again."

Suddenly she didn't ever want to leave this stupid elevator. Someone could send them food down the emergency hatch. Food and wine and Owen. They could eat and drink and have a ton of sex. The bathroom could be a problem and she would need a shower, but those seemed like minor issues.

God, she was not doing this again. She was not going to confuse good sex with emotional attachment. Nope. This was why she'd taken the two years off, and she was damn well going to learn something from it.

They came from completely different worlds. This had been a moment out of time, and she couldn't make more of it than there was.

Without another word, Owen slammed the phone down.

The elevator immediately started moving, and Becca heard a squeak come from her mouth. She pulled her skirt down as fast as she could.

Owen grabbed his shirt and dragged it over his head before picking up her cardigan. "Sorry, love. We're busting out of this place. Here." He held it out for her, helping her into the plain cardigan she sometimes thought she wore like armor. He smoothed back her hair and placed the sweetest kiss on her forehead. "You look perfectly respectable."

Something about how chaste that kiss was made any potential

embarrassment fly away. This didn't have to be awkward. It had been the single best sex of her life, and she would think about him for-freaking-ever. She grabbed her bag and turned to the doors as they slid open.

"Thank you," she whispered, a secret smile turning her lips up. "It was good to meet you, Owen Shaw."

He was right beside her, their hands brushing but not quite tangling together as they faced the seventh floor. A small crowd had gathered. Her coworker Carter Adams paced at the back of the crowd. River and Jax and the man she'd seen earlier dealing with the moving van were there. He was an attractive man, like Jax, but neither could hold a candle to her Owen.

Not hers. He'd only been hers for a moment, and that was okay.

"And you, Becca Walsh," he said in that deep, sexy accent.

"We heard you were stuck when we got back from our run. Carter told us," River was saying as she exited. "I was worried. I would freak out if I spent four hours in that tiny box."

"I had good company," she said, her smile widening. "Good night, guys."

Carter fell in beside her. She should have known he would hear about the elevator. He was friends with Colin. Carter had been one of the first people she'd met when she'd moved here.

He could also be a bit of a busybody.

"Who was that man? Are you okay?" Carter asked.

She didn't want to spend her evening listening to Carter complain, because that was mostly what he did. "I'm perfect and that was Owen Shaw. He was perfect, too."

"Who is Owen Shaw?" Carter glanced behind them, probably looking at the man again.

"I think he's new in the building." They'd had more important things to talk about than which apartment he lived in. Maybe he was one of the new guys.

"There was a delivery for you," he said. "I put it on your bar."

They'd exchanged keys when they'd gotten to know each other. Sometimes she locked herself out and he could be helpful. He also accepted packages for her when she wasn't around. "What was it?"

"Well, it wasn't from that guy, I'll tell you," he retorted. "I think it's from Cathy."

Ah, the surprise she'd mentioned. She opened her door. "'Night, Carter. I'll see you in the morning."

She let the door close behind her and turned. A brilliant arrangement of flowers was sitting on her bar.

Cathy had remembered. Today was the anniversary of her hiring at Huisman. Two years to the day.

Those gorgeous blooms reminded her that she'd made a new start. She caught a glimpse of herself in the mirror and smiled.

Maybe that promise she'd made to her mother wasn't so far away after all.

Chapter Five

Owen grabbed his bag and followed Robert off the lift. He was in an oddly good mood. He was about to get his arse kicked, and it had been worth it.

She had been worth it, and the truth was he couldn't wait to see her again. Allowing her to walk away from him had been an indulgence. His instinct was to tangle his fingers in hers and tell her to take him back to her place so they could do things right and proper this time.

Not that it hadn't felt right. Nothing in his life had felt as right as getting Rebecca Walsh up against a wall and shoving his way inside her.

She'd been hot and tight around him. He could still feel her nails digging into the flesh of his shoulders and back. He wanted to see the marks she'd left there.

He hadn't marked her. She might like a bite of pain. He would definitely like to look at her shoulder or the nape of her neck and see a mark, one he'd put there. He loved the fact that her nails had scratched down his back, damn near drawing blood.

He would explore it with her the next time they got together.

Because there was definitely going to be a next time.

"Are you all right?" Jax was walking behind them, but he'd noticed River was back at the door to the apartment she shared with her husband and their big mutt.

She winked her husband's way and they disappeared inside.

"I'm fine, mate." He wasn't supposed to know Jax either, but Jax seemed to have forgotten that fact. "I think I'll take the stairs next time though. I'm Owen."

Jax stared down at his hand. "She's gone, man. We're safe."

Owen lowered his voice. "You can't know that."

He started down the hall toward the flat he was supposed to share with his lover. They needed to put some distance between them and Becca. Once he'd rounded the corner, she wouldn't be able to see them.

The door to his flat was open and Ezra Fain stood there. Well, well, the gang was all here. "Yes, we can. While the elevator was down, we were able to wire this whole floor. All we had to do was monitor the stairs. We managed to get into her apartment. We didn't stay long, but we've got it bugged now. Dante thinks he can get into her office tomorrow night. But getting into her lab is going to be more difficult. Tucker, what's she doing right now?"

"She's smiling at herself in the mirror." Tucker looked up as they walked into the flat. He sat at the kitchen table, a laptop in front of him. "She went inside, put her stuff down, and now she's kind of staring at herself."

Sasha sat beside him, a glass of what looked like water, but was more than likely vodka, in his hand. "She looks incredibly pleased with herself. What did you do, Owen?"

Luckily, Robert ignored Sasha altogether. "Give us an update on everything that happened with her. I'll be honest, we weren't entirely sure she was the person with you in the elevator until that kid Colin came in. We thought you might be alone. Jax was about to go into the shaft and rescue you."

"I'm good at fixing things," Jax admitted.

"But then Colin, who looks a lot like the human version of a chihuahua, came in," Ezra explained. "Apparently Dr. Walsh is vocal in the residents' association meetings. Colin is scared of her, but then I think he might be scared of a stiff breeze. Are you okay?"

"I've been in a lift for four hours," he said because he had something to take care of. He couldn't have simply pulled the thing off and tossed it aside. He'd been trying to be a gentleman around Becca. "I'm hitting the loo before we have this debrief."

Because the debrief could turn into his firing. Could they fire him?

They didn't actually pay him, so they probably couldn't fire him. Of course they could kick his arse out on the street.

And he could show up at Becca's. He might be able to worm his way in. She was lonely. He was lonely. They could not be lonely together.

Shouldn't he be more worried about how they would take things? Apparently righteously good sex put him in a mellow mood.

"Need to clean up, do you, Romeo?" Sasha asked with a deep chuckle.

He turned and headed to the bathroom because he hadn't exactly gotten rid of the condom and it was starting to feel nasty.

He handled his business and washed his hands, looking at himself in the mirror. Was this what Becca was doing? Staring at herself because what had happened in that lift seemed to have changed her somehow? He felt it. Something had shifted in his life, but in this moment all he could think about was his past and how far he'd had to come to get to the second he'd held a hand out and opened the lift doors for the woman. The horrible rash he'd had from the drugs he'd been given had faded over the long months. He was back to being strong again. It had taken him almost two years, but he could hold his own in a fight. He'd had to relearn how to walk practically, and that hadn't come from his memory loss.

Becca would call it a side effect. Dr. McDonald's drug would almost surely have a black box warning. *Side effects may include complete and utter loss of self, rashes that decimate the skin, and overnight atrophy.* That meant his muscles stopped working. At least he thought that's what the doctors had meant.

He had a handsome face, but it was different from the one he'd had before. There wasn't a lot of light in his eyes. He didn't smile the way the bugger in the photos did—like he hadn't a care in the world. Except he had. He should have cared about the fact that he was a disloyal bastard who should have trusted his team.

Did any of them actually trust him?

Should Becca Walsh trust him?

He picked up his bag and strode back into the room where his whole team seemed to be arguing. Apparently the movers had done their job and the decent-sized apartment was filled with boxes and furniture.

"It's not a bad thing," Robert was saying. "Being alone with her probably allowed Owen to lay the groundwork for our cover. Unless they didn't get along, and then we're fucked."

"I would be surprised if that's the case. River and I like her a lot," Jax replied. "She's easy to get along with. You'll see. We're having her over for dinner. It's good that she'll already be comfortable with Owen."

"I bet she's incredibly comfortable with Owen." Sasha was staring at the laptop screen.

"I don't know." Ezra paced in front of the fireplace. "There's a reason Tag put him in a backup role."

"Owen can handle himself," Robert replied with a confidence that Owen was pretty sure he was about to shake because he couldn't hide this one. "According to all his records he was good in the field."

"Yeah, well, he doesn't remember a damn thing and he didn't get the training the rest of you had," Ezra pointed out.

"You mean the training where we were tortured and forced to commit crimes?" Jax's arms had gone over his chest and his stare was steely.

"The training where a crazy bitch doctor pumped us all full of drugs and then proceeded to force us to try to kill each other? That training?" Dante walked in from the kitchen, a beer in his hand.

Yeah, he hadn't been forced to survive that. What had happened to him had been brief. She'd only managed to dose him once, though it seemed to have been enough.

Then why have you started to remember things you shouldn't? Little things like how it feels to stand in a surf with the sun on your face?

He shoved the thought aside because Ezra had his hands up, obviously conceding the point.

"I get it," Ezra said. "It was hell, but it also trained you all on how to conduct yourselves during an investigation."

Dante put a hand on Sasha's shoulder. "Yes, this one learned how to nap so his coworkers must clean up all the trash."

Sasha shrugged it off. "You're better at it than I am. And Owen knows exactly how to conduct an investigation into what kind of underwear a woman wears."

His eyes came up, the only one who realized Owen had walked

back in the room, and that made him wonder how observant the resident drunken Russian really was. Sasha always seemed to not care, but then he knew things the others didn't.

Robert sighed and waved for him to come back into the living room. "Let's get this started. We'll be alerted if Dr. Walsh leaves her apartment. We're safe meeting here, but after today Tucker, Sasha, and Dante have to be extremely careful about when they come into this building. You're working at Huisman. You can't be seen here by Walsh. It would be far too much of a coincidence."

Tucker leaned back in his chair. "I've been at Huisman for a couple of days and I haven't even come close to meeting the big boss."

"That's not necessarily a bad thing," Ezra pointed out. "I don't want you to engage her too heavily. Keep your head down. Get us an idea of how the foundation works. I want to know how deep the ties to McDonald went. Hope was getting her money from somewhere after Kronberg let her go."

Kronberg was a large pharmaceutical company that had been involved in a group known only as The Collective. When Taggart had taken down McDonald, he'd also dealt a mighty blow to that group, though from what he'd read, The Collective had cut ties with McDonald long before that day.

Tucker was staring at Ezra. "Uh, bank robberies? You remember the part where a couple of us are wanted by Interpol for robbing places? I think that's where she got the money."

"I do know what she made you do." Ezra sank down to the couch, crossing one leg over the other and getting comfortable. "But I also know roughly how much was stolen and Phoebe, the forensic accountant Taggart uses, doesn't think it came close to paying for the high-tech facility in France we found you, Dante, Sasha, and Jax in. Despite the fact that the Huisman family is Dutch, they have heavy ties to France as well. When they moved their base of operations to Canada fifty years ago, they were originally in Montreal."

"Just because they speak French and the facility happened to be in France doesn't prove anything," Robert replied. "And you shouldn't have sat on that couch. Apparently Buster's found his new happy place. You're going to be covered in dog hair."

Jax sent Ezra an apologetic grin. "Sorry. The boy knows comfort when he sees it." He looked back at Owen. "Did the two of you talk about work at all? What did you think of her? She's not as serious as she comes off in the reports, right?"

"She's funny and smart," he allowed. And sexy as hell. So fucking sexy. What would it be like to be able to have her in a proper bed, with all the time in the world to explore that gorgeous body of hers?

Jax nodded. "She is. I like her."

Ezra turned his stare Jax's way. "You're not out here to make friends, and if River is going to have trouble separating the mission from her friendships, we need to talk about shipping you both back to Dallas."

Jax's jaw had gone tight. "We know what the op is and we know how important it is. Don't forget I'm the one who sacrificed to get us here."

Robert moved to Owen's side as Jax and Ezra argued. His voice was low as he ignored the sniping. "Did you have a good talk with her?"

"Yes." And a good shag. A nice hearty bang with the tightest pussy he'd ever been in. Well, that he could remember being in. "She's a smart lady."

He wanted to see her breasts. He'd felt them and they'd been soft and full against his palms. They'd felt perfect crushed against his chest as he thrust up inside her.

Fuck, he was getting hot just thinking about it. About her.

He didn't like the fact that Sasha was staring at her on the laptop screen.

"Did she seem like the kind of woman who wants a diverse set of friends?" Robert was asking. "Everything we have on her says she's had gay friends in her life before. She was particularly close to a man and his husband when she was doing her residency in Boston."

"I'm sure she's very open minded." How open minded would she be? She'd responded beautifully when he'd taken over. She hadn't minded being the aggressor, but she'd practically melted in his arms when he'd topped her.

How would she like more exotic play? How would she respond when he tied her up and tortured her with his tongue, playing with her pussy and her clitoris and her sweet arse?

He wanted to see that, too. He wanted her naked and laid out on the bed, a feast for his senses.

"You remembered our back story?" Robert asked.

"I remembered it." How to explain this to him without getting into an immediate fistfight? "She knows I'm a bodyguard."

Ezra and Jax seemed to have ironed out their differences.

"Excellent. So everything is in place," Ezra said. "It might actually be better this way. She'll get to know both of you, but let Robert take the lead."

Because Robert was the smart one. Robert was the one who hadn't betrayed the team in another life. Robert hadn't turned over a couple of Taggarts to the wicked witch. Big Tag liked Robert, precisely why he'd wanted Robert in charge and not Owen.

"I'll take over from here," Robert assured him. "Now that she understands we're a couple, I can go over tomorrow and thank her for helping keep you calm. I'll tell her I was worried because you can be claustrophobic."

"Did she keep you calm?" Sasha had a knowing look on his face.

Fucker. "She ain't going to buy that we're gay, Robert."

"Of course she will. Don't stereotype. We can be manly and gay," Robert said with a prim quality to his voice.

"Yeah, well, gay blokes don't usually fuck a lady in the lift." There. It was better to just shove it right out there.

The whole room went silent and then Sasha laughed.

"I told you," he doubled over. "I knew it the minute he walked in the door. Pay up."

Dante shook his head and pulled out his wallet. "Asshole texted me a couple of minutes ago. Last time I take a bet from him without investigating myself."

Wankers.

"You did what?" Ezra had stood up. He might have been more intimidating had he not been covered in dog hair. The man liked to wear black, and now his all-dark look was covered in white fur.

"It wouldn't have worked," Owen started.

"It obviously worked, if we're talking about your dick," Robert shot back.

His dick had totally worked. It wanted to work again. "She was attracted to me."

"A lot of women are attracted to you, asshole." Robert started pacing like a caged tiger ready to pounce. "Then they actually get to know you and they run the other fucking way."

"Robert," Tucker began.

Robert wasn't having it. "Do you understand that you've fucked this whole op up? Are you so arrogant that you had to have this one? Ian had reasons for shifting this to me."

Before he could say a word, Robert was off again, explaining in minute detail every single way Owen had screwed up and put the team at risk. He was worked up in a froth, his face going red.

The man was going to have a heart attack. He bet Becca could handle that. She worked with brains, but she probably knew a lot about hearts, too. She would be pretty when she did CPR. Her breasts would bounce while she did the compressions. And her sweet mouth would come down on his while she tried to breathe life into him.

Not Robert. If Robert had a heart attack, Tucker could save him. He wasn't letting the bastard watch Becca's breasts bounce.

"Have you heard a single word I've said?" Robert asked.

"Of course. I'm a right bastard and I fucked everything up." He didn't have to listen to a ten-minute rant to know that. "But it wouldn't have worked. If I had played things the way we talked about, she would have run the other way the minute the lift doors opened because she wanted me. She might have been friendly, but we wouldn't have gotten her to spend time with us. She's not a masochist and she wouldn't have willingly spent time with a man she wanted and could never have."

"You think pretty highly of yourself." Robert had his hands on his hips, challenging him.

And Owen felt a growl start in the back of his throat. He had no idea where it was coming from. He was the quiet one, the one who sat back and didn't give anyone hell because he was never sure of his place in the group. The alpha was challenging him, telling him to back down, and bugger all he wasn't going to do it. "Well, I am the one who fucked the lady a few hours after I met her, so I think I might have just become the expert here."

"Good for Becca," Jax was saying. "She seems really stressed."

"She isn't stressed now," Sasha said, still laughing.

"How exactly are we going to explain my presence?" Robert asked, his eyes still steely.

Shite. He'd taken Robert's op. Owen took a deep breath and tried to soften his expression. "It wouldn't have worked, mate. I'm sorry you feel like I screwed everything up, but I had to make a call and I was alone with her. Two seconds into meeting her and she was flirting with me."

Robert shook his head with a long sigh of frustration. "That doesn't mean she wants you to fuck her."

"No, but her asking me to kiss her and clawing at my shirt to get it off sent me a real fine signal. You want to see the marks she left on my back?" Robert needed to see that the original plan wouldn't have worked. "If I'd turned her down, she would have walked the other way the next time she saw me. She would have been embarrassed."

"And you think she won't be now?" Robert asked, but his tone had changed to something close to a grudging acceptance.

"Becca is pretty confident," Jax said. "At least that's how she comes off. I watched her trip over her own feet on the street and she just got up and bowed like she'd meant to do it. I also think if Owen had turned her down, she would have walked away and not looked back. I don't know her well, but I think I have a pretty good read on her."

"We have a way in. Do we need to fight about it because it wasn't the one we thought it would be?" Tucker moved in, obviously willing to play the peacemaker. "If Owen is dating her, we'll have a lot of access. Jax and River can play the friendship role. Sasha, Dante, and I will operate from the Huisman Foundation building. This still works."

"All she knows is I've recently moved to Canada," he explained. "I'm sure she assumes I'm a resident in the building, but I didn't talk about my roommate. It's a simple thing, man. Instead of you working for a bank, we both work as bodyguards. We share the place because one of us is usually working."

Robert seemed to think about it for a moment. "It could work. It's a new job and we're both single men. The job would likely require odd hours, so maybe the company put us together here for a couple of months until we figure out the lay of the city, so to speak."

"Or you could go with the boyfriend thing and offer to share her," Sasha said with a smirk.

"Over my dead body." He hadn't meant to say that. Certainly he hadn't meant to sound like a crazy person.

Sasha chuckled. "Sorry. We spent too much time in that Bliss place. Of course you wouldn't want to share a woman you just met with a man who is your friend. It's perfectly logical that you would already be incredibly possessive." He stood up and stretched. "I'm going back to the house. It's obvious you don't need me. Dante, come along. We have a few days before we have to be back at our shitty jobs."

Dante started to follow him. "He means that literally. The toilets there are horrific, and I won't even go into handling medical waste. I want to be the one who gets to fuck the girl in the lift next time."

"That wasn't part of his job," Ezra pointed out as the duo opened the door.

Owen let the door close before turning to Ezra. "I'm not sorry." He couldn't apologize for it. He knew he should in order to keep the peace, but somehow he couldn't make the words come out of his mouth. "I did what I had to do."

"Tell me you're not more involved with the woman than you should be." Ezra brushed some of the dog hair off his pants.

He couldn't lie but he did have an excellent distraction. He wished he'd had a chance to look at the file he'd snuck out of her bag, but he would always have turned it over. This was a job. Yes, she'd been hot as hell and he couldn't wait to spend more time with her, but this was a job. "I wasn't so involved I didn't nip a file from her tote bag. And before you nag at me, that bag was overflowing, and it would have been easy for her to drop it. Unless she stopped between the subway and the apartment building and checked to make sure it was still there, she'll have to conclude it fell out or got pinched while she was on her way home."

"That bag she carries seems to be an issue," Jax acknowledged. "River said she's helped her pick stuff up when it fell out at least twice. But I'm not sure what her medical research is going to do for us."

Tucker stepped up. "I'd actually like to get my hands on it. So far all I've done is cleanup work and getting the researchers coffee and lunch. I'm not sure why I needed to fake I'm in med school for that."

"Internships are more about making connections than actually learning the technology," Ezra said. "But I would like to see what you get from her files, too."

What Ezra really wanted was to see how far Tucker's medical knowledge went. He couldn't forget the fact that Jax had discovered a Dr. Reasor had worked for McDonald. They'd looked for the man and couldn't find a trace of him.

But then McDonald had been good at making people disappear.

He put his bag down on the coffee table and reached in. "I haven't looked at the files. Being in such a tight space bothered her. She did this meditation thing and that's when I slipped this out of her bag. I would have gone for more, but she's not good at meditating either. It only lasted a minute or two and then she was back to talking about comic books and her favorite TV shows."

He pulled the folder free and opened it.

Shite. Not medical research at all.

"What is it?" Robert asked, stepping in.

"It looks like financial reports." It was a bunch of numbers and accounts. Nothing at all that would tell them about Becca's research.

He'd fucked up again.

Ezra held out a hand. "Let me see it."

He passed the folder to his boss. "Sorry. It's not what I hoped it was."

Ezra opened the folder and started to look through the paperwork.

"I wish you hadn't done this," Robert said.

"I followed my instincts." He hated feeling this way. It was especially hard because while he'd been in that lift with Becca, he'd felt different. He'd felt like he mattered, like he belonged somewhere.

"Your instincts are crap." Robert shook his head and backed away. "I'm going across the street. I need a drink. I'm sure you can deal with unpacking the same way you took over the op."

He turned and walked out.

Tucker grabbed his jacket. "Don't take it hard, Owen. He's been touchy as hell since he realized Ariel wasn't in London. Until she flies back and he knows she's safely at The Garden, he's going to be a wreck and he's going to take it out on everyone."

"She's perfectly safe," Ezra said, his eyes not leaving the pages in his hand. "And I don't hate having her here to do some sessions after what happened in Colorado."

He hated sessions, hated having to talk about his feelings, going over the same things again and again and again because his life never changed.

Except it kind of had now. Becca was in it. He would have to talk about her. It might be worth it if Ariel could give him insights on how to manage easing his way into Becca's life.

"I'll work on the flat," Owen offered. "Maybe if I get things in order, he won't be so angry with me."

Jax looked up at him. "Are you sure? You usually hit a pub by this time."

He usually found the bottom of a bottle by seven or eight at night and then opened another. He found the idea unsatisfying tonight. "No. Go on with the others. I've got work to do here."

Jax gave him a smile that let him know that he wasn't merely surprised, but somewhat pleased, and left.

Or was he mistaking suspicion for surprise?

"This is accounting for the last quarter." Ezra moved toward the table, sitting down and starting to spread out the papers. "I wonder why she's bothering with balancing the accounts. She has an accounting department for that."

"I got the idea she was a hands-on kind of manager." She seemed fairly type A when it came to work. She would need someone to force her to relax, to enjoy her downtime. She'd needed him to take over before she'd given up and allowed herself to simply take the pleasure he was offering her.

It struck him forcibly that she was exactly the type of woman who could use a Dom.

"I find it interesting that she's only looking into one account." Ezra glanced up. "This could be nothing at all, but I'll send a copy down to Phoebe Murdoch."

Owen moved to the box marked clothes. It wouldn't be full. None of them had much to speak of. He found the plain T-shirts and jeans and hauled them out. Robert had some suits somewhere. He would hang them up before they wrinkled.

"Are you sure you did it for the right reasons?"

He glanced over and his boss was staring at him with intelligent eyes. He could never forget that Ezra Fain was a predator, and he often killed what he caught. "I made a call. I think it was the right one. I'm not going to lie to you. The lady is sexy as hell and I enjoyed myself, but I understand that this is a mission."

"That wasn't what I was worried about. I'm worried you did it to prove yourself."

He shrugged. "I didn't really, but would it be so bad to prove

95

myself? Big Tag still hates me. He's never going to see me as anything but the man who betrayed his brother. Tell me he doesn't think I'm the one who gave us up in Colorado."

"We don't know anyone gave us up," Ezra argued.

"Levi Green knew our location. He knew when Jax walked into those woods and he was waiting for him and River. There's no way that was a coincidence."

"Levi is a tricky one," Ezra allowed. "Never underestimate him. And if anything, I think it was Solo who gave us up."

"That's not what Big Tag thinks." He knew exactly what Big Tag thought because he'd overheard him one day at McKay-Taggart. "Big Tag thinks it's one of us."

"We disagree on that." Ezra gathered the papers and placed them back inside the folder. "He can be paranoid and he hasn't spent as much time with the team as I have. Owen, I don't think you would betray us."

"Well, history might have something to say about that."

Ezra strode over and put a hand on his shoulder. "You didn't do it for money, man. You did it for your family. You should have trusted your team more, but I can understand. It's time to forgive yourself for something you can't even remember doing and move on."

He wasn't sure it would be that easy for him, but as he started to unpack, he thought about Becca and, for a moment, his life didn't seem so bad.

Chapter Six

The next morning, Becca searched her bag for the folder again and bit back a curse. Damn bag. She was switching to one she could close up. It had to have happened on the train. The train had been full, as it usually was at that time of day, and she hadn't gotten a seat. Right before the Spadina stop, she'd dropped the damn bag and it had spilled over everywhere. She'd had help gathering it up, but she'd lost the folder she needed.

And she hadn't figured it out until this morning because she'd spent the whole evening thinking about Owen Shaw. She'd dreamed about the man last night, and he'd been on her mind all morning long.

She was not doing this. It had been a hot moment, but she wasn't falling head over heels for the first man she'd slept with. Fucked. Fucked hard and good and well, and she hadn't even seen him naked.

Shouldn't she at least see him naked?

She grabbed her bag and walked out of her apartment. If she hurried, she could grab a coffee before she headed to the office.

The elevator dinged and opened, but she was so not doing that. Stairs were her friends.

Would she get in if Owen had been the man stepping into the elevator? She'd only gotten a glimpse of the tall man with brown hair entering, but he definitely wasn't Owen. Did he even live in the building? She hadn't asked. It seemed like a big oversight. He could have been visiting friends.

She might never see him again, and that was a good thing because she wasn't falling madly in love with some guy she'd met two minutes ago.

Jogging down the steps, she felt a smile slide across her face. It really had been good.

Maybe that had been her problem the first time. She'd equated commitment with happiness because that was what she'd grown up with. Not everyone got a happy marriage, and it seemed harder to find it when two careers came into play.

So maybe for her, happiness would be found in good work and good friends, and the occasional hot night with a guy she liked.

No commitment. No ties. No promises that could be broken.

The heavenly scent of coffee hit her. She loved the city, loved the fact that she had everything she needed within walking distance.

The new girl was standing behind the counter. It was too early for the café to be truly busy. She walked right up when she would normally spend ten minutes in line.

Nina smiled at her. "No fat latte?"

She had that every single morning of her life. It was simpler to have a usual order. Sometimes she got lost in choosing and wasted tons of time.

But the night before something had changed inside her. It had been good to break out of her shell. She wouldn't stand here and debate calories. What sounded good?

"What's your favorite?"

Nina's eyes widened in surprise. "Oh, uhm, I love the caramel latte, actually. It's got great flavor. It's not too sweet."

"I'll take that." New things. She was going to try new things.

"I'll have whatever she's having," a deep voice said.

A shiver of pure desire went through her because there was no mistaking that voice. He was behind her. Owen. Deep breath. This didn't have to be awkward.

Why should it be awkward? She wasn't ashamed of what they'd done. She didn't have to live by some stupid society rules that said sex had to happen one way or she turned into a slut while he was more of a man.

She liked him. He'd been nice to her, really nice to her. She turned, giving him a warm smile. "Hey, Owen. How are you?"

He was gorgeous. Ridiculously gorgeous. The man was so hot, every woman in the place was looking his way.

And that was another reason to keep this light.

He smiled down at her, his stunning eyes sparkling in the early morning light. "I slept well last night despite the fact that it was my first night in a new place. I managed to unpack a bit and went to sleep with no problem. I wonder why."

For the same reason she'd slept like a baby. "I'm glad I could help. So you live in the building? Somehow we didn't cover that. I'm on seven. I suspect you took over the Holder's place. They were nice and quiet. Everyone likes a quiet neighbor."

He put a hand over his heart as though making a sacred vow. "I promise to keep all my keggers on mute."

"See that you do. Well, you got to know the building properly then if the first thing that happened was the elevator died on you," she replied, already feeling warm and comfy with him. He was easy to talk to. "Hopefully you don't have the plumbing problems I have. I swear I would move, but I'm super close to the station and to work."

"At the research place," he said as though trying to remember the details. "Houseman?"

"Huisman. It's named after the family that founded it," she explained. "I work with one of the sons."

"Owen works with people, too," a deep voice said. There was a hint of Western drawl to this one. He was all American, with dark hair that was a tiny bit shaggy but did nothing to hide his obvious masculinity. If he hadn't been standing next to Owen, she would have found him devastatingly attractive. As it was, she acknowledged his handsomeness but couldn't quite take her eyes off the Scot.

Owen winced, but his lips ticked up in a heartbreaking grin. "This is my mate, Robert McClellan. We're sharing the flat for now. We worked together back in London before we took the transfer here. It's only for a couple of months while we decide where we want to live. Apart. I'm just saying I'll have my own place soon."

Robert coughed, obviously covering his amusement. "I think he's trying to explain that he's not a thirty-six-year-old man who needs a roommate to cover half the rent."

"Oh, I was thinking it must be nice to have someone to talk to when you come home at night." She didn't even have a pet. She'd started talking to her plants.

He shuddered as though she'd said something distasteful. "We're mates, love. The most we say to each other is *pass the beer*. Do you mind if we join you?"

Oh, if she sat down with him, she might not get back up. She had to view him as an indulgence. "Sorry. I'm on my way into work." She took the coffee from Nina and handed her the payment. It was definitely time to head out. "It was good to see you, Owen, and nice to meet you, Robert."

Surprise was stamped on his handsome face.

She bet he didn't get the brushoff often. He was likely used to women falling all over themselves the minute he walked in the door, and there was the slightest satisfaction that she could put that look on his face.

"Hey, I was hoping we could maybe have dinner tonight," he offered.

Going out with him would likely be a mistake. Despite their incredible sexual chemistry, she knew they didn't have a ton in common. It wasn't that she wouldn't see him again. She would likely see him a lot, and that was why she needed to keep her distance now. "I have plans tonight. Maybe some other time."

She backed away.

"You having trouble, Dr. Walsh?"

Carter stood in the doorway, his bag over his shoulder. He was dressed for the office. "Not at all. I was just saying good-bye to my new friends. You heading in?"

He nodded, though his eyes were still on Owen and Robert. "Yes. Dr. Klein has me doing a bunch of paperwork this morning. He's got a conference next week. And I have to reshuffle the intern schedule. Ally's father is ill and she's going back to Ottawa for a few days. I'm hoping the new guy can take her shifts."

She glanced back and Owen had a cup of coffee in his hand, his eyes steady on her. He tipped his cup her way and smiled that incredibly inviting smile before turning back to his friend. Her breath had caught in her chest because that smile promised that he would be there if she needed him…for anything.

He was a dangerous man. She turned her attention back to her safety net—work. "How do you feel about the new interns? Are they going to work out?"

"Well, Annie is a moron and I have no idea how she got into medical school," he began complaining. "Hannah thinks more about her boyfriend than she does her work. She'll be spitting out kids the minute they get married."

"That's kind of sexist." She strode toward the subway station.

"Well, it's also true, and to show you I'm fair, I also hate Dillon. He's an overprivileged moron who only got the job because his family is country club friends with the Huismans, so I'm sure he'll be my boss soon. Tucker is cool," he allowed. "He's smart and hard working. He seems solid, if you know what I mean. I'm hoping he'll take Ally's place. The cancer team's double-blind finishes on Wednesday, and we'll need all hands on deck to get that data together."

Carter was a logistical genius. Despite his youth, he was excellent at dealing with the various teams he needed to juggle.

"Well, you'll do a fabulous job with it. Let me know if you need anyone else to help out," she offered. "Cathy can input data like a pro. Because she actually is a pro."

Carter slowed his gait to allow her to keep up. "I think we can handle it, but thank you. Speaking of data, how is yours coming along?"

A deep sense of satisfaction came over her. "It's good on both fronts. Elaine's aphasia has almost completely disappeared."

Elaine was one of her patients. She hated thinking of the people she worked with as subjects. It dehumanized them, and she couldn't do that. They were people in trouble. People like her mom. People who suddenly found the very power of speech taken from them by a greedy disease.

"That's amazing," Carter said with a smile. "She could barely speak when she came in."

"The therapy is helping rewire her brain." It was slow, but once she had the drugs that would speed up the healing process ready, it would be much faster. What could take a year to repair could be done in a matter of weeks or maybe days. "If everything goes well, I'll be ready to go to human trials next year."

And then she would start the real fight. It bubbled up inside her. She was getting there. She was going to take the fucker down, and then no one would have to go through what her mother had.

"I like it when you get that look in your eyes," he said with a shake of his head, as though he was surprised the words had come out of his mouth. "Sorry. The work you do is important and when you get that look on your face, I know you're in the zone, so to speak."

She kind of *was* in the zone. She felt more settled than she had the day before, and that probably had a whole lot to do with the man she'd left behind at the café. "I'm feeling good about a lot of things today."

"I'm surprised you turned that man down." He opened the door to the Spadina Street Station, allowing her to enter. "He was the one stuck in the elevator with you, right? I thought I recognized him. You must have made an impression if he wanted to see you again. I guess getting stuck together is one way to have a date. I should try it sometime."

The one thing she'd noticed beyond the fact that Carter seemed to have a problem with many of the interns under his charge was that he also complained about being single. A lot. "As guys to get locked in with for hours go, Owen's a pretty good one."

"So you're going to see him again?" Carter asked.

"I don't think so." Had she wavered? "I mean, no. I'm sure I'll see him around, but we don't have anything in common."

Except for raging sexual chemistry.

He didn't know any of the shows she liked. She didn't work out a lot and he'd admitted it was one of his main hobbies. That and stepping in front of people if a bullet was flying. She didn't like the thought of him getting hurt.

Was that why she was hesitating? Because he had a dangerous job and she couldn't stand the thought of losing anyone else?

No. She was being logical, and she wasn't ready for a relationship. She might never be ready for one. She was married to her work.

And he made her feel. Not merely physical things. He'd made her want to reach out and hold his hand, to let him take control. For a moment she hadn't had to be anything but Owen's lover.

Booty calls were about all she could handle right now. Lover meant something, something serious.

This was her time to have fun and play the field.

"Besides, I might have a date in a couple of days," she admitted. She was going to get out there, play the field. She wasn't going to spend all her time mooning over Owen Shaw.

He stopped, his eyes widening with surprise behind his glasses. "I thought you swore off dating."

"No," she corrected. "I took a sabbatical from interpersonal intimacy." Not intrapersonal though. She'd had an excellent relationship with her vibrator and various porn sites.

She'd dreamed of being on her knees the night before, looking up at Owen, and when he'd smiled down at her, she'd known that he valued her for so much more than sex. In the dream, he took control in much of real life, too, allowing her to concentrate on her work while he handled their daily life.

She groaned inwardly. She really was dreaming of having a wife.

If only she was attracted to other women.

Her heels clicked along the tiles at their feet and she couldn't help but notice Carter had gone quiet.

"Cathy's got a plan to set me up," she explained. "You know she's kind of a matchmaker."

He huffed with obvious disdain. "I'm sure she thinks she is. The dating scene isn't for me. Women don't want a smart man. They want a steroided-out asshole who looks like he should be on a movie screen."

She wasn't touching that one. "Okay, then. I will not put you on her list of available men."

"I'm married to my work," he insisted. "I certainly don't need some clingy female. If I date, she's going to be my intellectual equal. You were smart to not accept a date with that Neanderthal. He's obviously not in your league."

Yep, he was totally not in her league. He was in the majors. Any woman who looked his way probably wanted him, and it was obvious he hung out with the cool crowd. He and his friend, Robert, were both gorgeous and cut, sexy as hell.

"Don't be a snob," she said, but her brain was in overdrive.

It was a bad idea to get attached to some dude she'd done in the elevator. It was better to leave it where it was and to relegate the event and the man to her fond-memory files.

"Sometimes being a snob is all I have," Carter admitted.

The train whooshed in and she was ready to go to work.

* * * *

"What the hell was that?" Owen watched her stride out of the café, her lovely backside swaying. She was back in doctor mode, wearing a different shirt and skirt combo, flats and one of those cardigans. He wondered how many she had. This one was bright yellow and shouldn't have been so wretchedly sexy, but he knew what she looked like trying to get one of them off. He remembered how she'd tossed it to the floor so it wouldn't come between them.

"That was her blowing you off," Robert explained, a cheery grin on his face. "It sounds like fun because the word *blow* is in there, but it actually refers to the opposite effect. That was her way of saying thanks for the sex, see you never."

"Sex?" Nina looked at Robert and then Owen before handing over their second cups of coffee. "I thought the two of you were supposed to be having sex with each other, not the target."

"It's a sad but common tale." Robert leaned against the counter. "My lover left me for a chick he found in the elevator." He sighed and put his hand over his heart. "Such a faithless lover. One look at her and he forgot all our years of sharing our lives. What will we do about our two point five children and our rescue mutts? And who gets the china?"

"I was stuck in there with her for over four hours. It wasn't like we looked at each other and went at it." But when they had gone at it, it had been intense. "I got to know her. She's a hell of a lady."

"Yes, she is, and that's precisely why you shouldn't play games with her," Nina said, her tone going frosty.

"It's not a game. It's a mission, and I'm not going to let her get hurt." He'd made that decision the night before. "I'm not going to promise her anything I can't make good on."

"You're actively spying on her, Owen," Nina replied, her voice going low. "I can assure you she will get hurt. Think about that. I have to get back to work."

He got the feeling he'd stepped into it with the new girl. And that she'd be updating Damon Knight as soon as she could.

Robert picked up his cup and tipped it Nina's way. "Don't worry about her. I think Rebecca Walsh can handle herself."

Robert started for one of the swanky couches. The whole café was done up like someone's living room with intimate spaces mixed in with traditional tabletops. Robert sank down as Tucker strode in.

"Morning, guys," Tucker said. "Hey, Nina, can I get a plain black and a couple of muffins? Turns out the boss doesn't do breakfast. Or buy groceries. Is there a reason I'm stuck with Ezra?"

"He needs a roomie and you're the only one available," Robert replied. "Jax gets bitchy when he can't do his wife on every available surface wherever he's living. Trust me. I stayed with them in Dallas. I did not eat off that table after I came home at a completely inopportune moment. Sasha and Dante are the only people who can stand sharing a room with the other, and Owen and I were in love until his dick took over. It was always going to be you and the boss."

Owen rolled his eyes and looked at his partner for this op. "What's got you in such a bloody good mood? Last night you were all prissy and today I'm getting the Big Tag treatment from you."

Robert shrugged. "I've decided to go with the flow."

Tucker sank down to the couch. "Ariel showed up at the bar last night and they made love eyes at each other for three hours."

Robert frowned. "We did not make love eyes. What the hell are love eyes?"

Tucker's baby blues went wide and he looked utterly ridiculous as he put his chin in his hand and batted his lashes Robert's way. "'Oh, Robbie, it's so lovely to see you again and to let you creepily stare at me when you think I'm not watching but I really am because the truth is I love you, too, but I have a degree in psychology and that means I can't sleep with the crazy ones. Oh, cursed fate!'"

He'd said it all in a terrible impersonation of Ariel's upper-crust British accent, but he was probably dead on when it came to everything else.

Robert's eyes rolled. "She's not in love with me. It would be ridiculous for her to be in love with me." A grin tugged his lips up suddenly. "She likes me, though. I think she likes me a lot."

"Yeah, she does," Tucker said as Nina strode up with a mug of coffee in hand.

"You are worse than any group of teenaged girls, you know that, right?" Nina gave them a judgmental stare.

Tucker merely shrugged. "We never got to be teens so we don't know how to do it. And Big Tag is right. Gossip is super fun."

"Gossip can kill a career. I should know," Nina said before winking Robert's way. "But she does fancy you. Quite a bit. Make sure you take care of her. She's my friend. I know how to take a man's balls off seventeen different ways, and they all hurt."

Tucker leaned over as she walked away. "I heard she used to be Interpol. Damon hired her after she got fired for sleeping with the wrong dude, like a dude who was spying on her. She does not like the idea of fucking for information."

"Ah, that's why she was so upset when she found out Owen slept with the lovely Dr. Walsh," Robert mused.

"She's lovely now?" He knew it was perverse, but he didn't like Robert talking about Becca like that. Robert should see her as smart and even attractive maybe, but only in a theoretical sense. "Just yesterday she was nothing but the target."

That slightly feline smile Robert got from time to time when he relaxed enough to be mischievous took over his face. "Well, she's way hotter than she is in her professional pictures. And she was incredibly hot last night. She kind of glowed. I thought it was because the elevator was hot or something, but now I know the truth."

Tucker set his mug down. "So when are you seeing her again? The dude I work for is practically in love with her. Carter. He's kind of an asshole. He's a prick to the female interns, but you would think Dr. Walsh walks on water when he talks about her. I can't wait to watch him implode when Owen walks in with her."

Before Owen could ask about Carter—because he thought that was the man she'd walked out with moments before—Robert was speaking. "The impending implosion will have to wait. It looks like Dr. Walsh has excellent instincts. She's like the mouse that got the cheese and was smart enough to get out of the trap."

"She liked my cheese. Why wouldn't she want more cheese?" It didn't make sense. She'd been happy with him the night before. He'd been able to feel it. Robert was right; she had glowed.

"She might be one of those mice who knows going back for a second bite of cheese is never the same as the first," Robert offered with a sigh. "She also might view you as a gorgeous muscular himbo, and she got what she wanted from you and now she's going to go find someone with like five degrees to settle down with."

It was what he'd feared. She was smart, genius-level smart, with a prestigious job, and he was a bodyguard who hadn't exactly showed off his intellectualism with her. He'd talked about taking bullets and being a solider.

Neither of which he actually remembered.

It hit him hard, the scent of sweat and the *rat-a-tat* sound of gunfire all around him. For the merest second he could feel heat on his face and he'd known, oh, he'd known he wasn't going to make it.

"Owen?" All amusement had fled Robert's expression now. "Are you all right?"

He hadn't talked to any of them about the strange flashes he'd started getting. But then he didn't talk to them about much anyway. It wasn't that they weren't his mates, but he wasn't sure how much right he had to be among them. They'd all been victims through no fault of their own. But he...

"I'm fine." He shook it off. There was no need to worry anyone. He was fairly certain they all got a flash from time to time.

God, he wished he could get a flash of his mum, of his sister. He wanted even the merest hint of what it had meant to love them so he could make sense of the wrong he'd done in their name.

"You didn't look fine," Tucker said. "Are you feeling all right? Is it physical or is it the pure horror of actually having a woman blow you off? That's not the same as blowing you. It's kind of..."

Yeah, he got it. "The opposite. Did McDonald combine your bloody brains when she was playing about in them?"

"You have to admit, not many women turn you down," Robert mused. "It's got to be tough on the old ego. I'm perfectly fine with it. I've been turned down lots of times."

"Only because you tended to go after unavailable women," Tucker pointed out. "I, on the other hand, go in for the kill. Not really a kill. By that I meant the sure thing."

"You mean hookers," Owen shot back.

Tucker didn't bother to look ashamed. He merely grinned. "They never turn me down."

Rebecca Walsh wasn't a hooker, and she'd totally turned him down. It rankled. No. It didn't rankle. He was at least going to be honest with himself, even if he lied to everyone else.

It hurt.

"She's going to Jax's on Saturday?" He wasn't about to give up, and it wasn't entirely about the op. Apparently she was bonding pretty well with Jax and River. It would be easy for them to keep her occupied while he and Robert searched her place. But that wasn't how he wanted this to go.

Because he wanted her.

"That's what he said," Robert replied. "She's told River she would be there. That's where we were all supposed to meet and show off what a great couple we were, how crazy our manly love was. Now I guess I'm going as your sidekick. Mostly I'm going to see if she blows you off again."

"I wish I got to go," Tucker said, a frown on his face. "River makes good lasagna. Did I mention Ezra doesn't have any food in our place? Do you think I could find a hooker who can also cook? I would pay extra."

"Get yourself a freaking frozen dinner like the rest of the single male world. You are a coddled baby," a deep voice said and Ezra Fain was suddenly there, like he'd peeled away from the shadows. No one Owen had ever met moved as quietly as Ezra. "And I thought I told you to stay away from here."

Yeah, he was starting to worry that having the lads around constantly would tip off Becca that something was going on. All they needed was Jax to feel the man vibe going on down here and heed its call to have them all in one place. He discounted Dante and Sasha since they didn't believe in rising before noon.

"Nina told us the doc always heads out before seven. I was safe enough," Tucker explained. "And Carter texted me asking if I can take a few extra shifts. He slid in that he was going in to work with Dr. Walsh this morning. He's got a thing for Owen's girl."

"For Owen's brief fling?" Robert was an arsehole who seemed to be enjoying this far too much.

Ezra frowned as he sat down next to Owen. "Brief? Because I thought that was our play now. Did Owen magically find our data? Did you go see her after I left last night?"

"Nope," Robert answered. "The woman in question got her lick of the lollipop and now is moving on to other lollipops. She's a kid in a candy store."

But she hadn't even touched his bloody lollipop, and he wanted her to. "She's playing with me, that's all. I'll go see her tonight."

Ezra shook his head. "No. You play this slow. If you go after her too soon, she might run the other way. Nod and smile at her the next time you see her and walk on. Saturday night you can make your play."

He could be patient. Sort of. "I'll have her again Saturday night. You'll see. If I don't get my hands on her again, I'll pay up on whatever bets you have going, and don't tell me you don't, you bastards."

They all tried to look innocent.

It was his turn to frown. "You, too, Ezra?"

The boss shrugged. "Hey, the days are long and Dante has cash stashed. I'm not getting paid by the government anymore. Speaking of the CIA, I came here to tell you that Levi Green's gone missing."

Shite. Exactly what he needed, that bugger running about town. "He's here then."

Ezra's curt nod let Owen know that he agreed. "We had a couple of McKay-Taggart agents watching him. They couldn't follow him past security at Dulles. According to passport services, he flew to Heathrow, but we all know he can manipulate those."

Tucker looked serious all of the sudden. "Then it's starting."

They'd always known Green had a game plan. They were his pawns. But pawns could be quick. Pawns could maneuver in ways none of the stronger pieces could.

If only they could see the whole board in front of them.

"He's using us to find what he can't." It was the only explanation.

"I agree. Theo Taggart is coming up this weekend," Ezra said. "Big Tag is apparently making more small demons with his wife and he said something about ovulation that I didn't want to hear, so he's sending the Baby Tag."

"I think we have to call Theo a mediumish Tag," Tucker corrected. "There are a whole bunch of tiny Tags crawling around now. Is Erin coming with him?"

"I'm sure she will," Ezra shot back. "Taggarts rarely travel without their wives. It's like they're tethered or something."

How much of Ezra's bitterness came from longing? It was a stupid thought and one he likely wouldn't have had a few days before, but now he wondered if Ezra had once been "tethered" to Solo and how much he missed the feeling.

But that thought was drowned out by another. Theo and Erin were coming to town—the very people he'd hurt when he'd betrayed his team.

His gut rolled. He'd been careful to avoid them while they'd all been in Dallas. It hurt to look at that family and realize what he'd almost done to them. Little TJ Taggart would have grown up without a mum or dad if McDonald had been successful. It didn't matter that Theo seemed unbothered by his presence.

As for Theo's wife, he was sure Erin would have slit his throat if she'd had the chance. She was the savage one in that relationship, her violent tendencies only tamed by her love for her husband and son.

There were days he wished she would do it, that he would wake up one night and Erin Taggart would be looming over him like an avenging angel, her knife promising him sweet release. And if she wanted to torture him for a while, to flay the skin from his bones as he screamed, well, that would start to pay back what he owed.

"So we need to have something to tell them," Ezra was saying. "I've got Jax trying to hunt down Levi."

"He'll be somewhere close to her, close to Becca," Tucker said.

Owen shook his head. "He won't get too close. If he could do this job himself, he wouldn't have sent us to do it for him. I don't think he'll be content to sit back and watch. He's got a plan."

"He certainly did while we were in Bliss," Tucker offered, but his light had dimmed. His jaw tightened, and Owen could briefly see the demons that lurked under his normally sunny surface.

It could be easy to forget that Tucker had a dark side. A seriously dark side. A side that had been tortured over and over again. And maybe he'd been on the other side of the needle at one point in time. Owen knew that was Tucker's greatest fear, that he'd been callous and heartless, cruel and indifferent to the suffering of those around him.

Owen didn't have to fear. He already knew he had that darkness in him.

He sat back and thought about the light he'd been in recently. When he'd reached out for Becca Walsh, there hadn't been an ounce of dark between them. She'd been sunshine and she'd warmed his soul.

As Ezra started in on what they needed to do and Robert started getting paranoid about Levi taking off with Ariel, Owen sat back and sipped his coffee.

And plotted the seduction of Dr. Rebecca Walsh. He would get her out of that pretty cardigan and then they would see if she blew him off again.

Chapter Seven

"Thank you for coming up on a Saturday." Becca smiled at the intern. Annie showing up to help her out in the lab on a weekend seemed to be one of the only things going right for her.

That wasn't true. The research was going great, and that should make her happy, but all she seemed able to think about was the fact that she'd passed Owen Shaw three times in the hall in the last few days and he'd said nothing but hello to her. And then walked on.

She should be cheering. She'd gotten away clean and there was no weirdness between them.

Yet here she was on a Saturday, hiding at work so she didn't have to see if he was going on a date. Which was perverse because she had a date tomorrow. She'd agreed to Cathy's plan and she was going through with it come hell or high water.

"They're doing great, Dr. Walsh," Annie said, who despite Carter's insistence seemed incredibly smart and focused on her job. The young woman couldn't be more than twenty-four, her blonde hair up in a ponytail and a ready smile on her face. "Kidney function is perfect in all the rats. The drug doesn't seem to be affecting the liver either."

Becca stared down at the reports. "Excellent. How did short-term memory perform?"

Annie handed her another set of files. "With the drug, they

managed to make it through the maze two times faster than the control subjects. After three tries, memory function made them ten times faster."

It was everything she'd hoped for. "Yes. That's what I want to hear. The nerves are repairing themselves. The connections are coming back online once the drug clears the plaque out of the system."

"Once *you* clear the plaque," Annie said. "Dr. Walsh, this is remarkable. Don't sell yourself short."

"A lot of people helped work on this," she murmured, uncomfortable with the praise. She didn't give a shit about the prizes that would likely come if this worked out. The notoriety she would receive would be the worst part of her work.

She wasn't looking for money and fame. She was in a war, and it finally hit her that she might be winning.

"Yeah, well, a lot of people didn't have your ideas," Annie said. "I'm going to be you when I grow up."

She glanced up at the intern. "I'm like five years older than you."

A slender shoulder shrugged. "Yeah, but you're an actual adult. You don't party and stuff. I'm still sowing a bunch of oats or something. That's what my nana says. My mom just slut shames me and wants to know when I'm going to find a husband. She then tells me no man is going to want me if I don't slow my roll." She leaned in. "She means sex. I think if a guy can sleep with a bunch of people and have fun, then I should be able to, too. Not that you should. You should be here working and making the world a better place and stuff."

Did everyone see her as some kind of boring, plain Jane, never-gets-out of the lab martyr? "I have fun."

She'd damn straight had fun a few days before.

She kind of wished Owen had been the stripper she'd teased him about being. Then she could call and request his services. She wanted to celebrate and couldn't think of a better way than watching Owen get naked.

Annie's lips firmed as though she was holding in a chuckle and she nodded. "Of course you do. You simply have a different version of fun than a normal person. You're a genius. You're different from the rest of us."

She groaned because she'd heard that her whole life. She was special. She was different because she'd been touched by God or something. Her big brain was a blessing and she had to ensure that she did everything she could to make herself worthy of it.

She was sick of being seen as some kind of goody-two-shoes brainiac. "Do you know what I did Wednesday, Annie?"

"Yes, Dr. Walsh. You came to work. You were in the lab most of the day and then you had to listen to Jimmy's complete and utter failure of a trial. I saw the chick who wants to kill him. Her nose hair grew. I mean all the rest of it did too, but I was impressed at how fast that nose hair grew. You had a turkey sandwich for lunch at your desk and Cathy called in a chicken salad sandwich for your dinner from the Spadina Street café." She shrugged again. "We all have your schedule in case Cathy has an emergency."

God, she was boring. Well, she would have to fix that. "Was banging a hot Scot in an elevator on Cathy's schedule? Because that was how my night went."

Annie's eyes went wide. "Seriously?"

She felt her face flush, but there was no going back. Besides, she wasn't exactly ashamed. "His name was Owen and he was incredibly good stress relief."

"I thought your shoulders seemed looser lately. Good for you, Dr. Walsh."

Her shoulders weren't the only thing that were loose. So was her tongue.

Annie leaned in, conspiratorially. "Who was he? I didn't know we had a doctor from Scotland here. I thought the closest we had was the guy who's really from Vancouver but does that bad British accent."

Finally something she could jostle the girl with. "He's not from the foundation. He lives in my building. He's a bodyguard."

Yep, those youthful eyes bore the stamp of pure shock. "You did a blue-collar guy?"

She had and it had been glorious. "I did. I'm getting back in the dating world, though I don't guess getting trapped in an elevator counts as a date."

"It sure seems to have ended like one," Annie said. "Are you seeing him again? You know you don't have to, right? It's perfectly acceptable for you to have your fun and move on to greener pastures."

"I've got a date tomorrow but not with him," she admitted. Lawyer Larry texted her this morning and asked if he could call. They'd had a nice chat and lawyer number one of a hundred professionals Cathy was likely to parade in front of her seemed pretty nice. "I'm having lunch with a lawyer. I think that's what I'll do. I'll take the alliterative approach to getting back out there. Lunch with lawyers. Dinner with doctors."

Boning with bodyguards. Boffing with bodyguards. Bedtime with bodyguards.

Bodyguard. Bad boy. Except that bad boy had been awfully good.

Damn that man was in her head, but she wasn't giving in.

"That sounds good," Annie said with a smile. "Definitely stick to doctors and lawyers. They're the only ones who truly understand the kind of hours we put in. Unless you're looking for a good time. Then I can introduce you to some guys from the university who know what they're doing."

"I scarcely think Dr. Walsh needs to meet your friends, Annie," Carter said from the doorway. She hadn't heard him come in. "If you're done with Dr. Walsh's reports, why don't you go and help in the lab. Dr. Holder had some patients coming in for baseline MRIs."

Annie's eyes rolled but she was all smiles when she turned around. "Sure thing." She started for the door and then turned when she was behind Carter's back and gave Becca the *call me* sign along with a far more juvenile gesture that let her know Annie was willing to hook her up.

With college boys.

Did Annie know any men with ridiculously broad shoulders and eyes as blue as any ocean? Did she know any guy rough enough to send a thrill along her spine and tender enough to make her stupid heart soften up?

She needed to work on her reputation if all anyone was going to send her way was either professionals looking for companionship or college boys who wanted to get laid.

"I apologize for her familiarity," Carter said with a long-suffering sigh. "I go through this with them in their training classes."

"She was being friendly," Becca replied. "You should go easier on the interns. There might be a couple we want to keep, after all."

"Certainly not Annie. She's not serious about her work. She'll find a husband, some meathead with a good paycheck, and settle down. I've seen it happen time and time again."

"I hardly think medical school is the place to find a husband and never work again," she shot back. Normally she would let it go, but there was something under her skin today. "She's worked hard and we should value that."

If her little show of temper bothered him, he didn't let her know. He simply laid out an envelope that had her name typed on the front of it. "I think you'll like Tucker. He's very respectful, and from what I can see, he knows his stuff. He's assigned to Dr. Huisman right now, but I'll snatch him up for you if I can. This came by courier."

"On a Saturday?" She worked most Saturdays, but one of the things she liked about it was how she didn't have to deal with administrative stuff. She didn't get mail on weekends.

"I suppose whoever sent it knows you don't take a lot of time off work," he replied. "It was a bike messenger. Not the usual. He didn't have me sign for it or anything."

That was unusual to say the least. In her world there was always paperwork. Sometimes she expected the vending machines to need a signature to deliver a can of soda. She looked down at the plain white envelope in her hand. It wasn't thick. Her name had been typed neatly on the front and there was nothing else distinguishing about it.

"Is there something wrong?" Carter asked. "I was about to run some errands. I'll be back around six and we can head out together. If you like we can talk about your calendar for the next month. I'd like to get that on the books so the interns don't make excuses about not having the schedule in time."

She glanced up at the clock. She was supposed to be at River's in a few hours. She was surprised to discover she wasn't even thinking of canceling. It was what she usually did when it came to social events. She would say yes with all the good intentions in the world, and then the day would come and she would find some excuse to not put herself out there.

She wasn't even thinking about it today. Today she was eager for some lasagna. It had been a long time since she'd had a home-cooked meal, and her stomach growled at the thought. "I'm heading out early. I have a party to go to."

A single brow arched. "Party?"

Yep, she was working on her reputation. "Yes, I go to parties." At least she did now. "I have one tonight, so I'll see you on Monday."

"You're taking Sunday off?" The poor man looked like the world had shifted on him.

"I have a lunch date. I told you about it."

"I would assume it won't last all day."

"Only if I'm lucky," she replied pointedly.

His face flushed and for a moment he seemed to not understand. Then he backed away and she could see the shock in his eyes before he buried it under the veneer of professionalism. "Well, I suppose I'll see you Monday then. You…have fun this weekend."

Carter left without a backward glance. He was such a prissy man, much like a lot of the academic types. He was more focused on the job than the people they were trying to help. She'd known a lot of Carters. Somehow he'd latched on to her when she'd come to work at the foundation, and he'd been helpful at first. It had been nice to have someone who lived in the same building and was willing to show her around, but over time she'd gotten to realize he was pretty much a misogynist asshole. If her newfound sexual freedom made him put her in the same basket as the Annies of the world, she would happily go and bring a bottle of wine.

She should bring a bottle of wine to River's. She shouldn't show up empty handed.

That thought made her glance down at the envelope again. She should head out and stop somewhere along the way to grab a bottle. Red went with Italian, right? She might ask someone.

As she thought about the dinner, she opened the envelope and drew out the single sheet of paper.

If you want to know where the money went, meet me at Casa Loma where the Duchess overlooks the troops. 2 p.m. Next Friday.

What the hell did that mean? She stared at the note. It wasn't signed and there was no Dear Rebecca. Just those words printed on plain white paper.

The money. Fuck. There was over a million dollars missing and she'd been praying it was nothing more than an accounting error. Now it looked like not only was it not some kind of mistake, but something sinister.

Had she lost that file? Had it fallen out of her tote bag?

Or had someone taken it?

She grabbed the note and shoved it into her purse, the one nothing ever fell out of. It was time to go and talk to the security guards, to see if they had any video footage of whoever had sent the note.

After running down the security guard, she had a name. The note had been sent over by bicycle messenger and the security guard had recognized the young man who'd brought it to him. Arik Wheeler was a frequent visitor to the foundation. She'd been told he worked for several courier services, but this time the paperwork had been from City Messenger Toronto, one of the newer companies in town. She'd tried to call, but no one had answered, the business closing early on the weekend.

This mystery would have to wait until Monday when she would go straight to the head of accounting and start unravelling whatever the hell this was. She wasn't an accountant. She'd wanted to get a grasp on what was happening before she brought in her bosses, but this had officially gone over her head.

If she wasn't an accountant, she damn straight wasn't an investigator.

Frustrated, she closed up her laptop. It was getting late, much later than she'd planned on leaving. She glanced out the windows of her office and noted the street lights had come on and evening had fallen across the city. From her office, she could see the sparkling lights of Toronto.

Saturday night in the city.

She wondered if Owen was out and about, enjoying his first few nights in a brand-new town. Her lips curled up as she imagined all the women who would likely think about fainting so the handsome Scot would catch them.

She packed up and for a moment thought about falling back into routine. It was right there, the instinct to call and explain that she'd changed her mind and couldn't do dinner this evening. She could stop at the café and grab a salad and watch the same movies for the hundredth time and fall asleep on the couch. In the morning, she would call Lawyer Larry and let him know she had a work emergency and she could spend tomorrow here, too.

It was comfortable. It was safe, this routine of being alone.

It was cowardly and not what she'd promised the woman who'd

given birth to her.

With a long sigh, she vowed to try. Tonight she would be all social and sparkly and meet River and Jax's friends. Tomorrow she would smile and see if Lawyer Larry was at least a lust match.

She put her purse over her shoulder and opened the door to leave. She stepped out into the hall and realized how quiet it was. It wasn't like she didn't leave after everyone else did on a regular basis. She was usually the last one left with the singular exception of the janitorial staff and Chuck, who ran night security. But there was always ambient noise. There was the hum of printers left running or the heater. Not tonight. An eerie silence filled the space, as if sound could have weight.

Becca stopped, listening for something, anything that might tell her someone else was in the building because in that moment she realized she was being watched. She could feel it, knew it as surely as a rabbit knew a wolf was around, its eyes searching for prey.

But she didn't hear a sound. No one moved or even breathed. There was absolutely nothing that let her know that instinct deep inside her was telling the truth. She glanced around and not a damn thing moved in the wide bank of cubicles that dotted the floor.

Of course those cubicles could also hide a person.

What the hell was she doing?

It was ridiculous. She shouldn't have watched that stupid horror movie with her stepmom the last time she'd come into town. Melissa loved them. They gave Becca bad dreams and apparently made her paranoid that there was a serial killer in her office.

Her shoes clicked on the marbled floors, echoing through the space.

That was the moment when the lights went out.

She stopped, the place going dark, and then she could hear someone breathing. It came from her left, low and rattling through the room. Someone coughed and she took off, her heart pounding, adrenaline coursing through her veins like wildfire.

She raced for the bank of elevators, the light above the doors the only illumination in the building. She wouldn't be able to get in the elevators, but it was the only light to be found so she ran for it.

She could feel it; something was there behind her. Something was chasing her and if it caught her…

The elevator doors opened and a flashlight beamed in the darkness.

She stopped, her feet planted to the floor, and for a moment she couldn't breathe.

"Dr. Walsh?" a familiar voice rang out. "We're having some problems with the lights on this floor. Are you all right?"

Chuck. Her hands shook as the lights came back on and the world went from terrifying to normal in the space of a heartbeat.

Chuck clicked off his flashlight and concern showed on his face. "Dr. Walsh?"

She took a deep breath. "I'm okay. I just got a little scared. Is anyone still here?"

He slid the flashlight back into the belt around his waist. "There are a couple of researchers working in the cancer center. And Frank from human resources is sleeping in his office again. I know I shouldn't let him do that but he's been having…"

She was being paranoid. She shook her head. "If I was Frank's wife, I would have kicked him out, too." He was a jackass, but he wouldn't scare her like this. "The lights went out and I could have sworn I heard someone coughing."

A sound rattled through the room and she nearly jumped.

Chuck sighed. "It's the heater. You don't notice it when everyone is here and talking. We need to have it fixed. I'm sorry, Dr. Walsh. Come on and I'll escort you down. I promise I'll talk to maintenance the first thing Monday morning."

She nodded and didn't argue with him. She did notice the heater. That hadn't been the sound that frightened her, but she was being silly. She started following him toward the elevator. She glanced back and could have sworn she saw a shadow move in the rear of the building.

But it was nothing more than her eyes playing tricks on her. She could describe easily how the brain filled in spaces, how memory could make the mind twist and turn and see things that weren't actually there.

She went through it in her head as she forced herself not to give into fear, not to look back to make sure that thing she'd felt before wasn't still there. Wasn't waiting for the lights to go out again.

She banished the fear and promised herself she wouldn't let it affect her.

Chapter Eight

Owen glanced up at the clock and realized she was late. Fifteen minutes late. The party had started at six thirty, with Jax mixing cocktails while his pretty wife laid out her appetizers.

Damn him, but he'd forgotten River was a vegetarian. There was cheese but no meat, and a shocking amount of green stuff.

He was hungry and it wasn't all about food. Since the day with Rebecca, Owen Shaw had realized how empty his life had been, and he suddenly wanted to fill it.

Fill it with her.

That woman had done something to him, and he wasn't entirely sure he was happy about that.

"She'll be here," Robert said before popping a marinated olive in his mouth.

Owen shrugged. "Or she won't. Maybe you were all right and I fucked this up."

He'd been thinking about it every second since she'd blown him off. He'd been careful when they'd crossed paths, merely giving her a smile and a breezy hello.

"God, don't get broody," Robert groaned. "I need one of the Euros to have a sunny disposition. Sasha threw a plunger at me earlier today, and I swear he was trying to impale me. I often wish McDonald had more carefully screened her experiments for personality."

Owen stared at him. A shiver went through him. He dreamed about it at night, about that moment he couldn't remember, the one that had changed him utterly. In those nightmares, he saw the needle coming his way and looked up so he could see the face of the doctor who would take everything away from him.

He'd talked to Ariel about the dreams. What he'd never told her was that every time he looked up to take in Dr. McDonald's face before she erased him, he'd seen his own staring back.

The person in his nightmares was always, always himself.

"I don't understand how you joke about it," he said quietly. "I know I laugh and play along, but inside I'm not. Inside I think maybe I'm more broken than the rest of you."

Why the fuck had that popped out? He hadn't even had more than two sips of the whiskey and soda Jax had placed in his hand.

Maybe that was the problem. He wasn't drinking enough. He wasn't following his usual pattern, and it was fucking with him hard.

He was about to chuckle and pretend he was joking when Robert put a hand on his shoulder.

"No, brother, it's only that I've been broken longer than you," he said solemnly. "I've been broken for years, and you'll find that if you let it, some of those broken pieces will heal. They won't be the same, but you'll find ways to cope that aren't about trying to obliterate yourself. Ezra talked to me this afternoon. He's optimistic that this is going to work better than our original plan."

"I don't know about that," he admitted, storing Robert's words for later examination. Was he trying to obliterate himself? Was that why he got drunk and thought about starting fights he knew he couldn't win? He'd been in a bar brawl in Colorado and a fierce joy had lit through him when he'd realized how serious the man he'd fought had been about trying to kill him. It had occurred to him that this might be an excellent way to go out.

Not fade away. Never fade. He should go out in a blaze of glory.

"Stop it with the doubt, man," Robert said. "There's no place for it. When Dr. Walsh gets here, you need to charm her. This is all about forgetting everything but the mission."

A gentle chime went through the apartment and he was shocked at how his whole body seemed to go on alert.

River winked his way as she headed for the door, Buster hard on her heels.

Jax had found something special in Colorado. He'd found a family, was building a home, and it had nothing at all to do with some house. Jax's home wasn't found in four walls and carpet. It was there in River. In the way she smiled at him, in how she believed so much in him she'd walked away from everything she'd known.

The life that had been Jax's nightmare was now an adventure.

"Hi, I'm sorry I'm late," Becca was saying as River let her in. She was wearing a white shirt and a black skirt that was somehow professional and righteously sexy. A sweet-looking black and white cardigan completed her uniform. Pink gloss made her lips shiny, and she'd let her hair down. It hung around her face in thick tendrils that made him want to sink his hands into it and force her to look up at him.

He hadn't topped her, and he craved that in a way he never had before. He'd trained at The Garden because it had taken up the lonely hours. He'd enjoyed the D/s sex he'd had, but he hadn't understood the need to be in control until tonight.

"You're not late," River said, accepting the bottle of wine with a gracious smile. "Jax's boss isn't even here yet. I barely put out the appetizers. You've met Owen, but I'm not sure if you know his friend, Robert."

He watched as Becca's shoulders went stiff and straight and she turned slowly. Her eyes were wide when she took him in. She had not been expecting him. And then he saw the moment she decided to brazen her way through. Her lips curled up in a smile and she reached out a hand to him.

"Hello, elevator friend. I didn't expect to see you here," she said and there was a hint of something in her eyes.

Something that told him this wasn't a pleasant surprise.

But there was something deeper, something almost afraid. Maybe more than almost.

Fuck. He could play the game. He would enjoy the seduction game with her, but if she was scared, he couldn't overcome that. He had no idea why she would be afraid, but he'd talked to enough women to know she might have her reasons.

He briefly took her hand and attempted to make his expression as gentle as possible. "It's good to see you as well, Dr. Walsh."

Her eyes flared briefly as though she hadn't expected him to use her title. "You can call me Rebecca. Or Becca."

He took a step back, not wanting to crowd her or make her feel like he was in her space. He had no idea what he'd done to scare her. She hadn't seemed scared of him when they'd passed in the hall, but she'd obviously changed her mind, and he wasn't going to push himself on any woman. Not even for a mission.

There was pursuing a woman who wanted to be chased, and then there was stalking a woman to make her feel small, to let her know she was nothing but prey. He wasn't ever going to do the latter.

But standing in front of her made him ache. He nodded her way. "All right then, Rebecca. I'm going to refill my glass. It's good to see you again."

He turned and walked back toward the kitchen, well aware that Robert was staring at him like he was insane.

He could hear Robert telling her hello as well and then River was there, smoothing things over and telling Becca about the menu for the evening.

"Hey, have you decided to play this low and slow or something?" Robert whispered the question as he entered the kitchen.

There was a swinging door between the galley-like kitchen and the living room, but there was also a large open space over the sink. He was sure it had been designed so whoever was left with cooking duties could still be a part of the activities in the living room, but it was also useful for spying.

Jax's head came up from where he was cutting limes. "Low and slow? Like a brisket?"

"Like a man who just totally blew off a woman," Robert replied with a frown on his face. "I thought you were going after her. I'm not sure both of you playing hard to get is going to work."

One of Jax's big shoulders shrugged. "Robert should know."

Robert's eyes rolled. "This isn't about me. This is about the op, and Dr. Walsh *is* the op."

"I think we might have to go a different route." He poured himself more whiskey. It might be time to go back to what worked for him. He'd never once scared away the whiskey. "She was afraid of me."

That seemed to flummox his friends.

"You're reading her wrong. I think she was surprised to see you." Robert grabbed a glass of his own. "Jax didn't tell her you would be here tonight. I told you sometimes women get skittish after sex. You have to go out there and be charming."

"No, she was afraid. Something scared her. That wasn't embarrassment." She hadn't been embarrassed at all when she'd walked away from him that night they'd been stuck in the lift. She certainly hadn't been the morning after. That morning she'd been in control. This evening there was something tentative about her.

"Why would she be afraid?" Jax asked.

"It could be anything." Robert stared out into the living room as though considering the problem. "Something her ex-husband did. There might be some trauma there. Ariel didn't mention that there had been violence in the relationship, but she can't tell everything from her files."

"Becca filed an HR report against one of the other doctors at the hospital where she did her residency." He'd spent the day going over and over her file, everything they knew about her. He'd even tried to read one of her papers, something on how plaque affected memory, but he had no idea what half the words had meant.

She was smart and dynamic, and she'd had a few bumps along the way. The HR claim, the divorce. Tucker had mentioned there was gossip about Becca and Paul Huisman at work. Some people said she was sleeping with him. Others said they hated each other because she'd taken his job.

A woman of her skill and at her level would always have enemies or people who were jealous. Had one of those people tried to hurt her? What would that have to do with him?

He had to also consider the fact that she was simply done with him.

"You should talk to her," Jax said. "Walk back out there and strike up a conversation. She'll make an excuse and leave if it's too uncomfortable."

"Remember that this isn't personal," Robert advised. "This is only about the op. Nothing else matters, and we should put everything else aside."

The doorbell rang again and he watched as River moved toward it and Becca was left alone. She bit her bottom lip and glanced over at the clock as though trying to decide if she could find a way out.

He was going to lose her. He had to find a middle ground, had to figure out why she was afraid of him suddenly. Had something happened today?

He could hide in here or he could try.

"What the hell?" Robert straightened up as Ezra walked into the apartment, his hand tangled with his partner's for the evening.

Ariel Adisa. She looked gorgeous in a green dress that showed off her curves. Her hair was in its natural curl, and there was no doubt she was a stunning woman.

Becca's beauty was quieter, but no less impactful. Of course, Becca wasn't holding on to another man. She wasn't grinning as she was introduced as someone's wife, her face kind of glowing.

No. Becca looked shy as she put her hand out to greet Ezra and Ariel.

"Why the fuck is his hand on her?" Robert's whole demeanor had changed.

Ariel was here tonight as Ezra's wife so she could get a better read on Becca. She'd explained that reading Becca's reports and her social media would only tell her so much. Ariel wanted to get to know the woman who might have worked with Dr. McDonald.

Who hadn't worked with that woman. No way. He couldn't even think of it. She hadn't known a damn thing. He couldn't believe it.

"I thought this was all about the op, man," Jax said. "She's Ezra's partner, not his lover."

Robert actually growled the minute the word *lover* came out of Jax's mouth.

"Seriously? You know you were supposed to be playing *my* lover, right?" Owen pointed out the flaw in his friend's logic. "You certainly weren't doing it to make Ari jealous. Or were you?"

Robert's jaw tightened as he obviously tried to gain control. "Of course not. She knows damn well I wouldn't sleep with you."

But he was worried she might sleep with Ezra. "She turned you down because she wouldn't sleep with a coworker. I know Ezra technically isn't on the payroll, but I assure you she thinks of him as a coworker."

"She didn't turn me down at all," Robert said quietly. "I did it. I kissed her back when I first started living at The Garden, and it got out of hand. And I realized how much I could hurt her. We agreed to go back to what we'd been before, therapist and patient. Friends, sort of, because of how we work together. I've come a long way. I can control myself now. I won't hurt her physically. But she's angry because I left her behind in London. I'm trying to show her that maybe we could try again after all this is over."

Jax hissed slightly. "Man, they do not like to hear things like that. Women tend to want to go through all the things. The good. The bad. All the stuff."

"You've been married for five minutes, Jax," Robert shot back.

"Yeah, but it's been a good five minutes." Jax sighed as though thinking about something amazing. "It hasn't been long, but I know one thing I've figured out. If you're a couple you're together no matter what. You don't give up because being together is the most important thing. River isn't merely a gift to protect. She's my wife and she's got a say in everything we do."

"Oh, you learn quickly, baby." River pushed through the swinging door and walked straight up to her husband, throwing her arms around him and lifting her face for a kiss. "Nothing is sexier than being a partner and not a prop." He lowered her back down and she grabbed a corkscrew. "I take it this man-talk is brought to us by the sight of Ariel with another man? I ask because I know this isn't about Owen. He's already running away and hard."

"I am not running," he complained. "I'm giving her space because she obviously doesn't want me here."

"She had a rough day at work and she's still unsettled," River replied, picking up two wine glasses. "Which you would know if you hadn't gotten all man hurt because she didn't become a puddle of goo at the very sight of your handsome face. Go and make her laugh. Be charming and non-threatening. Try not to look like a crazy caveman. If you need tips on how to do that, look at Robert right now and then do the opposite of him. Now if you'll excuse me, I'll try to get Ezra back here and then Ari and I can solve the case while you guys gossip."

She strode out to the living room, the door swinging behind her.

Jax grinned after his wife. "She gets sassier with age."

She was definitely a far cry from the woman he'd first met. She'd been sad, closed off and suspicious.

If Jax had walked away the first time she'd rejected him—over a misunderstanding—they wouldn't be here. That wasn't how it would work out for him and Becca, however he could do his job and still be good for her.

But not if he let her walk away because he didn't even try.

From his vantage he could see her through the opening between the kitchen and the bar. She hadn't put her purse down. She was glancing around like she was trying to find a way to get out of this gracefully.

He couldn't give her the chance. He grabbed a second glass and poured out two fingers of whiskey. "I'm going in."

"Damn straight you are," Jax replied. "Ask her. She won't be expecting it because almost no one in this world is open and honest when they feel vulnerable. I was too stupid to know how to behave and it saved me. Be bold."

Bold. He could do that. He clutched the glasses and strode out to make his play.

* * * *

How to get out? It had been a mistake to come tonight. Maybe if she hadn't walked in and seen Owen she could have gotten through dinner, but seeing him again had thrown her off kilter.

She could fake a text. She was a doctor. Everyone knew doctors had emergencies all the time. A research emergency. That might work. Something could have gone wrong in the lab and she needed to get back. Except there was zero chance she was going back there tonight.

Damn it. She hated being this wishy-washy, hated not having a plan in front of her.

It had been an hour since she'd left the office and she couldn't find her calm. She could tell herself that the feeling she'd gotten while standing outside her office had been nothing but a trick of memory, but it still sat there in her gut.

She'd hated that feeling. Vulnerable. Fragile.

Seeing Owen had made her want to run because she was close to the edge and she didn't have any right to ask him to put those big, strong arms around her.

It would be a stupid thing to do. She'd just met the man. She wasn't going to pour her heart out to him.

She'd had sex with him, but somehow talking about how scared she'd been, leaning on him for something other than an orgasm was more intimate.

"Did you say you were a doctor?" the gorgeous woman with a British accent said. She'd been introduced as Ariel, Ezra's wife. She was tall and graceful, with brown eyes lit with intelligence. "Medical?"

"Yes," she replied out of politeness. River was busy opening the bottle of pinot noir she'd grabbed at the café downstairs as her husband's boss spoke to her in low tones. "I work in research with the Huisman Foundation."

"You're Rebecca Walsh? The Rebecca Walsh?" Ariel smiled broadly. "I'm sorry. I bet you don't normally meet fans outside of a conference. I guess fan is an odd word. Admirer is more posh, perhaps."

"I don't normally meet anyone who knows me outside of the medical world." There was a reason those eyes were so intelligent. "They didn't introduce you as Dr. Fain."

"I go by my maiden name, Dr. Adisa, but honestly, unless I'm working, I don't use it. I'm around a lot of Ezra's circle most of the time and they are not impressed with education. Well, not the university kind. My husband knows an awful lot of computer experts. I'm a clinical psychologist. I work particularly with intense PTSD and trauma." The psychologist smiled brightly as she spoke, practically lighting up the room. "Obviously one of the problems can be memory loss, both short and long term. Your paper on new therapy techniques in reconnecting memory function was brilliant. I use several of your methods with my long-term patients. I thought you were in Boston."

"I took a job at Huisman a couple of years ago," she explained. "They gave me a whole department and pretty much free range on whatever I wanted to work on, so I moved here."

"They've got deep pockets and some incredible connections," Ariel agreed. "It's such a small world. You should know that your work is helping people on many levels."

She loved hearing that and on any other night she would question the doctor, asking her about her research and practice. She'd often found that the doctors who used her work as a base came up with possibilities she'd never thought about. But tonight, that note was still in her bag and the shadows seemed to be chasing her. Tonight, praise might be a good transition to exit. "Thank you so much. I would love to talk to you about how you've used them. Perhaps we could have lunch sometime. I'm afraid I'm going to…"

She stopped when Owen stepped up beside Ariel, two glasses in his hand.

He was even more gorgeous than she'd remembered. Her dreams had nothing on reality. He was big and strong and those eyes pierced through her. His reddish and gold hair was slightly shaggy, and he had the hint of a beard across that chiseled jaw.

She kind of wanted to kiss that jaw.

How could she go from needing to be alone to wanting so desperately to be alone with him?

"I brought you a drink. I remember you didn't mind whiskey," he said, holding out the glass.

She took it and her first instinct was to down that sucker as fast as she could.

Her second was to wonder about that note she'd gotten and the way she'd felt earlier in the evening.

How well did she know this man? How well did she know any of the people in this room?

Owen offered his free hand to the lovely psychologist. "I'm Owen Shaw. I live across the hall. Just moved in this week."

"Ariel Adisa," she said, readily taking his hand and shaking it. "It's good to know my husband and I aren't the only strangers in a strange land. My husband works with Jax. We moved from DC, though obviously I'm a Brit like you."

Owen's brow rose. "I'm a Scot, love."

She sighed. "One of those. I should have known. Are you in the medical profession as well?"

She didn't like how pretty Owen looked with Ariel. But then he would probably look good with anyone. She didn't like how long Owen held the other woman's hand.

A very good reason to run because she shouldn't get possessive about some guy she'd spent a couple of hours with.

That was when she realized that while she'd been watching that place where Owen's hand held the other woman's, his gaze had been on her. She looked up into his vibrant eyes. He glanced down at the glass in her hand and she could have sworn she saw a hint of hurt there.

"Darling, could you come and tell River about the new gallery you found in Junction Triangle?" Ezra put his hand on his wife's back, gesturing her toward their host. "She and Jax have had a hard time decorating this place. Apparently they have different tastes."

Ariel chuckled. "I'm afraid I can't help Jax's sad preoccupation with dogs playing poker paintings, but I can help River." She sent Becca another of her brilliant smiles. "I'm so happy to meet you and to know you're in my little circle. See you in a bit."

And she was left alone with Owen. Not alone, exactly. They were in one of the apartment's corners, but River, Ariel, and Ezra were already talking animatedly across the room. Jax and Robert walked in, bringing more drinks.

It was a party. A normal thing.

She could still feel her heart beating.

"Give me that," Owen ordered.

She realized he was talking about the drink in her hand. The one she hadn't touched. He took it and downed it in one long swallow before setting it on one of the coasters River had set on the tables in the room.

"Jax will pour you another one and you can watch him do it," he said, his voice low but gentle. "We've been drinking from that bottle all night. He opened it in front of me. Now tell me what I did between Wednesday and tonight to put that look in your eyes and make you worry I might hurt you."

He thought she thought he'd tried to drug her drink? She was about to protest, but she *had* considered it. She'd looked at him and wondered honestly why such a gorgeous man would want her the way he seemed to. She'd thought about the fact that two weird, frightening things had happened in the days after she'd met him.

But he'd been here for over an hour, according to River. He'd come early because his laptop wasn't working and Jax had offered to fix it for him. While she'd been terrified, he'd been trying to get better Internet.

She was being utterly paranoid.

He'd seen right through her.

She stole his glass and took a long swallow, the whiskey burning through her in a pleasant way. "I had a rough day."

"And walking in on your…it wasn't even a one-night stand was it? Walking in to find out you're having dinner with me couldn't have helped."

"That wasn't exactly how I viewed it."

"Robert said you were probably embarrassed," he said with a frown. "I don't understand what you have to be embarrassed about."

She felt her cheeks heat and she forced herself to swallow her second mouthful of whiskey. "You told Robert?"

It was his turn to blush. "I did. I wasn't supposed to? I guess I didn't think about it. It was the best thing that happened to me in a long time. I wanted to talk about it."

Those words did strange things to her heart. And he was right. A little of her tension seemed to seep away. Maybe it was the whiskey, but she kind of thought it was the man. Now that she was standing here alone with him, she remembered how comfortable she'd been with him. They'd been stuck in that dumb elevator for hours, and it had been easy to be with Owen. He hadn't flinched at all over her dweeby talk about science fiction shows she loved or rolled his eyes when she started feeling tight in her own skin. He'd shared her dinner gratefully and offered her half of everything he'd had.

And when she'd needed it, he'd kissed and fucked away every ounce of stress in her body.

"I told some people too," she admitted with a half-smile. She would probably tell Cathy. She'd definitely talk to Melissa about it. "Well, I told one person and this other guy overheard, but I didn't really care because I would tell anyone who asked. Your friend is wrong. I wasn't ashamed." She glanced over at Robert and frowned. "Is he unhappy? He looks angry."

The man had the fiercest frown on his face and he seemed to be staring at Ezra, Ariel, and River like he might murder one of them. Or all of them.

Jax had walked over with a plate of crostinis. "Who's angry?"

Owen's brows went up and he looked over at his friend with a grimace. "Robert. And not at all. That's just his face, love. He's one of those guys who can't seem to smile much. I'm absolutely sure it's not because he can't stand to look at a couple who's obviously in love because that would make him a crazy man."

Jax sighed. "Definitely just his face. I'll tell him to watch the resting bitch face. Dinner's in ten."

He turned and walked back to the other group.

She wouldn't call it resting bitch face. Maybe resting serial-killer face. She watched as Jax walked up and whispered something to the man and his face flooded with red. He sighed and turned to his friend.

"So you're not afraid of me then?" Owen's words brought her attention back to him. "When you walked in, I thought you looked scared. I couldn't stand the thought of you being afraid of me."

She wasn't. Well, not in a physical way. Emotionally she was worried he might wreck her in a way her ex never could, but she wasn't going to let that happen. Maybe they could enjoy each other. Why not? As long as they were both open and honest about what they wanted, why couldn't they have some fun?

Of course, she might be reading him wrong. He might be simply trying to be friendly.

"Not afraid. Not of you," she admitted. "Something weird happened at work and it freaked me out a little."

"What happened?" His gaze sharpened and she could buy that this was a man who'd been honed in battle.

"It was nothing. The lights went out when I was about to come home. I was alone and it scared me," she replied simply.

"Was it the darkness that frightened you?"

She shivered as she remembered that feeling. "It was nothing. Primal fear of the unknown, I suspect. It's weird. I don't hate being alone. I like it most of the time. I've lived alone here for two years and I'm usually one of the last people out of the office at night, but today something felt different. Like I said, it was dumb instinct."

"Instinct isn't dumb," he insisted. "Fear isn't something to be ignored. Fear is the lizard part of your brain, the part that concentrates on survival."

She stared at him. "Are you seriously mansplaining the amygdala to a neuroscientist?"

His lips curled up in the sexiest smirk. "I got no idea what that is, but it's sexy when you say it." He sobered a bit. "And you might be the brain expert, but I assure you, I'm the expert in fear and survival. So let me soldiersplain this to you. Fear is the first ingredient to survival. You can't survive an attack if you don't know it's coming, and fear is the first sign. Did you feel like you weren't really alone?"

She nodded, the hair on her arms standing up again.

"Then you probably weren't," he replied. "Have there been any crimes around your building? Break-ins? Assaults?"

"Not that I'm aware of." He looked so serious, so concerned, that

132

she found herself reaching out to him, putting a hand on his arm. The minute she touched him, she felt herself relax fully. It was okay. She wasn't back there. She was here with him, and Owen knew what he was doing.

"You work in research," he mused. "How secretive is it?"

She hadn't considered that. "I publish my research. I talk about it pretty openly, but my data is kept secret until I'm ready to publish. The pharmaceutical companies who fund me get the updates, but those are quarterly. There's always different foundations and competing research groups who wouldn't mind knowing exactly what I'm doing and how far I've gotten."

"They might not be patient enough to wait. I've learned that corporations aren't patient at all, and they don't mind bribing employees to get what they want. If there's a spy, he's likely in your midst. Or she. Saturday evening would be a good time to have a look around."

That made more sense than someone waiting to hurt her. Having a logical explanation let her take her first deep breath in hours. "We have security. I'll have them check and see if anything odd happened and who was in the building at the time. But I'm sorry you thought I was worried about you. I'm not at all, Owen Shaw."

"You weren't happy to see me. I didn't imagine that."

"I was surprised. It took me off guard seeing you here," she admitted. How to explain? "I think I could get my heart broken by you. I think I could get serious about you fast, and that's not something I'm ready for. I don't know that I ever will be again. I think what happened in the elevator was a crazy connection, but I'm not sure we should take it further than that. I have a date tomorrow. I'm not planning on getting serious about him either."

He seemed to think about that for a moment. "Is that why you said no when I asked you to go to dinner with me?"

"I had to work late that night."

A hard glint hit his eyes and she was surprised that it didn't frighten her off at all. That dark look on his face made him hotter because she didn't believe for a second that he would hurt her in a physical fashion, though she wondered how rough he would get if he let himself off the leash.

Sex with her ex had been good. They'd been quite compatible, but she'd taken the lead in most of it. There had been something about the way Owen Shaw had asked her to let him take over, and then when she'd agreed how he'd mastered her body, that she couldn't stop thinking about. It had been a hurried affair. What if they'd had a whole night? How would Owen Shaw make love to a woman when there were no time constraints?

"That's a lie," he said, his sensual lips forming a flat line. "I don't like it when you lie to me. I would prefer honesty. You don't want to go out with me at all, do you? Just tell me, and I'll back off."

But she didn't want him to back off. "All right. You want honesty? I don't want to be exclusive with anyone, Owen. I'm not in a place where I can have a relationship. I would like very much to be friendly with you, but I think you're the kind of man who could get possessive."

"And I think you're the type of woman who won't be able to hold herself apart no matter how much she wants to." The dark look on his face was replaced with sensual amusement. "Are you saying you aren't opposed to repeating the experience?"

Just like that she could feel her nipples perk up. Damn, he was a sexy man. She wanted him, but she heard herself saying, "I don't know."

He reached out and his fingertips brushed back her hair. "When you figure it out, why don't you let me know. I think that we're both adults with demanding jobs. We likely don't have a ton of time to date, but I know I for one wouldn't hate having someone to go to bed with at night or to share an occasional meal with. I definitely think I would like a woman who appreciates what I can give her in bed, and I'm not just talking about my cock. I'm talking about more than mere sex. Do you understand? I want you to think about this while we're having dinner. Actually, for the next few days if you need them."

She was back to not being able to breathe, though it was a pleasant experience. Anticipation. Longing. Curiosity. "What do you mean it's more than sex?"

"I want more," he said, his voice a husky temptation. "I want a few nights a week where we play. Do you understand what I mean by play?"

She hadn't lived under a rock. Melissa had dragged her out to that movie she'd been crazy about. She'd sat there in the darkened theater filled with a crowd of swooning women and she hadn't admitted that she wondered what it would feel like. Not the all-day stuff. Not letting some man pick her clothes and tell her what to eat. That would make her punch the asshole.

But the sex stuff... Not having to think for a few hours a day. Trusting her lover enough to give him control of her body and her pleasure. Exploring with him.

"You're talking about dominance and submission," she whispered, trying to ensure no one else heard them. "I would assume it's your dominance."

He was staring at her lips. "Aye. And your submission."

That accent had gotten so much thicker and he'd said "aye" not "yes" the way he normally would, as though the very thought of it made him somehow more primal.

"I've never...played before." But she'd thought about it.

"That's not a problem. I've played enough for both of us. All you have to do is follow my commands. I'll ensure your pleasure, your relaxation. On a night when we play, you will belong to me and I *will* be possessive. The good news is you can tell me no and I'll walk away. If you tell me to stay away, I will. This is only good for me if it's good for you."

"You would spank me?" The question didn't come out shocked because she wasn't. And that kind of shocked her. She was a genius at the top of her game.

She was also a woman who needed sex and emotion and connection, even if it was only for a few hours a week.

"Only if you like to be spanked."

She had to push him before she made the decision. "But I know there's punishment."

"Only if you need it to feel happy and complete," he explained. "Or if you wanted accountability for something."

River walked up, a smile on her face. "It's time for dinner, you two."

He nodded her way. "We'll be right there." When their hostess had walked away, he turned his attention back on Becca. Such focus. When he looked at her like that, she felt like she was the only woman in the room. "Think about it, Becca. I'm willing to play with you. I'm more than willing. I want you. If all I can get is a night a week, I'll take it. As long as when you're with me, you're with me, then I won't ask

135

questions about the rest of your social life."

He wouldn't care that she was dating other men. Or he might care, but he wouldn't give her hell for it. He would likely date as well. They would be free to explore sex with each other, but also free to explore outside their relationship.

This was dangerous, but she couldn't seem to help herself. He was offering her everything she wanted. No holds barred. No strings attached.

But there might be rope.

"Think about it." He took a deep breath and stepped back. "We should go."

"Yes," she said, her decision made. "We should." She took his hand. "River, I'm so sorry. I have an emergency."

The whole room was staring at her, but she knew what she needed and it was absolutely him.

"An emergency? Is everything okay?" River asked.

She started to lead Owen toward the door. "Everything will be. Thanks so much for inviting me. And Owen. He's got to help me with my emergency."

It was weak, but she honestly didn't care. She'd spent the last few hours feeling vulnerable, and this choice seemed to have brought her strength back.

"It's definitely an emergency," Owen affirmed in a low drawl. "It might take most of the night. Thanks for the party, Jax. River."

She grabbed her purse and when he took the lead, she followed.

Chapter Nine

She led Owen into her apartment and silently thanked Cathy for the flowers that spruced the place up. Décor hadn't been a priority since she'd moved in.

Of course, the prettiest thing in her place right now was the large predatory man glancing around, taking in his surroundings.

She took a breath and then let it out. Where was the panic? Shouldn't she be asking herself what the hell she was doing? Shouldn't she be questioning why she was about to talk about submitting to this man sexually?

Her lateral frontal pole was perfectly silent, having given way to her limbic system with a big old thumbs-up. As though the most sophisticated part of her brain had just told the primal part, "you go, girl."

"Do you want another drink?" she asked, putting her purse on the foyer table and joining him in the living room.

"Do you need one?"

She didn't take offense. She considered it for a moment. "No. I'm okay with my level of calm right now. I think another might dull the experience."

He settled onto her big comfy couch. Big? She kind of got lost on it, but Owen's body took up all the space. "I'm glad to hear that. I'm not going to drink for the rest of the night either. I want to focus on you. Come here and sit on my lap. We need to go over a few rules first."

Rules. Yes, she'd heard this whole lifestyle thing was about communication. As long as it ended with his penis communicating with her pussy, she was okay with it. And his lap looked awfully comfy.

She kicked off her flats and crossed the space between them. "I don't do a lot of lap sitting. Should I call you 'Sir' or something?"

His eyes narrowed slightly. "Tell me you don't read those books. Every bloody sub I know reads those books. They're not like real life. In real life dungeons are in someone's creepy basement. Well, unless they're owned by multimillionaires or men who spend way too much money on dungeons."

Oh, she would like to see one of those. "Do you play in someone's creepy basement dungeon?"

His eyes lit up. "Not at all. I'm going to admit I know way too many of the multimillionaire types. I've done most of my play in lavish dungeons, but I get in because it's part of my employment package. The multimillionaires often need security. I'm good at my job, and many of the men and women at the firm I work for are involved in the lifestyle, so they're happy to give us access. You would be surprised at the high-powered people who enjoy playing."

She moved in, awkwardly settling herself onto his lap, but when his arms went around her she felt her whole body relax. He was like a warm blanket, covering and surrounding her. "It doesn't surprise me at all. Sex is an excellent way to relieve stress, and having rules and protocols would be attractive to type A personalities. I know I've thought about it. But I have to admit, the creepy dungeon might be fun, too."

His lips curled up in that smirk she was coming to adore. "You might not have to wait long. Robert will likely find a house soon and start converting his basement. There's a pervert for ya. Love him like a brother, but he's got his quirks."

"Do you have quirks?" She loved being so close to him. This was what they'd missed in their single encounter. They'd had all the talking and getting to know one another. Because of the nature of their location and the specifics of their situation, it could possibly have subbed for two or three dates' worth of getting to know each other. They'd had the incredibly hot sex. But they hadn't had the sensuality of touching and caressing and kissing before the hot sex. There was something tender about sitting in his lap, listening to the deep rumble of his voice.

"A couple," he admitted. He looked content. His body was relaxed, as though he genuinely loved being exactly where he was. "I don't talk about my past much. I prefer to look to the future. Couple of things you should know. I've never been married. Haven't had a steady girlfriend in a long time. I work too much, drink too much."

"I work too much," she replied, liking his openness. "I hide too much, too. I get lost in routine. I could explain why. It's got to do with the primal brain and comfort, but that's also the part of the brain where addiction forms. Addiction can be to more than drugs and alcohol. It can be to patterns of behavior that hurt us. I'm worried I'm getting addicted to not feeling things."

His hand slid up her hip. "Like pain?"

"Like anything." It felt good to talk about it. She couldn't with her coworkers and she didn't want to worry her family, but this was something she'd thought about for a long time. "I feel like sometimes I'm not present at all. Even when I'm with my dad, I'm thinking about work. I'm glancing at the clock and wondering when I can go back because in that lab I don't have to be anything but a doctor looking for a cure."

"All right, then. Here you don't have to be anything but a woman." His other hand found her knee. "When we're playing, you're to let everything else go and concentrate on pleasing me. I'm going to do the same thing. When we agree we're in a session, nothing else intrudes. You're my only focus and I'm yours."

That was exactly what she wanted. When they were together, they were together. When they weren't, they were friends. He would be her retreat. "I assure you I'm wholly focused on you, Owen. But I would like to know the rules. I'd like to talk about them. I'm one of those people who likes to know what's expected. I might or might not behave, but I don't want to be caught off guard."

That hand of his moved higher on her leg. "No high protocol and curse me all you like. For me that's not a sign of disrespect. I'm a Dom because I like it, because I'm wired to take control, not because I need respect. If I do something you're scared of or you find distasteful, tell me you're yellow. I'll stop and we'll talk. If I hurt you in a way that doesn't enhance your pleasure, you tell me red and it stops then and there. I'll back off and I won't touch you again until you're comfortable."

It struck her that he was offering her the best of all worlds. He would take control, but only until she didn't want him to. She could explore how pain and pleasure and control intermingled and enhanced the sexual experience, but in the safest of ways. And he wasn't an asshole about it. She'd read somewhere some dominant partners wouldn't let their submissives touch them without permission. He wouldn't do that to her. She wasn't sure why she knew that, but she did. It made her bold, let her reach up and gently scrape her palm across his scruff. Sexy scruff.

She could swear that man purred for her.

"Affection will go a long way with me, love." His eyes closed briefly as she rubbed a hand over his cheek and down to his neck. When they came open again she would have sworn she'd never seen blue eyes that hot before. "We're starting now. Are you feeling all right about it?"

She nodded, watching the way his lips moved. Plump and sensual, she wanted to know how it felt to have them on her breasts and at her core. "I'm feeling very excited about starting. It went so fast the first time. I liked it, but I wanted more."

His hand was warm between her thighs. Possessive. Not a word she loved, but it felt right now. "I did, too. I wanted to kiss you more, touch you more. I wanted to feel your mouth on me, put mine on you. Can I stay the night?"

She shouldn't let him. She had a date tomorrow. Was she really going to get up from bed with him and get ready to go out with another man? Yet it was what they'd agreed on. What did she want? Couldn't she indulge herself? "Yes."

It would be a good way to figure out if this thing could work, if they could be…whatever they were talking about being. Fuck buddies. Booty calls.

Lovers.

"Good, because what I want to do is going to take a while. But first, I'm going to kiss you, Becca. I can't stop thinking about how good it was to kiss you."

"I want that, too."

"All right then from now until either you tell me we're done or we leave this apartment, I'm in charge. You'll do as I say. You can ask any question you want. You can stop it, but give it a chance. From now at least until dawn, you belong to me. You're my gorgeous fuck toy, and I assure you I'm going to use you well."

Somehow every dirty word that came out of his mouth pulled her tauter, like a bowstring waiting to let fly. "Okay."

A stupid word, but the only one she could think of at the moment since his hand was so close to her pussy. She couldn't see his hand because she was still in her now too-tight skirt, but she could feel it, feel his heat and intent. God, she wanted him to stroke her.

She wanted to be his fuck toy all night long.

"Now you're in for it, girl," he said before his mouth covered hers. He kissed her long and slow, as though trying to show her how the night would go. Long. Patient. Luscious.

"I'm going to teach you something, Becca." The words shimmered against her lips. "I'm going to teach you how to fuck like a man."

She giggled. She couldn't help it. "Do I get a strap-on?"

He growled at her, but it was a playful sound and his arms tightened. That hand on her thigh finally skimmed over her pussy and she shivered at the touch, heat flashing through her. No man in the world had ever gotten her so hot so fast. If he'd wanted to, she would have allowed him to shove her on the couch, push her skirt up, and fuck her right then and there.

"You'll never get a strap-on, love," he said against her ear as those clever fingers of his started teasing their way inside her panties. "That's not what I meant. A man doesn't think about anything but sex when he's fucking. Well, unless he's trying his damnedest to make it last and then he'll think some boring-as-hell thoughts. But mostly all he thinks about is how he feels. How do you feel right now, Becca?"

"I feel like I want you to keep kissing me."

"No, that's not what I mean. Let go of what's going to happen and concentrate on the now. I don't want you to think even a minute ahead of right now. We live in this second when we're together. How do you feel?"

How did she feel? Not what did she want? How did it feel to be surrounded by him, overwhelmed by him? That wasn't what he was asking either. She had to go smaller, narrow down her field of study. How did it feel to have his mouth close to her? His hands grazing her clitoris? "I feel desired. I feel wanted. I feel good."

"And I feel like I'm ten feet tall. I feel needed, and that feels really bloody good." He put his teeth on the lobe of her ear, nipping her and sending a thrill through her body. "Keep that focus. Think about what I'm doing to your body." His hand came out from under her skirt. His arm unwrapped from her waist and he sat back. "Now take off your clothes for me."

She had to hold on to him for a moment, trying to find her balance. Jerk. She'd actually been pretty close. All it would have taken was a couple of strokes and she would have found her first orgasm of the evening. But no, the Dom had to play with her more. "I'm feeling frustrated."

"But you're looking gorgeous, my darling," he said with the sweetest smile. "Off with your clothes."

She got to her feet because she'd signed up for his bossiness. She started to unbutton her cardigan.

"Go slow with that," he commanded.

"With my clothes?"

"With the sweater."

Pervert. "My cardigan gets you hot?"

"That cardigan makes you look like the sweetest librarian in the world. Between that and those sexy fucking glasses you're wearing, I want to toss you up against the nearest stack of books I can find and fuck you until you can't see straight or think at all. And we'll have to be very quiet about it because we'll be in a library. Hush. Will you be able to keep quiet while I impale you on my cock?"

She wasn't sure she could keep quiet around him at all. She slowly unbuttoned the first two buttons. "You have very specific fantasies. Were you madly in love with your school librarian?"

A cloud passed over his eyes, but it was gone so quickly she would have sworn it was a shadow. "Not at all. I wasn't big on school, but damn me, I love a smart woman. How many do you have?"

Cardigans? "Probably ten or so. They're easy. They're kind of like a uniform for me, I guess."

One she'd never considered sexy, but it was obvious they did something for Owen. When she'd unbuttoned completely, she eased the sweater off her shoulders and made quick work of her blouse and skirt.

Owen watched her like a lazy tiger who knew damn well he was going to get his dinner, and he didn't mind playing with it. His eyes roamed over her body, taking in her white cotton bikini panties and utilitarian bra. If he thought they were boring, it didn't show in his eyes.

"Come here."

She hesitated. "I thought you wanted me naked."

"I want to finish the job. Don't question me about this or I might see how you like spanking right here and now." He sounded like he was slightly on the edge, like he couldn't wait to get his hands on her.

The man knew how to make a woman feel wanted. She liked her body. It wasn't perfect, but it served its purposes. Now she kind of loved her body because it was putting that look in Owen's eyes. She liked being this woman. Not afraid. She walked across the room and placed herself in front of Owen, holding still for his…well, for anything he wanted to do to her.

He moved forward, putting his hands on her hips first. His eyes came up and then seemed to make a map of her body. Everywhere he looked, she felt her skin come alive. Her nipples tightened as he stared at her breasts.

Then she felt his fingers trace up to the back of her bra. With an easy maneuver, her breasts came free and he tossed the bra away. He breathed out, a sigh that seemed like admiration.

"Damn but you're beautiful," he said. "I tried to picture them, but you're far more lovely in person. You're the sweetest handful."

He proved it, cupping her breasts in his palms. Heat flashed through her and she arched herself against him. He hissed slightly and then his hands were on her waist, pulling her in close.

"I wanted to do this. I wanted to do this the minute you walked into that lift. I thought you were the prettiest thing I'd seen. Then I realized you're a bit crazy and I knew I wanted you." He brought her in close and she couldn't breathe as he licked her nipple, a slow dragging of his tongue.

"Well, I thought you were hot enough to be a stripper." She wanted credit. She'd known the minute she'd laid eyes on him that he was the most gorgeous man in the world. Her building kind of seemed flooded with them lately, but he was the pinnacle of that beefcake.

And he was sweet and nice, and she found that sexy, too.

But all that mattered in that moment was the fact that he sucked

143

her nipple into his mouth. She felt it all through her body, liquid pleasure coursing through her. She let her fingers sink into Owen's silky hair as he lavished her with attention. She clutched him close, reveling in every suck and nip and lick of his mouth. He bit down gently, and she shuddered as the tiny pain turned to pleasure.

Callused hands worked their way down her back to skim the edge of her panties.

She lost herself in feeling, in the way their bodies seemed to flow together. It didn't matter that she was practically naked and he was fully clothed. He'd gotten her to a place where she didn't have to think about the worries of the day or whether or not she was making a mistake. This wasn't a mistake. It was an experience, and she felt so much for the man giving it to her. He dropped off the couch, getting to his knees.

"These come off now." The low command was followed by his fingers dragging at the waistband of her underwear.

She lifted her feet and then her undies were being tossed to the side where her bra sat. He kissed his way down her body, lips making a trail from her breasts down to her belly. He licked at her belly button, and she'd never once considered that to be some erogenous zone. Owen was finding all kinds of new ones since everywhere the man licked or kissed seemed to come alive.

"Put your right leg on the table."

She came out of the fog of lust. "What?"

He didn't seem to want to repeat his commands. He gently gripped her right leg and showed her what he wanted. She balanced against his shoulder and allowed him to shift her.

A shudder of anticipation went through her as she realized what he was doing. It had been so long since she'd had any attention at all down there. She could give herself an orgasm. A vibrator could take the place of a cock, but nothing ever felt quite like a man's tongue devouring her, his hands holding her still while he feasted.

There was zero hesitation in the man. The minute he had her where he wanted her, her pussy open for his exploration, he leaned in and rubbed his nose right in her labia. He breathed her in like she was the sweetest perfume.

"You're so ready." That accent had gone deep again. She could practically see the man in a kilt, a sword at his side. "I could fuck you right now and my cock would slide in no problem."

"But you're not going to do that, are you?"

His eyes came up, heavy lidded with pure lust and willpower. "No. I'm not letting you off that easy this time. This time you're mine to do with as I will. This is my will, love."

He leaned over and set his mouth on her and it took all she had to not cry out at the sensation. He licked her in long, slow drags of his tongue. She couldn't see anything but his head at her core, sucking at her, pulling at her clit in the sweetest way.

His tongue fucked up inside her, thrusting the way his cock would. Over and over he tongued her and his thumb found her clit, pressing down and rotating.

She went over the edge, clutching at his shoulders and calling out his name.

It was over far too soon and he was backing away, his lips glistening with the evidence of her orgasm.

"Now, love, it's my turn."

She took a deep breath, ready for whatever came next.

* * * *

Owen had to force his hands to stop shaking. She'd been everything he'd dreamed of, hot and ready for him, so sexy he couldn't stand it. Her body was curvy and intensely fuckable. Even in his brief life, he'd had many women, and none of them moved him the way she did. Not a single one of the subs he'd played with kept him up at night, thinking about her. Not a one of them had managed to chase away the demons that plagued him.

He'd spent the last several days thinking about her, plotting how to have her again. He might have looked calm on the outside, but inside the woman was turning him into a madman.

He was worse than Robert about Ariel, and that was saying something.

But Robert hadn't just shoved his tongue up his woman's pussy and made her cry out his name. Robert couldn't taste his woman on his lips, smell her all around him. Damn but that scent was the sexiest thing he'd ever known. Becca smelled like sex and need and comfort.

He kissed her one last time right on her soft, plump pussy and

145

promised himself he would be right back there soon.

She was fooling herself. She might go on that date tomorrow, but he would be the one in her bed that night. He would make sure of it.

He'd put on his sheep's clothing. He could play the modern man, but his wolf would come out in the end. His wolf would howl until he had what he wanted—her.

She looked sweetly disheveled, her hair brushing the tops of her breasts, her skin flushed a pretty pink. "Your turn. What do you want me to do?"

Everything. All at once. She was responding beautifully to his topping her. She hadn't seemed scared or self-conscious about her body. She'd strode up to him bold as brass and offered herself to him.

He got to his feet and helped her balance as she moved that shapely leg back down to the floor. Fuck but she was gorgeous. She was gorgeous and smart and way too good for him.

And it didn't fucking matter because he'd figured out he did have something to offer her. She'd been scared tonight. She'd been disconcerted, and it had all drifted away when he'd topped her. She wasn't thinking about what had happened at the office now. She was utterly focused on him, and that was exactly how he wanted it.

For the op, of course. Not because the way she looked at him did funny things to his soul. Not because he'd already started thinking about how he might keep her.

Jax had. Jax's wife now traveled with them. River was part of the team.

River didn't run a research facility. River wasn't a bloody doctor. There was no way Becca Walsh would walk away from everything for love. She had a career.

This wasn't going to end the same way Jax's op had. And that was a very good reason to enjoy her while he could. He might find what he needed tonight. After she fell asleep, he could search her place, find the package, and the bloody op would be over. They would move on and he wouldn't see her again.

"Take my shirt off."

He wanted to feel her hands on him. His cock was dying, but there was no way he would give in so easily. He would fuck her long and hard, but if this was the only time he had with her, he was going to play.

She was breathless as her hands went to the buttons of his shirt.

He'd fucked her so fast the first time, there was no way she'd gotten a good look at his chest. At his skin, really. The doctors had done an excellent job of clearing up the terrible reaction he'd had to the drugs Dr. McDonald had pumped through his system. His skin had been ravaged for months, and he still had some scarring.

Would it bug her?

She unbuttoned his shirt and eased it off him, and he saw the moment she caught sight of the scarring. It was faint now, but it would be on his skin forever. It had gotten as light as it ever would, he'd been told.

She draped the shirt over the edge of her couch and turned back to him. Her fingers skimmed over his chest and the sides of his torso, where it was worst. "This was an allergic reaction."

He had a story prepared. "When I was younger I had a bad reaction to a drug I took after I was injured. It's nothing. It's a whisper of something that happened."

"What was the drug?" she asked.

He wasn't going into this. He would get caught in a lie. "Becca, nothing but feeling tonight. Take off my belt."

"But most drugs don't have dermatological reactions like this. At least not ones on the market." She was staring at the scars.

He wasn't going to become some research subject for her. He'd already been that. She might not know it, but she'd played a part in the drugs that had scarred him for life. He didn't blame her. He was almost certain she had zero knowledge of what her work had been used for, but he wasn't about to indulge her curiosity now that she'd gotten some relief.

And she'd given him an excellent excuse to find out how she liked the disciplinary aspect of D/s.

"Turn around, grip the side of the couch, and present yourself to me."

Her eyes weren't on his scars anymore. "What?"

Damn but she was cute when she was confused. He brushed her hair back and leaned in close. "I said grip the couch and present yourself to me. Your ass is going in the air. Before you give me some smartass remark like it's already naked and air is on it, think because my hand is about to be on it, too, and how hard I slap that pretty piece of flesh is up to you."

Her mouth came open and then she wisely shut it and turned around. Only when she'd done as he'd commanded did she speak again. "I was curious. I'm sorry."

"And I told you I don't talk about my past," he said, not unkindly. He couldn't possibly be unkind when he was staring at the prettiest arse in history. At least in his mind it was. Her bum was a thing of perfection, round and luscious. It was going to look even better with a pink sheen to it. "How are you right now?"

"I'm feeling worried that I won't be okay with this and I might run out on you like she did in that movie, but she used the elevator and we fucked in the elevator, so I should probably take the stairs if I'm going to run, but it's my apartment. It would be weird if I ran and left you here in my own apartment. And she got her clothes on really fast in that movie. I don't know that I..."

He smacked her right between her cheeks, the sound cracking through the air.

There was only one way to shut that gorgeous mouth of hers. He'd noticed when she got nervous she could talk a mile a minute. He actually found it adorable, but he didn't have time to go over all the ways she might run out if she couldn't handle a spanking.

"Best to get right to it, love." He slapped her arse again, holding his hand against her silky flesh. "How are you now?"

She gasped like she needed air. One and then two gasps, her body moving with her lungs. "I'm a little pissed. Shouldn't you give me a warning?"

Another smack, this one slightly harder because her words didn't match her actions. She wasn't trying to get away from him. She was holding as still as she could. It was obvious to him she hadn't made up her mind yet, and she was giving the experience a chance. "I rather thought telling you what I was going to do would be warning enough."

Another breathy sound, but she was relaxing against the couch, her shoulders lowering as she became more comfortable. "A countdown would be nice."

He picked the undercurve of her left cheek to smack this time. If he had time he would spend days getting to know every inch of her body. He wanted that time with her. "I'm going to educate you. What you're doing right now is called topping from the bottom, and it's going to get you in serious trouble. You don't get to tell me how to spank you. You merely get to tell me whether it works for you or not. Do you like how this feels? Do you like the fact that my whole being is focused on you right now? Do you like knowing that I'm hoping you're the type of woman whose body turns the little tweak of pain into pleasure, and that your pussy is already aching for me again?"

Her right cheek got attention this time, and he felt her shudder.

"Yes," she managed. "Yes, I like knowing all those things, Owen."

Again and again, his hand cracked down. He gave her a little more each time because she didn't seem anywhere close to spitting out the word red. He wasn't even sure she was yellow anymore. "I like knowing how you feel."

She whimpered at this smack, a wholly sexy mewling sound. "It hurts, Owen. And then it doesn't hurt so much."

He brushed his fingers along the pink swaths of her flesh. "And then?"

"And then I ache."

He was starting to ache for her, too. "Is it a good ache?"

"It's the best ache ever."

That was what he wanted to hear. "Tell me something. Have you ever had that pretty arse fucked?"

Her head turned, and there was a shocked look in her eyes. "Arse isn't sexy."

He winked her way and gave her another smack. "This one is. Answer my question."

"I was talking about the word. And no." She was back to staring straight ahead. "I'm not sure I want to try."

"You don't have to do anything you don't want to," he said. "But I'll try to change your mind. I'll try to give you so much pleasure when we're playing that you'll trust me to take you anywhere." He gave her one last smack and then wrapped an arm around her waist and dragged her up against his body.

They had all night. His dick was going to explode if he didn't get inside her soon.

And did he really have to search her place tonight? He should spend the evening building a bond with her. This op required subtlety. If she caught him looking around tonight, she would kick him to the curb and they would lose everything. But a week or two down the line, she would buy most any excuse he would give her because she would trust him with more than merely her body.

"You did well," he whispered against her ear. He could still smell her. He let his hand drift down and found that pussy drenched in fresh arousal. No, he hadn't been wrong about her. She'd responded to a bite of pain, and he knew exactly how to give it to her.

Her head fell back against his shoulder. "I liked it. I didn't think I would. I like how it hurts. I think that makes me a freak."

"It makes you perfect." Perfect for him. He hoped her date tomorrow was some buttoned-up, completely vanilla, never-thought-of-sinking-his-cock-into-her-arse bastard of a man. He let go of that line of thinking because it wasn't going to happen. "And a sub as perfect as you deserves a treat after her discipline."

He sank his fingers inside, his thumb finding her already ripe and ready to go clitoris. She shook in his arms as he fucked her with his fingers, his free hand cupping her breast and holding her against his chest. It didn't take long before he felt her come around his fingers. The spanking had her primed.

He knew he should play with her longer, show her how much control he had. But he couldn't stand it one more second. He had to get inside her or he was going to lose his mind. He'd meant to have her completely undress him, but he didn't care now.

"Grip the couch again," he ordered. "And spread your legs for me."

"Yes, Owen." There was a smile in those words, a deliriously happy smile.

He'd made the doctor purr like a happy kitten. He'd done that. No one else. He pulled on his belt, his hands shaking like he was some teen and this was his first time. It took effort to find the condoms he had in his wallet and roll one on. His dick was so hard he worried the minute he touched the damn thing he might go off. It didn't. His cock knew exactly what it wanted. He shoved his slacks down, not bothering to take them off. He needed her too badly.

He was out of control, but if she was worried it didn't show. She turned her head back, her eyes still soft.

"One of these days, I'm going to see that cock, you know," she promised. She wiggled her arse his way. "But not this second. Fuck me, Owen. I want to feel you inside me."

That was an invitation he would never refuse. Not from her. He moved in between her legs and lined up his cock. She was perfectly wet and ready for him, and still it was a delicious fight to get inside her.

She was tight around him, and he gripped her hips to steady himself as he slowly impaled her on his cock. Her back flattened and she pushed against him as her hands gripped the side of the couch.

"You feel so good," she said on a shuddering breath.

Good didn't begin to cover it. He forced his cock in until he couldn't go any further and he held himself still against her, letting her heat surround him, suffuse him.

She wriggled, tempting him to move. He dragged his cock back out and thrust in again. She moved in perfect time with him, catching the rhythm quickly.

He fucked her hard, reveling in the way she took everything he gave her. The orgasm hit him like a flash fire. It poured through him and he held on to her as she shook and called out his name for the third damn time that night.

He staggered back and she managed to stand up and turn. She was stunningly gorgeous, obviously flushed from sex.

And he had his pants around his ankles, a condom still on his softening cock.

She simply smiled his way. "If this is how you play, Owen, count me in. Let's go to the bedroom for the next round. And I swear I'm getting you out of your clothes this time."

She turned and began to lead him to the back of the apartment.

He pulled up his damn pants and practically ran after her.

So much for being the one in control.

Chapter Ten

Becca came awake to the heavenly smell of coffee. She felt a grin slide across her face. It was coffee she didn't have to make herself, and she so wasn't organized enough to have a preset coffeemaker. Nope. There was a Scottish sex god making coffee in her kitchen, and if she was lucky, he didn't have on any pants.

A shaft of sunlight filtered in, warming her face. It was the kind of thing that would normally annoy her since she would have been up late going over reports and Sunday was the only day she allowed herself to sleep in. But she didn't want to sleep in today. Not unless Owen was cuddled around her.

After they'd made love again, this time in an actual bed, he'd ordered pizza and they'd shared a bottle of wine and watched an old movie on TV before he'd turned it off. He'd given her that look she was starting to understand meant he was in charge again and then the things he'd done to her body…

She opened her eyes and ran her hand over the place where he'd lain beside her the night before. She'd never had anyone in this bed with her.

She'd liked it far too much.

But why shouldn't she? They'd laid out all the rules. They would be together when they were together, and when they weren't they were both adults and free to do whatever they like.

It was a logical arrangement. It was precisely what she wanted.

Yep. That's what she wanted. She wasn't going to fall for the whole relationship thing again. It didn't work. This was the best way to deal with her physical needs. A casual relationship where she enjoyed the men in her life and she didn't become some puppy hanging on every word he said.

"Becca? Becca, are you awake?"

She was up and out of bed in a heartbeat, grabbing for her robe. "I'm coming."

She slowed down because she hadn't meant to do that. She hadn't meant for her heart to race at the very sound of his voice, and she definitely hadn't meant for every cell in her body to seem to come alive at the thought of seeing him.

It was oxytocin. Being around Owen Shaw rubbed at the pleasure center of her brain and released all those hormones meant to trick her into fulfilling her biological function. She was already addicted to it and it had only been one night.

"I mean, I'll be there in a moment." She forced herself to slow down and make sure her robe was firmly tied around her body, that she wasn't all flushed and breathless with anticipation. She was going to be normal, like this was something that happened every day.

It's totally normal to be crazy about the insanely hot guy who played your body like a freaking violin master.

Her primal brain wasn't going down without a fight, but she didn't have to listen. She could be a reasonable adult who knew that this road only led to heartache. It was like that old saying about the definition of insanity—doing the same thing over and over again and expecting a different outcome.

She wasn't going through that again. She was having a perfectly normal, adult relationship in which one of the partners sexually dominated the other. In which one of the partners had the most spectacular penis in the world. Not that she'd had the largest study of them, but she was a doctor. She knew a perfectly made body part, and Owen's was thick and long, and when she'd pulled back the foreskin she'd seen a beautifully made cockhead.

She wanted to have sex again. Like all-day sex.

"I don't understand why you're here." That hadn't been said by Owen. A familiar voice floated down the hall. "She wouldn't have given you a key to her apartment. Dr. Walsh is a careful woman. I'm the only one with a key. She locks herself out from time to time."

She rushed into the living room where Owen stood with a cup of coffee in his hand. It was from the café downstairs, and she spied a brown paper bag sitting on the bar. He'd gone down and gotten them breakfast. The only thing marring the situation was the fact that Carter was standing there looking up at Owen with suspicious eyes.

"Well, you're not sleeping with her so I guess you can give that key to me and I'll take care of her from now on," Owen shot back, and it was easy to see from the tense set of his shoulders that this morning was not going the way he'd planned.

Damn it. "Carter, you met Owen. He's my guest. Now what's going on?"

Owen passed her the coffee. "Not a thing for you to worry about. I went downstairs to get you some coffee and breakfast. It's a vanilla latte and a couple of croissants. The lady who works down there told me it's what you have on Sundays."

She nodded, taking the coffee. "Thanks. I love their croissants."

Not that she ate them often. Only one a week.

Was she going to parse her time with Owen out like that? Only once a week, and never more than a few hours. Wasn't that the smart play? Indulge lightly but never so much that he could hurt her when he inevitably left?

"I hope you enjoy them. And I used this because I didn't want to leave the door unlocked. You left it sitting on the bar." He held up her keys briefly before placing them on the bar beside the croissants. "I'm glad I did, too, because this one was hovering around when I came back. He's called the cops. You're going to have to deal with that one, love. I have to get to work."

He was leaving?

Carter had called the cops?

She was confused, but oddly the idea that Owen was leaving and he was irritated with her took precedence. She followed him to the door. "It's Sunday."

He turned, his hand on the door. "Yes, it is. And I have to work. I was going to stay and have breakfast, but I don't think that one is going to make it possible. Watch out for him. He's not the friend you think he is. He's got a thing for you and he doesn't like me. There's more to this

154

than you think."

She reached out to him. This morning he seemed untouchable, distant, but then she wasn't sure how she would feel if she'd been confronted with a guy who'd called the police on her when all she'd been doing was getting her boyfriend some breakfast.

Not her boyfriend.

"Besides, you have a date in a couple of hours." He leaned over and kissed her swiftly. "I'll see you soon."

He walked down the hall. She stood in the doorway and watched as he strode down the hallway. She couldn't see his apartment from her vantage. It was past the elevator.

"This is very dangerous, Rebecca," Carter said from behind her. "What do you know about that man?"

"I know he was a guest in my home and apparently you called the cops on him." Irritation rose swiftly inside her as she closed the door and rounded on her unwelcome guest. "You want to explain that thought process?"

Carter blinked once and then again. "I saw a strange man trying to break into your apartment. I didn't realize he had a key."

Was Owen right? Had she been misreading the signals Carter had been sending to her? He always seemed so uptight and prissy. She'd never once thought about him as anything but a colleague who was likely getting close to her because she was a department head. He was obviously ambitious, but he was also a man. Honestly, she'd kind of thought he wasn't interested in her entire sex. "He doesn't, but he certainly had permission to use mine. I wish you had talked to me before you involved the police."

He huffed, a frustrated sound. "Well, the next time I think someone is going to break into your place and rape you, I'll remember to ask your permission to call the police before I do." He shook his head her way. "I never thought for a second you would…"

"I would what?" They should get this all out in the open now. "Say what you need to say, Carter."

His face flushed. "I didn't think you would get involved so quickly. You seemed like a careful lady. I didn't think you would hop into bed with the first guy to come along."

"I've been celibate for two years." She didn't owe him an explanation, but she couldn't seem to stop herself. Her brain was still working on the fact that Owen had left. He'd reminded her about her date and then he'd gone away. It was perverse because it was everything she'd thought she wanted. "I assure you Owen isn't the first man to come around."

"That's because it's easy for women to find sex," he said under his breath.

"What?"

His head came up. "It's easy for a woman to find a man. A man will take anything that comes his way. At least a lesser man will. But if you're not some muscular caveman, most women won't even consider you." He stopped and took a long breath. "I'm sorry. I recently found out some unsavory things about a woman I was interested in and it's unsettled me."

"I didn't know you were seeing someone." She didn't want to have this conversation with him, but they had been friendly for the last couple of years.

"She's one of the doctors at work," he admitted. "She's on the nephrology team. She's not the doctor I thought she was. I won't go into it, but I don't like her ethics."

She'd never worked with that team. "She's doing something morally wrong?"

He'd flushed again. "It's a philosophical difference, that's all. We view the world quite differently, so it won't work the way I hoped it would. It's extremely disappointing because I thought she was the one woman in the world who might see the real me."

"I'm sorry to hear that." She wasn't sure any woman would fit with Carter. He seemed to have incredibly exacting standards. He was excellent at his job, which was why she put up with him, but she'd started to wonder about how he treated the female employees. And she wasn't stupid. "Careful" wasn't the word he'd been thinking. She was certain if she'd cracked into his head he'd been shocked that she'd turned out to be such a slut.

He could fuck himself for all she cared, but until she had something on the man to get him removed, she had to work with him.

He shook it off. "It's fine. I don't need a woman. So you're dating that man?"

She was done. "Carter, it's none of your business. I think we should take a step back because I don't want to harm our work relationship. And I think I would feel more comfortable if you returned my key and I gave you back yours. I'll give one to River."

Hurt was stamped across his face before he managed to clear his expression back to the look of bland arrogance he normally wore. "Of course. If that's what you think is best. I'll go get it. After all, you're the boss."

He started to move for the door.

She had a sudden thought. "Carter, where were you yesterday around five?"

"I was running errands," he said. "Why?"

It would be easy enough to check. He would have used his card to get in and out of the building. "Something happened. Someone was hanging around and hid in the cubicals while I was leaving."

She'd thought about it and decided Owen was right. There was nothing jumpy about her. She didn't see shadows and think someone was out to get her. Therefore the most probable reason she heard the things she did and felt the way she had was that someone had been in the room with her, someone who hadn't wanted to be seen.

His lips firmed as he looked back at her. "I certainly wouldn't be hiding in the cubicals, Dr. Walsh. It's obvious you think very little of me. Good luck with that man. We'll see how long he can keep up with you. I'll bring your key by in a while."

He threw open the door and two big cops wearing black uniforms and hats with red trim came striding up.

She really should have gotten dressed.

* * * *

Owen walked into the apartment and frowned Robert's way. "I want a complete workup on that little fucker who lives next door to her."

Robert looked up from his cereal and the tablet he'd been reading on. "Jax? He's not so little, but I agree with the fucker part. After you left, he and River went at it in the kitchen. I walked in to help with the dishes, also because Ezra had started talking about his days in the Agency and he's way more boring than Big Tag, and they were making out on the island. There was food prepared there. I don't think that's sanitary."

"I'm talking about Carter what's-his-name." He should remember the bugger's name, but right now all he could think about was the fact that the arsehole had talked about Becca like he had some kind of claim on her.

No one did. Certainly not him, and it rankled. It twisted in his gut that she was going on a date with another man this afternoon and there wasn't a bloody thing he could do about it.

Unless he assassinated the man. He'd noticed the note she'd left on her bar with a restaurant reservation and time, and the reminder to ask for a table on the patio. If he found a nice perch across the street, he could take Lawyer Larry out with one shot. He would make sure to angle it right so the splatter didn't hit Becca. Maybe he would even wait until she went to the loo and do it then. That way she would be traumatized, but not too traumatized. She would likely need someone to hold her, and he could be that man.

"I would not like what you are thinking right now," Robert mused, sitting back in his chair. "Did it not go well? Might I suggest a trip to River and Jax's kitchen island. It seems to inspire them."

"Will you stop going on about that damn island," a familiar voice said as a red-haired woman rounded the corner and entered the kitchen. "You don't understand how it is when you're first married. You gotta get all the sex in you can before the kids come. I told River that at her bridal shower. Not that it was much of a shower since they have to live out of suitcases and shit, but we all gave her advice. Theo and me didn't even get that time because his fool ass got killed, and TJ was already here by the time he was smart enough to come back to life. Is there coffee?"

Erin Taggart. She was wearing boxer shorts and a too big T-shirt with the Top logo on it, her red hair up in a messy bun.

His stomach took an immediate nose dive.

"I made a fresh pot of coffee a couple of minutes ago." Robert glanced up at him, concern on his face. "They got in late last night. I let them stay in your room. They're finding a hotel this afternoon."

"Are you sure about the coffee?" Erin's husband walked in behind her. Theo Taggart was technically the youngest of the four Taggart brothers, but only by a few minutes. His twin, Case, had been born first, a state that led to Theo being called the tiniest of the Tags. Looking at the six-foot-three-inch tree of a man, it was hard to think of him as tiny.

Erin's right brow climbed over her eyes. "Are you serious? You know I've done this before and you haven't. One cup a day isn't going to kill me. You might know that if you'd been around the first time."

His hands came up. "Peace, woman. You're a beast without a little caffeine. Hey, Owen. How's it going?"

Theo held a hand out and Owen forced himself to shake it. It was odd to stand in front of the man he'd betrayed. He knew deep down that he didn't deserve to shake the man's hand, but it was expected of him.

Erin was pouring a cup of coffee. "From what I hear it's going pretty good since Ezra told me you took the target home last night. She lives on this floor, right? Should Tucker be coming and going like he lives here? Are you supposed to know each other?"

"She can't see us from here and Tucker takes the stairs," Robert explained. "Oh, he whines and complains about it, but he does it. Wait until he starts talking about his quads."

Was Theo working on something else or was he really here to check up on him? Did they already think he was mucking things up? "She's got a tag on her purse and her phone," Owen explained. "I've also placed a device on her front door that lets us know when she's entering or exiting."

Robert held up a tablet as the thing chimed. "Like now. What's up with the cops?"

Erin turned to him. "She called the cops? What did you do?"

Yes, there was the judgment he always expected. It wasn't like she didn't have the right to it. "I didn't do anything. At least not anything she didn't want me to do."

"Ah, that's why you want me to check into the neighbor," Robert said, his eyes on the tablet. "I saw him hanging around. He didn't look happy to see you going into her apartment after you went to the café. That security camera is perfectly placed. Sasha did an excellent job with that. I think he actually does better work drunk off his ass. Dude, those cops are getting an earful. Your girl is not happy."

He moved around so he could see the image on the tablet. Becca was still in her robe and she was pointing to her left, toward Carter's apartment, her face angry as hell. At least she was blaming the proper person.

Robert had fed the security footage through all their systems so they would be able to know when it was and wasn't safe to move around the building. Becca didn't know it, but her every move was being monitored.

It made him feel a little sick to think about how he'd tagged her phone while she'd been sleeping. He'd rolled out of the bed he'd taken her in again and again, only to sneak to her purse and make sure they could keep track of her, stealing every vestige of her privacy because he'd also planted some bugs so they could listen in.

"You're doing it as much for her as for the rest of us," Theo said solemnly, as though he could read minds.

Or he was so damn transparent anyone could tell what he was thinking. "I'm not sure she would agree."

"She will when we keep her from falling into Levi Green's clutches. I think he sent us here to do his dirty work. He's trying to find leverage to make her work for him, but we're in Canada and he has to be careful. If she'd been in Boston, he wouldn't have bothered with us at all," Erin said with a wrinkle of her freckled nose. "I hate that asshole. I've been thinking about numerous ways Kay and I could mess him up. I think he requires female justice."

Theo frowned. "*That* you will give up. I don't care that you need a little violence in your life. You can kill again after you give birth, and that is a hard damn limit for me, baby. I can be indulgent, but I can also find a way to very gently make it so you can't sit for a week."

"Promises, promises," Erin tossed back at her husband with a wink. "Fine. No bloody vengeance until the miracle baby arrives."

The door came open and Tucker hustled in, carrying two brown bags. "Timmys for everyone." He looked up at Owen. "Well, not you. I thought you would be eating with the doc. Did she throw you out?"

Before he could reply, Erin was taking the bag from Tucker. "I'm starving. Throwing up all morning makes me hungry. Did you get the sour cream glazed donut holes?"

Tucker shook his head. "Nope. They're called Timbits, and if you don't call them that they...well, they're Canadians. They just smile and correct you."

"This is a strange land, my friend," Erin said, but her eyes lit on the bag of donuts. "Theo, you going to explain why we're here or are we waiting for Ezra to show up?"

"I was going to wait until we had a proper meeting." Theo grabbed a cup for coffee for himself. "My brother always does this kind of thing in a room with a projector and everyone sits around in the half dark and there's a bunch of file folders."

Erin's eyes rolled. "There's a reason he does that. Your brother sleeps through most of those meetings. He says it's about being high tech, but if you listen closely, you can hear him snoring in time to the hum of the projector. Truly, it's one of his great talents."

"He sleeps? But he's got his eyes open," Theo pointed out.

"Another one of his talents." Erin turned to them. "We've tracked Levi here and we think he recently had a meeting with Paul Huisman. Hutch found some traffic cam footage of Huisman being picked up in a limo. No ID on Green, but we did catch one of his CIA lackeys on film. Unless Donnie Lennox has taken a second job as a limo driver here in Toronto, which I doubt since he's still on the Agency's payroll."

Fuck all. "She said something scared her yesterday. She said someone was in her building when she was alone, and she felt like whoever it was he was stalking her."

Tucker sighed and set down his breakfast sandwich. "Well, we knew he was planning something."

"I'll have Jax pull CCTV from around the building. He can get it to Hutch for facial recognition," Robert said, picking up his mobile and starting to text. "Dante can get the internal feed. Was she in her office when it happened? He said there's a camera right outside her door and another one in the hallway."

"Yes, she was going home. The lights went out." When she'd told him the whole story, she'd been lying in his arms. She'd been relaxed and seemingly happy. He'd managed to get that haunted look out of her eyes. "I want to know who went up those lifts or who took the stairs up to her floor right before five p.m."

"We'll get it done," Robert promised.

He couldn't help but turn to Theo and Erin. "Is that all? Because that seems like something you could have told us over the phone."

That brow of Erin's rose again, but Theo was waving a hand as though he could hold off his wife's wrath.

"You know why he's asking. He thinks we're here to monitor him," Theo explained in a patient tone. "He thinks Big Tag is pissed because he took over the op."

Erin's smile was entirely predatory. "He *is* pissed."

Theo sighed. "And he also thinks Owen can handle this." He turned Owen's way. "Did you make a call in the field?"

He felt like he would never stop explaining this. "She wasn't going to buy what we were selling, man. If I'd walked away from her, she wouldn't have talked to me again. She's got a very narrow focus. Right now, I'm her focus. As a friend, she would have easily prioritized work over me and everything else."

"All right," Theo said simply. "This should always have been your op. My brother overrode Ezra because he's a stubborn bastard. Erin and I are here for different reasons. We're following up on a lead."

"A lead? On this case?" Why hadn't he been informed?

Theo's eyes hooded, and Owen knew there wouldn't be a lot of information forthcoming. "I'm following up on something else. I've got some intel about Dr. McDonald's former associates. I'm meeting a man who thinks he can get us in touch with someone who can give us new information. He wouldn't come to the States. It was here or Mexico City."

"Spicy foods don't agree with me right now," Erin said before popping one of the sweet treats in her mouth.

Theo had a wholly masculine look of self-satisfaction on his face as he put a hand on his wife's barely there baby bump. "Don't worry about us. This is a last-minute thing and Erin and I decided to make a mini-vacation out of it. TJ is currently showing his cousin, Heath, the ropes. Case thinks he's super dad now. He has no idea how hard taking care of an infant and a toddler is going to be. Good luck with that. Anyway, we're going to follow up on this lead and stay out of your hair. We'll be at the Shangri-La for a couple of days if you need us."

"I'm going to enjoy it," Erin said, a sparkle in her eyes. "The last time we stayed at a luxury hotel, I got pregnant. I can't get more pregnant, but I can order all the room service since it's on Big Tag's dime."

"You can't be sure you got pregnant at any one time unless that was the only time you had sex," Tucker pointed out. "It's a myth that women can tell."

He expected Erin to argue, but a secretive smile transformed her normally tough expression into something infinitely feminine. "I know when this one was conceived. I know it in my bones. We stayed at the Joule downtown for our anniversary. We were going to try to get the bridal suite, but someone had taken it. I know it sounds insane, but I could feel something coming from that room." She shook it off. "It was weird, but I've never had such crazy sex as we had that night. Theo was on, if you know what I mean."

Theo grinned, obviously used to his wife's oversharing. "I ran down to grab a couple of bottles of water and ran into this dude in all white. He told me he hoped I liked little girls. At the time I kind of thought I should call security, but now I think…well, there are more things in heaven and earth, Horatio and all that."

Erin snorted. "Don't think he came up with that himself. When we told Jesse and Phoebe the story, Jesse thought we'd had too much to drink and Phoebe merely pointed out that we don't know everything. Still, we thought TJ was a miracle. I wasn't supposed to be able to get pregnant again and here I am. I think this one is a girl and I'm naming her Devon. I don't know why, but that's this kiddo's name."

Theo's hand tightened around her waist. "I thought we weren't talking about names until…"

She turned in his arms, her hands coming up to cup his face. "It's fine, babe. This one is sticking. I don't know how or why I know it, and if Tucker says one damn thing about feminine intuition being a myth, I'm going to make his balls a myth. It's fine this time. We're good, baby girl and me, and we're going to stay that way."

Theo leaned in and kissed his wife.

"Feminine intuition is a beautiful thing," Tucker said with a nod.

He was a smart man.

"All right, then." Robert looked like he was definitely ready to move on to more professional matters. "How did things go last night?" He winced a little. "I do not need a rundown of the actual act. I saw enough of that last night on the island."

Erin groaned. "He's got a one-track mind, and he's prissy about sanitary food practices. But he's got a point. You're here awfully early for a man who had a good night. You playing hard to get?"

He felt his face flush. "It went fine."

Tucker held up a hand. "I know what that means. Fine means not fine. Ever. Which makes me wonder why we have the word at all."

Robert stood, crossing his arms over his chest. "What went wrong, Owen?"

"Not wrong, precisely." He didn't want to have this conversation.

He wanted to write it up in his daily report and then not talk about it at all. *Subject enjoyed coitus and then wanted to see if she would enjoy it with someone else.* Fuck. "She's got a date."

Erin's eyes went wide and then she was stifling a laugh. "She blew you off."

If he never heard that phrase again it would be too soon. "We've agreed to keep things casual. She's been out of the dating game for a while and she wants to see what's out there. That's all."

Robert seemed to consider the problem. "Okay. We need to figure out how to change her mind."

"I don't think I can," he admitted. "I promised her that we could see each other and have a sexual relationship without strings. When she's with me, we're together, and when she's not, we're free to pursue whatever we like. I didn't know how else to make her comfortable."

Erin sighed and kissed her husband again. "This one is all yours, babe. If anyone knows how to deal with a skittish chick, it's you. Take Owen to your man teat and let him suckle at the fount of your knowledge."

"You are in so much trouble," Theo whispered to her before giving her arse a nice smack as she picked up the bag of Timbits and strode toward the bedroom. "Don't think I'll forget that, She-an."

She laughed as she walked away.

"She-an?" Tucker asked.

"She and Ian." Theo was shaking his head but there was a smile on his face. "It's what I call her when her resemblance to my brother becomes creepy. I apparently have a type. Some women marry younger versions of their father. Same with men and their moms. I married the feminine equivalent of my oldest brother. Why couldn't I have gotten She-Sean? At least she would have cooked."

"I heard that, Taggart," she yelled from the bedroom.

Theo didn't seem phased. "But she's right about me understanding skittish women. Unfortunately, you don't have a couple of years to wear your stubborn chick down. Dr. Walsh went through a divorce, right?"

"Yes. He cheated on her." He'd considered this. "It's why I'm playing it cool. I'll let her come to me next time."

"That's where you're wrong, my man," Theo said, taking a seat at the kitchen table. "Taking a step back could make it obvious to her that you're serious about compartmentalizing. Maybe if you had all the time in the world that would work, but the clock is ticking here. Especially with Green in town. You need to up your game. So did you start a completely casual relationship with her?"

"I started a part-time D/s relationship with her."

A wolfish grin lit Theo's face. "And the parameters were?"

He was starting to see this in a different light. "When we're together, we're together. We didn't put limits on it or say when we would or wouldn't see each other. We merely said that when we wanted to, we would see each other and then she was mine until we ended the session."

"So a session could start at any time," Theo mused. "How did she respond to you topping her?"

A vision of her leaning over that couch and offering him everything he wanted echoed in his brain, and he wished he hadn't gotten out of bed at all. He could still be there with her tangled around him. He could have fucked her again and maybe she would have forgotten all about the lawyer. "She's sexually submissive and she's not ashamed of it. I don't know that she ever considered a relationship like this before, but she's not opposed. She's eager to experiment."

"Excellent. Then this is all about ensuring you have the opportunity to help her experiment," Theo said. "What do we know about her date?"

"It's a blind date," he explained. "She was set up by a friend of hers. I'll be honest, I expected her to cancel it this morning. I meant to convince her to spend the day with me instead, but that prick showed up and I walked out because that note of hers was staring me in the face. I found a note this morning on the bar. It had all the information for her date written on it."

"It bothered you?" Theo asked.

"It would bug me," Tucker said, pulling out a chair and taking a seat. He unwrapped his breakfast sandwich.

Owen rarely ate breakfast. He wasn't sure why. It didn't intrigue him, but this morning he'd gotten two croissants because he'd wanted to share them with her.

"I don't know why." Robert completed the circle, relaxing back into his chair again. "Your dates literally have men lined up, Tuck. Like she has to ask you to leave because her next appointment is there and she needs to clean up."

"I wasn't talking about hookers," Tucker replied, though he seemed to talk about them an awful lot. "I was saying if a lady I was interested in basically kicked me out because she had some other dude coming over, I would be…hurt. Sorry. I had to think about that for a minute. If one of the other Tags had been here, I would have said something more manly like I would have been pissed or jealous AF. No. I wouldn't have said AF. That's probably hipster or something. What does Big Tag have against hipsters?"

The youngest of the Tags ignored Tucker. "Are you already in deep with this woman?"

Was he? He liked the hell out of her. He wanted her. He wasn't sure he was capable of anything beyond that. "I enjoyed my time with her. I like the thought of topping her on a regular basis. She's smart and sexy as hell."

"See, that would be AH. Like why is as hell okay but AF isn't?" Tucker mused. "The last time I used the phrase Big Tag slapped me upside the head and told me I wasn't twelve. I don't think twelve-year-olds are allowed to say fuck. Do you think that's why they use AF?"

"Eat your breakfast or I'll send you back to Ezra's," Robert promised.

"You know you're going to walk away at the end of this, right?" Theo seemed very capable of ignoring Tucker's antics.

He nodded. "Of course, I am. I'm either going wherever we go next or I'll go home."

He wasn't sure where home was. When all of this was over, would he end up back at The Garden, working and watching as Nick and Hayley and Damon and Penny grew their families? Would he be the weird "uncle" to Brody and Stephanie's son? Would they always watch him, waiting to see if he would betray them again?

"Have you considered at all that this is the one woman in the world who might be able to fix you?" Theo asked.

"There's no fixing us," Owen replied. "Not those of us who got the later doses. You and Robert, for sure. But I thought the theory was the rest of us got the final drug."

According to their research and the few documents that had been smuggled out of McDonald's labs, Robert and Theo had been considered part of the A Team, the group she took care of above all others. Dante, Sasha, Tucker, and Jax had been the ones she initially experimented on. She'd meant to use the final drug on Theo that day, but Big Tag had been smart and had embedded an operative deep inside McDonald's team. So Owen had been the last man to get it, the last to fall prey to her dark games. The final drug was the one supposed to wipe the memory completely.

"Just because she said it would work doesn't mean it will," Theo said, his voice deep. "According to what we've discovered, she'd only started testing that final drug. We don't know how it's going to work long term. Rebecca Walsh might though. She might be the one who can break it. Have you thought about sitting her down and asking her?"

Only every minute he'd lain beside her the night before. "I don't think she was ever knowingly involved with McDonald. This woman is kind. I don't think she can fake it. But I also don't know how she would react if I introduced myself as an operative looking for a bunch of old files of a colleague of hers. The way she tells it is this is a collaborative business, but there's always someone trying to get a leg up, if you know what I mean. Her own ex-husband tried to take ownership of her work. Do you honestly believe she'll buy that we were experimented on? No. She'll look us up and find out most of us are wanted for one thing or another and she'll call in the authorities."

She was a law-abiding woman. It was in her nature.

Robert chuckled, though there was little humor in it. "Maybe that's what Levi's angling for. If the Canadians call the Americans in, he can operate freely and take Dr. Walsh back to the States and force her to do god knows what, all with the blessing of the CIA and the president. President Hayes can't ignore a request from Canada."

"I hate Levi Green," Tucker said sullenly.

"Put that aside for now," Theo insisted. "If we're going to get that material and sneak it out under Green's nose, we need you close to her. But if you think it could actually work between the two of you, I want you to consider backing off or talking to Ezra about potentially making the gamble and bringing her in."

How the hell could it work between a brilliant scientist who was trying to cure a terrible disease and a man who'd fucked up so entirely it had cost him his memories? He had nothing to offer her, not even his past. "No, we're not a good match, but that doesn't mean I don't like her. It doesn't mean I want her hurt. But I think she knows it won't

167

work between us. She's smart. She knows I'm a bad bet. That's why she's putting me in a box and taking me out when she wants to."

"Because you're giving her all the power," Theo insisted.

"She's got the right to say what she wants." He couldn't throw her over his shoulder and run away with her. No matter how much he wanted to.

"Are you giving her the option?" Theo asked. "Did you give her the option this morning? No. You got annoyed and your back was against the wall and you walked out. So give her the choice."

"You want me to call her and ask her to go out with me instead?" He could do it. He had to find a way to not beg the woman, but maybe he could manage it.

A slow smile spread across Theo's face. "Nope. We're going to do something much more fun. A woman likes a grand gesture. What I'm thinking of isn't so much a gesture as it is a really cool entrance. It's a bit theatrical, but if you play it right, then even if she turns you down, she won't be thinking about the guy she's out with."

Music thudded from the hallway, a bouncy pop song starting to play.

He looked up and Erin was holding out a phone, the volume turned up to dance party levels.

Theo's eyes narrowed on his wife.

"Well, it's time for the makeover, right?" Erin asked, her lips curled up in a mischievous grin. "You need music for your makeover. You can giggle and talk fashion and maybe get a mani pedi, and I'll follow you around so you have a soundtrack. Theo's phone is full of Taylor Swift and Kelly Clarkson. Was that Ariana Grande I spied on your playlist? We've got your girl-power jam right here for hours, buddy."

Theo stood slowly, his shoulders squaring. "Gentlemen, I'm going to have a talk with my wife. I'll be back in a second. Well, maybe not in a second. This might take some time." He stalked toward her before turning briefly. "But she's right about the makeover. Sort of. We'll talk about it when I finish disciplining my incredibly smartass sub."

Theo chased his wife down the hall, her laughter ringing through the place.

God, he loved the way Becca laughed.

Maybe Theo was right. He hadn't asked her this morning if she wanted to spend the day with him. He hadn't given them enough time to bring the subject up. He'd left her alone to deal with Carter and the police. Not exactly the signs of a man who was interested in altering their bargain.

There was nothing in their agreement that said he couldn't try to lure her away from some other guy.

She'd seemed disappointed when he'd reminded her of her date this morning. There had been a moment when hurt had flared in her eyes, but he'd dismissed it because he'd been hurt, too. He was acting like a jealous boy, not a bloody operative. If he wanted her in his bed, he would have to work for it, tempt her into it.

Theo thought he needed to make an entrance. He might be able to do that. "Do you guys want to help me with a project?"

Robert frowned. "You really want a makeover? Like we go through your clothes and stuff?"

He rolled his eyes. Bugger all. "No, I want to go down and talk to a bloke about a motorbike. I can't get to my clothes. Two Taggarts are likely already fucking on my bed. They better change the sheets."

Robert nodded. "See, that's how I felt about the island. Could they make sure they clean that? Or burn it down? Sure, let's go out and talk about a new plan. I don't know that I can listen to more fucking. I'll get dressed."

Tucker sighed. "I'll join you, but can we use the elevator? My quads are killing me, man. Have you seen them? They're getting huge. Every day on this op is leg day. What's up with that?"

Owen groaned, but his mind was spinning.

She wanted a bad boy? He could give her that. After all, it was practically his profession.

Chapter Eleven

She was going to murder Cathy. She was a doctor. She could do it about a hundred different ways. It didn't have to be painful, but she was going to make sure Cathy never set up another human being again.

Because she was terrible at it.

"Well, I told her she didn't get Lacey for both Thanksgiving and Christmas," he said, glancing up from his menu. "It's not fair. Our custody agreement clearly states that we split holidays, and she already had Lacey for Victoria Day."

It was a stunningly gorgeous afternoon. The sky was a beautiful baby blue with big puffy white clouds floating overhead. The sun was warm on her skin, but there was a nice breeze that cooled everything off. The restaurant was lovely and the patio was the perfect place to spend time talking with friends or getting to know an attractive, intelligent man.

Lawyer Larry was definitely attractive. He had thick, dark hair and soulful eyes. He looked fit and healthy. He was damn near her perfect type until he opened his mouth and couldn't stop talking about his divorce and the ex-wife who was keeping him from his beloved daughter. It had taken her about fifteen minutes before she understood he was talking about a pug. Not that pugs weren't cute or even that she didn't feel for him missing his dog, but it was a lot to throw out there in the first couple of minutes of a date.

He winced as though he'd finally figured out she wasn't

responding as readily as she should have. It was good that he could at least pick up on social cues eventually. "I'm sorry. I'm talking too much and not about the right things."

"Not at all," she lied. "I understand the pain of divorce, though we didn't have any pets."

And now she thought that was a good thing. She loved dogs and cats but had always worried she worked far too much to give a pet the proper attention. Now she knew Fido could have far-reaching consequences.

He sighed and sat back. "Yeah, I'm afraid I got off the phone with my ex right before I came here. I swear she's got a sensor or something that goes off the minute I'm going to do anything happy in my life. Do you see yours often?"

"I moved." To a whole different country. "I needed a clean break, so when the job at the Huisman Foundation came up, I jumped at it."

She'd been right to take a break from the emotional stuff, but she was starting to wonder if she was being too rational about Owen. She'd missed him. All morning she'd thought about going down to his apartment and knocking on the door. She hadn't. She'd forced herself to stay away, but now she was wondering why.

Why did she have to play the field? Why couldn't she play in Owen's field? There wasn't some dumb rule that said she couldn't have a relationship with the first guy she felt something for, and if there was then she could break it.

"God, I wish I could have a fresh start," Lawyer Larry was saying. "It's impossible when there are children involved. We'll be tied together as long as Lacey's alive, and honestly, we've been talking about potentially breeding her. She's such a light in the world that I can't stand the thought of not having a piece of her with me for the rest of my life."

He started going on and on about how difficult it was to find the right sire or something. It was a lot of information. Way more than she ever wanted to know about breeding dogs.

She smiled gamely and wondered where the waitress was. They'd put in drink orders but she was ready to eat and run as fast as she could. She'd been ready to order the quiche and salad, but if they made them individually that could add time to the process. Turkey sandwich it was. It took no time at all to slap some turkey between two pieces of bread and call it a day. She could choke it down in record time.

"And the breeding fees can be ridiculous," he continued. "But I want the best for Lacey. It's one more thing Jane and I fight about."

Why hadn't she come up with some kind of signal? She should have had a friend she could text 911 to and then she would call and save her, claiming some kind of emergency.

Could she fake a text? Was that rude?

Or she could fake a heart attack. That would get her out of here fast, but it also might get her an ambulance ride, and then everyone would freak out.

Her cell phone trilled and she breathed a sigh of relief. Cathy. Excellent. Cathy had gotten her into this. She could get her out. Holding her phone, she pushed back her chair. "I'm so sorry. I have to take this. I won't be more than a moment."

"Of course," he replied, frowning at her. "I'll see if I can wave down a waitress."

She settled her purse over her shoulder and moved back into the restaurant. When she was out of hearing range, she slid her finger across the screen to answer the call. "Hello, Cathy. Would you like to know about the high cost associated with breeding your precious pug?"

A long sigh came over the line. "I was worried about that."

"In the first fifteen minutes of this date, I know more about Larry's divorce than I know about my own. Mine now feels like a beautiful mystery to me."

"I'm sorry, Becca. Look, you're only the second woman he's gone out with since he and Jane broke up. It takes a while to get back into the swing of things."

"He's literally the first person I've dated since I got divorced." Owen didn't count because what they'd done hadn't been dates. They'd been sexual encounters. They'd been hot and sweaty and perfect. And she'd enjoyed talking to him.

It hadn't been all about sex. There had been an easy intimacy between the two of them she hadn't felt in…she'd never felt it. Not once. When she'd met her husband it had taken months before they'd slept together, and while it had been good, she'd never once laid around in bed naked and eating pizza and watching movies with him.

"I know but men take divorce harder than women do," Cathy was saying.

"Really?"

"Okay, I'm coming up with excuses, but it's because he's a successful guy. He's on your level. It's hard to find someone who can keep up with you professionally," Cathy admitted.

"What does that mean?" She glanced out and it looked like Larry had found a waitress. He was talking to the blonde woman and shaking his head, gesturing back toward the entrance as though complaining about his date.

Yeah, she was cool with that.

Something crashed on Cathy's side of the phone and there was a muffled call for order and not playing with hockey sticks in the house. "It means I can't pull out my virtual rolodex and set you up with the first blue-collar guy I see. You need a serious man."

She looked out over the patio. She'd made the argument to herself when she'd agreed to this date. She'd made it again when she'd decided she couldn't throw herself into a relationship with Owen. "I was married to a serious man."

What about Owen wasn't serious?

She moved back to the door that led out to the patio. There was a beautiful wrought iron fence that surrounded the patio, a gate that would allow diners access to the street. In the distance, the CN Tower rose above the skyscrapers. She'd lived here for two years and never been. How much of life was she missing because she took herself so seriously?

"You were married to another doctor," Cathy pointed out. "I think you need a white-collar guy who won't talk about the medical profession every single minute of the day."

She continued on about all the things Becca needed, but Becca's attention was suddenly on the street. An old-school motorcycle pulled up and stopped in front of the iron gate. The man on the bike wore a proper helmet, and she couldn't help but notice there was a second helmet secured to the bike, a smaller more feminine-looking helmet.

Cathy would probably tell her any dude on an old motorcycle wasn't a proper date for her, but she thought the bike looked cool. Not that she would ever ride one since she knew quite well the ramifications of a motorcycle accident.

The man on the bike put his feet down, balancing it. Was he picking up his girlfriend after her shift? He was wearing jeans, and a leather jacket covered his broad shoulders.

She was in a skirt and button-down and a cardigan. Perfectly normal clothes for her, but as she'd dressed she'd thought about whether or not Owen would like her navy blue cardigan with white piping and gold buttons. Would he think she looked like a sexy librarian? She pushed her glasses up and sighed as the man on the bike started to unhook his helmet.

"I'm going to cut this off at the pass," she said, forcing her eyes away from the guy on the bike. He probably wasn't as hot as he seemed. He would take that helmet off and just be a normal, average dude. "I'm sorry if this gets you in trouble, but I can't spend the afternoon with this guy. It's not fair to either one of us."

If she hurried, she might be able to find Owen.

Or she could go to the office because it wasn't like Owen had wanted to spend the day with her. He'd left her with the cops. He might be annoyed with her. He might have decided she was too much trouble for a booty call.

Another sigh came over the line. "I'm sorry. I'll do better next time. I've got an accountant I think you'll love. Now, he's divorced and still a little bitter, but I think you can turn him around."

The helmet came off and she caught her breath as she recognized that gold and red hair, the sexy line of his jaw, those godawful gorgeous lips of his. And his scruff. It was the hottest thing she'd ever seen. Owen. Owen was on that bike.

She shrank back because Owen was here and he was obviously looking for someone.

His blue eyes took in the patio.

Did he have a woman he was picking up here? That was a coincidence. A big one.

Or he was a sexy bastard who'd seen the note she'd left on her bar. Well, he'd told her he didn't play fair. Had he come out here to offer her an alternative?

She could hide and maybe save herself some embarrassment or she could walk out there and find out if Owen Shaw had come to save her. Her knight on a shiny bike.

"Hey, Cathy, don't ever set me up again. I think I have this handled." If he wasn't here for her, then at least she'd get a look at her competition. Because she wanted him. Only Owen, not some random setup that might or might not lead to a super-professional happily ever after.

She hung up the phone because Cathy would keep her on it forever and she needed to get out there before Owen thought he'd missed her.

He was here for her. She was sure of it now. It was there in the way he was studying the patio, his eyes catching on Larry and staring.

She stepped out into the sunlight and waited.

"I sent the waitress away because you weren't here," Larry said, irritation flavoring his words. "You know it's rude to pay more attention to your phone than your date."

Owen's gaze caught her and the slowest, sexiest smile crossed his face. The man actually made her catch her breath. A single brow cocked over his eye as if to ask if she was staying with the lawyer or fleeing with the bad boy on the bike.

She wasn't the kind of woman who walked out when she'd made a commitment, but she was the kind who knew a good thing when she saw it, and that man was a good thing.

"If you didn't like me answering my phone, you're really not going to like what I do next," she said, never taking her eyes off Owen. "Bye, Larry. I hope things work out between you and Lacey and whatever doggie dad you pick. Bye."

"Hey, where are you going?" Larry stood up.

But she was already jogging for the gate. She tossed it open and Owen was suddenly standing in front of her, the extra helmet in his hand.

"You done playing the field, love?" he asked.

She loved how tall he was, how petite he could make her feel. She moved through her days treating her body like the tool it was, but Owen reminded her she was a woman who needed attention and physical affection. And that she was a woman who needed to take a couple of risks. "Yes. I told Cathy not to try to set me up again. I don't think she knows what I want."

He towered over her. "Good, because I know exactly what I want and I don't want to share. Walking out this morning was the hardest thing I've had to do in a long time. I'm going to be honest, I don't like the idea of you seeing other men. I don't have any interest in other women."

"Okay." She was done pretending and done playing by any rules other than her own.

"Just like that?" He put the helmet on her head, checking carefully to make sure it was secure.

"Just like that." She went up on her toes and brushed her lips against his.

"What are you doing?" Larry stood on the other side of the fence, his hands on his hips.

"Diving in," she said as Owen settled on the seat and held the bike for her to get on the back.

"She's with me, mate, and I'm not giving her back," Owen said, revving the engine. "Better luck next time. This one is mine."

She wrapped her arms around his waist and held on for the ride.

* * * *

Paul Huisman wasn't sure exactly what he was dealing with. His new "friend" was an odd one. Levi Green sat in a huge wingback leather chair that at one point in time had been Huisman's grandfather's and he looked over the gorgeous raven-haired woman who'd shown up exactly when Green had said she would.

His father's mistress was also a spy. It was kind of hard to believe, but she'd dropped the sweet, shy act the minute she'd seen Levi Green.

It was rather odd having two spies in his office.

"What do you want? Obviously you know who I am," the woman with the raven hair said. "And I'm not foolish. I know exactly who you are, or at least who you say you are, Levi Green."

Green tipped his head her way, taking a sip of the ridiculously expensive Scotch Paul himself almost never drank. It was there for show, but apparently Green believed in enjoying the finer things in life. "Ah, Mo Chou, it's good to know my reputation precedes me. So what is MSS interested in at the Huisman Foundation?"

"Well, we would have been more interested in the son had we known he has dealings with the Agency." She looked Huisman up and down, assessing him with dark eyes. "I didn't expect that of you. The way your father talks you can barely tie your shoes."

Humiliation burned through him and hardened his resolve. If Levi Green could take his father and that bitch Walsh down, he would give the man anything he wanted. Especially since what he seemed to want was Dr. Walsh herself. "I assure you, I can do more than tie my shoes."

The foundation would be his and then that mansion his father occupied would be his, too, or his father could see how much he enjoyed prison. It would be fun to have the man at his mercy for once.

Mo Chou sank into the seat beside Levi, turning her attention to him. "What do you want? The fact that I don't have Canadian police knocking on my door means you want to deal. The fact that you're here with Paul Huisman means you know what I want."

"I suspect you're interested in many of the high-tech medical research here, but more specifically in the treatments for cancer. Someone's close and that could mean trouble for big pharma. What's R&D up to now? You've got six of the top thirty-three pharmaceutical companies with research and development centers in China now. I would bet they might pour more money in if you could give them a heads-up on what's coming down the pipeline."

"Seven," she corrected. "It's an up-and-coming industry and one that we will take over. The jobs are better. It's rough keeping the peasants down, you know. We need to offer them a bigger economy and more opportunities. Also, wouldn't it be nice if our own state-run research managed to find a cure?"

"Yes, I can see that," Levi agreed. "It would likely make China look more and more like a world leader. Unfortunately, I play for the other team. I can't give you what you want."

She stood. "Then have me arrested. I don't care. There'll be another one just like me here in a week. Hell, there's already several of us in place, but I suspect you know that. I take it you're planning a coup so you can get the intel for yourself."

"Not exactly," Levi hedged. "I do want something from the foundation, but not what you think. I need your help setting it up. Or rather setting her up. Mr. Huisman had his own plans in play, but I like to call an audible in the field every now and then. Would you care to explain what you've been up to, Paul?"

He would have thought this was all an elaborate plan to catch him red handed, except he'd witnessed Levi and his bigger, more muscular partner torture the security director of the Huisman building the night before. He'd been behind a two-way glass so there was no way for his employee to know he'd been there. The security head had yielded all the passwords needed to erase the camera footage from the night before. No one would be able to see Levi Green sneaking into the building, hiding from Dr. Walsh, and then searching her office.

He'd been certain in that moment that Levi had no plans to turn him over to his father.

He'd been just as certain that if he didn't give the man what he wanted, he would be the one in that chair, and he wouldn't come out of it again.

"I find Dr. Walsh to be in the way," he said, trying for a perfectly bored tone. "In *my* way, specifically. She's brilliant but she's not much of a team player, if you know what I mean."

Mo Chou gave him a roll of her eyes that could have come from any American female. She'd been in the West for too long, it seemed. "You mean she's smarter than you and more capable, and you don't stand a chance against her in a fair fight so you're going to play dirty." She shrugged. "It's not a bad play. I would do it if I ever found myself with someone smarter in the way. Ask Levi here. It's his standard move. Didn't you fuck your rival's wife? I liked that one. Solo always thought way too much of herself."

"Maybe I fell madly in love with her and wanted her for myself," Levi said, his voice steady, though there was something about the way his shoulders had stiffened that made Paul wonder if this wasn't a difficult conversation for the man.

It was the first time he'd seen the agent shake even the slightest bit.

"I doubt that. I would believe you would do it for revenge before I would believe there's a beating heart in your chest. Everyone knows you're the reason Fain got burned," she said, obviously relishing having the CIA operative unsettled. "You're not one to let anything get in the way of the job." She turned back to Paul. "So how were you planning on getting rid of her? She's got a sparkling reputation. I should know. I've done a careful study of every doctor in that place. I'm concerned with a couple of new hires, though."

"Taggart plants," Levi said.

Mo Chou nodded as though that explained everything. "Then this is about that crazy bitch Hope McDonald. Is he still trying to figure out who those boys were?"

"That's irrelevant," Levi insisted. "What's important is that I want access to Rebecca Walsh and I want it now. She's got something I need, and it's more than a bunch of old research, though I want that as well. I need her in my custody and ready to work."

The Chinese operative waved a hand as though it should be simple. "Why don't you just do what the rest of us would do? Kidnap her and smuggle her out of the country."

"I like subtlety, besides I have some very stuffy people watching me right now. I have to be careful. This president is a little squeamish about torturing American citizens. Hopefully we can get his ass out of office soon and go back to the easy way. Until then I have to play this cool and that means finding a way to make Rebecca Walsh come to me."

"That's where I come in." Paul was happy with the even tone of his voice. He could handle this. Yes, he was caught between vipers, but he had fangs of his own. "I began setting up Dr. Walsh a little over a year ago. She's got a charitable foundation. She pays attention to the actual work she does, but she's not as careful with the money. Over the course of the last year, I've managed to take around a million dollars from accounts Walsh has access to for her research at Huisman and funneled them to her charitable foundation as donations."

Mo Chou's scarlet red lips tipped up at the corners. "Aren't you a sneaky one? Still, there are ways for a forensic accountant to track that back to you."

"Well, I didn't intend to actually have her arrested," he admitted. "I intended to find the crime and have her fired. You know most of the time crimes like this aren't reported to the authorities. It tends to cause our donors to worry we've been lax and think twice about backing us. I would have taken over the department and her research would have remained here at Huisman."

"That's changed," Levi explained. "I need her arrested."

Mo Chou nodded. "Ah, and you'll be waiting right there to 'save' her, I suspect. You'll agree to help get the charges against her dropped in exchange for her returning to the US and working for you. She might not. This isn't exactly a hellhole. What's Canadian jail like? I bet it's the politest general population in the world. You would have better odds if we were in a Third World country. Or Russia. Fucking Siberia is the worst."

"Jail is jail, and this is a woman who's never faced a moment in her life when she wasn't the smartest, most accomplished person in any given room." Levi seemed much more comfortable now that he wasn't

179

talking about some woman named Solo and they'd moved on to his evil plans.

"I agree," Paul added, feeling confident in this as well. His original plan to rid himself of Rebecca Walsh meshed beautifully with what the CIA agent needed. Once it had been explained to him, he'd understood how they could help each other. "She'll do anything to stay out of jail. She's been very sheltered."

Mo Chou shrugged. "Well, I don't care. What I care about is what you need from me, Levi, and what I get out of it if I can't take the cancer research back to my bosses. I don't see why I should help you."

"I didn't say you wouldn't get anything out of it," Levi said simply, as though he knew he held all the cards in this particular game. "What would you say if I offered you Ezra Fain on a silver platter?"

"I would say I would rather have the research," she replied. "I could pick up a burned CIA operative in a heartbeat. Besides, he's working with Taggart, and that man gives me a headache. You get him involved, you get his wife involved, and those other sarcastic bastards. Now, if you would like to kidnap Kayla Summers, I'll kill her myself. That's one I'd risk Tag's wrath for."

"Kay's too much in the public eye now," Levi replied.

Mo Chou's eyes narrowed. "I want a copy of the research McDonald left behind and I want one of those boys. Shaw will work. Taggart will believe he could turn on the team. After all, wasn't he the one who turned in Tag's brother and sister-in-law? We can set him up while we're setting up Walsh. I know our doctors would love to get a look at his brain, to see how the drug affected him."

A chill went up Paul's spine. They were talking about people. They were bargaining with real human lives.

They were powerful.

Levi held a hand out. "Done. I never could stand Shaw anyway. And if you get a chance to shoot Ezra when things inevitably go bad, do a guy a solid."

"I don't know," she said, shaking his hand and thereby sealing the deal. "I kind of like having the two of you at each other's throats. Or rather at Solo's…"

Levi sat back, his eyes going cold. "Leave her out of this. And I expect you to follow my instructions to the letter. I need you to meet with Walsh next week. I've set everything up."

They were acting like he wasn't even here. He'd been the one to set the plan in motion. Without him, they would have nothing to back up the narrative they intended to build. "I want something, too."

A single brow rose over Levi's light eyes. "I rather thought getting rid of Walsh was your prize."

Yes, but they'd made him think so much bigger. "I want to get rid of my father. Permanently."

"I'll kill him on my way out," Mo Chou agreed with a wave of her hand. "I don't mind. Really, I hate the bastard and he's a terribly selfish lover. And if he called me exotic one more time I was going to kill him anyway."

"Then it's a deal," Levi said before leaning forward and explaining the plan.

Paul sat back, a calm coming over him he hadn't expected. Control. He was taking control for the first time in his life.

He would have what he wanted, and then the world would see who the truly strong Huisman was.

He sat back, thoughts of revenge playing through his head.

* * * *

Owen stared down at her, her head in his lap as he sat back against a tree in Clarence Square Park. They'd found a bit of shade, but there was a chill in the air so she was wearing his leather jacket.

"You're sure you don't want to find something better than hot dogs." He'd taken her from a gorgeous, upscale café and they'd driven all around Toronto. They'd stopped in Yonge-Dundas Square and eaten from a street vendor, sitting underneath the red umbrellas, the city rising around them.

"I liked it," she said with a sigh. "And I like it here. It's pretty."

What she seemed to like most were the dogs. There were plenty of them here. She'd stopped and petted a couple, talking to the owners in an open, friendly way.

He put a hand on her head and smoothed her hair back. He loved this intimacy with her. Anyone who walked by would see nothing at all out of the ordinary. They would see a couple spending a lazy Sunday together, enjoying the lovely weather.

Why couldn't they be exactly that? What would the world be like if he hadn't made that single mistake? If he'd been able to meet her as the old Owen Shaw? Would he have fallen for her quirky beauty and brought her home to meet his mum and sister?

Or would he have been the bastard who couldn't see through her cardigans and glasses and intellect to the raw woman beneath, the one who seemed to somehow complete him, bring him some semblance of peace?

"I like it here, too." But he had to remind himself over and over again that he had nothing to offer her. He would be in her life for a few weeks and then if everything went perfectly, he would disappear. He could leave her with an explanation, that his job was going to take him back to the States or even Europe, and sure they might talk sometime, but he wouldn't see her again.

He'd enjoyed the afternoon with her far too much for his peace of mind. There had been a few moments when he'd worried she was going to sit back down at that table with her date, but otherwise the day had been perfect.

Except that he knew what was happening back at her place. Ezra and Robert were going through her apartment. They were invading her privacy, stealing her secrets, and he was the one making it happen.

Guilt gnawed at him when her eyes opened and she looked up at him, completely trusting. "I thought we were playing it cool, Shaw."

That brought about a genuine smile. "Never believe a man who wants to get under your skirt, love. He'll tell you anything you want to hear. I never wanted to play it cool. I see something I want and I do what I need to make it mine."

"That is very caveman like of you," she said with a smile.

"I never said I was much of a modern man." But he was. Or at least he had been. According to what he'd learned about himself, he'd been perfectly happy to fuck and send whoever he was fucking along their happy way so he could fuck someone else. He'd broken more than one heart, that man he'd been.

"I don't want to see anyone else, Owen," she said quietly. "I thought I should, but I couldn't stand that man, and it was about more than the fact that he talked about his dog so much. It was because it felt wrong to be on a date with him when I couldn't stop thinking about you."

Well, in this case he didn't have to lie. "I spent every moment between the time I left and the minute you hopped on my bike thinking of ways to see you again. Robert gave me the most terrible time for it."

It had really been Erin, but Robert had gotten his punches in, too. Sarcastic bastard. Maybe he should have gone easier on him about the whole Ariel situation.

"So we're going to try this thing?" She asked the question so seriously it would likely have made the old Owen flee in terror.

All the new Owen could think of was how much he wanted to really try with her. "Yeah, I think we are. I'm not interested in other women. You're all I can handle."

"And I'm never letting anyone set me up again. Ever. I'm only dating men I meet in the elevator," she said, a sparkle in her eyes.

Brat. He let his hand shift under the leather jacket, giving her nipple a nice twist that had her squirming.

"Owen!"

"No one was looking until you yelled, love," he replied, knowing damn well there was a smirk on his lips.

Her face was flushed as she sat up and wrinkled her nose his way. "We're in public."

"Then don't be a brat." He reached over and pulled her onto his lap. It made it much easier to nuzzle her neck. And to whisper into her ear. "Don't think I won't take what's mine wherever I want to. The minute you got on the back of my bike, you became mine."

She leaned back into him. "I thought that was only during play."

"We'll always be playing." He kissed her neck and wondered how much time Robert and Ezra needed. They were supposed to text him with the all clear. He wanted to get back to her place and get naked with her. They could spend the evening together. She would be back at work in the morning and he would be lonely without her.

Damn it. He would be lonely. He was a stupid arse, but he couldn't seem to help himself.

"Are there new rules?" She didn't seem truly fazed by his changing things up on her. She seemed perfectly content to sit on his lap and let him breathe her in.

"Absolutely." He was a bastard but he was going to take every single minute he had with her. She was interested in D/s, and he was definitely interested in topping her. "Like I told you, I'm mostly interested in being in charge in the bedroom, but there are a few places

I want control of as well. Not places, exactly. There are times and situations where you need to let me take the lead."

Her body stiffened slightly. "What are those times?"

She was thinking of something specific. Something was working in her brain and he was fairly certain he wouldn't like it. Was it Carter? What had happened after he'd stormed out and left her alone with that asshole? "If you ever think you might have a hint of danger, I expect you to tell me. I expect you to let me handle it. It's my job. I take bullets for people I don't even like. I damn well won't allow my woman to be in danger on her own. If we're going to be a couple, we play to our strengths."

She twisted slightly and her hands came up, cupping his face. "So you'll listen to me when it comes to the medical stuff and I let you handle the weird stuff where I don't understand exactly what's going on."

Yes, he was right. Something was happening, something she hadn't mentioned. "Yes, that is absolutely what I mean."

She was quiet for a moment, her hands running along his jawline. He let her make the decision. He was silent as she figured out how to tell him what she needed to say.

"I think something is happening at the foundation, but I'm not sure how dangerous it is," she said finally.

Not what he'd expected. "Tell me. I've done investigative work before. I can help you."

And if she was in danger, he could get her out of it. This was something he could offer her. This was one thing he could give her in exchange for all the gifts she'd given him.

"From what I can tell there's roughly a million dollars missing from the account my research is funded through," she said with a sigh as she laid her head against his shoulder.

He wound his arms around her, needing her to know she was safe with him. The missing money. That's why she'd had the accounting documents with her that night. He'd known she hadn't had anything to do with it. Someone was fucking with her work, and now he could find out who without a bunch of restraints. "All right. Who has access to the funds?"

"Please understand that I'm not even sure it was stolen or misappropriated," she answered. "There are only a couple of people who could access the funds directly. It could be an accounting error."

He doubted that. "I have a friend who's a forensic accountant. Let me have her take a look. You can talk to her. She works for a company called Miles-Dean, Weston and Murdoch Investigations. They typically work missing persons cases, but she was with the CIA for years."

All true, though he didn't tell her that Phoebe was already looking into it. He wasn't about to let her know he'd stolen the documents that first night.

"I would like to talk to her." She seemed to relax a bit. "I'm not an accountant. I'll be honest, I'm pretty bad at paying attention to that sort of thing. The accounting department of the foundation audits us regularly, but they give us a pretty free hand in spending. It's one of the reasons I was interested in moving up here. Huisman has always been a place that lets researchers work without a ton of red tape."

"What you're telling me is it would be easy to move money around?"

"We can spend pretty freely. If we need a piece of equipment and we've got the budget for it, we buy it. Not every team has the kind of funding mine has. The honest truth is I'm pretty far along on my research. If I need money, someone will give it to me, so I don't think about it a lot."

"How did you catch the discrepancy?" he asked.

"One of the accountants is a friend of my assistant's. She's prepping for the quarterly audit and she pointed it out to Cathy, who brought it to my attention. I was sure all I would have to do was track down the order forms, but there was an incident yesterday that makes me think something weird is going on."

He didn't like the sound of that. "The same day you think someone was in the building watching you?"

"Yes. I didn't think about that. I got this odd message about finding out where the money went. It was couriered over. Do you think they could be connected?" She sat up, turning again so she could look him in the eyes.

He would be shocked if they weren't. "I don't believe in coincidence. What's the security like in your building? How do you protect your research?"

"We all have key cards to get into the building. The elevator requires them, too. There are a couple of places in the building that

185

require biometrics."

"What kind?" He was surprised a high-tech facility like Huisman used key cards instead of biometrics for everything.

"Iris recognition on the actual labs," she explained. "That's where the real research happens, but honestly the data is on computers. We use the highest security so we can ensure that nothing happens to ruin the experiments and the studies. Believe it or not there are people who will wreck research either to help out their own or because they don't believe in what we're doing."

He thought about it for a second. "But other than the actual laboratories, I could get in by nabbing your key card?"

"There's a security guard on site twenty-four seven and we have tons of CCTV. I've already asked them to get the footage from that night," she explained.

He would like to see that footage. "What were you saying about a message? Is that the weird thing that happened?"

"Well, the first weird thing that happened was that I lost the documents accounting sent over," she mused. "I thought they'd fallen out of my bag on the train. It's a giant tote bag and it doesn't close. But now I wonder if maybe it was stolen because the note I received yesterday told me if I want to know what's happening with the accounting, I'll need to meet someone at Casa Loma where the duchess resides. I know Casa Loma is the big mansion the crazy dude built, but I don't know that a duchess ever lived there. Isn't that weird?"

It was more than weird and it made him very curious about who would show up to meet her. "I want to track down who sent that. You said it arrived by courier."

She nodded. "But they're closed today."

"I'll give them a visit in the morning."

"So you'll, like, do everything and I don't have to worry about it?"

Yes, he definitely had something she needed. He leaned forward and kissed her forehead. "You worry about your research and I'll handle everything else."

A look of pure relief spread across her face. "Thank you because I've got a big week ahead and the last thing I need to worry about is weird treasure hunts. I'll talk to accounting and let them know we're looking into it. Cathy can go through all the requisitions of the last year in case it's an error."

He would bet a lot that it wasn't an error, but he was curious as to why it was happening now. Levi Green was in town and he would make his move sooner or later. Was this part of his move?

She started talking about everything she needed to do the next week and he let her enthusiasm drift over him.

He couldn't let her out of his sight. Not until they knew what Green's game was.

He felt his mobile vibrate and knew beyond a shadow of a doubt that it was the boss giving him the all clear, but he didn't make a move for his phone. It was too nice to sit in the open with Becca, to listen to her plans like he was nothing more than her boyfriend.

He would keep her close and if they needed to figure out who wanted to meet her, he would make sure she was safe.

He wouldn't let her out of his sight. Not until the moment he had to.

Chapter Twelve

Three days later, Rebecca stared at her computer screen, but the data kind of swam in front of her eyes.

All she could really see was Owen and how he'd smiled at her and kissed her when he'd dropped her off earlier this morning. She'd found a new schedule. Wake up to Owen kissing her, shower with Owen, have breakfast with Owen, ride to work with Owen. Think about Owen. Count down the time to when Owen would pick her up. Have dinner and hot sex with Owen. Scream out Owen's name until she passed out. Start all over again.

Yep, she was like a teenaged girl with her first crush. Well, except for the very adult sex stuff.

"I have never seen you zone out," Cathy said from the doorway. Her assistant was standing there with her hands on her hips, her eyes wide as she stared at Becca.

"Maybe I was concentrating," she tried. It was good to see Cathy. She'd been out with a sick kid, and Becca had been reminded of how much she relied on her.

Cathy stepped inside and closed the door behind her. "Nope. That's not your concentrating face. You get a little more brow action when you're concentrating on work. And you didn't get in until nine. You haven't been in early all week. That is not your schedule. You're always in by six thirty. Are you all right?"

At six thirty this morning she'd had Owen's head between her legs and she'd been forcing herself not to scream out in pure pleasure. She'd woken up with his hands on her body, coaxing her to open for him.

They'd had breakfast in the café with his roommate, Robert, who was a funny, friendly man, and then Owen had driven her to work with the promise that he would be back to pick her up at the end of the day. They'd argued about what time the day ended. She'd said seven. He'd wanted her done by five. They'd agreed she would be out front at precisely six this evening.

"I'm fine. I've had something to do the last couple of mornings." Owen. She'd been doing Owen. She'd taken all of Sunday off. She normally would have at least come in during the afternoon, but she hadn't thought about work at all. The only thing that had mattered was him. They'd gone out a couple of nights, taking in a movie once and going to some nice restaurants. She'd seen more of the city in the few days she'd been with him than the whole two years she'd lived here.

She was thinking about going to another tourist destination on Friday. Oh, she'd put it all in Owen's lap, but there was a big part of her that wanted desperately to see who would show up to that meeting. Something was going on. She could feel it, and she was starting to trust her instincts.

Paul Huisman had smiled at her this morning. That man never smiled. Ever. It had been the kind of smile a predator might give a small furry thing right before it feasted. Maybe it was her imagination, but she hadn't liked the way that smile had made her feel.

"Is whatever you were doing the reason why you're wearing your cardigan inside out?" Cathy asked with a knowing wink. "Please tell me it was the man you left Larry for. I still haven't heard the end of that."

Damn it. How had neither of them noticed? She stood up and quickly fixed the problem. "His name is Owen and he works for a security company. He moved into my building a week ago."

Cathy leaned against her desk. "Is it true you showed up for work on a motorcycle? The ladies down in reception were all talking about it. They said he was gorgeous."

"He's a very careful driver." She would get lectures on motorcycles and head injuries and how the neurologist probably shouldn't be riding a death trap, but some things were worth the risk.

189

The feeling of freedom she had as he drove her around the city was definitely worth it. He treated her like she was something precious.

"I'm happy for you," Cathy said with a broad smile. "It's good for you to get out of this office once in a while. Is that why Carter is in such a foul mood? Did he finally figure out you're a woman under all that intellect?"

"He wasn't happy the first time Owen spent the night at my place." Had everyone seen the Carter problem except her? "He was pretty rude about it. I haven't talked to him since then. We've given each other a pretty wide berth. I think we should look into how he treats the female interns."

Cathy nodded. "I've heard some rumors. I'm glad that's out in the open. He's had a creepy thing for you since the day you hired on. At first I thought he was a groupie."

"A groupie?"

"An industry junkie. They all either love you or they're jealous of you. Did you know Carter studied medicine?"

"Of course," she replied. "I've heard all about it. He studied neurology, but he has a fine tremor in both hands. It's not Parkinson's. It's an essential tremor. When he couldn't perform surgery, he switched to medical admin. I don't know why. He could have done research. He could have been a GP."

"He's the type who doesn't compromise," Cathy explained. "I think in some ways he was punishing himself for not being able to do what he wanted to do in life."

"You're playing the armchair shrink?" It wasn't so surprising. It was kind of what Cathy did, and she was often right.

Cathy shrugged. "I've seen pretty much everything, and trust me I know the medical types. He's angry. Like I said, I hoped it was all hero worship, though that inevitably goes bad. Knowing how he reacted to you dating makes me think he put you on a pedestal for a different reason. It's okay. I'll manage him from this end and I'll start looking into how he treats the interns. Trust me, after dealing with a sick kiddo for days, I'm ready to bust some balls."

"How is Billy?"

"Not happy to go back to school," she said with a sigh. "But I was so happy to come back to work."

"The stuff with Carter will have to wait. I have another job for you." While Owen's friend in Dallas was looking into it from an accounting end, she would have Cathy start searching for the paperwork trail. There had to be one.

Unless someone really had stolen almost a million dollars from her research account.

She explained the problem and Cathy took some notes, promising she would handle it.

"There must be something going around," Becca said, getting to the second problem she was having, the one Owen was pushing her on. "Chuck's been out for a couple of days, too. Can you go down to security and see if he's back in the office? I've been trying to get some CCTV footage from last Saturday night, but the others said they couldn't get it to me without clearance from Chuck. If he's not in, maybe we can get him on the phone."

"Did you not hear?" Cathy had gone a little pale. "Chuck quit. He left a message with Paul and said he wasn't coming back."

"Are you serious? I heard he was sick."

"Yes, no idea why. He's worked here for twenty years. He was supposed to retire soon. I can't imagine why he would walk out. Security is kind of chaotic right now. Paul said he'll have someone new in a few days, but for now the only person who can do the job is John, and he's barely twenty-five."

"Can you get me Chuck's phone number?" Again her instincts were flaring. Right as she needed to talk to the head of security, he mysteriously decided to quit a job he'd claimed to love? It didn't make sense.

"Of course," Cathy promised. "And I'll pull any requisition that matches these numbers. It's probably that the account number was wrong and the other teams got it screwed up. It's happened before. Don't worry about it. Now, you've got a meeting with your team at noon. The new round of data is in and I've heard it's phenomenal."

She'd heard she would be happy with it, too. She was so close to being able to really push this new therapy.

It would be all right. Owen would help her figure out what was going on, and by this time next month, she would be writing up her paper and potentially taking on a wave of new research money. Then the big trials would begin and she would be one step closer to fulfilling the promise she'd made to herself the day her mother died.

She was already closer to the promise she'd made to her mother. Owen was making her happy, and she needed to concentrate on that.

Still, her curiosity was getting the best of her. "Could you clear my calendar for Friday afternoon?"

A brilliant smile crossed Cathy's face. "Of course. You're seeing your man again?"

She hoped Owen could take a long lunch break. She wasn't dumb enough to go alone, but she needed to know who was going to be waiting for her there. "Yes, I'll definitely be seeing him."

Cathy started to talk about plans to have a double date night or to possibly have Owen out for dinner. Becca wasn't completely sure that meeting Cathy and her crazy family wouldn't make Owen run, but she nodded. Out on the floor, her team was buzzing around, prepping for the meeting later on.

Her eyes caught on a man delivering mail. It was just a glimpse of light brown hair and broad shoulders. There was something about the man that made her go still, pure terror seizing through her.

You should run, Dr. Walsh. Or I might have to show you why they call me Razor.

Bile rose in her throat and when she looked again, the man was gone.

"Becca? You went white." Cathy stood in front of her, blocking her sight of the place where he'd stood.

Except he couldn't stand because he was dead. Dead and gone. Now she was seeing ghosts.

She shook off the feeling. She was being paranoid. It was all about what had happened that Saturday night. It reminded her of the other time she'd been sure someone was stalking her. Of course that time, she'd been right and she'd run.

She wasn't going to think about that man…that monster again. He had no power over her. "I'm fine. I had too much coffee, that's all. I'm going to get ready for the meeting. And thanks for trying to look up that paperwork."

She stayed there while Cathy went to work. Becca sat there trying to convince herself that the past was in the past.

After all, she'd just found her future.

* * * *

192

"What do you mean the money leads back to Becca?" Owen felt his whole body go tight as Phoebe's words sank in.

"I mean the money was moved from her research accounts to her charitable foundation. It was run through a Swiss account, but the numbers match up," Phoebe replied over the connection through the computer. She was sitting in her beautifully decorated office in the middle of downtown Dallas. Phoebe Murdoch was a lovely woman with dark hair and intelligent eyes. She was wearing glasses and looked far more like the accountant she'd claimed to be for years than the CIA operative her accounting job covered for. She had a degree in accounting and had worked many jobs untangling financial data for both the Agency and then McKay-Taggart.

She reminded him a bit of his Becca, but he did not like what she was saying.

It wasn't true.

"You haven't had a long time with that data," Robert pointed out.

The gang was all here. All except Tucker and Sasha, who were working at Huisman, and Nina, who had a shift at the café.

"She's had days with it." Ezra sighed and sat back. They were at Ezra and Tucker's place across town. It was a nice-sized apartment with a view of the CN Tower. Tucker was right. Ezra was definitely a minimalist. There was no furniture in the living room, merely this long table and a bunch of folding chairs. It was his version of a conference room on the run, Owen suspected. There were two large white boards on wheels. One tracked where the central players were and everything they knew about Hope McDonald's operation. The other had information on Rebecca Walsh.

He hated that board, hated the fact that she'd been pared down to nothing but facts and theories about how involved she'd been in McDonald's research.

He could answer that. Zero. Zilch. Nada.

Phoebe leaned toward the camera. "Owen's right. I've only had a couple of days with this but I wanted to let you know the preliminary results. According to what I've found, that money moved from one of her accounts to a single Swiss account, and then to her charity in the form of donations. They were done as wire transfers, so I can't compare signatures, and obviously the Swiss do not share information on their account holders. Adam might be able to figure it out, but we try to keep the boss out of jail for hacking."

Jax might be able to do it, and it wasn't like he wasn't already wanted for even worse crimes. But the truth was he didn't need to see someone else's name on the account to know that it wasn't hers.

"She didn't do it," he insisted. "If she did it, why would she have asked me to come to you? She gave me the data. She gave me permission to give it to you."

"I don't know," Phoebe replied. "Maybe she's being set up. Does she have enemies?"

He held on to that thread. "Of course she does. The same one we have. Levi. This is his plan. He's going to go to her and offer to not turn her in if she hands over that damn box McDonald sent to her."

"It sounds like something Levi would do," Ezra agreed. "It's straight out of his playbook. He knows how to gain leverage and then use it to his own ends."

Phoebe was shaking her head. "These go back almost a year. I thought you said Levi didn't find out about the package until a couple of months ago. Whoever is doing this has been planning it for far longer than a few months."

Dante leaned forward. "Could Mr. Green have known about the doctor for longer? Solo got us the intelligence, right? Could she have lied?"

He didn't want to believe that of her, but he certainly didn't believe Becca was a thief. "We have to consider it."

Robert gave him a "what the hell" look. "I don't think Solo would lie about this. She doesn't have a reason to."

"She's always got a reason," Ezra said, his bitterness soaking through his tone. "However, I still have some sources at the Agency I trust and they confirmed what Solo told us. Levi didn't know there was anything but a professional connection between Walsh and McDonald until a few weeks before the Colorado op. Not even that fucker can backdate bank transfers. Not in that way."

"I'll keep looking into this," Phoebe promised. "It doesn't make sense that she would turn this over to a forensic accountant if she knew she was the one who'd done it. But I will tell you that her charity foundation was on shaky ground before this influx of cash. I'm not sure how she wouldn't know about the money and question it."

"You said they were donations." He wasn't about to explain that Becca's attention was on her research and she struggled to divide her focus. She wasn't a multitasker. She gave everything she did one hundred percent of her attention. From what she'd told him, she was close to making her breakthrough. She wouldn't question the donations. "Were they done anonymously?"

"Of course," Phoebe replied. "Another thing that should have made her suspect something was going on. Large anonymous donations should have tipped her off."

She didn't think that way. "Rebecca is naïve about a lot of things. She's also an optimist."

"She's let you believe that," Ezra pointed out. "Owen, you've known the woman for a week, but you're acting like she's utterly incapable of doing anything wrong."

He was on thin ice. He could practically feel it under his feet. One wrong move and they would pull him. He couldn't let that happen. "I was giving you my opinion. I might not have known her long, but the time we've spent together has been intense."

"The time you've spent together has mostly been in bed," Dante pointed out.

"What Owen is saying is he's the only one who knows her on any kind of an intimate level," Ariel said. "I only know her from what I've read and the brief period of time I got to spend with her before Owen dragged her off."

"She was the one who dragged me," he corrected. She'd known what she wanted and she'd gone for it. That was Becca Walsh.

Ariel sent him a wry smile. "Nevertheless, I didn't get to spend the time I'd hoped to with her. Still, I think I would tend to agree with Owen on this. She's too smart to give herself away like that. I think her morality is like many highly intelligent people. I'm not saying she isn't a good person. She absolutely is. She gives a lot of herself to her work, and her work is good. She believes in her work. She believes in it to the point that she could have some situational ethics concerning it."

Ariel was right. She only knew Becca on paper. "No, she's not that woman."

"Owen, we know she worked with McDonald," Dante said. "That's a fact. From the report Solo sent Big Tag, she spent time with McDonald in Europe. A whole summer working with her."

195

"She was working at Kronberg Pharmaceutical. McDonald just happened to be there, too," he pointed out.

Ezra leaned toward the laptop. "Phoebe, I would love for you to delve deeper into this. If someone is setting up Dr. Walsh, I'd like to know who and why. And if you can come up with any way this helps out Walsh, I'd like to know that as well. I'll let you get back to work."

Phoebe nodded. "Of course."

Owen understood the underlying message. Ezra wanted whatever he said next to stay in the family, so to speak. Phoebe was connected to them, but she wasn't a part of the immediate team.

When the screen cleared, Ezra looked to him. "Did you read the same report I did?"

"Of course he did." Robert was always stepping in front of anyone who fucked up. The big brother of them all.

He couldn't hide behind Robert this time. "I did read it. I understand that she likely had some kind of a working relationship with the woman, but Becca Walsh wouldn't have supported McDonald's research. She didn't even stay the entire summer. She walked out in late July and gave up her grant."

"Which means she might have gotten a hint of what McDonald was working on and left," Robert agreed.

Dante shook his dark head. "Then why on earth would McDonald have sent her that box?"

He was sick of hearing about that bloody box. "We don't know what's in it. It could be shite Becca left behind for all we know."

"Levi Green doesn't think so," Ezra pointed out. "He wouldn't be here if he didn't think whatever is in that box is important. The only thing McDonald did that was important was her research and the formulary for the drugs and protocols for the therapies she used on you and the others."

"You're wasting your breath. He won't believe you," Dante said nonchalantly, as though he didn't particularly care about the outcome of this fight. "He's too far gone. He thinks he loves the girl."

"I like the woman," Owen corrected. "I like her a lot and I've gotten to know her."

Dante leaned in, his dark eyes pinning Owen. "Like she's gotten to know you? You've gotten to know the real her? Have you considered for one moment that she could be playing you the same way you're playing her?"

Robert held out a hand, trying to stop Dante from pushing this confrontation further. "Give him a break. He didn't go through what the rest of us did. He doesn't think everyone is out to get him."

"How does he explain that the CCTV of the night she claims she was being stalked has been erased?" Dante asked. "Something happened that night and she's covering it up."

He knew what they'd found, or rather hadn't been able to find. "Then why mention it to me?"

"You are naïve then," Dante said with a shake of his head. "Or you're thinking of finding a way out. This could be a way to leave this shitty life of ours. And if she was a wealthy doctor who happens to have something the very man who could ensure no one comes after you wants, then that would obviously work."

"What exactly are you accusing me of?" Because there was no way to mistake that for anything but an accusation.

"Hey, calm down," Ezra said.

Robert looked like he was ready to get in between them if he needed to. "No one is accusing anyone of anything."

"Oh, I disagree," Owen said, watching Dante. "I think he's got very specific thoughts about what I'm doing. Say it out loud, mate."

Dante shrugged and sat back. "I'm merely pointing out the obvious. You aren't one of us. You got stuck with us. You don't have the same problems we have and you have a history of betrayal. A man like you would take the first chance he can find to get out."

"That's not my assessment of Owen at all," Ariel said, her voice going cold for once. "And you should understand I knew the man before he lost his memory. I worked with him. He was a good man who made one mistake, and he made it out of love for his mother and sister."

Dante's eyes took her in. "You think the rest of us don't know there's a traitor among us? Ezra thinks he's so quiet when he speaks, but I hear him. I hear him talking to Damon and Taggart. Some of the things that happened in Colorado… Levi Green knew exactly where to be, and that means someone told him. One of us. We were the only ones who knew."

Robert had moved closer to Ariel, as though he thought Dante might attack her.

197

It wasn't Dante Robert should worry about. Anger rolled through Owen. Anger and guilt made a toxic cocktail in his gut. They'd been talking about him? He knew there had been questions about what had gone wrong with the Colorado op. Levi had seemed to know where they were at all times. They'd been careful about covering their tracks, but somehow Levi had shown up or sent his men in to show up at precisely the right times and in the right places.

They thought it was him. Of course they did.

"We weren't the only ones who knew," Ezra corrected. "Levi had a plant and so did the Agency."

But Solo hadn't known all their plans. She hadn't been there every second of the day.

"Solo knew Jax was going into those woods," Ezra continued.

"She didn't know exactly where he was going," Dante pointed out.

"Neither did Owen," Robert said tightly.

"Ah, but he was there at the end. He made sure he was." Dante sat back as though enjoying himself. "If I remember correctly, he was also the one who helped Jax put together his pack. It would have been easy to slip in a tracking device. He then could have retrieved it at the end."

"I helped Jax, too." Robert's whole body had gone stiff and Ariel stood up behind him, her hand going to his shoulder. "You want to accuse me?"

"Ah, but you were far away at the end," Dante crooned. "You weren't in the two places where it would have been easy to cover your tracks. Owen was."

"Owen is the only one of us who can fly a fucking helo." Ezra's voice had gone low.

It didn't matter. He could point out the logic all day long, but the truth was he had betrayed them all and they would never forgive him.

"Yes, he's excellent at using his resources." Dante wasn't giving up. "Now he's going to use the good doctor to save himself. Rebecca Walsh was in on it. That's why she's hidden the box. We've looked for it everywhere. In her home and her office. She's protected it because she's going to use it. She's not some innocent. She's a bitch like her mentor, and Owen is going to ride her all the way home."

He wasn't sure what happened next. He saw red, a violent mist that shut out everything else. He went over to the table and had his hands around Dante's throat in a heartbeat. It felt good. His throat was warm and muscular, but Owen had righteous anger on his side. He slammed Dante to the floor and held the man down as he started to choke the life out of him.

Yes, he was seeing red at the moment, but he wanted to see blue. He wanted that fucker's face to turn blue.

Someone was yelling, but that didn't matter. All that mattered was that Dante's mouth couldn't spout shite about Becca again. He didn't care what anyone said about him. He'd earned their scorn, their mistrust, but she hadn't.

"Owen! Stop it," Robert was saying.

"Owen, I need you to calm down." Ariel knelt down beside him. Her voice was soothing. "You don't want to kill Dante. Not really. I know who you are, Owen Shaw."

No one knew who he was. *He* didn't fucking know. He wanted to be the man Becca thought he was, the one she could count on.

Dante's eyes had started to bulge and the fight he'd shown was slowing down, but Ezra had an arm around Owen's neck. He managed to snap his head back, making hard contact with his boss's chin and causing him to curse and let go. Pain flared but Owen didn't let up.

"Owen, please," Ariel implored. "If you do this, you can't go back to her. If you do this, Ezra has to turn you over. Becca will be alone. She won't have you to protect her."

Those words seeped into his brain. They worked some kind of magic on his hands as he fell back, letting Dante go.

Dante coughed, but was on his feet in a heartbeat, trying to come after him.

Robert caught the other man. "No fucking way. You are going home. Now. I'll have Tucker stop by your place to check on you."

Dante looked savage as he stepped back. "Don't bother. I can take care of myself. It's obvious whose side you're on, Robert."

Ezra sighed as he got to his feet. "There are no sides, but it's obvious we need to have some serious talks. Come on. I'll take you back to your place. And Owen, you can't tell Rebecca Walsh what we found out today. I want a couple of days for Phoebe to figure out what's happening before you tell Walsh what we know. And that's an order. I expect you to follow it."

He shot Robert a look that plainly told him to take care of it from this end.

Owen didn't know that he wanted to be taken care of, but Ariel had been right about one thing.

Becca needed him. He might have to protect her from his own team.

Except they weren't his team.

"Owen, do you want to talk about it?" Ariel got to the floor, sitting down beside him.

"Man, you have to know we don't think that of you," Robert said.

Did he? Hell, if he was in their position, he might think it, too.

He forced himself to get up. "No, I'm fine. I'm going home. I have to take a shower. I have to pick up Becca soon."

He walked away without looking back.

Chapter Thirteen

Something was wrong with Owen, and she couldn't put her finger on it. He'd been perfectly sweet. He'd been waiting for her at the time they'd agreed on. He'd taken her to dinner and asked about her day, listening patiently as she likely went way too much into how plaque was formed in the brain. Way too much.

It had been an exciting day and it had taken her too long to figure out that his smile didn't come close to reaching his eyes.

Now they were ensconced in her apartment and she wondered how to tell him she planned on going to the meeting Friday afternoon. She was wondering if she should tell him at all since there was something in his eyes that told her he'd had a rough day.

Maybe it was time to play the submissive. Wasn't it her job to soothe him? He protected her. She soothed and calmed him. That was the exchange they'd agreed on, and he'd definitely done his job. She wasn't sure she'd been doing hers. She'd been far too into the sex and pleasure and affection to remember he needed things too.

He locked the door behind him. "I think I might head to my place for the night, love. I've got a headache and I worry I'll keep you awake."

Yes, something had definitely gone wrong with his day. "Or you could sit down and let me take care of you. After all, I am a doctor. Can you describe it to me? The headache, that is?"

A faint smile crossed his face. "He's six foot, dark hair, bloodshot eyes. He's an asshole of the highest order and I have to work with him."

Oh yes, she could handle this. "I know a couple of those myself. Owen, please stay with me. I don't mind if you toss and turn. I can handle it. Sit down."

His eyes caught hers and she realized she'd made a mistake. If he'd had issues with someone at work, it might have made him feel small, and now she was ordering him around. That wasn't how to handle a man like Owen.

"Please." That was a better plan.

His gaze softened but he didn't move toward the couch. "I'm on the edge tonight, Becca. I don't want to go into it, but work was hard today. I think I could push you tonight if you let me. I don't want to scare you."

She moved into his space. "I'm not scared of you at all."

His eyes seemed grave as he stared down at her. "Maybe you should be."

She shook her head and put her arms around him, resting her ear on his chest. "No. I do not want to be afraid of you. Not for a second." She was quiet for a moment because his arms had wrapped around her and he seemed to relax. It was peaceful to breathe him in and listen to the steady beat of his heart. "I wanted to be here all day."

"I thought you had a good day." One of those big hands of his moved over her back.

"I did." The results of the latest test had been spectacular. But she'd still thought about him. He was a distraction, but one she wasn't willing to let go of. She'd worked all this time thinking of nothing but her research. Maybe Owen was her shot at having something outside of work. She knew it was too early to start thinking like that, but she'd been super careful when it had come to her ex-husband. Careful hadn't worked. She was following her instincts this time. "But the whole time I was waiting for six o'clock."

Now that hand came up and cupped the nape of her neck, cradling her to him, and she knew she had him. He wouldn't be going anywhere tonight. "You have no idea how much I felt the same today."

"Do you want to talk about it?" He rarely talked about himself. He would let her go on and on, but he tended to turn the conversation when it was about him.

He was silent for a moment. "I screwed up a job a couple of years back. I screwed up badly and it put two of my teammates in danger. They came out of it all right, but it's when I got injured and had that bad reaction to the drugs they had to give me."

She went very still because she'd learned this was not something he talked about. He was touchy about the scars on his body. She could have told him they did nothing to detract from how gorgeous he was, but he obviously hadn't wanted to hear it.

"The reaction was bad," he continued. "It went far beyond what you see on my skin. It made me weak for a long time. My boss…well, I think he felt so bad about what happened that he couldn't fire me even though he should have."

"I can't imagine you would do anything that would require you being fired."

"Then you, love, don't have a good imagination," he replied quietly. "I assure you, I deserved it and more. But I've tried to redeem myself. I was reminded today of everything I did wrong and that some people don't believe I can change. I also might have tried to kill someone."

She brought her head up, or rather tried to, but he gently held her down. "What?"

"Hush. I didn't do it. I was reminded that I have things I care about now," he replied. "Besides, he deserved it. Sorry. My work isn't like yours. We're a bunch of barbarians at heart. It's all right."

"Did you get hurt?"

"He never had a chance, though I suspect he'll try something nasty soon," he admitted. "I'll be ready for him. Now, are you sure? Are you sure you want me to stay because I'm still raw. I think it might be best if I go home and Robert and I beat on each other."

That sounded like a terrible idea. "Or you could play with me."

She felt the groan go through his body, felt his cock get hard against her belly.

"I won't go easy on you. I need too much tonight." His hands tightened around her. His words told her she could go, but those hands begged her to stay. Commanded her to stay.

"Do you need me?" She could handle anything he threw her way if he did.

"I need you more than I could have imagined. I need you more than I should." His voice had gone deep, hoarse, as though he was right there on the edge and all it would take to push him over was a little help from her.

She rubbed her cheek against his chest and let her hands find the globes of his amazingly muscled ass. "I need you, too. Tell me what you want from me, Owen."

He tugged on her hair, gently forcing her to look up into his eyes. "Everything. I want everything."

"Then let's play." She wanted to be the reason he relaxed tonight. Whatever had happened, it had all come back to him today. And he wasn't the only one. She couldn't tell him the story of what had happened to her that summer. It didn't matter because everyone who was guilty was dead. Everyone but her. She wanted to wipe those months away, and she knew exactly how to do it. "I don't want to think for the rest of the night. I don't want to be Dr. Walsh. I want to be yours."

"Take off your clothes. You won't need them until morning. Take them off and kneel at my feet. This is how we begin formal sessions."

"Is this a formal session?" So far they'd been fairly casual. She had to admit she was intrigued.

"This is a learning session. If you ever want me to take you to a club, you'll need to learn certain protocols. Do you want to go with me to a club? I would like to take you to one. I would love to show you off, to let everyone know how pretty my sub is."

There was a whole world out there to explore. There was a world where she could relax and be someone other than the doctor she had to be during the day. There could be a whole other Rebecca. Owen's Rebecca.

Owen picked up the key she'd left on the hook by the door. "Go to the bedroom and get undressed. I want you to get on your knees and wait for me there. I'm going to grab something out of my apartment."

"Sex toys?" She was joking. It was probably condoms.

"Yes," he replied absolutely seriously. "Now stop questioning me or I'll get the canes out. I've got a lovely set of them. Would you like to be introduced to those tonight? Or do you just want to take the plug I bought for you?"

She felt her eyes widen. "Plug? I...what part of me are you...oh, my bottom."

That got him smirking. "Aye. Your pretty arsehole, love. How did you expect to take my cock? I certainly didn't plan to shove it in without any preparation."

Okay, so the after-hours Becca was definitely going to explore new things. "What if I don't like it?"

"Then I stop. All you ever have to tell me is no."

She was safe with him. Safe to explore crazy sex stuff. "Then I will definitely take the plug over the canes. Though I'm sure they're perfectly lovely canes."

She turned and hurried back to her bedroom. In the end it was all a game. That was precisely why they called it playing. But she wasn't risking the cane part.

The lamp was on, casting soft light across her bedroom. She pulled her clothes off, tossing them to the side. Her bedroom was fairly utilitarian. She didn't think about it much but she was going to have to reconsider because the hardwoods under her knees weren't very comfy. A thick rug might be helpful if she did this often. And maybe she should move from her queen-sized bed to a king, because Owen took up an enormous amount of space.

She couldn't help it, her mind flashed back to the last time she'd been on her knees. She was right back at Kronberg. That day the floor had been cold under her knees. She'd tripped as she'd tried to get away from the man who'd threatened her. She'd panicked and fallen and Dr. McDonald had walked in, looking from him to her.

What have you done?

"Spread your knees, love." Owen's voice brought her back to reality.

It took her a moment but she did as he asked, spreading her knees wider.

"What happened? You're tense and you weren't before," Owen said, his hand finding her hair.

She didn't want to think about that day, tried to not ever think about it. "Nothing. Just nervous about the plug. Not that I'm not willing to try it. I am."

His fingers tangled in her hair, tugging her until she faced him. "Don't lie to me."

"I saw someone today who reminded me of a man from my past.

205

Then I remembered when I was trying to get away from him, I tripped and my knees hit the floor. I'm okay. It just reminded me."

"Someone hurt you?" The question came out on a low growl and she had the impression that their session might be interrupted by some bloody revenge if Owen had his way.

"He threatened me," she corrected. At least she thought he hadn't hurt her. It had all been a dream when she'd been sick. That's what she'd told herself. The threat, however, had definitely been real. "He scared me, but he didn't actually hurt me. I made sure I was never alone with him after that day. I left a project I was working on."

"I would like a name, Rebecca."

She breathed out and let the old fears go. "He died a few years back. It's fine. Like I said, I saw someone who reminded me of him today. It's a whisper, that's all. But you need to know that I want to be out of my head tonight every bit as much as you do. Please take me out of my head."

His face was still tight, as if it was an indulgence for him to let the conversation go, but he stepped back. "All right. Spread your knees wider and if you argue with me, I'll start the discipline for the evening."

She moved her knees as wide as they would go and realized why he was insistent on this position. It made her vulnerable. It made her deeply aware of her pussy. Cool air caressed her and she was open to him.

"Yes, that's what I want." He stood in front of her, his eyes going straight to her pussy. "Straighten your shoulders."

She did as he asked. The position made her breasts thrust out. Her nipples were already hard and aching for attention. Despite the coolness of the room, her body was warming up nicely.

"Now place your hands palms up on your thighs. Like you're offering yourself to me because that's exactly what you're doing. You're offering me your body and your trust." When she'd done as he asked, he stood in front of her. "Do you have any idea how beautiful you are?"

She hadn't thought about it in a long time. Her whole life was spent inside her head, her intellect so much more important than anything else about her. It still was. Her mind was a gift, but it was good to feel something physical, too. "You make me feel beautiful."

"You are beautiful, love. Inside and out. Don't ever forget it. If there's one thing I can teach you, it's that. And I accept what you're offering. I accept it with gratitude. Now, I want you to shift positions and get on your hands and knees and let me have access to that pretty arse of yours."

He was really going to do it. And now. Somehow she'd thought he would wait a while, play a while, but he was reaching for his small leather bag, pulling out a tube of lube and a...yep, that was an anal plug.

He stepped away into her bathroom and she heard water running.

She shifted and then she really felt vulnerable. She'd only thought she knew what vulnerable meant, but being on her hands and knees, waiting for her lover to shove a piece of plastic up her asshole, was something else entirely.

"Do you know why I want to fuck your arse?" His words floated in from the bathroom.

"Not really."

"Because I want to have you every single way a man can have a woman. I want to know you in every possible way I can. And because it's going to feel like heaven. I'm crazy about your pussy. I promise, I'll fill your pussy up every chance I get, but your sweet arse is going to be my indulgence." His every word was a dark promise. Of pleasure. Of intimacy.

He stepped back in, that plug in his hands. He'd taken off his shirt and shoes, leaving him in nothing but a worn pair of jeans that hung low on his hips. He was a decadent dream Dom.

He sank down into the plush chair she usually read in before she went to bed. He sat back like a king on a throne. "You're a very obedient sub. I can see you're going to make it hard on me. I'll have to find reasons to spank you. I'll do it because there's nothing I'll like more than having you over my lap. That's an idea. Come over here and drape yourself over my lap."

She would have thought that crawling across the floor toward a man would make her feel small, but she imagined herself a sleepy cat. A wild thing in need of attention. His cock was bulging against the denim he wore and his eyes were hot as he watched her move his way. She felt every muscle in her body, every inch of her skin as she crossed the distance between them. Her breasts felt heavy, but it was a good feeling. They were heavy with want she knew would soon be fulfilled.

She felt graceful and sexy as she placed herself across his lap. Between the rough feel of the denim against her belly and the warmth of his hand on her back, she was caught in sensation. The last of the stress and fear of the day seemed to leach from her system, and she was wholly ready to be his, open to the experience he was going to give her.

"Or I could simply slap this arse because it's mine."

She gasped at the sudden pain that wracked through her as he brought his hand down. It was sharp and sent a wave of pure heat roaring across her.

"I'll slap it because I love how hot you look when your cheeks are pink and perfect."

Another smack had her holding on to his leg and gritting her teeth, but she knew what was coming after. The pain and the heat, and then a rush of lust. It shot directly to her core and she was getting wet and ready for him.

He smacked her cheeks again and she realized she could get addicted to this. Owen Shaw might become her drug of choice if she let him.

She gritted her teeth as he continued to spank her. It was a ritual. Grit teeth. Moan. Let the heat sink into her bones. Yearn. Begin again. Over and over he put her through it, punctuating each slap of her flesh with sweet words. He told her how gorgeous she was, how much he wanted her, how he thought about her every minute of the day. The words sank in as much as the physical sensation. Something infinitely warm had opened up inside her.

"You like this," Owen said, his hand moving between her legs.

She forced herself to breath as his fingers brushed against her pussy. It was a light thing, so much less than she needed. And yet she found herself arching against him. "I love it. I've never felt anything like it before."

"And I know you like this. Hold still or I'll stop what I'm doing." His fingers pressed against her pussy, sliding in because she was so damn wet. "I love how hot you get for me."

She'd never been this hot for anyone before. It took everything she had to remain still as he fucked her with his fingers. His thumb came up and rubbed against her clit.

"I want you to come for me. I want you to come all around my fingers and then it's going to be my time. You'll do anything I ask tonight, won't you, my sweet sex toy?"

She would do anything at all for him tonight as long as he kept doing this to her. "Yes, Owen."

"That's what I want to hear." He picked up the pace, fucking his fingers deep inside her pussy and rotating them as he pressed down on her clitoris.

It wasn't more than a few moments before she was clutching his jeans and calling out his name as the orgasm pierced through her.

She was still shaking, coming down from the high when he pulled his fingers out.

"I bet you've never felt this either." There was a deep chuckle to his words and she gasped as he parted the cheeks of her ass. "Hold on, love. It's just a little lube."

And it was cold. She whimpered at the sensation. She'd never played this way before, never even thought she would want to, but she couldn't deny him. Her whole body felt boneless in the wake of her orgasm.

"I love the sounds you make," he said as he started to work the lube in.

She was back to shuddering. The sensation was odd, jangled. It wasn't painful, but she certainly wasn't sure it was pleasure. Pressure hit her when she felt him place the plastic tip to the tight ring of her ass.

"Hold on to me," he said, his voice hoarse.

She did as he asked and realized how relaxed she was. It would be okay. She didn't need to tense up. Becca took a deep breath and let herself feel. She cataloged every sensation, from the cool air on her flesh to how her backside ached in the sweetest way. The plug was opening her up little by little and his cock was rock hard under her belly. One hand held her in place, giving her balance.

"Tell me where you are," he said, the plug rimming her. He pressed in and then pulled out, gently gaining ground.

She was with him. That was all that mattered. "I'm good, Owen. It's not painful. It's a little weird, but I can handle it."

"Good because now that I've seen how pretty it is, I have to have it. I can't wait until it's my cock fucking this pretty hole." His accent had gone deep again.

She'd certainly never thought of an asshole as being pretty, but she was glad he liked hers. He was an outrageous man. From what she could tell the man had no shame when it came to sex, and that was one of the sexiest things about him. And she'd helped him tonight because he obviously did feel shame about other things. She'd hated the guilt in his voice as he'd talked about screwing up at work.

He wasn't thinking about that now. He was here with her. While she found a safe place with him, he was doing the same thing with her. It felt good to be necessary to someone in a personal way. Being with Owen pointed out all her problems with men before. Not a one of them compared to her research. Not a single one, even the man she'd married, had been able to take her out of her head and let her be a woman.

His woman.

He slid the plug in. "That's it. Relax for me. It's not so bad."

It wasn't bad at all. Now that he'd managed to coax it inside her, she wasn't sure what she'd been afraid of. She felt full. "I don't hate it."

"I'm glad to hear that because you're going to wear it for a while. Clench it, love. You need to concentrate to keep it inside. I've got to clean up. I want you to lie on the bed and wait for me. I'm not even close to being done with you yet."

She wasn't close to being done either.

* * * *

Owen washed his hands and looked at himself in the mirror.

Fuck, he didn't recognize himself, and it had nothing to do with what had happened to his memory. He'd looked at himself in the bloody mirror every day. He saw an attractive man who couldn't quite connect to anyone around him.

Not tonight. Tonight, all he could see was a man who hungered. The man in the mirror hungered for something and it wasn't his next glass of Scotch.

It felt good. It felt fucking perfect. She was everything he could want in a woman.

He was lying to her at every single turn.

He dried his hands. It didn't matter. She never had to know. He could handle this and handle her. He didn't have to give her up.

He wouldn't give her up. She was the one good thing that had come out of his pain. He wasn't about to let her go now no matter what Ezra said.

It was okay. He still had time with her.

Time to steal more of her privacy. Time to lie to her.

She didn't deserve any of this.

He opened the door and every single bit of guilt fled because she was lying on the bed, her head tilted off the edge, her gorgeous body draped over the comforter. He had to smile because she was in an awkward position. Sexy, but awkward. It was like she'd tried to center herself on the bed and gotten it wrong. She lay across the bed, but not like she would to sleep. She was parallel to the headboard and her head was slightly off the mattress.

His cock twitched in his jeans and he knew it didn't matter what he'd done before or what he would do after. All that mattered was this moment and this woman. It didn't matter that he didn't deserve her, that he'd lied and cheated to have her. She'd given herself to him and he was going to keep her no matter what.

He stood there for a moment, his eyes taking in every inch of that golden skin. Her tits were perfect. Round and tipped, with ripe pink berries. His palm itched to touch them, to feel that silk under his skin.

"I kept the plug, but that was pretty much hell on earth, Owen. It doesn't want to stay in," she complained. "I had to roll on the bed and I ended up like this. Can you grab my ankles and pull me down so my head isn't falling off the mattress?"

But he could see the possibilities of her position. She was laid out for his enjoyment. He unbuttoned the fly of his jeans and shoved them off his hips, kicking them to the side. He wouldn't need clothes for the rest of the night, either. He was going to spend every second of it skin to skin with her.

Doing disgusting, perverted, glorious things with her. "I like you exactly where you are."

It struck him that he hadn't felt her mouth on his cock. He'd been too eager to get inside her, but he could certainly make up for it now.

Her hair fell in golden brown waves. "You like it? I'm not sure how…" She bit her bottom lip. "You want me to suck you, don't you? You want to shove your cock into my mouth and play with my breasts at the same time. That's why you like it."

211

It was a good thing that she could read his intentions. He couldn't keep her like that forever. She would get woozy, but he could enjoy her for a few moments. "I like it because you're laid out like a feast for me. Are you going to do it, love? Are you going to suck my cock?"

"Yes, Owen. I've been dying to." Her legs slid against one another, like she couldn't help but move.

He crossed the space between them. The bed was at the perfect height. It brought her luscious mouth in line with his cock. "Open for me."

She did as he'd commanded, and he felt the first long lick of her tongue on the underside of his dick. It was enough to make his eyes roll to the back of his head. The position wasn't one he'd been in before, doubted she had either, but she took to it with enthusiasm.

Her tongue rolled over him. It was a tight fit. Her mouth was small, but she managed to work his dick with sweet enthusiasm. He fucked in and out of her mouth, loving the way her teeth scraped against him. Yeah, he didn't mind that tiny bite of pain. There was something primal about having her like this. It wasn't normal or natural, and yet she was giving him everything he desired.

Maybe it was normal and natural to go wherever he wanted as long as he was with her. Topping Becca felt right. He did have something to give her. If he hadn't insisted, she would be in a lab at Huisman working away instead of spread out with a cock halfway down her throat. She would forget that her body needed attention too.

And protection. Something was happening and she had no idea what was coming for her. He would protect her when it all went down. He would stand in front of her and take anything that came her way.

Maybe then she would forgive him.

He let the thought go and reached for her breasts. The position she was in left her whole body open to him. His playground. He cupped her breasts, feeling the nipples against his palms. She continued to work his dick, moaning around him when he tweaked those pretty nipples. He rolled them between his thumbs and forefingers, pinching lightly. Every groan he elicited from her rolled over his cock.

He felt her hands run along the outside of his thighs and he reached for her pussy. He wasn't about to come in her mouth. He wanted inside her pussy too much, but she could get another orgasm out of this. She was so hot, and that plug would make her even tighter than normal. He wouldn't last long. It was imperative to give this woman every second of pleasure he could. He needed to get her addicted to the pleasure he could give her and then maybe they would have a shot at coming out of this together.

Her nails rasped against his thighs when he touched her clit. It was swollen, her pussy soaking wet with her previous orgasm. He could give them to her all night long.

So responsive. She shuddered underneath him as he started to work her clit.

"Give me another one," he commanded.

She squirmed beneath him, her hips catching the rhythm of his hand.

Her mouth sucked at him hard and he wasn't sure how long he could hold out. She felt past good. The sensation was brilliant, like nothing he'd felt before, likely because there was emotion behind this. He'd fucked before. As soon as he'd physically been able, he'd started looking for partners, but those had been nothing but pure sex. This was more. This was what Jax talked about. This was why his brother couldn't keep his hands off River, why he shoved his wife onto a kitchen island and had his way with her. Not because he needed sex. Because he needed her.

Becca's body went stiff and he could feel her arousal coating his fingers. She moaned, the sound purring across his dick as she came again.

He pulled out because his cock was pulsing, ready to go off. He looked down and groaned as he saw her swollen lips and heavily lidded eyes. Sex. She was the picture of sex, of a woman who was well taken care of.

It was okay to take care of himself now. Owen tore open the condom and rolled it on. He stalked around the bed. It was okay that it was small now. Oh, when he had to curl himself around her to sleep…well, he would be okay with it then, too. He reached out and gripped her ankles, pulling her toward him. A gasp came from her throat, but she was utterly submissive as he spread her legs. He was too far gone to properly enjoy the sight. Nothing mattered except getting inside her.

He thrust in hard. She was tight but also incredibly wet and ready for him. The plug. God, the plug was a hard drag against his cock.

"I feel so full." Her voice came out on a dreamy sigh.

He could fill her up. He could do it every damn night of his life. "You feel like heaven."

He pressed up into her, loving how her eyes widened when he joined them fully. He was as deep as he could go, his balls rubbing against her. Damn but this was where he always wanted to be now. The world fell away when he was with her. He could be the Owen he wanted to be, not the one who'd fucked up in the past or the one who couldn't seem to find a future, but Becca's Owen. He could be the man who took care of her, who protected and sheltered her.

He set a brutal pace, his heart pounding in time with his cock. It was too good to last. She tightened around him and called out his name, and it sent him right over the edge.

He poured himself into her, fucking up inside her again and again until he had nothing left.

He fell on top of her, giving her his full weight. Her arms came around him.

Sometimes she was the one who sheltered him. That felt good, too.

"Owen, I lost the plug," she whispered in his ear. "That's okay, right? I couldn't clench when you were doing all that stuff to me."

Oh, he was okay with it.

He kissed her neck. "It just means we start all over again, love."

Starting over seemed like a perfect thing to do.

Chapter Fourteen

"Why the hell is there a massive castle in the middle of Toronto?" Owen asked, glancing around the balcony at the grounds below. It was another gloriously beautiful day, with powder blue skies and fluffy white clouds that made a stunning contrast to the vivid green of the gardens below.

And the ultra-modern buildings all around them. He would have expected this gothic mansion in the middle of London, but not here.

Becca stared out at the fountain and the large trees. "It was built by Sir Henry Pellatt before World War I. He was the financier who brought electricity to the city."

She said the words but there was a distance to her tone. He hated that.

He moved in, putting his hands on her shoulders. "If you're nervous about this, we can leave right now. I promise we can figure out who sent that note to you without having to face him or her down."

He wasn't particularly happy about this mission of hers, but he'd seen the stubborn gleam in her eyes when she'd asked him to go with her. The fact that she'd asked him and not simply gone off on her own had made him reluctant to argue with her.

Still, he wished they were here to do nothing more than take the place in like the tourists milling all around them.

"I think this place is cool. I've been here all morning, and you

215

should go down to the stables. They were the first thing Pellatt built, and during World War II, they were used to conceal Canada's research for sonar devices that could detect U-boats," a voice only he could hear said.

He touched his earpiece, the one he'd concealed even from Becca, and wished Robert wasn't listening in. It was one more betrayal, but he couldn't help it this time. If this was some kind of trap Levi Green had set, he couldn't be here without backup. Becca hadn't questioned the small device in his left ear, so he was fairly certain she hadn't noticed it.

"Well, I've seen nothing of any interest," a deeper voice said. Sasha was here as well. They'd decided Becca wouldn't recognize him when he wasn't wearing his janitorial uniform. He was walking the grounds with a camera. Sasha would be the one on the third floor when the time came.

"I have to do this." Becca had turned and stared up at him.

It was hard having two completely separate conversations going on. Becca had zero idea he had another one going on in his ear, and she would likely be pissed as hell at him for bringing in his crew. He focused on her as Sasha and Robert argued in his ear about how interesting this place was. "You don't. I told you I'll handle this."

"If this is a whistle-blower, then I need to be strong enough to face whoever it is," she said resolutely.

They'd had this argument over breakfast. She had a theory that whoever had anonymously left the note requesting her meeting here was some kind of whistle-blower who'd discovered something nefarious going on at Huisman. There was definitely something going on, but he wasn't at all sure they were dealing with a person of good intent. "Why not simply come into your office and tell you what they need to say? Why all the subterfuge?"

She glanced down at her watch. She'd been doing it all morning. Only ten minutes to go. He'd convinced her they shouldn't simply stand around at the meet-up spot.

"Because whoever this is, he or she is afraid," Becca replied. "It's the only explanation."

He could come up with another couple of explanations, none of them good. "They posed it as a riddle. A person who was scared wouldn't want to confuse you."

She waved off the argument. "It's a little dramatic, but it was easy enough to figure out. A million dollars is missing, Owen. What if someone from one of the other teams is siphoning money off my accounts and hoping I wouldn't notice? I do have one of the biggest budgets at Huisman, and I'm not known for being that great about keeping up with spending."

"Because you're a brilliant brat and people throw money at you all the time." He'd definitely learned that about her. She was one of the single most sought after researchers in the world. He'd seen all the events she turned down, the numerous speaking engagements and offers to host her at various universities and hospitals around the world.

"The money isn't important."

"You can say that because you've always had it," he replied, his stomach clenching at the sensation of being hungry. It wasn't so much a visual memory that stroked across his brain but rather a feeling of pure guilt that came from knowing his mum was hungry while he and his sister were eating. He could feel himself pushing a plate toward her, trying to get her to take his portion because he would get food at school.

"Are you okay?" Her hands were suddenly on either side of his cheek. "You went pale."

Something was definitely happening in his brain. The sensations came more and more often, that feeling of déjà vu that had started to make up his memory. Or rather replace it. He couldn't trust it.

"I'm fine," he replied. "And we're going to have to work to help you pay closer attention to detail so this can't ever happen to you again. Phoebe told me she'll have something for us by the end of next week. She thinks she can figure out where the money went. She might not be able to give us a definitive who, but she'll point us to where we should look." Another lie. He was piling them on. He'd lied to her about work just this morning, saying it was his day off. He didn't bother to tell her she *was* his work. "And that's an excellent reason we don't need to be here."

A stubborn look hit her face, and he knew he wasn't going to win this. "I want to look this person in the face and let them know I'm here to help. I'm not afraid. If someone thinks they can get away with this by stealing from my funds, I have to handle it. I'm already going to have to deal with Paul, and that's not going to be a fun conversation."

Yes, he was interested in Paul Huisman. Huisman had met with Levi Green. Green had disappeared after that first day, but that didn't mean he was gone. Showing up in front of the Huisman building felt like an announcement of intent to him. The question was what was his intent. The fact that they hadn't managed to find Green again meant the game was definitely afoot.

He really hated Levi Green.

"This would be an excellent time to feel out her relationship with Huisman," Robert pointed out, his voice coming through loud and clear over the earpiece.

It was a reminder that he hadn't done that before now. He should have pressed her for information over the last couple of days, but he'd been too busy making her scream out his name to gather useful intel. He slid his hand into hers as they started to walk back into the majestic house. "Do you think he could have anything at all to do with this?"

"Why would he?" Her arm rubbed against his as she walked close to him. "He's rich all on his own. The Huisman family is incredibly wealthy. He lives in this massive house, and here in the city that means something."

"For some people there is never enough money," Sasha said. "By the way, I'm in position. You've got five minutes to the meet. I'm in a good place. She can't see me, but I should be able to hear, and that means you should as well."

It was good to know they were ready. He wasn't. He wasn't at all ready to step back and let her walk into this without him right at her side. "Does he like you?"

"I wouldn't say like," she admitted. "I think he respects me. At least my research. He's always picking at me about how I run the team. He thinks I'm sloppy about admin duties, but then we all know he's right."

It wouldn't matter if she could do what she said she would, but it was something a man like Huisman might use if he wanted to get rid of her. "Would you consider yourself rivals?"

"We don't work on the same things." She followed him as they rounded the corner and found the stairs that led up to the third floor.

"I thought you both were neurologists."

"We are, but we're working on different things." She frowned as she moved up the stairs. "Okay, so it's pretty close when you think

218

about it. We're working on the same group of diseases, but our approaches are different, if that makes sense. Our focuses are different. He thinks he can solve the problem purely with drug therapy. There's a reason we keep our projects separate but we share a lot of the same funding. I use occupational therapies as well because the human body is an amazing thing. Especially the brain. Often if you give it the right stimulation it can heal itself."

"Was he upset when you were put at the head of the department?"

"Yes, but we both know why they did it. The Huisman name is already on the foundation doors. They wanted my name to help bring in donors," she explained. "I get the foundation a lot of attention."

"I find it interesting that she is a...how do you say...rock star in this world and yet she does not tour," Sasha mused. "She hasn't left Canada for anything but to go home and visit her family in two years. It's odd. Most of the doctors around the building travel a lot. There are rumors that she's afraid of flying. There's always gossip about her."

Yes, he was sure there was plenty of gossip about the young rock star of a neurologist.

"So you're kind of the face of the foundation?" He was interested in why she didn't travel. From what he could tell before that summer with McDonald, she'd traveled quite a bit. At least four or five times a year, and to fairly exotic locales.

"Not really," she admitted. "I think that might be one of the reasons they hired me, but I want to work on my research. A few years back I got way too invested in being...I don't know what the word is...celebrated, maybe. When I was fresh out of med school, I worked on a project that led to a new therapy for stroke patients. It kind of made me a celebrity in the medical world. I got a little lost in that."

"I'm afraid I don't understand what you mean." He knew exactly what she meant, but he was supposed to be a bodyguard, not an operative who'd studied up on her.

"There are a lot of opportunities out there." There was a hesitance to her tone that let him know she was reluctant to talk about this. They reached the top of the stairs and she moved to the side. "There are conferences and retreats. You get invited to work with various projects. They pay for everything and treat you like a celebrity. It's easy to let that go to your head if you're not careful. I lost myself in it for a few years. My ex-husband and I would go all over the world. He would come with me most of the time, and he made a lot of connections that way. When we divorced, I decided it was taking the focus off my own research, so now I'm staying put for a while."

"She stopped traveling after she left McDonald's project," Robert whispered in his ear.

A lot had happened around that time. He thought it went deeper than merely a job going wrong or her husband cheating on her, but he couldn't push her on it. He needed to figure out how to get her talking about her time with McDonald, but he couldn't ask her outright. He would get her in bed and figure something out. She was more open when she was naked and sated. He would push her about her past projects and see where it led.

"There she is. The duchess." Becca turned her face up to him. "You can't be too close or they won't come talk to me."

He nodded and she stepped away, walking to her right. The third floor of Casa Loma served as the Regimental Museum for the Queen's Own Rifles of Canada. There were portraits and displays all along the hallway that led to the stairs. It hadn't been difficult to figure out where the "duchess" resided. A quick Internet search had brought up the fact that HRH the Duchess of Cornwall, Camilla Parker Bowles, was the colonel-in-chief for the regiment, and a large portrait of her was displayed at the end of the hall.

Becca moved toward that portrait. She stopped briefly at a couple of the paintings of the military men who'd served the regiment.

"She's not very good at this," Sasha said.

Owen looked down the hall and sure enough there was the big guy at the edge of the balcony overlooking the floors below. He *was* good at "this." If Owen hadn't known who he was, he would think the man was nothing more than a tourist taking photos of Casa Loma. He had a professional-looking camera, and he moved around as though trying to get exactly the right shot.

"I'm in place," Robert said. "And Jax and Ezra are monitoring the security cameras in case Green shows up. Relax, Owen. He won't nab her here, and we might have a better idea of what he's planning."

He wished he could calm down. He would feel better once he'd gotten Becca talking about her time with McDonald. It might slip out where she'd stashed the box McDonald had sent her, or he might find out she'd gotten rid of the damn thing. He actually wouldn't mind that being the outcome. He wanted to clear her name and make it obvious to everyone that she had nothing to do with McDonald and couldn't be used for her knowledge because she didn't have any.

Maybe then he would breathe easy.

He forced himself to move into the rooms that housed the exhibits. He wouldn't be able to watch her, but he had eyes on her. And there were plenty of weapons. He'd walked into a whole room filled with antique weapons dating back to World War One. They wouldn't be functional to shoot with, but a couple of them had actual bayonets, and he wouldn't mind a good skewering if Levi Green was the one being skewered.

Robert was in the adjoining room. He nodded Owen's way. From where Robert was standing, it appeared he could see out but Becca wouldn't be able to see in.

She was safe. As safe as he could possibly make her.

"Have we considered the fact that Green might make the same play he did with River?" Robert asked when he got close enough they could speak quietly. It was odd to hear the conversation both with his actual ear and through the earpiece.

"We should be able to hear the conversation. If it starts to go bad, I'll move in." He'd thought about this. It had kept him up half the night wondering how he would handle it if she found out he was lying.

"She's in position, but there's a woman standing in front of the portrait. Sasha, play it cool. We can take her picture off CCTV. Are those working?" Robert asked quietly.

They were alone in the exhibit room, but a few people were milling about in the hall outside.

"We've got a good view." Jax's voice came over the line. "I'll pull stills off the feed of everyone she comes in contact with. It looks like she's having a conversation with the other tourist."

They went still because he'd planted a bug on Becca's handbag so they could hear the meeting.

"I like her suit," an unfamiliar voice said. "It's fitting somehow."

"I was thinking it was a bit dour," Becca replied.

"I don't know. It kind of fits with the whole colonel-in-chief thing." He could practically hear the shrug in the woman's voice. "The British are an odd lot. Of course where I originally come from the politics are even weirder and much more deadly. Our president is practically a king, so I think it's good to be Canadian. Oh, I'm so sorry. I didn't mean to bump into you. I'm a klutz."

"I'm all right," Becca said. "No harm done."

He wanted to see what was going on.

Robert held out a hand. "She's fine. The other woman stumbled a little. She's in incredibly high heels."

"We have another problem," Jax said. "I didn't catch him when he came in. I'm sorry. This place is huge and there are a ton of cameras to watch. He's a tenacious asshole."

Fuck. Green was here. He'd known it would happen and he still wasn't ready for it. His first instinct was to haul Becca into his arms and run with her.

"Green?" Robert asked.

He could hear the woman Becca had been talking to wish her a good day.

"No, and there's a reason for that," Jax said. "Ezra was informed a couple of minutes ago that Green is at CSIS."

Canadian Security Intelligence Service, the closest thing Canada had to the CIA. Was he checking in or something more nefarious?

"Carter?" Becca sounded surprised.

It appeared the whistle-blower had shown up, and it wasn't at all who they'd expected. Carter Adams was here, and it looked like he had something to say. Well, there was a reason he'd been following her all week.

Owen started to go out, to help her. He wasn't leaving her alone with a man who obviously had an ax to grind.

Robert held out a hand.

And then Carter said something that had Owen standing still, his whole soul in complete shock.

* * * *

"Oh, I'm so sorry. I didn't mean to bump into you. I'm a klutz." The pretty woman with the long black hair who'd teased her about the difference between Canadian and Chinese politics had bumped into her, and naturally she'd dropped her bag.

The lady in the insanely high heels knelt down, grabbing the bag before everything could fall out of it. Becca only had to reach for her keys and the protein bar she kept around but never quite convinced herself to eat.

The woman handed her back the bag and wished her a nice day before walking off.

She was alone again. Owen was wandering around somewhere, and she was waiting here like a spy or something. Was he right? Owen thought this was pretty crazy, but she couldn't let it go. She couldn't get rid of the feeling that something was wrong.

Except for the night when Owen had made her feel like a sex goddess. She'd learned that even incredibly awkward positions could be made superhot when she found the right partner.

Her backside still ached from where he'd spanked her. After she'd lost the plug, he'd started everything over again, though the second time he'd taken her to the shower. He'd cleaned her up and then proceeded to get her dirty as hell all over again.

She was going to let him do it. She was going to let him have her in a way no one else had and she was shocked that it was something she was looking forward to.

She glanced around. Was she going to stand here all afternoon? She needed to be back at the office, writing up the latest round of test results, but no she was here playing the spy because she couldn't let it go. It was something she needed to deal with because her control issues were becoming a problem.

And she'd recently discovered that giving up control could be a good thing.

Another ten minutes and she would go find Owen and put this all firmly in his hands. She would go back to work and wait for him to figure this thing out.

She glanced over at the stairs and wished she'd come here for the right reasons. The place was incredible, and she would love to learn more about the history of it. Next week she was taking the whole weekend off and she was going to explore this city with her new boyfriend.

A familiar face came into view.

What the hell was Carter doing here? She felt her eyes widen at the sight of him as she settled her tote back over her shoulder. Now she realized her crappy choice of accessories wasn't the worst thing that had happened to her today. Carter was here. He'd obviously come straight from work. He was in his normal uniform of pressed slacks, a button-down he'd buttoned up, and shiny loafers. She'd avoided him all week, but it looked like she couldn't now. He looked up and down the hall and his stare found hers. He turned and there was no doubt in her mind that he wasn't surprised to see her.

"You sent the message." She tried to wrap her head around any other explanation for why he was here. He didn't have anything to do with accounting and he could easily have dropped all the drama and had this conversation with her anywhere else. They lived in the same building. No one would have listened in on them there.

"I didn't send you anything." He stared at her, his arms crossed over his chest. "But I did need to talk to you away from the office. I've been trying to have this conversation for a solid week, but you're always with that ape-man boyfriend of yours. I decided this place is crowded enough to risk it. I doubt that asshole will try anything in public. One of the interns overheard you talking about being here this afternoon."

Damn it. She'd talked to Owen on her cell phone this morning. She remembered one of the interns being in the room at the time. This was why she wasn't a spy.

"Did you think you could get away with it?" Carter asked in a cold tone.

"With what?"

His eyes narrowed. "I know you're planning on getting rid of me. God, and to think I believed you could be the one woman in the world for me."

"I thought that was some woman in nephrology." He'd mentioned that he'd grown disillusioned with a woman.

"I lied. It was always you," he returned. "I'm embarrassed to say it now, but from the moment I heard you were coming to the foundation, I thought we could have something special. You have a great mind and I have all the resources to make you even greater. We could have made an excellent team. We *did* make an excellent team."

"I never gave you any reason to believe we could be more than friends, and this is an inappropriate conversation. I need you to leave." Why had she told Owen to stay away? She wasn't comfortable with Carter. The hallway was public, but there was only one tall man in a ballcap at the end of the balcony railing. He was taking pictures and paying absolutely no attention to the drama playing out behind him. Owen was back in the exhibits waiting for her to come for him.

"Of course you did, but then that's what women like you do," Carter hissed. "You get what you want out of a guy like me and then go find some asshole with muscles to fuck."

She wasn't going to let him do this to her. He'd obviously set this up. She didn't completely understand why, but he hated her deep down. "I'll be having a talk with the foundation human resources when I get back to the office. Don't bother me again."

He leaned toward her, his voice a quiet snarl. "I'll have a talk with them, too. I'll have a long talk with them about Project Tabula Rasa."

The words stopped her in her tracks. Tabula Rasa. It was Latin for blank slate. She forced herself to turn. Tabula Rasa was what Hope McDonald had privately called her work. It was a nickname and not anything that would have been on her formal files or the work she might have tried to publish about it. McDonald had been working for a pharmaceutical company at one of their European labs at the time. "What about Tabula Rasa?"

The project had taken place in the lab she'd run from and sworn to never go back to. The universe seemed intent on reminding her of that terrible day.

He stared at her for a moment and then something dawned over his face. It was as though he'd figured something out, some puzzle piece falling into place. "Well, now who holds the cards? I know about what you did when you worked with Hope McDonald. They kept it quiet, but I know what she was really working on."

"She was working on memory function," Becca replied. McDonald had been creepy and a little weird, but she hadn't been the problem. Her staff, on the other hand… She wouldn't think about it. Dr. McDonald had been almost worshipful of her patients, especially the ex-military ones.

"She was working on how to erase memory," Carter said. "And you helped her."

Heat flashed through her. It had always been there, the idea that McDonald wasn't what she seemed. Hadn't that asshole told her that?

You've got no idea what's really happening here, do you? They say you're so smart, but you can't see what's right in front of your face. Let's see if you're good for anything at all…

225

"I helped her with her research and her research was all about restoring memory. She did an enormous amount of good for soldiers with retrograde memory loss. She was dedicated to them." The whole McDonald family had been about service. Hope McDonald had specialized in helping soldiers with brain injuries and memory loss. Her father had been a senator serving on the Armed Forces committee, and her sister Faith worked with various medical charities in Third World countries. Hope and her father were gone now, but they'd done their part to help. "You should think before you start trying to ruin the reputations of people who aren't here to defend themselves. But I am, and I'd like to know exactly what you're accusing me of, Carter."

"I bet you would." An infuriatingly smug smile appeared on his face. "I think the ethics board at Huisman would be interested in your part of that project."

"My part was to help her understand how plaque is formed and new ways to destroy it," she shot back. She had no idea what he was talking about. He was playing a game. He couldn't possibly know something about the project that she didn't.

"How are you going to explain what you did to Tomas?"

She shook her head. "Tomas?" A memory flashed across her brain, a vision of a handsome young man with sandy blond hair and blue eyes that held his pain. "Tomas Miller? He had long-term memory loss brought on by a combination of injury and PTSD. He was a patient of Dr. McDonald's. I treated him for a few weeks. I couldn't manage to make any headway with him. It was a frustrating case. What does he have to do with anything?"

"So much, but it's obvious you're going to play the innocent. Think about that before you try to get me fired. I know things about you. Things that could kill your career. I think we'll have to talk about this again. Privately," he said, a leer in his eyes. "I have a much better hand than I thought I did. I'll see you back at the office."

He turned on his heels and walked away.

What the hell had just happened?

She forced herself to take a deep breath. She wasn't going to talk to Owen about this. It was lucky that he hadn't seen Carter here. He already didn't like the man, and she wasn't going to give him an excuse to go after him. Owen could get in trouble if they got into a fight.

Then there was the fact that she didn't want to ever talk to Owen about what a coward she'd been. He never had to know. It was one of the great things about dating a man who wasn't in the business. He wouldn't know to ask why she'd left such a prestigious position.

He didn't have to know that she'd run and never looked back until yesterday.

Except Carter seemed to know something. Who had he talked to? There were plenty of people who knew about the project, but not many who'd known what McDonald had called it. She'd been a bit paranoid about her research. She'd thought someone was watching and waiting to steal it. It was over the top, but Becca had written it off as the doctor had been in the corporate jungle for far too long.

Tomas. Guilt rose hard and overwhelming when she thought about the man. He'd needed her help and she'd failed him. She'd thought she might be getting somewhere with him when the incident had happened and she'd left. She'd left him behind. He was alive out there somewhere, but why would he talk to Carter about her? Could he even have remembered her? His retrograde memory loss was one of the worst she'd ever seen. Tomas could forget the previous day.

She would never forget the hollow look in his eyes, like he knew his whole world was right there but he couldn't touch it. McDonald have been so devoted to helping him. She'd brought him into the lab many times, escorting him herself.

Did Tomas miss Hope McDonald? Or had he utterly forgotten the doctor who'd tried to help him.

She should have looked him up. She shouldn't have let fear lead her when a patient might need her. Who had taken over his care after McDonald died?

She stood there because she wasn't sure how she would react when Owen questioned her. And he would question her.

What had happened to all of McDonald's patients?

Bile rose in her throat. She'd wanted to never have to think about that summer again, but it looked like she couldn't help it.

She had to figure out what Carter thought he had on her. What unethical thing had she done? And how did this have anything at all to do with the missing money?

"Rebecca?"

She turned and Owen was standing there. It took everything she had not to walk into his arms. Owen looked big and safe and she wanted him to hug her, but there was something about his stance that made her hold off. He seemed to be in full-on bodyguard mode, and it put a coldness in his eyes. "Yes?"

"It's been longer than we agreed on," he said, glancing around as though looking for a threat.

She'd already met the threat and it was time to go and figure out what the hell was going on. "I'm sorry I wasted your time."

She couldn't tell him about Carter. Not yet. She needed more information. But she also needed him. Her hand was shaking so she held it out.

He stared down at it for a moment and she had the most horrible fear that he wouldn't take it.

The expression on his face cleared and his hand encompassed hers. "I'll take you back to work."

She wanted to ask him what had put that dark look on his face, but it might open up questions she didn't want to answer right now.

"I think I should probably work late tonight." She needed to do some research. It might be time to face those months of her life and what had happened during them. But she couldn't do that with a building filled with curious doctors. Gossip had already bitten her in the ass once today.

She expected an argument from him. Earlier, she'd promised him she would be home for dinner every night so they could spend sweet time together. He'd made it plain that he wanted attention, and she had been more than willing to give it to him.

"I think I need to work late myself," was all he said.

They walked down the stairs, utterly silent.

Chapter Fifteen

Owen sat in Ezra's bare bones apartment and tried to let everything that had happened sink in.

Tomas. She'd not only known that name, she'd admitted to treating him. He'd known she'd been there at the same lab as McDonald. He'd even sort of known they'd likely collaborated, but he finally understood she'd been working on the same project. Rebecca Walsh had aided in developing the drug that had wiped out his memory. The one that had turned him into a blank slate.

Tabula Rasa.

"I don't remember her, but that's not shocking." Theo Taggart was staring down at the photograph they had of her. At both of them. The doctor and the woman who played superhero for little kids. Both photos showed a gorgeous woman. He wished they had a picture of the woman who lied, who worked with monsters.

Erin stood beside her husband, a hand on his back as she looked to Ezra. "You're saying Dr. Walsh treated Theo? Why would McDonald have brought him out into the open like that? Why would she risk it?"

"Theo was the anomaly," Robert replied. "The drug didn't work on him the way it did the rest of us. He was always able to fight it better than anyone else. She might have been trying to figure out what went wrong. Dr. Walsh was known for being able to figure out the complexities of drug interactions, especially when it came to memory function."

"I don't remember any of it," Theo admitted. "But this was during a time when she was regularly dosing me. Even if I remembered something one day, I would forget it the next. I've gotten a lot of my memory back but it's almost all from before I met McDonald. I don't even remember how I got shot. I don't remember moving into our house. I sure as hell don't remember a couple of appointments at a lab."

Erin's hand ran up and down her husband's back. "It's okay. I'll let you do all the work for the new nursery. And I've been meaning to replace that horrible recliner of yours. We'll get all new living room furniture and skip on the delivery. You can shove it all in the back of Case's truck. It'll be exactly like when we moved in."

Theo turned and stared down at her. "I remember the first time I kissed you. And I remember the first time I spanked your pretty ass. I can recreate that, too, my sarcastic love."

But he was smiling. Erin had done her job and she winked her husband's way before turning back to the group. "So now we think Dr. Walsh is the bad guy?"

The bad guy. The evil doctor. Or rather assistant evil doctor.

Could she have not known? How could she have not understood what was happening? All he knew was if she'd had an inkling of what was going on behind Dr. McDonald's project, she hadn't mentioned it. "What do we know about the lab she was at?"

Ezra had his laptop up. "McDonald was in and out at the time. This was in the months before Kronberg shut her down and she went on the run. Naturally they kept it all quiet. They announced that Dr. McDonald was leaving to pursue other opportunities. The last thing they wanted was the world to know who McDonald was. It could have opened them up to lawsuits. Hell, even her death was covered up. The papers announced it as an accident and said nothing else."

"Given the time period, I would have thought we were in Argentina, not Germany," Theo said.

Ariel walked in with two mugs of tea in her hand. She placed one in front of Robert, her hand briefly touching his shoulder before she sank into the seat beside him. "She had the Argentine base long before she was forced out of Kronberg. Her father had been funding those portions of her research. Are you certain you heard correctly? I have a hard time believing Dr. Walsh knew what exactly was going on."

He did, too, but it was obvious she'd known something and she'd said not a word. "I know what I heard. Sasha sent Jax a digital recording before he went to work at the foundation. You can listen to it yourself. She states plainly that Theo was a patient."

"No, she said Tomas was a patient," Robert pointed out. "She likely had no idea he wasn't exactly who McDonald said he was."

"There's an easy way to figure this out," Erin said. "Theo and I walk into the foundation."

"And see what happens? See how she reacts?" Ezra nodded. "That could work."

Erin moved out from behind her husband. "You didn't let me finish. Theo and I walk into the foundation, put a gun to her head and tell her to talk or we'll blow it off. She's a brain surgeon and all that. I think she'll know what happens to the old brain pan when a bullet hits it."

Ezra stared at Theo. "Your brother puts up with this, why?"

"Big Tag loves me," Erin said, pulling out a chair. "Okay, how about we consider calling her and setting up a meeting. We say Theo is still Tomas and would like to talk to the doc who helped him years ago."

"We don't know how deep into this she is." Owen felt the need to take the lead in this. He'd been the idiot to push them all to trust her. It was definitely time to take a long step back. "If she knew what was going on, this could tip her off and she could run."

Ariel set down her tea, a look of concern on her face. "Owen, she could have known absolutely nothing about the true nature of McDonald's research. You have to remember that Hope McDonald was a sociopath, and a brilliant one at that. She was excellent at covering her tracks."

"You said she left early," he pointed out. "I happen to know Rebecca Walsh doesn't walk away from anything early. She gets the job done. She walked out for some reason. She knew something and she didn't bother to get the word out. Have you considered that if she'd reported McDonald, none of what we went through afterward would have happened?"

Theo would have come home years before he had. Jax and Tucker, Dante and Sasha wouldn't have been forced to commit crimes. Robert wouldn't have suffered. Theo would have been home for the birth of his son.

His mum and sister would be alive. He would have his memory. He would still have a bloody home. He would never have betrayed his team.

Theo stared across the table at him. "You can't go down that road. Believe me, I understand. I think all the time about the things I could have done, but we can't go back. We can go forward, and right now that means trying to figure out what's going on."

It was easy for Theo to say that since he had a family who loved him and a home. He could have pride in himself.

Ezra sat back. "I listened to the tape Sasha sent. First of all, I want to know how Carter knows what he does. If he's been talking to someone, I'd like to know who that is. It's obvious this wasn't as well buried as we thought it was. I didn't even know she'd called it Project Tabula Rasa."

Theo shrugged. "I can put a call into Ian and Case. No one knows more about McDonald than my brothers, perhaps with the singular exception of my sister-in-law. Mia's been dying to write the whole thing as a tell-all. So far Case has managed to keep her under control because of the whole classified-material thing, but she's never stopped researching. If this Carter guy has a connection to McDonald, she might know about it."

"I don't see how." Owen had gained a lot of knowledge on Carter Adams. "He's been working at Huisman for the last six years. He's never been out of the country. He's spectacularly ordinary. But I definitely think we should look into any possible connections between Carter and McDonald. Sasha and Dante are going to search her office again. They can't get into her lab. No one is allowed in there, and I'm starting to worry we need to. Apparently her private office in the lab is protected with biometrics. We would need a retinal scan to get in."

"I can get that for us," Erin said with a savage grin.

He stared back at her. "Don't touch her. I'm still the man in charge of handling her and not a one of us is going to physically harm her."

"I always knew you were soft, Shaw," Erin said, sitting back. "So what did she say to you about Carter showing up? How did she react?"

There was a knot in his gut that twisted at her words. "She didn't say a word about it. She told me no one showed up. I was supposed to stay in the back of the museum. She has no idea I was listening in the whole time."

She'd lied directly to him, and when he'd prodded her, she'd lied some more. Of course he was lying to her as well, but he had his reasons. What were hers? Was she covering up the fact that she'd helped to develop one of the most dangerous drugs in the world?

"I listened in with Ezra," Ariel began. "If I had to guess, I would say she was afraid and confused. I would like to see the CCTV footage. If I could read her body language that might help enormously. Jax is supposed to be getting it to us soon."

"Who is still at the foundation this afternoon?" He needed to keep eyes on her. He should have stayed and staked out the foundation building, but Ezra had wanted a report. "I'm supposed to pick her up at eight, but I don't trust her not to leave the building without me. Not anymore, I don't."

"Tucker is there along with Dante and Sasha. Sasha's on night duty. Dante gets off at six along with Tucker." Robert's arm moved casually around the back of Ariel's chair and it made Owen wonder if the last few days had gone well for those two. Or he would wonder it if his own misery wasn't twisting his soul. "Dante's staying after his shift so he can get some pictures and video footage of the labs. It might take some time, but I can't imagine Chelsea and Hutch can't figure out a way around those biometrics."

How much time did they have? It felt like a net was tightening around them.

"I'm going to text Tucker and ask him to stay late, too." He pulled out his mobile. "I want to know where she is at all times. Have we figured out why Green paid a visit to Canadian intelligence?" He quickly texted Tucker.

"I don't like it," Ezra admitted. "Something's happening and I can't see it."

The door came open and Jax rushed in, a piece of paper in his hand. "Guys, you need to see this. I pulled some stills from the CCTV at the museum and Sasha got a couple of pictures, too. He told me he was suspicious of the woman who bumped into Becca."

"I couldn't see her." Owen looked down at the picture. Jax had blown up a shot of the woman's face. She was stunning, her beauty more obvious than Becca's subtle loveliness. "Did you find a name?"

"Yes," Jax said, his voice steady, but there was tension to it. "She's

233

here under a Chinese passport as Zhang Li Na. She lives in Quebec and surprise surprise, the condo she lives in is owned by Jean Claude Huisman."

Ezra frowned. "That's awfully coincidental. And Becca didn't seem to know her?"

A nasty feeling took root in Owen's gut. "What else, Jax? There's something else."

"Her real name is Zhao Mo Chou and she's MSS, according to Adam," Jax said.

The room erupted in discussion about the new information. Before he could start asking his own questions, a text came through from Tucker.

Will do, but something's going on. I overheard someone talking about security shutting down some doctor's access. I think it might be our girl. Any thoughts?

Any thoughts? It all fell into place.

"He's going to arrest her," Owen said, adrenaline starting to pump through his body. "Green set her up. He went to Canadian intelligence so they'll facilitate handing her over to the US. I don't know what's going on with the money, but I know that Green is going to use it. He's the one who drew her out today, and it was all to get a picture of her with a known Chinese operative."

Ezra stood up, cursing under his breath. "He'll have her accused of selling secrets to the Chinese, and I'm sure Levi has offered the Canadians anything they like if they'll turn her over quietly. He can take her anywhere. He will not take her back to the States. I promise you that."

Even though he was blindingly angry, he couldn't let that happen. In his rational brain he told himself it was because if they lost Rebecca, they lost her knowledge and the possibility of ever finding out who the lads really were.

"We have to get her out of the building now," Ezra ordered. "Robert, call Sasha or Dante. They need to take her into custody before Levi walks in that building. Ariel…"

"I'm calling Tucker now," she said, stepping away from the table.

"Owen, go and pack a bag for her," Ezra ordered. "I'll find a place for us to hole up. We're going to have to move and quickly, and assume Green's got eyes on us."

"I'll get us a place," Robert said.

Theo and Erin were on their feet, Erin checking her gun and looking ready for a fight.

Owen moved, following Jax. They would head to the building they lived in and grab their go-bags and River. They were on the run. Again. But this time they would take Becca with them. They would get her out before Green could get his hands on her.

Deep down he knew he couldn't let her go. He couldn't. He could scream at her. He could accuse her. He could punish her.

But he could never let her go. He might never be able to let her go.

* * * *

"Are you sure you don't want me to stay?" Cathy asked, her purse on her shoulder as she stood in the doorway.

"No, I'm fine. I'm going to clear up some paperwork." And make a few calls to some of the doctors she'd worked with on the McDonald project. The ones who were still alive. God, why hadn't that hit her before now? There had been a team of docs working on Tabula Rasa, and most of them were dead. They'd been a fairly young team so the fact that three out of four of them were gone should have tipped her off that something was weird.

She'd had her head up her ass for years when it came to that summer. It was time to start figuring out what had really happened and why so many of those team members were dead.

She'd called the head of Kronberg's research, but she'd been told there had been several changes made to their staff and she would have to wait for a call back. There had been one research assistant, Veronica Croft, a young American interning for the summer. She'd seemed close to...it was hard to think his name. She'd been close to Dr. McDonald's assistant. She might have known something.

How would Carter know what he knew unless he'd been talking to Veronica or one of the others who'd been close to the project?

"Are you sure?" Cathy's voice brought her back to reality. "Did something happen at lunch? You left with a smile on your face and came back...well, you weren't smiling when you came back."

Because her whole world had turned upside down and she wasn't sure where she'd landed. It didn't make sense. How did any of it fit together? She had a long night ahead of her and she still had to figure out how to talk to Owen about all of this. The last thing she needed was Cathy getting involved. "I'm fine. I've just got a headache. Too much caffeine. I'm trying to wrap up this report so I can take the weekend off and spend it with Owen."

That got Cathy's face to light up. "Well, I can't tell you how happy that makes me. He's a charming man. All right, you call me if there's anything at all I can do for you."

She gave Cathy what she hoped was a bright smile. "Have a nice night."

Cathy waved and then turned before bumping into someone. "Oh, hello, Dr. Huisman. Did you need something?"

Becca groaned inwardly. She did not need a confrontation with Paul.

"Not at all," Paul said, sounding more chipper than he usually did. "I was simply coming by to congratulate Dr. Walsh on the latest round of testing. I've heard it's spectacular."

Cathy grinned, her pride showing. "Oh, they're spectacular. Expect our girl to bring in the cash next quarter. She's going to shake up the medical world with this. Maybe we can convince her to travel a little, get out and show her face to the world. She needs to start networking if she's going to win her first Nobel Prize before she's thirty-five."

"Whoa, let's tap the breaks on that." She didn't need more pressure on her.

Paul looked amused as he leaned against her door. "Yes, let's slow down. We have to get the drug and the therapies approved first. We've got a few hurdles before she takes over the world."

Cathy shrugged. "She'll do it. If you don't need anything else, I'll say good night."

Paul nodded her way. "Good night." He turned back to Becca. "I hate to do this to you, but can you stay another hour or so? Maybe two? There's a courier bringing in some legal paperwork and they'll only accept a signature from me or you. I would stay myself, but I need to pick up Emmanuel from school."

"Of course." It wasn't like she hadn't been planning on staying anyway. She glanced up at the clock. It was almost six. "I thought school let out earlier."

She would have sworn there was a surprised look stamped on his handsome face, but it cleared quickly. "Emmanuel stays late to work with a tutor. He's a brilliant child, but he struggles with focus. I've found having him complete his homework in a classroom environment helps."

Sometimes she felt for poor Emmanuel Huisman. He didn't talk much and when he did, he was awkward and seemed too focused for a child his age. Perhaps it was because his father pushed him to be far older than his years. She understood that. "No problem. Homework is important. I was staying late anyway. I have to get through all this data I want to present next week when your father is in town."

He huffed, a sound somewhere between amused and annoyed. "Yes, well, I'm sure my father will be thrilled to see it. I'll let security know you're going to be here in your office."

"Okay," she agreed. "Anything I should be worried about? You said it was legal paperwork."

"Just some cleanup on staffing situations," he replied with an odd smirk. "You know how my father likes to cover the foundation's ass on all fronts. Feel free to look at it if you like, or you can ship it straight on to HR after signing for it. Good night. I hope it's a fun evening for you."

He slipped away before she could say anything else.

And she was left alone with her thoughts, and they weren't all that good. She really did need to work on the report, but the numbers scrambled in front of her.

She should have told Owen what happened. She should have gone to the café at the bottom of the castle and sat with him and told him everything.

Or she should consider the fact that they'd only slept together a couple of times and she was putting a whole lot on him.

No. He cared about her. She felt it. They were together and that meant she couldn't leave him out of important things. She expected him to let her know if he was in trouble because he had to know she would move heaven and earth to fix things for him.

She loved him.

A low groan came from the back of her throat, and she put her head down on her desk. It was stupid. It was everything she'd worried it would be. This was precisely why she'd tried to stay away from the man in the first place. She'd known she would fall for him and hard.

Owen Shaw was her damn knight in shining armor, and she was an idiot if she didn't call him. He probably knew investigators who could handle this. She would pay him back in ridiculously kinky sex and give him all the love and affection he so obviously needed.

She sat up and felt better having made the decision.

She stood up. She needed a cup of coffee and then she would call Owen and ask if they could talk. Maybe she would ask him if he could come up here and sit and wait with her for the courier. Then they could pick up a six-pack and some takeout and talk about all this in bed.

That was what she truly needed, his arms around her. Once she talked this through with him, she would feel better. It had been a mistake to keep it from him.

The floor was quiet as she stepped out of her office. Across the way, she could see the sun starting to sink, the dying light shining off the buildings. The elevator doors opened and she hoped it was security escorting the courier up. If she could get out of here fast, she'd go to Owen's work and surprise him.

Except she wasn't sure where his building was.

A man strode out, his pace nearly a jog. "Dr. Walsh. Dr. Walsh, I need to talk to you."

She froze where she stood because she knew that voice. It sent a chill down her spine. The last time she'd heard that voice had been when the man attached to it had threatened to rape and murder her.

Dr. Reasor. Except Dr. Steven Reasor had died. He died. It had been the only reason she'd felt safe.

"Hi, my name is Tucker and I'm an intern downstairs." He strode her way and his hair was longer than it had been when he'd worked for McDonald, but there was no way to mistake those blue eyes. At first she'd thought he was handsome, but she'd seen how cold those eyes could go. Arctic. Like the coldest winter day.

He was dead. They'd told her he was dead. Dr. McDonald had told her. It had been an accident, and that had been the first time she'd been able to breathe.

He was coming for her. He was saying words, but all she could hear was the ones he'd said that day.

You really should run. Maybe I'll catch you. Maybe I won't. Either way, you should run.

She turned on her heels and took off toward the stairs.

It was pure panic, and it came from PTSD. It came from him turning into the nightmare she had for weeks afterward.

He'd promised if she ever got caught up in his world again, he would come after her. She'd believed him.

Don't think about it. It hadn't been real. It hadn't been real. Couldn't be real.

She ran, screaming out for help. Fear ruled her. It caused her to be irrational, made her see things that weren't there. Probably.

It didn't matter. She had to get to a place where she would be safe. She would call Owen. She would lock herself in a room and call Owen. He would come for her.

She just had to get somewhere safe.

He was shouting behind her, but she didn't stop. She hit the door to the stairwell, her arms slamming into the metal with a hard *thwack*.

He was still behind her. She had to think. She had to know the building better than he did.

How long had he been here? How long had he been stalking her?

Would he take her back to that place she'd gone to? To that hell she'd convinced herself couldn't possibly have been real?

Couldn't go back. Couldn't go back.

The door came open as she rounded the corner and saw a man with dark hair. He wore the uniforms the janitors wore. He was tall and broad, and in that moment, he looked like the best thing she'd ever seen.

"Please help me," she said.

He frowned. "Of course. Are they already here?"

She stumbled coming off the last step and he caught her up in his big arms. "They?"

He set her on her feet. "Yes, the men who are coming for you."

Confusion started to pierce through her fear.

"They're not here yet," that familiar voice said. "But you need to get hands on her because she's running from me, Dante. I have no idea why, but she's running from me."

Steven Reasor was jogging down the stairs. And he was talking to the janitor.

She turned to try to get away, but the man he'd called Dante grabbed her. He pulled her close even as she fought. She brought her elbow up and back and then stomped on his foot. The man didn't move, didn't even grunt.

"Are you fucking serious?" Steven asked as he closed the distance between them. "Do you carry one of those around? Shouldn't we talk to her first?"

Something sharp stung her neck and her vision immediately went fuzzy.

It was happening again. The devil was back and she was going to hell. She wouldn't wake up this time.

"You're going to be okay," he said, looking down at her.

Someone had picked her up. Her legs didn't work anymore. She wasn't going without a fucking fight. She wasn't going into that darkness without letting him know. Hate mingled with fear.

"Fuck you, Reasor. Fuck you."

The last thing she saw were his eyes widening in what looked like shock.

As the darkness clouded her vision she prayed Owen would come for her.

Chapter Sixteen

Becca sat down at the table and stared at the mug in front of her.

"It's not poisoned or anything," her red-haired captor said. "It's Earl Grey. It's all they have. I'm afraid this place isn't well stocked. It's beautiful and remote, but not a lot in ye old pantry, hence the Earl Grey but without milk or sugar. Someone better go find that or we'll have trouble later."

Like she was going to touch anything these people gave her. "Not a problem. I can absolutely get that for you."

"Tough girl," the woman said with a nod. "I didn't expect that."

She'd woken up an hour before to find herself in some kind of prison. From what she could tell she was in a cabin, and they weren't in the city anymore. It was dark outside. She hadn't had the chance to run because the redhead had been there when she'd woken up. She'd been told to do whatever she'd needed to do in the bathroom and then come with the woman.

Now, here she was sitting at a folding table across from a woman she'd never met. A woman who had a gun in a shoulder holster. She wasn't trying to hide the fact. That gun was there as a warning. Or maybe they believed in foreshadowing.

Becca forced the bile down her throat. Her hands were still shaking. "What kind of sedative did he give me?"

"The kind that works," Red shot back, opening a file folder.

"Sorry, I don't know what Dante puts in those things. I'm a little worried that he carries them around. Have you had any problems with serial killers in the last couple of weeks?"

Becca simply stared.

"Too soon? Okay, let's get down to it. My name is Erin and I'll be your interrogator this evening."

She was so not interested in sarcasm. "I'd like to see a badge."

"I bet you would. We made damn sure you wouldn't." Erin sat back. "Would it surprise you to know that there's a warrant out for your arrest? This is a copy of the legal paperwork that would have been shoved through court in order to quickly push your extradition to the States through."

She looked down at the papers. They didn't make a lick of sense. Why would she be arrested? And why would anyone want to extradite her? She wasn't a lawyer, but it looked like she might need one. Lawyer Larry would come in handy now. "I'd like a lawyer. I don't think I should say anything else until I talk to one."

"I'm sure we'll get you an attorney if it comes down to that," she said. "Unfortunately, we're in Canada and I don't know a ton of people in Canada, so we're going to have to work on it. Next time you get in trouble do it in Dallas. Or London. Or New York. Mostly any place but Canada."

"Who are you?" It was obvious this woman wasn't with the police.

"I told you. I'm Erin. I work with a group of former military and intelligence officers who investigate bad shit that happens. Sometimes we work with the Agency. Sometimes the Agency sucks and we find ourselves on opposite sides, like tonight." She slid a photograph across the table. "Have you ever met this man?"

She shook her head, but not in response to the picture. She didn't bother to look at it. "I want to leave this place. I want to make a phone call and have my boyfriend pick me up. I don't know what kind of game you're playing, but I want no part of it."

"I'm sorry for the way we had to bring you in, but if we'd left you there, you would be in police custody right now. That warrant is real. We barely managed to get you out in time. There's nothing on the news yet, but I imagine they'll have to say something at the foundation tomorrow to cover up why you're gone. I'm interested to see how they play that one, but we've had to pull our guys out so we'll hear secondhand."

"Your guys?" She was confused. More than confused. "Look, if you aren't the cops, then I want out of here. I want my phone."

"You're not going to listen to me, are you? I told them it wouldn't work and we would have to bring the big guns in, but do guys ever listen? Nope. Sometimes I think they'll try anything besides a woman's very reasonable suggestion just to try to prove me wrong." Erin's lips curled up. "Yeah, I bet you will, baby."

That was when she realized Erin was wearing a small device in her left ear.

Someone was listening in. A cold chill went across her skin as she glanced around the room. The small room was sparse, with only the table and three chairs to decorate it. Except for the cameras mounted in either corner.

What the hell was going on?

Was Reasor somewhere in this cabin? Was he the one who'd decided to play this game with her? She hadn't woken up the way she had the last time. Whatever he'd given her that night had produced the worst dreams of her life, dreams of never-ending pain and torture. She could still remember the day. Unless…

"How long was I out?" Could she trust anything this woman would say?

"A couple of hours."

"What day is it?"

Erin frowned and managed to look slightly concerned. "It's the same day, Dr. Walsh. It's eleven o'clock on Friday. You didn't lose a day."

Then it had to have been a different sedative since the one Reasor had given her the first time had caused her to forget a whole day. One minute she'd been walking in the cafeteria and then…then she'd had her time in hell.

"All right. Let's start with the basics," Erin said. "Would you like to explain how a little over one million dollars was funneled from your research accounts at Huisman to your charitable organization?"

The bottom threatened to drop out of her stomach. "What?"

Erin flipped a folder around and pointed to what appeared to be copies of bank drafts and a report. She recognized the name. Phoebe Murdoch. Owen's Phoebe. How had they gotten that report? Were they watching Owen, too? Had she gotten him involved in her problems?

"This is a report from a forensic accountant," Erin explained. "She managed to track the funds from the account at Huisman to a Swiss account. Naturally we can't know who owns that account, but I find it interesting that the money was then transferred from that account into the account your charity uses in the form of several large donations."

She was going to be sick.

"Take a deep breath," Erin said. "If you go, I'm sure to go, and I've done my vomit-time today."

She barely managed to keep it down. "I didn't take any money. I sure as hell wouldn't take money from my research account. I need that money."

"Everyone needs money."

"I don't. I have what I need. I don't need to steal."

Erin's shoulders moved up and down in a negligent shrug. "As it so happens, I agree with your assessment. This is a setup. It's been going on for over a year. Do you have any enemies?"

It was a harsh word, and not one she'd ever thought applied to her. "Enemies? Of course not. I'm a doctor."

"Trust me, I've met a doctor who had enemies. I *was* her enemy. She's not here anymore," Erin said, an odd pleasure to her tone.

This was a dangerous woman. A predator. She was probably the kind of woman who worked with a man like Steven Reasor. "You work with him, don't you?"

"I work for a couple of men," she said. "You'll have to be more specific."

"Dr. Reasor." She said his name, forced herself to say his name. "I assume he's why I'm here."

"The Dr. Reasor who worked with Dr. Hope McDonald?"

They were going to dance around the subject? "Yes. I saw him today. Is that why I'm here? He was supposed to be dead."

"How did he die?" Erin asked.

Frustration threatened to well over. "He didn't since he was in my building earlier today."

"Who told you he died?"

She wasn't playing this game. "I'm done. I want to make a call."

"Who are you planning on calling?"

"My boyfriend. He'll come get me." She needed to see Owen.

Tears pierced her eyes and she fought hard not to shed them.

"Are you sure about that? It might be better to leave him out of this," Erin replied. "I've found that bringing men into a situation does nothing but complicate things."

Becca stood up. "Fine. Shoot me, but I'm leaving. I'm not playing this game with you and I won't let that man hurt me again. I won't. Owen will look for me. He's probably looking for me right now, and he's smart and strong. He'll figure out where I am, and then you should watch your back."

A look crossed Erin's face. It almost seemed like sympathy. "Things aren't always as they seem, are they, Dr. Walsh? Remember that."

The door opened and her heart threatened to stop. Owen was here. She didn't even think about it. She threw her arms around him and sobbed. He was here. She was safe. He'd come for her and now he could figure this whole terrible situation out and they could go home.

It took her a moment to realize he wasn't hugging her back. She clung to him and he was simply standing there, his arms at his sides.

She looked up, and his face was an icy mask. "Owen?"

"Dr. Walsh, if you'll take your seat we can continue."

She stepped back, feeling the tears coursing down her cheeks. "I don't understand what's happening."

His voice was as cold as the look in his eyes. "I didn't want to give up my cover, but it's obvious to me you won't cooperate until you realize no one is coming for you. I know you won't believe me, but we saved you earlier today. You might deserve prison, but we won't be the ones to put you there. You have information we need. Cooperate and this will be over soon."

"I don't understand." She didn't seem capable of moving past those words.

He took a seat beside Erin. Like the redhead, he held a file in one hand. He placed it on the table in front of him. "Sit down, please. You won't be allowed to leave. I'm with a group investigating Dr. Hope McDonald."

"You said you were with a security company." The words felt dull in her mouth. She had to force herself to say them. Her whole body felt numb in a way that had nothing to do with the sedative she'd been given.

245

"I am," he admitted. "And I've certainly done bodyguard work before. However, that wasn't the focus of this job."

It was beginning to penetrate her brain. "No, I was the focus."

"Yes," he agreed as though he'd never touched her, never put his mouth on her, never held her all through the night.

He'd done all those things, but now she understood that she'd been a job to him. Nothing more.

She was still sleeping. That was it. This was a dream and she would wake up and Owen would be beside her in bed. She would tell him about the dream and they would laugh. He would make love to her again and she wouldn't go to Casa Loma. She would stay with him.

She would wake up soon.

"Dr. Walsh? Becca?"

She turned to him and sat down. It was okay because this was all a dream and she had to get through it. "Why are you here?"

"Because you worked with a woman named Hope McDonald. Because she was working on a drug that erased memory and acted as a time dilation mechanism. Because Hope McDonald tortured at least fifteen men, ripping their memories and lives from them, and I think you helped her do it."

"Time dilation?" It was a theory, that drugs could trick the brain into thinking more time had passed than had in reality.

If someone was administered a time dilation drug, he or she could be tricked into feeling as though days had passed in a moment's time. Whatever was being done to them under the influence of the drug would seem to go on forever.

Like what had happened to her.

She couldn't stop it now. She wasn't dreaming and she hadn't been back then. It had all been real. What she'd gone through had been real.

Pain flared through her as she hit the floor hard. She crawled to the trash bin in the corner and emptied her stomach.

"Fuck," Erin said before the door opened and slammed closed again.

"Becca? Becca, let me help you." Owen was on his knees beside her.

But she wouldn't accept his help. She wouldn't accept anything from him again.

She was alone, and she had no idea what he was going to do to her.

Becca held on to the trash bin and prayed she made it through the next couple of hours.

* * * *

Owen had never felt so helpless. He tried to touch Becca, wanted to help her, but she shrank back from him.

She'd gone so pale. What had he said that made her go so pale?

You told her everything was a lie, arsehole. You ripped the rug from under her feet and you're surprised she fell?

She looked up at him. "Get out. I don't want you here."

He stared down at her. "Rebecca, you're sick. It could be a reaction to the sedative. I'm sorry about that. He wasn't supposed to do that unless it was absolutely necessary."

"It's not the sedative," she said, her skin pale. "It's being kidnapped. It's finding out you're an asshole. Go away."

"I'll get you a cold rag." Wasn't that what she needed? Nick's wife Hayley was pregnant and he always got her a cold rag when she was feeling sick to her stomach.

He turned and walked out the door, careful to lock it. She was sick, but she was strong, too, and he wouldn't put it past her to try to run.

"I need Tucker," he said. Becca was sick. She needed a doctor and they were three hours away from Toronto. Tucker would have to do.

"He's about fifteen minutes out. I just got off the phone with Sasha and he said there's something wrong with Tucker." Jax glanced up from his laptop. He'd set up in record time. The living area of the cabin they'd rented was covered in high-tech stuff. The minute they'd gotten here, they'd set up security equipment and then the interrogation room where Becca was currently shaking.

He'd made her sick. He'd seen the minute she'd realized he hadn't come for her, that he was the enemy. A light had died in her eyes.

Ezra strode in from the kitchen carrying a can of soda. "Erin wasn't lying about the sympathetic nausea thing. Theo's locked up in the bathroom with her. Where is everyone?"

When they'd realized what Green was planning, they'd scattered. Erin and Theo had gotten the cabin, and along with Jax and River, had gone out to open it up. He and Ezra had gone to the Huisman building to collect Becca. Dante, Sasha, and Tucker had handed her over and

247

then gotten in their own vehicles to throw off anyone who might be following them.

"Robert's driving Ariel and Nina in, but they're about an hour out. Tucker dumped his truck. Dante and Sasha have him. They should be here any minute." Jax stood up, looking at Ezra. "You know we don't have long. Green is going to figure out where we are and he'll come after all of us. If it comes down to it…"

Ezra put a hand on Jax's shoulder. "If it comes down to it, you take River and that big mutt of yours and you run. Go to Bliss. They'll protect you."

Jax took a deep breath. "Ezra, I don't…"

The boss shook his head. "You owe your wife everything. I know these men are your brothers, but you made vows to River."

Hadn't he made vows to Becca? Not the legal kind, but his body had made a promise to hers. He'd made promises to her. He'd done it with kisses and caresses and words. He'd told her he would take care of her.

And he'd fucking done it. He'd ensured she didn't end up in Levi Green's hands. What else was he supposed to do? Was he supposed to forgive her for what she'd done?

"I'm not going anywhere," a soft voice said.

Jax turned to where his wife stood, Buster sitting at her side. "You damn straight will if this goes to hell. I might have to stay. I might have to deal with the fallout of what McDonald made us do, but you will be safe in Bliss if I even get a hint that Green is on his way."

River simply joined him. "I believe the words for better or worse were spoken. You'll find I take those words seriously." Her face fell as she looked at Becca. "Oh, what did you guys do to her? I told you putting Erin on her was a mistake. Can I go talk to her?"

Ezra shook his head. "Absolutely not. I'm not happy that Owen went in there. We have no idea how she's going to react or how deeply she's involved in this. Until we figure out her place and where that box is, I would prefer we keep her exposure to the team to a minimum."

"She has to know Robert's involved," River pointed out. "And if you're planning on questioning her and letting Ariel talk to her then she's going to know Jax and I are involved, too. Or we just had a dinner party where we happened to invite the whole team investigating her."

"She's got a point," Jax said.

Ezra cursed under his breath. "Fine. You can talk to her, but later. We need to ask her about the box, but first I would like to know why she mentioned the name Reasor and what she knows about him."

"Damn it. Does Tucker know she mentioned that name?" Owen asked.

It was Tucker's greatest fear, that he was the man mentioned in Hope McDonald's private notes, the man named Reasor. The trouble was Reasor apparently had a nickname among McDonald's less savory associates. He'd been called Dr. Razor because he cut so deep. Ever since the day a mercenary had called him that, Tucker had been dreading finding out anything about his past.

"I don't know," Ezra said. "He didn't say a word when we picked her up, but then we had to move quickly. I assume we'll discuss it when he gets here. Now, we have to go back in there and get her talking. So unless you want Dante or Sasha in here questioning her, it's got to be you and me. Can you handle this?"

No. He wasn't at all sure he could. He'd nearly broken down when she'd asked for him, and when she'd shuddered in his arms he'd felt her relief at seeing him. It had taken everything he had not to wrap his arms around her and tell her it would be okay. It had been easy to be cold until he'd seen her in Dante's arms. He'd carried her out the back even as the police had walked in the front, and that fucker Green had been with them. They'd managed to get her out with mere moments to spare.

He'd taken her from Dante's arms and held her in the back of the van Ezra had driven. All the long drive, he'd held her close and gone over all the reasons he should strap her in and stay away from her. She'd lied. At best she'd been quiet about a project that hurt people. At worst, she'd known exactly what she was doing.

It hadn't mattered. He'd been the one to carry her into the cabin they'd found. He'd been the one to lay her down on the bed, and he'd sat there until he'd noticed she was starting to wake.

Now he was the one who couldn't stop wanting to hold her.

"She needs some time." He looked down at Jax's screen. She was sitting with her back against the wall, tears streaming down her face, but there was a stubborn set to her jaw. She was weak but she wasn't out. If he had to bet, he would say she was scared.

"We don't have time. I think we need to be ready to move in forty-eight hours tops," Ezra said. "If we decide she's worth the risk, we'll take her with us. If she can't help us, we'll leave her behind."

"For Levi Green?" The thought sent a wave of anger through him. "I'm not allowing him to arrest her. We have no idea what he'll do to her. Or rather we do. He'll take her someplace where he doesn't have to follow Geneva Convention rules."

Ezra's gaze was steady on him. "Then we should get her talking."

He got it. He had a day or two or Ezra would force them to leave her behind. Just moments before he might have agreed with that plan, but seeing that look in her eyes…he wasn't sure what he was doing. He needed to be cold.

"Be honest with her," River said. "I've been where she is, and Jax didn't win me back by being a bastard."

"I did it with sex," Jax admitted with a grin.

River's eyes narrowed on her husband. "You did it by convincing me you loved me."

"I don't love her." Owen couldn't love her. It would be dangerous to love her. Dangerous for her. Damn dangerous for him. He couldn't love the woman who'd had a hand in doing this to him and his brothers. She couldn't love a man who'd betrayed his team.

River looked at him, disappointment stamped on her features. "Then be kind to her because it's the right thing to do. Having some kind of revenge on her won't help any of us now, and yes, it's easy for me to say because I'm not the one who lost her memory. But it's still the truth. I know that if I was in her position, you would have two choices. Convince me to help you by showing me your cause is just. Or torture me until I have to talk."

"No one's bloody well touching her." The words came out before he could think about them.

River and Jax shared a look. Yes, he'd just given away more than he'd wanted to.

There was the sound of a car coming up the gravel drive and it had Owen reaching for his pistol.

Buster sat there and thumped his tail.

"It's fine," Jax said, looking down at the monitor. "It's the boys."

Ezra unlocked the door and Dante strode in followed by Sasha and Tucker.

"You will have to talk to him," Sasha said, shaking his head. "He's now absolutely certain he's a serial killer."

Dante huffed. "So much drama. If you were a serial killer then be happy that now you are not. Stop whining about it or I might become the serial killer."

Tucker's jaw was tight. "She knew me. She took one look at me and she ran. How could we have been wrong about that? She called me Reasor."

"Hutch checked on the passports Hope might have used on each of you," Ezra said. "It's obvious we missed something. But we couldn't find any evidence that a doctor named Reasor ever set foot in Kronberg. That name isn't on any accounting or human resources documentation. As far as we can tell, Dr. Reasor never existed."

"Except I did," Tucker insisted. "McDonald erased me. She erased my memory and then she got rid of my existence."

"It doesn't work like that," Ezra replied. "She didn't have that kind of power."

"But she worked with people who did." Tucker was pacing the floor, his hands shaking slightly. "She worked with The Collective. They could do things."

"It's very difficult to completely erase a person," Ezra said quietly.

"You don't think we've pointed this out to him?" Dante sank down to the couch. "We spent hours on the road trying to explain this to him. But he's right about one thing. She was terrified of him."

He had a few words to say to Dante. "Maybe she should have been terrified of you. Did you even think before you sank that needle into her neck? You had no idea what kind of reaction she would have to that drug."

If it bothered Dante at all, he didn't show it. He merely shrugged and sat back. "I decided she would react more poorly to being taken into custody." He frowned suddenly, looking to Ezra. "I had no choice. I had very little time to make a decision, and if you'd seen her, you would have done the same thing."

"She wasn't in her right mind." Sasha backed up his friend. "I've seen people with that look in their eyes. She was ready to fight like a wild cat, and she wouldn't have listened to reason. Dante did the only thing he could."

"Don't do it again," Owen warned.

Dante's eyes flashed. "You're not in charge of me."

He needed to make a few things clear to the man. "I'm bloody well in charge of her, and you'll do well to remember it."

Dante sent him his middle finger. "Fuck you, Shaw. You shouldn't be here in the first place. I should have known you would take her side."

"She was there," Sasha argued, pointing toward the screen that showed Becca staring at the door as though wondering when they would come back, what they would do to her. "She was in that lab. No one who wasn't there would have said those things. She worked with McDonald. Hell, she worked on Theo and you're defending her?"

"We don't know what she did there." It was perverse, but he couldn't call back the words. He was well aware that moments before he'd made those arguments himself, but that was before she'd cried in relief at the sight of him.

"We know that she ran away and never spoke of the experience," Sasha said. "If she found out what was happening and she didn't tell the world, she's just as guilty as McDonald."

"We have no idea why she ran, if she ran," he shot back.

"He learns," River said.

Those words seemed to stop everyone in the room. They all turned and looked to River.

"I'm the only one here not so involved in this that I can't see straight," River said, her arm going around her husband's waist. "I understand that you heard a couple of sentences she said, and you've found her guilty without even asking her the questions. Ask her why she walked away, and don't do it like you're the damn police. You're not. Tell her who you are. Explain to her why it's important that she tell you the truth."

"And if she's still working with them?" Ezra asked.

"Then we're not any worse off than we were before. If she's working with them it doesn't matter if I walk in there and offer her a drink because they already know who I am and whose side I'm on." River looked to Owen. "I understand that I've never been in your position. I haven't been through what you have. I didn't lose what Erin did. But I do know where Becca is, and if you want to have any chance that she'll end the night helping us, don't walk in there as avenging angels. Owen, walk in there and explain why you did it. Tell her you didn't mean to hurt her, but you got in deep with her. Let Jax explain how he lost his family. Let Robert talk about how hard it is to have no idea who he is. Tell her your story. And then listen to hers. That's the only way we've got a shot at getting that box."

"She was terrified, Owen," Tucker said, his face grim. "Have we considered the fact that it might not have been McDonald and the drug who made her run? It might have been me. I need to know. I need to know if I'm some kind of monster."

He turned to his friend, trying to let what River had said sink in. He'd gone about this all wrong. He'd heard a few words and declared her guilty without even asking what had happened and why. Tucker couldn't make the same mistake about himself. "You are not a monster."

"How can you know that?" The question sounded tortured coming out of Tucker's mouth.

"Because I know you. I can't begin to understand the forces that shaped you before you lost your memory. I can't say who you were then, but I know the man you are now. I know the man who those forces didn't touch. This is who you are without the influence of anything else. That's not right. This is who you chose to be despite the pain she put you through. When you had your mind erased, when you were tortured and forced to do another's will, this is the man you chose to be. Kind. Helpful. Hopeful in a way I try to understand so I can find it for myself. Tucker, we need to figure out who you used to be but only because it could help us move forward in clearing your names. Not so you can pay for some crime you committed for reasons you'll never remember. This is who you are. That person, Dr. Razor, he's dead and he's not coming back. You're Tucker. You're who you are right now, and that's a man I'll fight beside. That's a man I'll let watch my back. That's a man I'm proud to call my brother."

Tucker looked up and there was such determination in his eyes. "Back at you, brother. Now listen to River and maybe we can save this thing. Maybe we can save a lot."

He turned to the door that separated him from Becca and wondered if there was anything left to save at all.

"All right," Ezra said with a nod. "We'll try this River's way. She's right. She's the only one who knows how it feels to be Rebecca right now, but we have to be careful. If she won't tell us where that box is, we could lose our shot at what's in there. I can't imagine Levi is giving up."

Levi Green would never give up, and now he had to wonder why Levi had sent them here at all. Were they still falling into a trap?

And how much would it cost them?

He took a deep breath and walked through the door.

Chapter Seventeen

Becca watched as Owen walked in. Walked? The man didn't walk. He strode. He prowled. He was a gorgeous predator, the perfect bait to a trap for a dumb woman like her. Had they staked her out? Done their homework and realized how lonely she was? Was that why they'd sent in the man meat?

"Let me help you up." He stood over her, looking perfect in his jeans and T-shirt. It was what he'd worn earlier in the day, and somehow he wasn't wrinkled or haggard. He hadn't just been sick as a dog. "Do you want to use the bathroom?"

"I want to go home." She turned her eyes away from him. How was she going to get out of here? She needed to get a look at the layout of the place. Maybe she should go to the bathroom. It would give her a chance to see where she was. She might be able to get a glimpse of the front door or out a window.

He sighed and got down to one knee in front of her. "I'm afraid your home is being searched right now by a police unit."

"Why would they do that?"

"Because you're at the heart of a conspiracy that's been going on for several years." He sounded so much warmer than he had before. "Because you worked for Hope McDonald and she did some terrible things. Did you know she was developing a drug that erased memories?"

"She wouldn't do that. I don't know what your game is, Owen, but I'm not going to play it."

"It's not a game."

She looked up and a familiar man was standing in the doorway. Jax's boss. Jax must be in on it, too. How many of them were there? And did they all have to be so gorgeous? "You'll excuse me if I don't believe you. I would like a lawyer or to be let go."

She struggled to her feet because she wasn't about to let Owen help her. At least she didn't have anything left to throw up.

"I can't do that," the man who'd called himself Ezra Fain said. "I'm sorry about how we started. You have to understand that everyone on my team was deeply affected by Dr. McDonald's work."

Damn it, she wasn't sure she could make it farther than the table. With shaking hands, she started to pull the chair out. Owen was right there, doing it for her. She didn't look at him as she sat down. Fain slid a green can her way.

It sounded way better than the tea had. And if they'd poisoned it, well, it wasn't like they hadn't already drugged her.

She started to pull the tab.

"Let me help you," Owen offered.

"If you touch this, I'll throw it on you," she promised.

He backed off but didn't go far. "Becca, I started this off all wrong. I was angry you lied to me."

She wasn't buying his new warmth. "It's Dr. Walsh, and do you understand the meaning of the word hypocrite? I would really like to understand how I lied to you."

"This afternoon," he replied. "You lied about Carter coming to see you while we were at Casa Loma."

"How did…" The truth hit her like a hard slap to the face. If only that had been the actual place he'd slapped her. "You had someone watching me."

"Yes," he agreed. "We've had someone watching you for a while now, but there were several of us earlier today. I was able to listen in on the whole conversation."

She let that sink in. The major question was why, and she could only come up with one reason.

"I want to know if he's here." She didn't *want* to know anything about Steven Reasor, but it appeared she wouldn't have a choice. What she didn't understand was why he would want her here. She'd done what he'd asked her to do. She'd run and she hadn't looked back. She'd left him alone with his precious mentor.

But now she had to wonder exactly what he'd done to her back then. Time dilation. McDonald had mentioned it while they'd had lunch one day shortly after she'd joined the team.

Think of the implications, Rebecca. If we could trick the brain, we could effectively become immortal. Forever young. Imagine all that time to do our work.

It was science fiction. It wasn't real.

But it explained so much. What was the old saying? Something about eliminating the impossible and whatever was left had to be the truth. It was impossible. Except very little was impossible when it came to the brain.

"Are you talking about the man you knew as Steven Reasor?" Fain took a seat in front of her. "I have some questions about him. Was he on Dr. McDonald's team at Kronberg Pharmaceutical?"

She forced herself to take a drink. She couldn't panic the way she had this afternoon. If she'd been logical, she might have avoided this trap. "He was at Huisman this afternoon. Are you telling me he doesn't work with you?"

Owen took the other seat, though he sat down with obvious reluctance. "No. A man named Tucker works with us. He might look like Reasor, but he's not the same man."

A laugh huffed from her throat. Even to her own ears it was tinged with the edge of hysteria. "Reasor has a twin? I think that's my nightmare. Hell, maybe there could be three of that psychotic son of a bitch."

Owen winced. "No one's going to hurt you here."

Anger threatened to overtake fear, and that felt good to her. "No one's going to hurt me? What the hell do you think you did, Owen? You think I'm not hurt? You think I'm having a blast figuring out that the man I've been sleeping with is some kind of criminal? I assume you're a criminal since you kidnapped me. What I don't understand is what you want from me. Is it money, since apparently I've got an extra million lying around?"

"I believe someone set you up. I know you didn't steal that money. A man named Levi Green is using that stolen money as leverage to get what we all want," Owen explained. "Hope McDonald's research."

"Fuck you. I'm not giving you any research." If that's what this was about, they'd come to the wrong place. They could kill her, probably would, but she wasn't giving in to them.

"Sweetheart, the police are after you for more than the money." He opened that ever-handy file folder and slid a picture her way. It took her a moment to realize it was of her. She was standing in front of the portrait of the Duchess of Cornwall. The lady she'd talked to was standing there, too. "This woman is a Chinese spy. She's also the mistress of the head of the Huisman Foundation. I assume she's sleeping with him to get information."

"There's a lot of that going around these days." But her brain was working. Something had been happening all around her and she hadn't seen it until it had been shoved in her face. She still didn't understand it. If the Chinese had targeted Jean Claude Huisman, there was only one thing they could be after—research. Or intelligence on the doctors who worked there. There was a reason they locked down the private labs. A lot of delicate research occurred there, things the doctors wouldn't want out in the world because it could potentially be twisted.

"She slipped something into your bag," Owen explained as though he hadn't slid the knife in. "It was a thumb drive."

"I don't have a thumb drive in my bag." She could remember how the other woman had bumped into her, had insisted on helping put everything back in her bag. It would have been easy to slip something small inside.

Had she been set up?

"I assure you that you do, and the police have likely already found it," Fain said. "They'll use it to prove that you're working with the Chinese."

"That's insane." She was cold. Why was it so cold?

Owen got up and walked out, the door slamming behind him.

"It's not, though I'll admit that I don't understand the way Green's mind works," Fain admitted. "But I can explain part of this to you. Years ago, Dr. Hope McDonald started working on a project called Tabula Rasa."

"I know that." She wanted to get to the heart of the matter. "Though she never called the project that in public. She used much more technical terms. Her project was specifically about helping people with profound retrograde amnesia. I was brought in because my own work deals with the same parts of the brain. Those memories aren't lost. They're stored in the brain, but the connection has been cut for some reason. We were studying ways to reconnect, to rewire the brain so the patient has access to the memories again. It's obviously more complex than that, but there it is in a nutshell."

The door opened again and Owen return with a blanket in his hand. "You're shaking. You can let me wrap this around you or let me hold you until you're warm again. Tucker is firing up the furnace and River is making coffee."

"Well, of course she's here." All her new friends were assholes, but she wasn't so stubborn she didn't take the blanket from his hands. She didn't trust that he wouldn't do exactly what he said he would, and she couldn't stand the thought of being wrapped in his arms.

"I want to ask you flat out if you knew anything about McDonald kidnapping men, wiping their memories, and forcing them to work for her. I need to ask you about her, for the lack of a better word, super-soldier program. Her goal was to build small military units whose soldiers would only be loyal to their employers," Fain said. "Although employers is the wrong word. Owners is a better word. Imagine it. Men who could keep their muscle memory so they would know how to fight, but they would have no ties, no memories of anything but their lives in the unit. And if they got troublesome, she could wipe their minds again and start over."

"That's ridiculous." Except Fain didn't look like he was joking.

"Do you remember a patient named Tomas?" Owen asked.

She nodded. "Of course. He had profound retrograde amnesia. He didn't remember anything before his accident. Dr. McDonald took him on as a patient. I actually thought I could help him. I worked with him for a couple of weeks and we made progress. He remembered he'd been in the Navy and that he had a brother. I read the report on the accident that occurred. It was traumatic. He was shot in the line of duty and barely survived. He had a traumatic head injury as well. That was what caused the amnesia."

"He has three brothers and his name is Theo Taggart. He wasn't in the military at the time of his injury, though he was shot in the line of duty," Fain explained. "He was on a mission to prove that Senator Hank McDonald was selling out US troop intelligence for cash. Hope

McDonald saved his life but put him into her program. Theo proved to be her problem child. She brought you in not to heal him but to try to understand why he wasn't responding to the drug the way the others did. The way Robert and Jax did."

This was utterly ridiculous. "I don't understand why you're doing this."

"The way Owen did," Ezra said solemnly.

She felt her stomach drop. Owen? She looked to him, but he was staring at the table in front of him.

He never talked about his past. He'd avoided it studiously. He talked about work, but never his family beyond the fact that he had a mom and a sister and they'd died.

She forced herself to take a deep breath. She couldn't be emotional about this. "What proof do you have?"

There was a knock and the door came open, and Erin walked in carrying a binder. The redhead glared her way. "I hope you're happy. That was terrible. I hate sympathy vomiting. Honestly, I don't like sympathy anything. Here's the full report. Alex gave us the go to show her. It's everything from Dubai to today."

It was a big binder.

"Thank you," Ezra Fain said before turning back to Becca. "As I told you before my name is Ezra Fain and I used to work for the Central Intelligence Agency. What you're about to read is everything a group called McKay-Taggart and Knight has on the McDonalds, specifically Hope McDonald and Project Tabula Rasa."

"All of which you could have made up."

A blond man walked in, propping the door open. She'd only worked with him for a few brief weeks, but he was impossible to forget. Big and broad and gorgeous, Tomas looked to Ezra. "I think I have someone who can explain this better than that report. Reports are boring. Hello, Dr. Walsh. I hear we've met before. I'm sorry I don't remember you at all. I've got a lot of my past back, but those months with McDonald are pretty muddy."

"I hope they stay that way," Erin muttered.

He was in on this, too? He hadn't been faking. She'd worked with too many patients to not know when a patient was faking. Her head was spinning, and not from the drugs she'd been given. "I saw your records. You had a traumatic brain injury."

"He didn't even hit his head when he got shot," Erin said. "I should know. I was there. I watched him die. No brain injuries. Just a big old hole in his heart." Erin's stare pinned her. "She fixed it and he's alive today. It's the only reason I don't regret shooting her quickly."

She looked to the redhead. "Dr. McDonald died in an accident."

"I shot her. I killed her in a lab in France where she was holding Jax, Dante, Sasha, and Tucker. And Owen, though he'll have to tell you that story," Erin said.

"Did you ever run the brain scans on me yourself?" the man she'd known as Tomas asked. "Or did you simply accept what McDonald gave you?"

"She was your doctor." This couldn't be real. "Of course she ran your scans. Or had someone do them. Most doctors don't run scans. We have techs who do that. We read them."

"Would you like to run mine? I'm sure we can figure out a way to do it," Theo offered. "You'll find I've never had a traumatic brain injury, but I still have issues because the drugs she gave me caused disconnections in my limbic system. Or so I've been told by a friend of mine. Did you ever meet McDonald's sister?"

"Faith? Yes, she's a lovely woman." She'd met the doctor while she'd worked with her sister that summer, and once since. It had been at a fundraiser. Faith was a general practitioner who ran a clinic in Africa and helped raise funds for health care in Third World countries. She was practically a saint. "Are you trying to tell me she's evil, too?"

"Faith?" Theo moved out of the way as Jax walked in carrying a laptop. Theo shook his head. "Faith is one of the sweetest human beings I've ever met, and she's one of the reasons I'm alive today. She believed us when we told her what her sister was doing. She helped us."

Jax set the laptop down and fiddled with the keys. "You there, sis? I'm afraid I'm bouncing this off a couple of satellites. The connection isn't the best."

River was standing in the doorway, Buster at her side. She gave Becca a hesitant smile. "Jax is Faith's half-brother. That makes him Hope's half-brother, too, but we don't talk about that much. It's why Hope erased his memory. Turns out his dad didn't want to claim him."

"Love children don't play well in elections," Jax admitted and then a big smile came over his face. "There you are. Hey."

A voice came over the computer. "Hi! It's so good to see you and to know you're not in police custody somewhere."

"Not yet, sister, and if we can get some help, maybe never. You know what to do?" Jax asked.

"Tell the truth and shame the devil. Or rather shame my sister," she replied as Jax turned the monitor to face Becca. "Hello, Dr. Walsh. It's good to see you again."

That was really Faith. What was her part in this? "I can't say I'm happy to see you're involved in this."

"I wasn't happy to find out what my sister was doing. And I certainly hadn't thought about the fact that she likely used your research to aid her own. It's always good to know how something works if you want to break it down." Faith leaned in. "I'm going to tell you the truth about my sister and what she did to these men and how she used you to do it. If you want to walk away at the end, if you don't believe me, then I'm going to ask Ezra to drive you back to your place."

"No," Owen said, finally looking at her.

She ignored him. Faith looked so serious. "Tell me."

Faith began her tale.

Thirty minutes later, she couldn't breathe. She stared down at the reports in front of her. Sometime in the middle of Faith's recitation of her sister's crimes, Becca had reached out and grabbed the binder Tomas…Theo had brought in. It played like a handout accompanying the most horrifying lecture she'd ever attended.

Hope McDonald had used her. The other doctor had used her work to rip apart people's memories. And then she'd had work all of her own, terrifying work.

"You've studied the time dilation drug?" It had been a part of McDonald's therapy, tricking her "boys" into thinking they'd been with her far longer than they had. When she thought about it objectively, it was an interesting theory. Erase memories. Replace those memories with pain. Let the subject know that as long as they obeyed, there would be no pain. Let them think this is how it is and always was. Surround them by others so it feels normal. Isolate them. Become their only source of anything.

It was a psycho's guide to building an army.

"No," Faith admitted. "One of the things the team is looking for is the formulary of the drug. We know it's out there, and if it falls into the wrong hands it could go poorly. My husband...she gave him the drug to torture him. My sister and my father tortured Tennessee. He'd worked for the CIA, but my father had him burned when he threatened his business interests. Ten doesn't like to talk about it, but I know he still dreams about it at night. I have to wake him up and convince him that he's here and not in that place."

That place. The one she'd been sent to. The one she'd thought was all a horrible dream.

If she'd had anything in her stomach, she would have been sick again.

"I need...I need to breathe." She stood up.

Owen was right by her side. "I'll take you outside."

She didn't fight with him. She simply followed him because if she sat there for one minute more, she was going to explode.

Everything she'd worked for...everything she'd needed...

She turned the corner and there he was. Steven Reasor sat at a table with two other men. There was a beer in front of him and he looked haggard.

She stopped and stared at the monster who'd haunted her dreams.

"Dr. Walsh," he began.

"She wiped your mind, didn't she?"

"I don't know." Three simple words, but there was a world of pain in them. "I only know that if I hurt you..."

She couldn't right now. She couldn't do this with him. Her heart started to race and her hands were shaking.

Owen picked her up. He hauled her up into his arms and carried her through the cabin. He managed to get the door open and she was outside. Cool air hit her and it didn't matter that he'd lied to her. It didn't matter that he'd used her.

All that mattered was that years of her life, her research, her soul had been warped and used to hurt others, used to hurt him.

A sob tore through her, making her body shake, and if Owen hadn't been holding her so tight, she would have fallen from his arms to the porch. He didn't let go. He kept walking, leaving the slight glow from the porch for the moonlight.

She sobbed against his chest. She'd been stupid. So fucking stupid. She should have seen what was happening, but she'd been flattered and then frightened.

She'd run like a coward and she hadn't looked back. Because of her weakness, a whole group of men had been confined to Hell, and she'd had a hand in putting them there.

"Keep going, love. You don't have to stop but I'm going to sit us down here."

He sat and she looked around. They were in a gazebo-like structure. He sat them down on a bench, and she could see silvery moonlight reflected on water.

She had no idea where they were, but then that wasn't a surprise. He could tell her where they were and it wouldn't mean a thing because she hadn't left the lab in years. Since that day when she'd fled Kronberg she'd buried herself.

Had she done it because deep down she'd known what had really happened? That was almost easier to deal with than the idea that she'd merely been a coward.

What would her mother think of her?

Owen's arms tightened around her as though he feared if he let go even for a second that she would disappear. "Forgive me. Please forgive me."

For lying to her? She shuddered and forced herself to sit up. "You thought I was responsible for what happened to you."

She wanted to stop talking. If they didn't talk, she might be able to stay in his arms. If they didn't talk, she might be able to pretend.

"You didn't know." His words were hoarse. "I always knew you didn't know. Forgive me for doubting you, Becca. When I heard you'd treated Theo, it triggered something in me. But I can easily see how she manipulated you. You're not the villain in this."

But she was. "I knew something was happening. I thought it was Steven. If I'd said anything at all, maybe she gets caught."

"Or the pharmaceutical company she worked for covers it up and she moves on and they very likely have you and anyone you'd talked to about it killed. It was how they worked. They only cut her loose when she wouldn't fall in line. I doubt any one person with one complaint could have taken her down."

"Let me up, please." It was time to put some distance between them.

His arms tightened almost painfully. "I don't want to let you go."

"You have to. You said it was my choice. Did you lie about that, too?"

His arms dropped and she stood, the wood of the gazebo creaking under her feet. Weariness invaded her limbs and when she looked back at him, his head was in his hands.

His eyes gleamed in the moonlight, and she could have sworn there was a sheen of tears there. "Forgive me. I didn't go into this with the thought to hurt you. It wasn't supposed to be this way."

"It doesn't matter now." She wasn't even sure what to do. Her life was in ruins. There was apparently a warrant out for her arrest. Everything she'd ever worked for was gone and all because she'd taken a job so she could spend time in Europe. All because she'd been arrogant.

"Of course it does."

She stared out at the water. It was dark, and she had no idea how deep it went. It looked peaceful on the surface. What horrors did it hide? "The scars on your body, you didn't get them the way you said you did, did you?"

He was quiet for a moment, the silence emphasizing the distance between them. "I had a bad reaction to the drug. I don't know if it was the one that wiped my mind. I think she used the other one on me, too. I don't know. I get flashes of things now, and I don't know if they're real or not. I hope some of them aren't. I hope they're dreams. From what I can tell I wasn't there for long. A little more than a day."

"If she gave you the time dilation drug, I assure you she could make a few hours seem like years. If she then wiped your memory, well, you might not remember it, not the way you're used to remembering things. It would be like something rippling under the water. You wouldn't know why you were afraid. You would likely convince yourself there's nothing to be afraid of, but it would be there. Always." Like it was for her. It was always there simmering underneath her shiny surface, and now it was out in the open, crawling up from the muck like some monster inching toward her. "Why does this Green person want me? Why go to all this trouble to set me up?"

She heard him moving behind her. "I think he wants to put you in a position where you'll work for him. Becca, there are things you should know about me."

"I can't do anything personal with you right now." If she did she would break down again. She could understand why they'd investigated her. She could even forgive them for surrounding her. When researching a disease, one had to isolate the cause. They'd thought she might have been a cause. But they hadn't had to send Owen to her bed. They hadn't needed to trick her like that. From what she could tell, they'd placed someone in every aspect of her life. While she'd been listening to Faith, Robert had shown up along with Ezra's wife, Ariel, who probably wasn't Ezra's wife since Robert seemed to have a hand on her the whole time. Even the lady who'd recently started making her morning lattes was in on it.

They hadn't needed to send her a lover who didn't love her.

"All right, but understand I'm not letting it go. You're only delaying the inevitable." He sighed and moved in beside her.

"Tell me what your group wants from me."

"Shortly before she died, Dr. McDonald sent you something. We believe it was a package that contained her research. We think she understood the net was tightening around her. Ezra has been working on this for a while now. He thinks she'd set up an escape hatch, so to speak. When Theo's brother raided her French laboratory, she had protocols in place to erase every computer in the lab."

"She destroyed her own research?" It was a foreign idea. Everyone she knew was obsessed with their own work and desperate for it to live on even after they were gone.

"I don't think so. Not completely. What was your relationship like with her?"

It was easier to talk out here. She didn't want to admit it, but it was easier to talk to him. "We were friends. Sort of. She was kind of a mentor to me. It was like she wanted to teach me, to mold me. That was why Steven had a problem with me. He liked being her protégé. He was very jealous of her. I thought for a while that they were lovers."

A shudder went through Owen's big body. "Please don't ever tell Tucker that. I don't think he could handle it."

Tucker. The name didn't fit him. "I don't know that I can handle being in the same room with him."

"What did he do to you?"

"I don't want to talk about it." She couldn't handle that confession, but she could make another one. "And I only thought they were lovers at first. I realized later on that they had an odd relationship. She used him almost like her bad cop, if that makes sense. He was mean. He was also brilliant, which isn't uncommon in my world. People put up with a lot when a researcher has brilliant ideas. We don't call them bullies. We call them quirky or eccentric. But they are bullies. Having a brilliant mind doesn't excuse being cruel. He was cruel, and she used that so she didn't have to look cruel. I realize that now."

"He's one of the kindest men I know," Owen said softly. "He was on a mission once with a friend of mine. He sacrificed himself to save a woman I admire quite a lot. He doesn't remember who he was. He won't hurt you."

"Or he's fooling all of you," she said quietly. She'd read the final report on McDonald's last day and the raid that took her out. "Have you considered the idea that he could have faked it? He could have seen what was happening and faked his own memory wipe?"

"Jax knew him. Jax and Sasha and Dante were in there with Tucker. If he was faking he would have to have done it for months. I promise I won't leave your side and I'll talk to him about giving you space."

He wouldn't believe her about Steven Reasor. That was obvious. It was one of the reasons she hadn't said anything at the time. She'd known they would all come down on his side.

She held her hands out to show him how empty this whole thing had been. "I don't have a package from her. She called me the week after I left Kronberg. She wanted to know why I'd gone and I told her. She said she would handle Steven and asked me to come back. I refused and we didn't talk again. She left me a voice mail a few months later telling me Steven had been killed in an accident and she could use my help. I did not reply. I didn't hear a thing about her after that until she died. There wasn't even any gossip about her."

And that told her a lot. There were powerful forces surrounding this whole mess if no one talked about it. Even in the research world there were sections that thrived on gossip. Yet almost no one talked about Hope McDonald after she died. It should have made her curious.

It had been far too easy to ignore all the clues, and now she would pay the price with her career.

She'd already paid the price with her heart.

She'd loved Owen. She'd fallen in love with him and she'd been nothing but a job to him. And a failed one at that because she didn't have the mysterious package they wanted.

"She didn't send me anything, Owen. Or at least I never got it," she said, every word dull. "Maybe these people you say are after me have it."

"No. There's no reason for Green to have sent us out here if he had the information he needed."

"Why would he send you out here at all? Why not come after me himself? He seems to have had a plan in place for a long time. That money started going missing almost a year ago. Didn't that CIA guy say they didn't know about me then?"

"Ezra is ex-CIA," Owen explained. "He was forced out over philosophical differences."

She could read between those lines. "His bosses wanted him to find the drugs so they could use them."

One shoulder shrugged. "I think every intelligence agency in the world would like to get their hands on her work. I won't say they would all misuse it. I'm sure some of them merely want to know how it worked and how to keep it out of the hands of the rest of the world. But someone would use it."

"It would be far too tempting," she agreed. "Even the best of intentions can get pushed aside out of sheer curiosity. I'm not saying I would ever do what she did, but I'm curious. I'd love to see that drug and how it works." She would love to know what it had done to her. She shook it off. "I would give you the package if I had it. I trust Faith. She said you guys work with Stephanie Gibson, too. I've never met her but she's got an excellent reputation. I would feel good handing it over to them, but I don't have it."

And that meant she didn't have any leverage with these people. They were here to do a job, and now that the objective wasn't achievable, they would move on. She would be alone to face the music because she doubted the problem would disappear. This Levi Green person might shrug and walk away, but the Canadian police wouldn't. Once it got out that she was under investigation for embezzling funds from her grants, there wouldn't be a place on the planet that would hire her. Not for research work, and she hadn't been a practicing surgeon for years. And then there was the fact that apparently she was being accused of working with a Chinese spy.

She would spend every dime she had fighting the accusations.

She would have to stand in front of her father and explain what had happened, why she'd broken the promises she'd made to him and her mother all those years before.

It was overly dramatic, but it felt like her life was over. The thought opened a deep ache in her heart because briefly she'd felt like she was starting all over again. For a few days it had felt like everything was coming together and she would be able to fulfill the promise she'd made to her mother, that she would be happy.

"Could someone give me a ride back or let me use a phone so I can call a cab?" She glanced around. It appeared they were by a lake that spread out before her as far as she could see. The cabin behind them was the only light, so there didn't appear to be any close neighbors. She might be hiking out of here.

He turned to her. "You're not going back. Do you understand what they'll do to you?"

"Yes, I think they'll put me in jail until I can make bail. They'll freeze my accounts so I'll have to call my father. He should be able to loan me the money. I don't know what I'll do about an attorney, but I'll figure it out. It's not your problem."

His hands cupped her shoulders and he turned her, forcing her to look at him. "I will not leave you alone. We're holing up here for a few days and then you and I will make our way to London. There's a place there where you'll be safe. I'll try to stay with you as much as I can. I have a bit more freedom of movement than the others. I promise I'll find a way out of this for you. I'll keep you safe and I'll clear your name."

There it was, the insane impulse to believe every word he said, to toss the whole problem in his lap and let him take care of everything.

He'd lied to her and she couldn't believe him. "I need to go home and face this. I'm not going on the run. Don't be ridiculous. I'm not a fugitive. If this Green person doesn't get what he wants, maybe the heat will come off me."

"It won't. He won't stop because you don't know where that package is," Owen swore. "He'll take you anyway. If he can't get the knowledge out of the box, he'll take it from your brain, and he won't ask gently for it. He never meant to take you back to the States. He'll get custody of you and take you somewhere no one cares how he treats you."

"I don't know how she did it."

"But you could figure it out. I think he's got enough pieces of the puzzle he figures if he gets a brilliant mind like yours on the problem, you could solve it. You could recreate the drug from the clues he has. Hell, for all I know he's got some of it and he wants you to reverse engineer it. I don't know. I only know that he wants you and I'm not going to let him have you. I'll die first."

There was such emotion in his voice that she had to step away. He didn't mean it. It only meant that he had something else he wanted from her. She had to hold on to the cold man who'd walked into that interrogation room earlier this evening. That had been the real Owen Shaw. He'd strode in with no warning because he'd wanted her to be shocked. He'd likely enjoyed it.

He probably deserved it since he'd lost his memory because of her.

"Becca?" He turned to her and seemed to force his hands back to his sides.

She shook her head, backing away. "I won't fight you, but don't talk like that again."

"I know I fucked up." His voice was like gravel. "I know I made a mess of things, but you have to believe me when I tell you this was real to me. You and me, we were real."

Of course they had been. "Do you not believe me when I say I don't know where the information is?"

"The information is meaningless. You're what's important."

"I asked you not to talk that way." She couldn't stand listening to those words coming from his mouth.

"Not to tell you I love you? I know I didn't say it before, but it's true. I love you, Becca. I'm in love with you. I don't know what I was like before, if there was some woman I cared for. I don't think so according to the people who knew me then. I think you're the only woman I've ever loved."

"Stop it." She shouted the words. The whole night seemed to crash in on her and rage suddenly made the velvety darkness of the night seem red. How dare he say those words to her? How could he lie again? He put her here. It wasn't fair or right, but her rational mind wasn't in charge. She'd held it in for the hours it had taken for the truth to sink in. She'd held in her rage at being used. He'd used her. He'd fucked her and called it something else. He'd promised her his kindness and given her…this. Protection and caring was what he'd promised to exchange for her submission.

He wasn't the first. Her husband had promised her much the same and then tried to steal her work and cheated on her with a more "womanly" female. She'd always been the youngest person in her class, and there had been a couple of assholes who'd tried to take advantage of that. Even fucking Paul Huisman made her feel small because she was female. She'd heard the way he talked about her, the way he'd told everyone on her team that she was too emotional. He constantly told her to calm down.

She wasn't sure how she made it across the gazebo, but she found herself hitting him, taking out her rage on him. Her hands were balled into fists and she was using them on Owen. She struck his chest again and again, hearing the way her flesh thudded against his. It wasn't right, but she couldn't seem to stop herself. It was too much. She'd lost. She'd lost her mother and her childhood and her husband and her self-worth. God, it had taken her years to get that back. Now she'd lost her career. Decades of work were down the drain.

And she'd lost him. She'd lost Owen. She'd lost the future she'd thought they could have had together. She'd lost the peace he'd promised her.

He wasn't fighting back. He took everything she had to give him without a single protestation. He stood there and let her use him like a punching bag.

God, she wasn't this person. She wasn't the kind of person who hit people when it wasn't in defense of herself or others. She wasn't violent. Her whole life had been about helping people, and all she would be known for was her part in violating the rights of her fellow men, in torturing them and stealing the most precious thing a human being could have—a memory.

A moan was heard, the low sound of an animal in pain.

It was her. Becca started to fall to the floor, her strength gone in that attack. She braced herself but didn't even come close to hitting the hard wood. Owen lifted her up and his arms were around her, holding her tight.

"I can't let you go. I won't let anything hurt you, but I can't let you

271

go." There was a fine tinge of panic to his voice. "You can hate me, but I can't let you go."

She shuddered in his arms, coming down from the adrenaline high of her rage. She was left with nothing but an aching sorrow.

Her arms finally went around him and they stood like that for what felt like hours, clinging to what briefly had seemed like a bright future.

Chapter Eighteen

Owen sat up in the godawful uncomfortable chair he'd been trying and failing to sleep in the moment he heard Becca cry out. He was on his feet in a heartbeat, staring down at her.

"You're still here." She groaned and sat up, pushing the covers away and then pulling them right back up because it was chilly.

It was downright cold and he didn't have a blanket to huddle under. He didn't have her to cuddle with.

"I told you I wouldn't leave you. Are you all right? Was it a nightmare?"

He knew he sounded like a mother hen, but he couldn't help it. Ever since that moment when she'd broken down utterly and he'd carried her out of the cabin, he'd known he'd likely ruined every single chance he had with her. And he'd also known he wanted that chance, all those chances. He'd known in that moment that he loved her with his whole broken and busted-up heart.

And he'd ached when she'd attacked him. Not because of her fists or her righteous anger. He understood that. He'd been oddly satisfied that she'd taken it out on him. He wanted her. All of her—her love, her body, her soul, her joy, her sorrow, and her rage. He'd stood there, willing all that anger to transfer from her to him. He would have told her he would take it all if it brought her a single moment of peace.

"I didn't have a nightmare." She rubbed her eyes and yawned. "I just woke up and for a moment I couldn't remember where I was. I'm thirsty."

"I'll get you some water."

A long sigh split the air. "I'm hungry, too. I didn't eat lunch and then well…I'm hungry. I had a protein bar in my purse but it's back at the foundation."

"Robert and Ari hit the supermarket in town on their way in. Come on. I'll make you a sandwich." He held out a hand. She wouldn't need to get dressed. Other than her taking off her shoes, she'd kept everything on, even the purple cardigan she'd been wearing. He'd tried to talk her into slipping into one of his T-shirts. He had two in his go-bag, but she'd refused.

After that blissful moment in the gazebo when she'd clung to him like she wouldn't let go, she hadn't touched him again. He'd had to be satisfied with the fact that she hadn't argued about him staying in the room with her. It had likely been shock, but she'd simply taken off her shoes, got under the covers, and fallen into an exhausted sleep.

"All right."

He was shocked when she put her hand in his and allowed him to help her up. She dropped his hand the minute she was on her feet, but she'd touched him. It had to be enough for now.

"I can get it myself," she said. "I'm not going to run or anything. It's not like I have anyplace to run to."

"I'm going with you," he returned, following her out the door.

"You'll do what you want to do anyway," she muttered as she turned down the hall.

The place was quiet except for the sound of keys clacking. The cabin only had two bedrooms and a tiny loft with two twin beds. He and Becca had taken one and Theo and Erin the other. River and Jax had bedded down in the back of the van while the loft held Sasha, Dante, and Tucker. He wasn't sure which one was sleeping on the floor, but he would bet it was Tucker, and he wasn't sleeping at all.

The living room was quiet, only the crackling sound of a fire in the hearth making any noise at all. Nina was curled up on the love seat while Ari and Robert had taken the couch. His friend seemed to be moving in the right direction this time. Robert was lying on his back while Ari had draped herself over him, her head resting on his chest. They were cuddled together under a blanket and looked warm and happy.

He was fairly certain he'd looked that way the previous night.

He led her into the dining room where Ezra's face looked ghostly in the light from the computer screen. He glanced up. "Everything all right?"

"She's hungry" Owen replied. "Everything's fine. How are the plans going?"

"We can't get a plane out until the day after tomorrow, but I don't think that will give Green time to track us." Ezra looked over at Becca. "We're going to take you to London, but we have to do it carefully. Jax is working on getting you a Canadian passport. I promise I won't let him pick your name. He's not good at them."

"When he made one for River, he named her Fjord," Owen said.

A hint of a smile crossed her lips. "Because it's water. Like a river."

"It's ridiculous," Ezra corrected, "because she's obviously not Nordic, and even Nordic people don't name their kids Fjord. Jax thinks he's creative. I need him to be realistic. Amber or Ashley is normal. Fjord makes security look twice, so River is Amber and you get to be Ashley. Regular Ashley. No two ee's or the p is silent."

"They argue about spelling, too," Owen admitted. He'd found it amusing. "Jax thinks fake names should be special. Ezra thinks they should be as boring as possible. What did he try to name Becca?"

"Sunny Brooke. Not joking. First name Sunny. Last name Brooke," Ezra said with a sigh. "I'm sure he was going to try to work the word farm in there somewhere. My question is how the hell does he know about *Rebecca of Sunnybrook Farm*. He knows next to nothing about the damn world. He can't tell me who the last president of the United States was but he knows a kid's book."

"It's Kay's fault." He adored Kayla Summers. She'd worked at the London office before she'd married her Hollywood sweetheart. Kay had been the one to take all the Lost Boys under her wing when they'd first showed up at The Garden. They'd been traumatized and unsure of what had happened to them and she'd sort of played big sister to all of them. "She would watch movies with us at night, trying to acclimate us to the culture. Unfortunately, she showed us the *The Shining* and then Sasha started sleeping with an ax, so then we had a whole week of kids' films. I still don't understand why they had to shoot that dog."

275

"Old Yeller was rabid," Ezra said with a shake of his head. "Like a couple of you. Anyway, Becca is now Ashley Jones from Ottawa. We'll take a private jet to Mexico City. From there we're going to split up. I'm sending Becca back to London with Ari and Nina." He held out a hand as though he knew what came next. "Brody and Nick are meeting them in Mexico. They'll provide security, although don't let Nina hear me say that. She's a badass all on her own."

"I thought she was a barista," Becca said.

"She makes a mean latte and can kill a man fifteen different ways. She's a modern woman," Owen explained. "But I would rather escort her. I'm not wanted by Interpol. I don't have a record like the others. I can go home."

"I don't think that's a good idea, but we'll talk about it later. I think you should feed her and get back to bed." Ezra nodded to Becca. "You need to stay in the house. The police are looking for you. There hasn't been any media coverage yet, but the Huisman Foundation has blocked your access to the building and they spent the evening searching your lab and your apartment."

"How do you know?" she asked.

"I know because I have sources." It was all Ezra would say.

Becca thought about that for a moment. "Did you have cameras on me? Did you put them in my apartment?"

Owen's gut churned, but he wasn't going to lie to her again. "Yes. We had to know where you were at all times since Tucker and Dante and Sasha came in and out."

"I wouldn't have known who the janitors were," she admitted. "That's shitty of me, but it's true. I would have known the other guy. I'm going to the kitchen. I won't like sneak out the back or anything. You can stay here and plan the rest of my life. I guess I should be happy you don't turn me over to the police and be done with it."

"We wouldn't do that." How did he make her believe?

She simply turned and walked to the small galley kitchen at the back of the cabin.

"It's okay," Ezra said quietly. "She can't get out without us knowing. The most she can do is walk through the kitchen to the other part of the cabin and get back into bed without you. If she opens one of the outer doors or windows, the alarm will go off."

So that's what Dante and Sasha had been doing while they'd been debriefing Rebecca. "I'm sure she's thrilled that she's locked in."

"Well, it appears she's accepted that she's staying. I'm glad she understands about Green and what he'll do to her." Ezra sat back and rubbed his thumb between his brows as though trying to stave off a headache. "He used us to do his dirty work. If we'd gotten that package, he would have found a way to take it, maybe even used the authorities. I'm a burned CIA agent and most of the crew are known and wanted criminals. He can fuck with us and no one will give a damn."

"Then why change up the game? Why not let us get it and…" It came to him. "He found out someone was setting her up and he's using it. He walked into a situation that was already going on and used it to his advantage. Someone was setting up Becca for a big fall. Do you think Green is working with MSS?"

He wouldn't put it past the bastard to work with Chinese intelligence if it furthered his own agenda.

"Or MSS was already in place and he used that, too," Ezra replied. "The fucker was always good at finding an advantage. I think this all fell into his lap and he shifted strategies. So we're going to do the same thing. We can't find that data. All right, we'll take the brilliant neurologist, pair her with Walt, who can learn almost anything in rapid-fire time, and see what we come up with. While they're working, we'll keep searching for what we need."

They would keep looking for a hint that anyone else had the drug and if they did, they would try to put a stop to it. They would look for leverage, for a way to save his brothers and get them any kind of normal life.

He would be away from her. He would have to work to get her back to her life, to a life that couldn't include him.

Ezra looked up, his expression grim. "Owen, it's obvious you want her. Maybe I was wrong about sending you with the others. Talk to her. You don't have to be here. You don't have to go with us. If you want, you can stay in London and try to find some normalcy."

But he was the only one of them without a global warrant out for his arrest. He was the only one who could show his face in certain places. "She doesn't want me. I'm needed here. I've spent the entire time I can remember trying to figure out my place in all of this, but now I know I'm supposed to be with this team. I'm supposed to make sure this group of men can live a life since I had a hand in taking their old one from them."

"Guilt will eat you up if you let it," Ezra said. "All that stuff you said about Tucker, you know it applies to you, too. You're not the same man."

"But he's still there, deep down. That selfish bastard still lives inside me. Do you know there was a part of me that was happy when we found out she can't go back?"

Ezra nodded as if he understood completely. "Because you want her in our world, and now none of us has a choice. I get that, but it's not like you manipulated things to get her here. Would you have done that?"

He wouldn't have taken her work from her. "No. Never. She's worked too hard to do that to her."

"Then you're merely adapting like the rest of us." Ezra sat back with a heavy sigh. "Do you know what my first thought was when I realized my ex-wife was working this case?"

"Was it something violent?"

"Maybe. She likes a bite of pain," he said, the words almost too quiet to hear. "I thought thank god it doesn't have to be over. How stupid is that? She was there to work against me and deep down I was okay with that because it meant I would see her again. I'm a stupid fucker. She cheated on me."

He and Ezra had different definitions of that word. "I thought you weren't married at the time."

Ezra was quiet for a moment. "Sometimes I feel like I've always been married to her and yet I know there was a time before Solo. Kim. I call her Solo because it's far easier to deal with the operative than the woman underneath. I wish I could separate them sometimes."

"I think she still loves you, if that's any comfort."

"Sometimes love isn't enough."

And it wouldn't be for him either. "Becca doesn't know me. She knows who I've shown her. She fell for a lie."

"Was it?" Ezra asked. "You didn't step into that elevator with plans to seduce her, did you?"

"No." But it hadn't taken him long.

"It would have been simpler for you to have introduced yourself the way you were supposed to. You know we had an argument about why you changed up the plan. Some of the guys thought you might have done it because Big Tag took you off lead."

"I didn't." He wasn't surprised they thought that way though.

"Tucker bought the whole line about how you realized she needed to be played differently," Ezra pointed out.

"I told you what happened. I wasn't lying."

Ezra chuckled and sounded a bit amused. "Oh, you were lying, but mostly to yourself. A couple of us knew why you'd done it. Me and Robert and Jax. We knew it had been about her. You see we all know what it's like to meet a woman and know. We might not have known exactly what we knew, but it was there deep down. Like a memory of something beautiful, a hint of some life we used to lead. You saw her and something clicked into place."

And he hadn't been able to say the words he should have. He hadn't been able to lie about his attraction to her. He hadn't been able to stop himself from kissing her. "I love her, Ezra."

"Yeah, I got that." The boss gave him a sad sort of smile. "It's okay. Stay with her. Stop punishing yourself. It's time to let that go."

"And how will she feel when she finds out who I was?" It was his greatest fear, that she would learn what he'd done and turn away in disgust.

"When she finds out you were so desperate to save your mom and sister that you made a poor choice? Somehow I think she'll forgive you for that. Everyone else has. Even Erin. Oh, that woman won't ever let you know it, but she disagreed with Big Tag about pulling you from the lead. And Big Tag didn't pull you because he was still angry with you. He pulled you because you stay in the shadows and show no ambition to move out of them. He pulled you because you let your guilt rule your life, and that means you're likely to do something stupid like sacrifice yourself at the earliest opportunity."

He would argue but the truth was Ezra was right. Big Tag was right. "I owe them. I owe the Taggarts a lot."

"Jesus, I hate these things." Erin Taggart sighed and pulled out a chair at the table, slumping into it. "Sorry, I can't sleep. The bed here sucks and Theo's mumbling in his sleep. Nothing scary. He's talking to Case about beer. I can't have a beer so I don't want to listen to him talk about beer. Then I come out here and you two are having a feels talk. Haven't I vomited enough for one day?"

He had no idea how to handle Erin. It was best to simply apologize. "I'm sorry."

"I'm sorry I didn't murder you. Doesn't change anything," she shot back.

"Erin." Ezra managed to make her name an admonition.

The redhead sighed and sat back. "Owen, we've all done shit we're not proud of. You should have trusted your team, but you panicked. She had your family. I personally would have let my brothers or father rot, but apparently you loved your family." She shuddered. "Fuck, I've been around Avery too long. My partner's wife is a freaking saint and I'm going to take a play from her book. You know what you owe me, Shaw? You owe me a good life. You owe it to me to try to find some happiness and to make better choices this time around. I forgive you and shit. Now can someone make some hot chocolate or something? It's going to be a long night. I hate this job."

She looked ready to move but he had a few things to say. He shifted so he was standing in front of her. "I'm sorry, Erin. I never said it to you. Not plain and direct. I'm sorry. I was selfish, and it could have cost you everything. I don't know what was going through my brain at the time. I can't remember them, but I must have loved them."

"I know you did." She sounded solemn for a moment. "And I think you love her. So don't fuck it up."

"I already did," he replied. "Even if she can forgive my past, she won't ever forgive me for lying to her. She won't forgive the way we met."

"I've seen couples survive worse," Erin replied before pointing to Ezra. "Not that one, though. He's super stubborn and does not consider an actual divorce to be a break. He and Solo are so not going to end up like Ross and Rachel. Be smarter than they are."

"Do you have to be such an asshole?" Ezra asked.

Erin shrugged. "I'm the chick who says what everyone's thinking."

"I was not thinking that at all," Ezra said before turning back to Owen. "If you want Rebecca, don't let up. I watched Theo's twin brother Case utterly ruin his relationship with Mia. And he could have accepted that. He could have laid down and accepted that it was over."

"He mostly whined and looked sad and shit." Erin's brows rose at the look Ezra gave her. "Hey, who had to put up with that? This girl. I had just had a baby and I swear Case cried more than TJ."

"Somehow I doubt that," Ezra replied. "I got to see it from the Mia side. You know what got them back together? Case didn't give up and he was honest with her. Even when it was painful. He told her everything he was feeling."

"Or you could do what Theo did and fuck her until she can't see straight. Sorry. I'm not good at the touchy-feely stuff. You should wake up Ari for that." She glanced back into the living room and when she looked back an infinitely sad expression crossed her face. "Or don't wake her. Let her sleep. It's sucks to be awake sometimes. Do what Ezra says. Talk to her. Tell her all your manly feelings. It does work for most chicks. I think it'll work for her. She already feels bad. You have to get through her guilt or it will eat her alive. Is she asleep somewhere? Should we like find her? You're a terrible guard. Feel bad about that."

Could he talk to Becca? He didn't talk to anyone. He barely talked to Ari and she was his therapist. He wouldn't know until he tried.

"You know you need help, right?" Ezra was asking Erin after he'd explained Becca was in the kitchen.

"No, I need a hot chocolate," Erin replied.

"I'll put a kettle on." It was the least he could do for her. And he could make one for Becca if she liked. Perhaps they could start some kind of dialogue. If there was even a chance at getting back to where they'd been. He'd failed her. When she'd needed him to take control, he'd used that control against her. He'd listened to his own anger and guilt and not to his instincts about her.

He walked into the kitchen and stopped because Becca wasn't alone.

* * * *

"We wouldn't do that," Owen said.

Becca didn't know what to believe. When she'd woken up only a few moments before, she'd found herself reaching out for him. It had been terrible when she'd remembered where she was and why Owen was sleeping in a too-small chair. Now standing here just outside the kitchen, she was reminded of all she'd lost.

Ashley Jones. She was going to have to change her name so the police couldn't find her. She would be stuck in some office in London, and who knew when she would see the light of day again.

She'd thought briefly about running, but that would be stupid.

How was her father going to feel? How embarrassed would her little sister be?

She didn't say anything to Owen, simply turned and walked into the kitchen. A sense of relief washed over her when she realized he was still in the dining room talking to his boss.

His boss, who happened to be ex-CIA. There were a whole bunch of ex-soldiers and operatives. Even her barista had worked for Interpol. She'd never had a chance.

She wasn't even certain why. That was what killed her. Why had Dr. McDonald chosen her to send this mystery box to?

"Don't freak out," a voice said from the gloom beyond her sight.

She reached out to find the light switch. A cone of light popped on from above the sink and she saw what she hadn't before.

Her breath caught in her throat and she really wanted to freak out. It was Steven Reasor.

He stood up, his hands out as though to show her he didn't have a weapon. "I'm sorry. I didn't have another place to go. Sasha snores and Dante sleep punches. I'll go sleep in one of the cars."

He didn't sound like Steven Reasor. Reasor was always in control. He always sounded like he was the smartest person in the room, and also the one who would stab you the fastest, and she'd learned he hadn't meant that figuratively.

Now that she looked at him, he seemed differently physically. Not that he didn't have Reasor's face. It was his face, just without the arrogance, without the hint of malice that had always hung over the young doctor.

She could do this. She could stand in the same room with him and ask a couple of questions. Owen could be in here quickly if she called out.

Was it stupid to think Owen would save her? Maybe if she thought it was about loving her, but this group wanted her alive. They apparently thought she still had something to add so yes, Owen would save her. It made logical sense. She could ask her questions.

Could she get some closure? Would standing in front of the bad guy make it easier to move on?

"You didn't think I would recognize you." She turned and forced herself to look at him. She was glad she'd turned down Owen's offer of his T-shirt. Being dressed for bed would have made her feel vulnerable.

His hands came down and he sank back into the wooden, straight-backed chair he'd been in before she'd turned on the light. There was nothing on the table. No drink or phone or tablet he'd been amusing himself with. He'd been sitting in the dark with nothing but his thoughts. "No. We missed something. Or we didn't have enough information to make a proper decision. We did try to mitigate the risk that you would know one of us."

He sounded so defeated, the words rolling out of his mouth like they were rote and bland. This man was answering questions not because he wanted to but rather out of a sense of obligation. Again, not the Dr. Reasor she'd known.

"How would you even start to do that?"

He glanced up and she could see the dark circles under his eyes. "We had a couple of known aliases. I was a part of what we call the B team. We mostly stayed in Europe where it was easy for us to move around. I think I was held somewhere in Asia once. I can't be sure. But that was what we had to go on. We couldn't find a man named Reasor who was close to her. I know the name. I know the nickname, too."

"Dr. Razor."

A shudder went through his body and his gaze was on the hallway. "Yeah. Dr. Razor because he cuts so deep."

"You liked the nickname." It was odd to be standing here with a man she'd thought was dead. Hoped and prayed was dead. "You bragged about patients giving it to you, but I convinced myself you were being an ass. You were often an ass."

His eyes came up again. "So I've heard. Can you tell me what I did to you?"

Could she? She wasn't even sure what had been done to her at all. "It doesn't matter if you're not you anymore."

"It matters. It matters to me. It obviously matters to you, too, since that was a look of terror on your face this afternoon. We'd been lucky that I hadn't worked for you before. I'd actually asked to be put on your service, but I was told I hadn't earned the honor yet."

Carter. Carter always placed himself on her schedule when he could. Right up until Monday when he'd sent in one of the female interns. She'd liked working with Annie. The young woman was funny and smart. Had Carter thought it was an insult to place Annie on her service? "It would have screwed up your plan."

She'd lost her appetite, but her throat was dry. She opened the fridge and pulled out a bottle of water. It looked like someone had stocked them up. There was lunch meat and a couple of bagged salads. Some cheese, grapes, strawberries and yogurts. Maybe she could handle the yogurt.

"Do you recognize any of the others?" Reasor asked.

Raspberry. She could do that. Her hunger was gone, fled in the light of her current company, but her weakness remained. "No. Except for Tomas." That wasn't his name. "Theo. I remember him. I saw a lot of Dr. McDonald's patients, but I remember him in particular because she seemed fascinated by him. It was kind of a shock and everyone gossiped about it when she would bring him in because that was a woman completely obsessed with her work."

"Did I hurt Theo?" The question came out on a tortured gasp, and it was easy to see he was trying to keep control of his emotions.

Was he faking it? Or was he the real deal? "She never left you alone with him." Why hadn't Theo known… "She must have used the drug on Theo after they visited the lab. Toward the end of the summer, she was in and out. She left you in charge most of the time."

"Of course, I was." He glanced up, his eyes wide and empty. "The spoons are in the drawer by the sink. Raspberry is my favorite."

She found a spoon and forced herself to sit across from him. "That's surprising. You used to be a carnivore. You made fun of the bunnies in the group. That's what you called them. You said there wasn't a point to eating something without a face. I often worried about your fiber intake."

He huffed, a slightly amused sound. "I'm not saying I don't enjoy the occasional burger, I do, but I like yogurt a lot. I don't eat a lot of meat around River. She's a vegetarian. Jax is pretty much one now, too. I eat whatever someone puts in front of me. I'm not that great in the kitchen but I'm trying."

"I don't know if I can believe you." She wasn't sure she even wanted to. She'd hated this man for so long that the idea he might be likeable was foreign. But if the drug did what she suspected it did, it could be true. If this man had the connections in his brain destroyed, he wouldn't remember who he'd been. He would have woken up and not understood what was going on. He would have been afraid. Perhaps not like she'd been afraid, but it was something they had in common.

"Please tell me what I did to you." It was a quiet plea, but she could hear the desperation behind it.

What would it be like to wake up in a strange place with absolutely no identity memory? Fear and sorrow and rage had been fueling her since that moment she'd seen Reasor, but curiosity was starting to swirl around in her brain.

What Hope McDonald had done was horrifying, but the need to know how she'd done it was there. It was like a physicist looking at the atom bomb. The man or woman looking at it would be sickened by what it could do, but the scientist…the scientist would need to know how it worked.

If she figured out exactly how it worked, could she reverse it? Could she give them back what was lost?

"You were cruel," she said quietly before taking a spoonful of yogurt. It was tart and sweet and cool on her tongue. She had to force herself to swallow. "To everyone really, but to me in particular. You were McDonald's star pupil. You didn't want anyone to take your place."

"Where did I go to school? Was I friends with anyone? I'm sorry. I have a lot of questions."

"Yale Medical," she replied. "At first I thought we would get along because we were both so young. We had a lot in common. We'd both gotten through school quickly and were considered real talent in our fields. At least that's what McDonald told me. I'll be honest, I'd never heard of you before. I didn't hear a lot about you after. You didn't have friends, per se. At least not on the team, but there was a reason for that. Most of the team came and went. Six weeks here, two months there. She had a core team of four researchers. Three of them are dead. Veronica Croft is the only one left. She worked with you quite closely."

"Veronica?' He leaned forward like that name was a lifeline. "Who was she?"

A vision of a pretty young woman with long, dark hair floated through her brain. "She was one of the research assistants McDonald brought over from Texas with her. She was fresh out of UT medical. From what I could tell, she wrote up a lot of the research for the group."

"Could we find her?"

She nodded. "Yes, but I don't know that you'll like what she says about you. She hated you. You were mean to her. Again, you were pretty much mean all the time. You ran the group while McDonald was traveling, and she traveled a lot. She had speaking engagements and conferences. Well, that's what she said she was doing. She said she worked with the US Army on some projects dealing with retrograde amnesia. I didn't ask for proof."

She should have, apparently.

He sat back. "She wouldn't want to talk to me." He seemed to shake it off. "Did I ever talk about my family? Did you know where I lived? We found evidence of a Dr. Reasor when we found McDonald's personal notes, but we can't find me. Anywhere. It's like I never existed."

And that was odd. "There's no record of you at Yale?"

He shook his head. "No. We checked all the medical schools. I know that sounds crazy, but the team I work with has a couple of excellent hackers. There's a whole company we work with. They do nothing but track missing persons. In this case they're working backward, but if anyone could find me, it would be them. Nothing."

"There can't be nothing," she said, her mind working. "You haven't looked in the right place yet. Hope's father would have had the power to change records perhaps, but he was dead by then. Why would she have erased your memory? Could you have seen something you shouldn't have? I don't think that's it. She let you have power over the project when she was gone. I was limited in what I could see of her research, but you often used her computer. I think you had to have threatened her in some way."

"Like I threatened you?"

She set aside the yogurt and put her hands on the table because she needed balance. This would be easier if Owen were here in the room with her, but she had to forget about him in a comfort role. She was certain all his talk was about keeping her under control. Pleasing her sexually had worked well once. He was simply going back to a familiar tactic. "Yes, you threatened me. You scared me so badly that I ran and I didn't look back. It was the only time I ever left a job."

"What did I threaten to do?" He seemed to brace himself as well, his shoulders squaring and spine straightening.

He was a lovely man. He always had been, but there had been a hardness to the old Steven Reasor, a sneer that seemed to dominate his every expression. There was none of that on this man's face. He seemed younger than Reasor. Despite the doctor's youthful age, he'd always seemed so much older than she was. Not so the man in front of her.

Maybe she needed to start thinking of him as a patient. If this man had walked in with a degenerative brain disease and had wanted to call himself Tucker, she would let him do that. She would allow him to do anything that made him comfortable.

And she would have had someone confront him with events that might spark his memory.

"You threatened to kill me." She was happy with how even her tone was. "Not before you'd sampled the goods, as you put it, but you promised that after you'd figured out what made me tick, you were going to kill me. I believed you."

"I threatened to rape you?" He looked sick at the thought.

"Not in so many words, but that was the gist." She needed to know a few things. Faith had talked about what had happened to her husband, but only in vague terms. "McDonald was there the last few days I spent at the Kronberg lab. You and she were fighting about something. I don't know what because she refused to acknowledge that anything was wrong."

McDonald had smiled, a gesture that didn't reach her eyes, and sent her back to work. *Nothing to worry about.* She would handle everything, and could Becca bring her the latest results on the primary testing?

"In her journal she talked about dealing with Reasor if she had to. She didn't say why, but she said if he continued to cause problems, she knew how to handle him." His eyes became steady, focused utterly on her. "Did I rape you?"

"No." She sighed. "I don't think so."

His breath hitched and he stood up, panic plain in every movement of his body. This was killing him, and she didn't think he was faking it.

"I don't think you did anything to me physically, but I had a dream the night before I left." It was past time to figure this out. "It was weird. I had dinner and I felt sick. That was the last thing I remembered. I woke up in one of the patient beds, and someone had given me IV fluids. The nurse on duty told me I'd had a terrible stomach flu and I'd passed out. She said it happened to a couple of us who ate in the cafeteria."

He shook his head as though the blows just kept coming. "You think I poisoned you?"

"I had dreams that night. The worst dreams I've ever had. They were so vivid. It felt like weeks passed and you were there. You tortured me."

"In your dreams."

She nodded. "And when I got back to my room, that was when you confronted me. You were angry because Dr. McDonald was talking about bringing me on full time. I was supposed to go on a trip to Argentina with her the week after, and you'd just found out. I guess you wanted to be the one to go."

His eyes narrowed. "Rebecca, Argentina was where her secret lab was located. That was where she held Theo. If she was taking you there, she would have kept you there, too. She likely wanted you to solve her Theo problem."

A chill went through her.

"Do you remember who was around you at dinner?" Tucker asked.

She shook her head. "Honestly, I don't remember much. I remember walking into the cafeteria and then waking up. They told me there was something bad in the salad."

"Or someone dosed you. We know she'd worked on the time dilation drug by that point. Tennessee Smith knows what that feels like." Tucker started to pace. "I don't understand why she would have done it if she was planning on taking you." He stopped. "I did it. I did it to get rid of you. I did it to keep my place."

It was easier to talk to him now that she could see a bit past who he'd been. The old Reasor never paced. He'd been almost preternaturally still. It had been unnerving. "You don't know that. The only way to know that is to uncover the memories."

He shook his head. "I don't want to. I know the others are hoping there's some kind of cure out there, but not me. I won't take it. I won't go back to who I used to be. Would you? Would you unlock your Mr. Hyde?"

"Knowing what you did for McDonald could help the others," she said, her doctor brain working on how she would do it. She would need scans and blood work. If McDonald had used Becca's own research to perfect her treatments, then she should be able to do something about it. "Have you tried hypnosis? The human body will always attempt to heal itself, and it can be shocking how much it can do given time and rest."

"Yeah, Ari's tried that with all of us. Some of the others get flashes sometimes. I get feelings. Like I should be doing something. Like I left something undone. I don't know why but I think about old-looking places. Places that look like London, but they're not."

She nodded. "That's because she can't erase your mind. She could potentially destroy the sections that deal with memory, but that would be a delicate procedure and one that would as likely hurt the parts she wanted to function as not. She needed to break down specific communication between brain synapses, and do it in a way no one has before. Not that anyone who isn't psychotic would want to. I'm trying to do the opposite. I'm trying to find a way to break down the plaque that cuts off…damn it. She found a way to build it up and very quickly. In a targeted way."

She could work with that. Especially if she had a lab. She needed those damn notes. McDonald wouldn't have gotten rid of them and she would have had a failsafe.

"I'm sorry." Tucker sounded tired.

The words burst through the momentary excitement of discovery, and guilt swelled inside her again. These men had been broken utterly and she was excited about a new project.

Because if McDonald figured out how to build up walls around sections of the memory center, then she had also known how to break them down. The key was here. She knew it was. It was held in these men and that research.

But the man in front of her was real, and she was shocked by the tears that ran down his face. Everything else about him was controlled, but those tears…

"You aren't the same man you were." That particular truth hit her soundly as she stared at him, unsure what to do. "You have nothing to apologize for because you aren't the one who did it to me."

"I don't know who I was, what I did. I meet people and I wonder how I hurt them. I don't ever want to know. I don't want to lose this me. I don't have any right to ask you this, but can you help me stay me?" His jaw tightened and he was obviously on the edge. "Please. I have to stay me or I need to…I can't go back."

She could walk away from him. She didn't have to promise this man anything.

Except he was giving her a chance to choose. If it had really been Steven Reasor standing in front of her, she could have walked away, but this was a man named Tucker and he wanted to be good. She had no idea what forces had molded Reasor into a man they called Razor, but this man was different.

And he was in pain.

She'd promised her mother that she would be happy, but happiness sometimes wasn't a choice. Happiness could be taken away, made into an impossibility due to circumstance. Maybe what her mother should have asked her was to always be true to who she was because then, even if her world got ripped away, she could be content.

She could hate this man for what he'd done to her in another life. Or she could see him as a man who needed help, and she'd dedicated her life to giving help when and where it was needed.

Becca stood and crossed the space between them. "I promise you, Tucker. I'll do what I can to help your friends, to help any of them who want to get back what they lost, and I'll make sure we don't need your memories. I can do it. I can make this work."

He broke then and his hands came out, as though he couldn't not ask for comfort.

When his legs went out and he slumped to the floor, she went with him. She let her arms go around him and finally let go of that day. She'd been a victim, and nothing she could have done would have likely fixed the situation.

"Get your hands…" Owen stopped when she looked up at him, his words halting and face transforming from anger to confusion as he looked down at them. "Are you all right?"

She nodded as she felt a shudder go through Tucker. "I am."

"I wasn't going to hurt her," Tucker said, his voice tortured. "But you should know that I did. I hurt her, Owen."

"You didn't," a feminine voice said. When Becca glanced up she saw they weren't alone. Ariel stood in the doorway next to Ezra, with Robert behind her. "You didn't hurt her, but someone who wore your skin did. I think we should talk about this. I'll make us some tea. Why don't the rest of you go back to bed?"

Go back to bed with Owen. That seemed like a bad idea. Even being in the same room with the man was dangerous, and after her talk with Tucker, she was on the edge again.

Ezra stepped away, pulling a phone from his pocket.

"Thank you, Dr. Walsh," Tucker whispered. "I'm still sorry. I'll try to stay away from you. I don't want to make you uncomfortable."

But he was the only one who knew anything about medicine, and she wasn't certain he would have forgotten what he'd learned from Dr. McDonald. That kind of knowledge could remain even when personal memories did not. She might be able to coax some of that information out of him and might lead them one step closer to a cure.

Sometimes bad things happened, and it was up to her to make the most of them, to try to see the positive that could come from it.

"I'm okay. You're Tucker. You're not Steven. And we're okay, you and I." She let Owen help her up. "Good night, Tucker. I'll see you in the morning. We can fight it out over the last raspberry yogurt."

"It's all yours." Tucker managed to make it back to his seat.

Owen didn't let go of her hand. "Good night. We'll see you all in the morning."

She followed him out, a piece of herself settling. But the larger piece was still in turmoil and it was all about Owen. Maybe it was time to have it out with him, too.

Ezra stepped back in. "We need to move out now. There's a team on the way. I don't know how the fucker found us, but he did. Big Tag says we've got maybe five minutes. Owen, take Dr. Walsh in my SUV. Ari and Robert, go with them."

Owen's hand found hers and he started into the living room.

"I'll go wake my sleeping prince," Erin said. "We'll stay behind and deal with the fallout. I can't wait to answer all those questions."

"Tucker, take Nina and hop in the van with River and Jax. I'll take Dante and Sasha," Ezra said, reaching for his backpack. "You know the protocols. Let's move."

Owen frowned at his boss. "You know what this means?"

Ezra nodded tightly. "I do. We have to deal with it later. Scatter now and implement a twenty-four-hour blackout on communications. See you on the other side, brothers."

It looked like her night was taking a turn for the worse.

Chapter Nineteen

Owen looked out the window from his place in the back seat, his eyes on the blue and red lights in the distance. Though they'd gotten miles away, he could still see how close it had been.

"Will Tom…Theo and his wife be okay? Shouldn't they have run, too?" Becca was looking at those ghostly lights, too.

"I assure you Erin will take care of the situation. Leaving two safe people behind will actually slow the police down. They don't know the whole story, and Erin will use that to her advantage. And to ours," Ariel said, sitting back. "There's no reason for the police to pick them up, and if they did, they have connections who would move swiftly to get them out. The Lost Boys don't have those. Big Tag can hide them, but he can't make global warrants disappear. If they'd caught Jax or Dante or Sasha, or even Robert, there would be trouble. Some of them have Interpol red notices out on them."

"Red notice?" Becca asked.

Owen took that one. "It's an international warrant for their arrests. Ezra explained how McDonald funded her research after she left Kronberg. She was involved in several criminal operations, including robbing banks. She didn't do it herself."

Even in the moonlight he could see the way she paled. "She used her strike team. She could get the money she needed and see them in action."

"I don't actually have an Interpol notice on me," Robert corrected, "but I am wanted for questioning about a couple of things, including my association with the others. Big Tag made sure Theo's records are perfectly clean. He's good."

"Though I assume this isn't about the lads," Ariel said.

"It's about me." Becca was holding herself apart. While they'd been rushing to the car, she'd let him hold her hand. The minute he'd closed the door, he'd felt a wall come up between them.

There was no forgiveness for him.

Robert pulled out onto the highway. They needed to drive at least a hundred miles, find a motel, and settle in for the night. Though he was certain he wouldn't feel settled. He wouldn't be comfortable until she was safely ensconced in The Garden and protected by people he trusted.

"How did he find us?" Becca asked. "They got rid of my cell phone. I thought everyone did."

"We were working off burners, anyway," Robert said. "No one except the team, Damon Knight, and Big Tag know the numbers."

"Then how did they find us? Do you think it was CCTV?" Becca's hands were balled in her lap, a sure sign of her tension.

He wanted to reach over and hold her hand, promise her everything would be all right, but she wouldn't take comfort from him. "Maybe."

What he wasn't saying, what Robert and Ari had to know, was that there was only one way Green could have caught up with them.

Someone had betrayed the team.

What did they really know about Nina Blunt? She'd hired on to McKay-Taggart and Knight only a few months before.

But then hadn't something gone wrong with the Colorado mission? Nina hadn't been around for that one. Pieces were falling into place, and he didn't like the way this puzzle was filling out.

"So you think he wants me for the same reason Ezra does?" Becca watched the road out of the window. "I would think I was useless without the actual drug. Do you think he has it and he wants someone to reverse engineer it?"

"He could have any number of people do that for him," Ari replied. "He needs you to figure out the protocols. Her techniques were about more than drugs."

"He wants me to be the new Hope McDonald. Why would I ever

do that? I'm certainly not going to sell my soul to get my career back. I love my work, but I would be dishonoring every vow I took when I became a doctor. He would have to kill me first. How does he think he's going to get me to help him?" Her eyes widened and she turned in her seat. "Owen, my family. What if he uses my family to get to me?"

"I've already got someone watching over them." It was the first thing he'd thought about as he'd held her in the back of Jax's van. He'd made the call to Big Tag and someone would be monitoring her father, stepmother, and sister.

"Levi has to be careful about how he works in the States," Robert pointed out. "He might draw attention to himself if he pulled a stunt like that. That's why we believe he isn't the one who was setting you up. Not only does the timing not work, if it could be tied back to him, he would be in trouble with his bosses. I'm almost certain he walked into the situation, assessed it, and decided his best shot was to use the embezzlement scam as leverage. Add in the fact that there was an MSS agent already working the head of the Huisman Foundation, and he cut us loose fast and quick."

Becca had no way of knowing what they thought. He was certain Ezra would likely want it kept that way, but she was part of the team now. Her life was on the line, and he wouldn't leave her ignorant. "Levi Green sent us here. We think he intended to let us do the dirty work and he would have shown up at some point and grabbed the prize."

Or let his plant grab it for him.

His mind sought any other explanation for what had happened tonight. Maybe they'd been unlucky. He didn't want to think about the fact that one of them could have been lying for years, waiting and watching for his time to strike.

"I don't understand any of this," Becca said with a long sigh.

"I'll answer any questions you have," Owen replied.

A long silence followed and he watched her in the moonlight, half her face shrouded by night. He should have told her everything that day in the lift. He should have trusted his instincts. There were so many places where he could have turned this thing around, and time and time again he'd missed the moment.

"What you did for Tucker tonight was amazing, Rebecca," Ari said, her voice soothing. She'd turned so she could get a glimpse of the woman she was talking to. "I wish they'd let me go with him, but I'm glad he's got River and Jax. I can't imagine how hard this is on him. He's been afraid of this since the moment he heard the name Razor."

"It wasn't him," Becca said, the words sounding dull out of her mouth.

He hated how the light in her eyes was dim again. Briefly he'd seen her come alive when she'd been comforting her enemy. He wanted desperately to see anything in her eyes but this grim sadness.

How much time would they have together? In twenty-four hours, they would get the new orders that would move her out of the country as quickly as possible. Somewhere Big Tag had a team together and they would be making plans that would separate him from her.

Was he willing to let her go without a fight? He wasn't sure she would be alone with him again. She might cling to Ariel, and he wouldn't have a chance to talk this out with her.

"I'm sorry, Becca. I need you to understand that I didn't walk into this with the thought of hurting you," he said. "It wasn't supposed to go down this way, and I'll do anything I need to do to make it up to you."

"There's nothing you can do." She leaned against the door, staying as far from him as possible. "This isn't like Tucker. You knew who you were when you walked into my life."

"He forgot who he was supposed to be really fast, though," Robert added, sounding cheerier than he did before.

Ari turned to Robert and send him a wilting look.

Robert shrugged. "It's true. One minute I had an exotic Scottish lover and the next I was a lonely man. I was looking forward to playing twink to his bear."

He was about to tell Robert to stop with the sarcasm, but Becca had sat straight up.

"What?" She leaned toward where Robert was sitting. "I thought he was sent in to seduce me."

It was the most animation he'd seen on her in half an hour. This could get embarrassing, but if it made Becca smile, he would suffer through it. "Not exactly."

"Not at all is what he means," Robert replied with something akin to glee. "He wasn't supposed to get close to you. I was."

"Really?" Her nose wrinkled up. "No offense, but you're not my type. I mean you're attractive and all, but I don't know that I would have responded to you."

A deep sense of satisfaction welled inside him. Robert turned women's heads wherever they went, but he wasn't Becca's type. Owen was. "She likes a bit of the bad boy in there. And she loves this accent of mine."

Becca glared his way. "I think I'll stay away from bad boys from now on since I got taken by one."

Before Owen could reply, Robert was chuckling. "I wasn't going to seduce you. I was going to befriend you, and trust me, you would have wanted to befriend me. I had plans. I bought board games and everything. A couple of rounds of Ticket to Ride, some wine and a nice dinner, and you would have been eating out of the palm of my hand. You would have been thrilled to befriend the new couple in the building. Of course we would have bonded over talking about my surly husband there. He wasn't going to talk much."

She finally glanced his way. "You and Robert were going in as a couple? You didn't mention that to me. When did that change? Did Ezra order it? Speaking of couples, why were Ezra and Ariel posing as a married couple when it's obvious she's involved with Robert?"

"I wouldn't say involved," Ariel began.

"Because I looked better with Owen than Ezra. I was the obvious choice, and no one consulted me about the whole married to Ezra thing," Robert continued as if Ariel hadn't said a thing. "I would have gone with sister."

Ari snorted. "Seriously, you think I look like lily-white Ezra's sister? And how would you explain the accent?" She shook her head, but there was a smile on her lips. "He's insane."

"He was also staring at the two of you like he was going to rip Ezra's head off that night at dinner." It was way better to talk about Robert's flaws than his own. He noticed Becca had moved closer to him. He wanted to reach out and get a hand on her, but he wasn't about to push his luck. "You two should be damn glad I got her out of there early because I think she would have figured out something was wrong if you'd spent the entire dinner glaring at Ezra every time he touched his wife."

"Everyone at that dinner was in on it." Becca sat back, her hands in her lap again. "The whole thing was done to trick me."

"The whole thing was done so I could get a feel for who you are as a person," Ariel corrected quietly. "I really am a psychologist. I wanted to spend time with you so I could evaluate whether or not I thought you were capable of working with McDonald on a project like Tabula Rasa. You have to understand that it was important to know who you were personally. All of these men's lives depend on who you are. On paper, I would have said no, but getting to know someone in person is important. I didn't get the chance because Owen hustled you out. And no one changed up the assignments. Owen did that because he couldn't keep his hands off you, and he knew it the minute you stepped on that lift. He could easily have given you his cover and that would have been the end of it. But he didn't because he'd been thinking about you since the moment he saw a picture of you."

He wouldn't have put it so baldly, but the words seem to have an effect on Becca. She'd turned to him and there was a softness to her expression.

Was this what Ezra had been talking about when he'd mentioned Case and Mia? Had he been talking about letting himself be vulnerable? It wasn't something he wanted to do, but she'd been made to feel that way and he'd had a hand in it.

"We had two pictures of you," he began. "One was the picture you use on all your foundation informational materials. You look very professional."

"And the other?"

He couldn't help but smile. "You're wearing spandex and your smile is so bright you reminded me of the sun. I think something about that picture brushed against those memories you say are trapped inside me because after I saw it, I could remember what it felt like to be in the waves with the sun on my face. I think that picture opened up a place inside me I didn't know I had."

"You didn't tell me you were getting flashes," Robert said.

"Not the point, dear," Ari said and they went quiet for a moment.

"Captain Neuro. It's stupid but I have fun with it," Becca said after a long moment. "Had fun with it. I liked being around the kids. I liked showing the girls they could be doctors and talking about science with the classes."

"I don't think it's stupid. I think you found a way to get them to think about science," he replied, hating the inches between them. It felt like miles.

"Yeah, well, it's gone now, and I won't be allowed to do it again. The funny thing was I didn't start it until I came here to Canada. I set up the charity years ago, but I didn't know what I wanted to do with it. After I left Kronberg, I came back to the States and that was when my marriage fell apart. I was having terrible dreams about…about what happened in Germany. I had them for a long time afterward. I thought I was a coward for running out the way I did. I guess you could say I was compensating and didn't even realize it."

"Or you were trying to help a bunch of children," Ari said, her tone gentle. "Sometimes a thing simply is. You tried to do good. Maybe subconsciously you chose the form of it as a way to empower yourself after a traumatic event, but you were still doing good."

"My mom was a professor and my father a doctor. It was a meshing of my role models, I suppose," Becca mused. "I thought I could help kids who don't have role models who could talk to them about working in the medical field. Paul always told me it was embarrassing. Asshole. I changed at the office once and he told me not to do it again because it wouldn't look good if any patrons saw me like that. I knew then and there that we weren't going to be…he did it, didn't he? Son of a bitch. I bet it was Paul. He's wanted to get rid of me from the moment they hired me. He knew about the charity and he would obviously have ways to get into my accounts since his family runs the place."

"If he's at the heart of this, Phoebe will figure it out," he promised. "I'll take care of this and you'll have your reputation back if it's the last thing I do. When we can call base again, I'll let Phoebe know where to look."

"What an ass," she said under her breath. "I can't believe he did this to me. He'll take over my research, too. I bet he was planning to force me to leave quietly. His father will be angry when my name gets plastered all over the news since if my name is out there, so is Huisman's."

It made sense. He'd worked a couple of cases while he'd been in London concerning corporate spying, and they always handled the spy with great care so word didn't get out and cause concern among stockholders.

There was a reason Paul was willing to take that particular bullet. Levi Green must have had a field day with him. "They're going to take down his father."

Robert nodded as he pulled off the highway and onto a country road. They were going to use as many backroads as possible. "They'll use the fact that he's got ties to Chinese intelligence to do it. I bet Green himself brought in the operative. I wonder what he's giving her for her cooperation."

"I wonder if we can find a way to prove he's working with her," Ari said. "I bet the Agency would be interested in that."

Robert said something about Levi being made of Teflon, but Owen was staring at Becca.

"I will do everything I can to get you out of this."

She wouldn't look at him, simply stared at the back of Ari's seat. "It's not your problem. I'm going to London and I'll be safe there. You can do what you want to."

"He doesn't have to be with us," Robert explained. "He's here because he chose to. Owen could have stayed in London and worked and rebuilt his life, but he chose to come with us."

His old partner, Nick, had tried to talk him into staying in London. They'd worked a couple of jobs together and he'd been perfectly competent, but it had felt wrong to stay. It felt like he owed these men.

Owed them? God, it hit him like a slap in the face. He'd walked away from The Garden out of guilt. Loyalty was in there, yes, but at the heart of everything was the deep desire to eradicate himself. Deep in his heart, he'd come out here because he'd thought he wouldn't come back. Suicide by martyrdom.

"I didn't do it for the right reasons," he said slowly, forcing the words out of his mouth. He didn't want to say them, but he had to. Becca deserved his honesty. So did the rest of them. "I did it because I don't think I deserve to live. I did it because I thought if I went out in a blaze of glory saving my brother, then maybe I could make things right."

Becca gasped and Robert's hands tightened on the wheel, but Ari turned and looked at him, sympathy plain on her face. "I know, Owen. I'm glad you realize that. Maybe we can work through it now."

Becca turned to him. "Why? Why would you do that? Why would you think that way?"

He should have known Ariel saw right through him. Now Becca could, too. "Because it's true."

"Owen, if you care for her, tell her. Talk to her about it." Robert didn't sound cheery now. He sounded grim and sure of himself. "Don't hold on to this because it's eating you up inside. If you won't tell her, you won't tell anyone."

But he didn't want to tell her. She already hated him. She already thought he was a liar and a user.

"Owen, I want to know." She was staring at him across the seat between them. "Why would you think you would be better off…sacrificing yourself?"

"You don't have to talk about it," Ari offered. "But if it helps, I don't think she'll blame you. I think Rebecca is a sympathetic person who will understand why you did what you did. They were your family."

"Owen, were your mother and sister really killed in a break-in?" Becca asked the question as though she already knew the answer.

He could say yes and leave it there. She would believe him. No one on the team would talk about it. The lads could be terrible gossips, but not about anything important. And then he would never give her anything of himself that was real. He'd loved every moment he'd spent with her, and every moment had been a lie because he'd been playing a part, one where he was whole and clean. "No. They were murdered by Dr. McDonald. She used them as leverage to get me to turn over Theo and Erin and their son."

A gasp escaped from her throat and she turned to face him. Her eyes shone in the moonlight that streamed in from the window. "She killed them because you wouldn't turn them over?"

"She killed them even though I did." He let the words sit between them, the silence lengthening like a chasm. She stared at him as though she couldn't quite understand what he was telling her. "I lied to my whole team. I don't know the hows and whys. I can't remember that, but I know I did it. They tell me I refused to turn over the baby, but how can they really know? Maybe I screwed that part up."

It was his fear, that they were all being kind or they'd misunderstood his intentions and he'd been willing to turn that child over.

"We didn't lie to you," Robert insisted. "You wouldn't turn the baby over. You made sure the baby stayed with Kayla."

Sure he had. They couldn't know what was in his heart that day.

"She took your family? Hope McDonald took your family?" Becca asked, though he'd already told her. It was like she was attempting to make sense of the words.

"Yes. Again, I don't know the hows. I know Mum and Hannah lived in Scotland and I was in England. I left them alone. I was in a position where someone could use them against me and I didn't protect them. I don't even remember if I loved them. All I feel is guilt. I look at their pictures and all I feel is despair, and I'm glad they aren't around because I'm pretty sure those women in the pictures wouldn't have been proud to call me kin."

She was still for a moment and then finally she spoke, her words coming out thin and tortured. "Do you hate me for that?"

"What?"

Tears began to slip from her eyes. "I was scared. I ran and I didn't do what I should have done. Owen, I was so scared. I didn't even understand what truly happened until tonight. I believe I was given a dose of the time dilation drug by Steven. He wanted me to leave because he thought Dr. McDonald was going to choose me over him. He didn't want to lose his place at her side."

His breath caught in his throat at the thought. He knew what that fucking drug did. He'd read everything he could, every report available. "What did he put you through?"

She went quiet. "I don't want to talk about it. I'm not even certain what happened."

"Depending on how he used it, what the dosage was and some other factors, it could have felt like a dream state," Ariel explained.

"A nightmare," Becca said, and he thought she was saying it more to herself than anyone else. She seemed to shake it off. "I'm sorry I don't know where the package is. I don't remember getting anything from her. If I had, I would have studied the material. This was right before I came to Canada?"

"Yes." He didn't want to talk about the mission. He wanted to drag her onto his lap and keep her talking. He wanted to assure her that he didn't blame her for anything, but she wasn't ready to listen. She might never be. "From what we've discovered, Dr. McDonald sent a package to you roughly two weeks before the raid on her compound in France."

"I believe she knew Taggart was closing in on her." Ariel's voice had gone professional again as if she understood they couldn't handle

301

any more emotion. "She might have sent you that material in order to try to protect it."

"Or it might be complete crap and we've done all of this for nothing," Robert said with a long sigh.

"It wasn't for nothing." He hadn't meant to say it out loud, but he couldn't hold it in. "Green would have come after Becca at some point. He believes there's something in the package, and he would have figured out that Becca has knowledge he can use. If we hadn't been here, he would have taken her one way or another."

"But she didn't send anything to me," Becca insisted and then she took a long breath. "Wait. How would she have sent anything to me? She didn't have my address at the time."

"It was before you moved here. You were living in Boston," he explained. "Wasn't that your address when you worked at Kronberg? They would have known your address."

She nodded, clearly thinking it through. "But Gary and I split up right after I got back from Germany. He had his affair while I was there and I found out when I came home unexpectedly. I moved out that day. Yes, Kronberg had that address, but Gary lived there at the time. Not me. He lived there up until a few months ago. Oh, shit. I know where it is. It's at my apartment. About three months ago, he sent me two big boxes of stuff I'd left behind. He'd put it up in the attic but I never made time to go get it. He and Britney decided to sell the house, and I asked him to mail me the boxes. I put them aside. I was busy and I honestly didn't want to look at anything that would remind me of that time. They're sitting in my guest room closet. It's got to be in there."

He hated what he had to tell her next. "It's not there."

She shook her head. "If Gary got mail for me that I didn't pick up, he would have put it in the box he sent. He even said something about having some packages I never came to get. Britney said she wanted my shit out of the place before she called a real estate agent. I would have told him to throw it all away, but he'd already shipped it. It's got to be there. I never opened the second box."

"But I did." He had to put it out there. "And by now Levi's gone through it, too. There was nothing there but some clothes, a couple of stuffed animals, and some books. There was no package."

She stilled. "Of course you did. That's what you were there to do. You waited until I was asleep. You did a good job tiring me out. I slept like a log when you were there."

Because he'd fucked her so long and hard and well, he'd wanted to sleep, too. Instead he'd crawled out of her bed and gotten his job done.

"If it hadn't been Owen, it would have been me." That was Robert, always trying to help a friend out. "We had cameras stationed around the building so we would know when you were coming and going. If Owen hadn't searched your place, I would have done it while you were at work. Sasha and Dante searched your office. They weren't able to get to your lab. They were moving into those shifts next week."

"Of course." She was staring out the window again. "The lab would have been a bust, though they'll take my research now. Paul will likely move forward with it on his own."

"I'll try to get it back for you." He could steal it. He could have Jax hack into Huisman and take it back for her. The data would be stored somewhere. It could be a team job.

Her face had settled into a stubborn expression. "I want to tell you to fuck yourself, but I need it. It will be helpful in my new work, my work no one will likely ever know about because I'm a fugitive."

"You won't always be," he replied, hoping she understood he wasn't going to leave her like this. "I told you, I'm going to fix it. I'll find a way."

"You also told me you wanted to be my lover. You'll excuse me if I don't believe you."

"I wanted to be your lover the minute you stepped into that lift. Maybe before. Is it really my fault you also happened to be the target?"

"Yes, it's your fault." At least she was looking at him again.

"I think we should take a moment," Ariel began.

"Stay out of this." Becca looked like she was ready to take them all on. "This is not a therapy session and while we're discussing it, how do you reconcile lying to people? You're a therapist and you help these guys put people into positions where they will inevitably need your services. That's quite a racket you have going."

"That is certainly not my plan, Rebecca," Ariel replied primly.

Robert chuckled. "Actually it is a great business plan when you think about it, babe. Tell me you weren't already planning Becca's sessions?"

Ariel frowned his way. "Of course I was. She's going to have trust issues. She already has them, and I've only recently realized that they

303

aren't merely caused by her childhood. They've also got an enormous amount to do with what happened to her at Kronberg. We'll need to work through that."

"I don't have trust issues." Becca argued, pointing Owen's way. "Well, I didn't until I met this one."

"That's not true," Owen replied. Ariel wasn't the only one who'd made a study of Rebecca Walsh. He'd gotten to know her, spent long hours thinking about her. He'd come to some conclusions. "You don't have friends, Becca, and you're the type of woman who needs them."

She seemed to think about that for a moment. "I have Cathy."

"How much does she know about your life?" Owen asked. "Think about this. You see her at work and you talk about research and what you're going to eat for lunch and how her children are doing. When do you tell her about your hopes and dreams? She set you up with the most boring lawyer on the planet and why? Because all she really knows about you is how hard you work."

The tears were back in her eyes and he hated the fact that he was the one who had to point this out to her.

"I wanted to take some time after the divorce," she said. "I guess I didn't realize how much I isolated myself."

"After a trauma, it can be hard to open up," Ariel said, her tone back to soothing. "It's not surprising that you kept to yourself. It would feel safe to keep yourself locked away, to not become intimate with the people around you."

"I'm bloody glad you didn't open up to that arsehole, Carter." If there was one good thing that could come out of this, it was getting her away from Carter. "I swear if I'd had more time, I would have had a long talk with him."

"Why?" Becca asked. "He's a jerk, but I'm pretty sure he's harmless. Or at least I thought he was until he basically blackmailed me. I knew he was obnoxious the day I met him, but I didn't think he was abusive."

A chill went through him as he realized something he'd missed before. He'd been so wrapped up in his own misery he hadn't been thinking. "How did he know?"

"Know what?" Becca asked.

"Owen, we have a problem," Robert said, his tone going dark. "Is everyone buckled in? I didn't see him before because he's got his headlights off and it's dark as hell."

Owen turned his head and saw what Robert was talking about. In the dim shadows given out by the rear lights, he saw the outline of a vehicle following them. His heart rate ticked up and he pulled his SIG, aware of how Becca's eyes widened.

"Maybe it's someone out for a drive," she said, looking around the interior as Robert passed Ariel his gun and she competently handled it.

"At three in the morning? In the middle of the country?" His revelation would have to wait. "With their lights off? I doubt it. Apparently Green was waiting for us, and now he doesn't even have to deal with the police."

"Yeah, I was thinking that, too," Robert said tightly. "Whoever set us up knew what they were doing. Green was probably watching us from a distance and he knew exactly which car to follow. Ari, if I can't lose him, I'm going to find the nearest police station and I want you to take Rebecca and run in. Give yourselves up. Big Tag will move heaven and earth to get you both out. You call the Dallas office as soon as you can. Owen, find us the nearest station."

"I'm not leaving you."

He'd expected Ariel to say that, but the words came out of Becca's mouth. She was leaning toward him expectantly.

He would have replied to her, would have told her that she damn well better do as Robert said, but that was the moment a shot split the air and the SUV careened to the side. He heard Robert curse, trying to stay in control as they lost one of the tires while speeding down a country road.

Something hit the back of the SUV, just a bumping of metal on metal, but it was enough to send them off the road and rolling. The world upended, and he heard a scream as metal crunched and crushed.

He reached out, trying to get Becca's hand in his, but his head snapped back and he saw stars. He could have sworn the world was twisting and turning. He saw Becca lurch forward and then back before her body went limp.

After what seemed like the longest time, the car stopped. They hadn't landed right. They were upside down. The car swayed briefly, as though it would make one more turn. But they stayed where they were, the world going startlingly still.

For a moment all he could hear was the harsh sound of his own breath sawing in and out of his body. Then, the sound of shoes crushing against the ground.

"Hello, Owen," a familiar voice said. "Robert, if you don't want me to kill your lovely lady, you'll drop that. You'll see I've brought a few friends. We can do this the friendly way or the hard way. I personally prefer friendship. Owen is going to make some new friends and I'm going to become very good friends with Dr. Walsh. She seems to be sleeping."

Owen was upside down, his weight hanging from the seatbelt. He'd dropped his bloody gun. He couldn't feel its weight in his hand. All he could do was dangle there. Though it hurt like hell, he forced his head around, to look for Becca. A low moan shuddered through his system because her eyes weren't open.

"Rebecca." He managed to get her name out of his mouth, a prayer, a plea, a recognition that if she wasn't alive he didn't want to be either. Somehow this woman had invaded his soul and taken up all the empty spaces. Everything he'd lost was somehow replaced because he loved this one woman.

"Don't hurt her." Robert's voice sounded tortured.

"It's okay. Why would I hurt her? Ariel's never done anything but been lovely to me, and you know I don't like to kill the beautiful things of this world." Levi's voice floated through the vehicle like a wraith about to strike them all.

It was so dark. He tried to let his eyes adjust, but his head was ringing. The gun. He needed to get it in his hands before they came for Becca. He couldn't let them take her.

"You, on the other hand, have been a pain in my ass for a long time, so I don't have a single problem shooting you," Levi said.

And then there was the tiny ping of a gun being fired through a suppressor.

Robert? Fuck all, Green had shot Robert and he was next, and then Becca would be alone. It was so hard to think. His brain wouldn't work. Pure panic shot through him as the door to the passenger side opened and big hands reached toward Becca's still form.

Was Robert dead? He'd fucking shot Robert and Owen had no idea how he recovered from that. But he had to because Becca was alive and he owed her. He'd promised her. He had a brief glimpse of Ariel hanging from her seatbelt, her whole body limp. Blood. There was blood on the seat. Robert's blood?

God, how would he tell Ariel he'd been hanging uselessly while Robert had died? Robert had been through so much, survived McDonald's experiments, and he'd died on Owen's watch.

Running on pure adrenaline, he managed to reach the buckle and winced when he dropped to the floor...ceiling. It was an awkward position, but he had to make it work. He had to get out of here, get Becca back. They were pulling her body out of the car.

Gun. He couldn't see it. It was too dark. He reached for it, trying to get that cold metal back in his hands. If he could get the gun, he might have a chance.

"Not so fast, big guy. I'm afraid you're going to have to come with me, well, with my friend," Levi said as something sharp shot into Owen's calf. "You're payment. You know no one does things just for the good of humanity anymore. They're all about the payment. You're going to have fun in Beijing, my friend."

He was still trying to reach for the gun when the world went hazy.

God, he didn't want to forget her. He couldn't forget her.

He held on to the thought of Becca Walsh as his vision went dark, and he prayed he wasn't being sent back to hell again.

Chapter Twenty

Becca came awake slowly, her body aching oddly and her mind reaching for any explanation as to where she was. What had happened? She remembered being in the car and Owen had asked her a question.

He'd asked her how he'd known. How who had known? And known what? They'd been talking about something and then...

"I don't understand why you had to bring them here," a familiar voice whispered, though she could plainly hear him. Paul. What was Paul doing in the car? "I can't have anyone know I was involved in this."

"And no one will," a deep voice replied. "We came in under cover of darkness and hauled our guests in through your very spacious garage. Ah, old money. Was that a Rolls I saw in there?"

"This is serious, Mr. Green."

A long huff was heard as though the man making the sound was incredibly bored. "I'm not about to call your neighbors, but where did you think I would take them until we're ready for transport? I certainly can't carry two unconscious people through the lobby of my hotel. And poor Mo Chou can't show up at her condo building with a couple of new friends she needs a bellman to carry up for her. There would be questions. Here, we're all alone. What's wrong, Paul? Getting a little real for you?"

The accident. Something had happened and the car had flipped.

Not an accident. Those brief moments of terror came crashing back in on her. Someone had shot out their tire and Robert had lost control of the car.

"You're a man who doesn't want to know where his food comes from, aren't you, Paul? You like it all wrapped in plastic so you don't have to see the dirty work. Did you think she would happily walk away with me?"

"I thought she would do it so she didn't go to jail," Paul replied.

There was a long pause before that deep voice spoke again. "And your father? Did you think he would, what? Maybe walk into Mo Chou's knife?"

"I'm going to shoot him," a feminine voice said. "Easier and I don't have to get dirty. Dry cleaning bills are expensive."

Becca forced her eyes open and gradually figured out where she was. Daylight streamed in through the windows. She blinked, the light far too bright. She was at Paul's house, the one he kept in one of the wealthiest parts of the city. She'd only been here a couple of times, but she would recognize that chandelier anywhere. His whole home was exquisitely done in old-world elegance. She looked up and saw the balcony across from her. There were two grand sets of stairs on either side of the house, and a balcony landing that ran from one wing to the other. She'd come for a Christmas party one year and wondered why he needed such a large house. There was only Paul and his son since his wife had left.

Where was Owen? Owen had been beside her in the car. Owen had been trying to get through to her. Owen had been offering her a life together, if she was only brave enough to take it.

"Ah, the good doctor awakens." A man's face came into view. She'd seen the man in pictures. He was handsome, with dark hair that swept over his forehead and chocolate brown eyes that should belong to someone less evil. He didn't look like a man who would kidnap people. "You might have a concussion. I don't know. I'm not the neurologist and Paul here won't check you out. I think he's sure if he touches you something bad will happen. The good news is you don't have any broken bones. You're probably going to bruise some though. When we get where we're going, I'll let all the doctors check you out."

He was actually smiling at her.

"Leave her alone," a deep voice growled.

Owen. Owen was here. She sat up and nausea rolled through her.

"Hey," Levi said, sitting down next to her on the leather couch she'd been laid out on. "Go slow, Doc. You're okay. He's okay. I know I played a little rough, but everyone's good."

"Robert isn't," Owen shot back.

She slowly turned her head. They weren't alone in the room. The woman she'd met at Casa Loma stood by the wall of windows that dominated the large office. She stood out against the white drapes that had been drawn. She wore all black, her hair in a neat bun. Beside her stood a massive man she'd never seen before. He'd gotten the all-black memo, though. She could see his shoulder holster and the hilt of a gun.

"Robert's such a baby," Levi said with a sigh. "One little gunshot and he's out of the game. I thought Big Tag raised them tougher than that."

"It's hard to be tough when you're hanging upside down in the dark and you've been in a bloody wreck. Note I didn't call it an accident." Owen sat in a chair they'd dragged in from the dining room. She recognized the highbacked antique chair from the evening she'd spent with Paul and his father and son. She remembered how small Emmanuel had looked sitting in the chair, how fragile he'd seemed. Owen wasn't small, but she was well aware of how fragile his body could be. He could have all the muscles in the world and one bullet could still kill his light. His arms wrapped around his back. She obviously wasn't such a threat as she'd been left free to move.

Her heart ached at the thought of Robert being dead. How had it happened? One minute they'd gotten away and the next she was waking up and Robert was gone.

"Stop looking at me like that, Owen," Levi said with a shake of his head. "He'll live. I didn't shoot him in the head or anything."

"Yes, I was surprised we left two survivors behind," the woman he'd called Mo Chou said, crossing her arms over her chest. "You know they're going to talk."

"Yes, well, dead bodies mean something to Taggart and Knight," Levi replied. "It's why I left Jax alive. I'm only turning Owen over to you because Tag won't care about him. And honestly, if Big Tag wants to even the score, he can take Donnie there and send him to MSS. With what he eats, it could bankrupt your entire intelligence program."

"Like we would want him," Mo Chou said.

The man named Donnie said absolutely nothing, simply stared at Owen like a predator waiting to pounce.

"Robert's alive?" Owen seemed to breathe a sigh of relief.

Levi stood up, smoothing down the vest he wore. "I left Jax alive, didn't I? I know how to play this game. Or maybe I left Robert alive for other reasons. Maybe I left Jax alive for other reasons. Or maybe it's one of those foreign boys. One of them had to have given me the information on where you were staying this evening. You moved quickly. I'll admit that I intended to negotiate with the Canadians for the doc's release into my custody, but this turned out so much easier. I originally sent you out here to get what I needed, and then my friend would have shared it with me and you would be none the wiser."

"But then he got greedy," Mo Chou added. "Like our friend Huisman here, and I'm worried it's going to bite us all in the ass."

Levi shrugged. "I realized that the doctor herself would be a much better asset. After all, what do I do if I don't understand the research? Shockingly, most incredibly gifted doctors don't end up working for the Agency. All it cost me was Big Tag's puppies figuring out one of them isn't what he seems to be. Not my problem anymore if I have the doc and the research. Game over. I win. We all find a new game to play."

She wanted to get up and cross the space between herself and Owen. Now that she was facing the idea of losing him, she couldn't stand the thought of never touching him again. "What do you mean you're giving Owen to her?"

Green put his hands in his pockets. He looked dapper and lean in his pressed slacks, crisp white shirt, and fitted vest. The only thing that marred the image was the gun holster around his shoulder and the hint of metal under his arm. "It's nothing you need to be worried about. Owen's taking a little trip to the East. You and I are going somewhere else, but I promise your every need will be met. This doesn't have to be a bad thing."

"I think kidnapping is usually a bad thing." He was the worst kind of evil, the one that didn't even realize he was bad. The man in front of her was charming, and if he'd shown up on her doorstep she wouldn't have been afraid of him until the moment he slit her throat. And he would if he had to. She believed absolutely everything Owen had told her about him.

If she believed Owen about that, why couldn't she believe him about the rest of it? Why couldn't she believe him when he said he loved her?

Green merely sent her a charming smile. "You call it kidnapping. I call it the necessary acquisition of valuable resources. You are the key to all of this. I figured that out too late to go after you myself. I take care of my people, Dr. Walsh. I'm sure Ezra and his group have filled your head with all sorts of lies about how I would hurt you, but it's not true. Play nice with me and I'll treat you like a queen. You'll have everything you could hope for."

"How about my freedom?"

He had the grace to wince. "You've got me on that one, but once you finish with the project, I'll make sure your reputation is restored and that you get full credit for all the good that's going to come out of this. And you know there *will* be good that comes from this. You'll thank me in the end when you win a Nobel Prize for medicine." He knelt down beside her, every ounce of his charm used to make her believe. "Here's something they don't know. I found something in Colorado that led me to another one of her facilities. I found one dose of what Dr. McDonald thought was the cure. I need you to break it down for me so we can move forward with this project."

"You have a cure?" That cure could be the key to Alzheimer's and dementia. If McDonald had truly figured out how to reconnect those neural pathways, it could open up a thousand doors.

"I think so. I'm not sure. I only know that I found something she thought was the cure," Levi replied. "She'd made it specifically for one of the men in Owen's unit. She wanted him to remember something. We can use it for something more, can't we?"

He knew exactly what to say to her. He knew how to get inside her head and coax her.

"Don't listen to him, love," Owen said.

"Wait a minute." Paul seemed to forget he was trying to make himself invisible. He strode across the large room, a steely look in his eyes. "I thought you were going to ensure she never had power again. Now you're planning on giving her one of the major finds of the century? You're going to hand over the cure to dementia? That was not our deal."

Mo Chou rolled her eyes. "I should have known you'd be

difficult."

Green stood again, facing off with Paul. "Our deal was that I wouldn't turn you over for setting up Dr. Walsh for embezzlement. You get her research and you get to take over the Huisman Foundation. You can be happy with that or not. It's your choice."

Mo Chou moved toward the back of the house. There was a hallway under the balcony that Becca thought led to the kitchen and the garage. "My team should be here in half an hour. We've got a plane ready. I'm going to make a phone call. Is that creepy kid still around?"

"That's my son," Paul said between clenched teeth. "Another reason you should have taken them somewhere else. I have a child. He can't be involved in this."

"Maybe you should have thought about him before you started doing criminal things." Becca was done with that asshole. She managed to get to her feet. "Maybe you should have thought about a lot of things. You won't get away with this. Cathy knows I wouldn't do this."

"Becca, darling, please sit down," Owen said, pleading in his voice.

Paul stepped into her space. "Cathy doesn't matter. She can fall in line or I'll deal with her, too. I'm done being everyone's whipping boy. I want this project." He turned to Green again. "I'm every bit as smart as she is, and we can do it all here. I have a whole foundation at my fingertips."

Her first impulse was to stand in front of Paul and let him know exactly how she felt. But Levi Green was speaking to him in hushed tones, and that meant he wasn't paying attention to her. She moved to Owen.

The massive man who'd spoken not a word stepped in her way.

"Please let me talk to him. I want to make sure he's okay. I'm a doctor." Maybe they would buy it. He didn't move an inch. She decided on a different tactic. "What do you think I'm going to do? You're right here. I don't have any weapons on me. I want to talk to him."

"Donnie, she's harmless," Green said. "And she likely has a few words to say to our friend. Why don't you stand by the door and make sure Mo Chou doesn't decide to take more than she's been offered? I can handle this."

She dropped to her knees in front of Owen, looking him over as best she could. She felt stronger now. At least her limbs moved. "Are you okay?"

He shook his head. "It doesn't matter. I need you to listen to me, Becca. You do whatever he wants, do you understand me?"

His eyes were clear, though there was a cut on his forehead. Someone had cleaned him up and dressed the small wound. "What are they going to do to you?"

"It doesn't matter." He stared at her as though he could force his will on her. "You do whatever he asks of you and you wait for the right time. Someone will find you and they'll come for you."

"Which is why we should kill them both and let me take over the project," Paul argued.

Green ignored him. "They won't come after either of you. I intend to give them something else to run after. I'll give them just enough of whatever I find to satisfy them. I have no intention of playing Hook. Yes, I know Tag calls you the Lost Boys. Hook was an idiot. By the time I'm done, we'll all be friends. They'll forget about you because you were never truly one of them."

"I assure you my team won't forget," Owen said.

Levi chuckled slightly as he started to approach Owen. "Your team? You know you're only a part of them because Knight didn't know what else to do with you, right? Your old partner, Nick Markovic, is the reason you didn't get kicked to the curb. The way I heard it, he fought to keep you with the team when Big Tag wanted to get rid of you."

She looked at Owen, her heart breaking because he was so strong and they were trying to bring him low. She'd been angry all day and she'd had a right to be, but somehow looking at him now, she couldn't work up the will to hate him. Maybe she'd never hated him. Raged at him. Been hurt by him. But under all of it there lay a deep and never-ending longing she'd never felt before.

"Doesn't matter," Owen said, forcing his head up to look at his enemy. "Doesn't matter what happens to me. They won't leave her behind. They'll come for her. You can kill me here and they'll still move heaven and earth to find her."

Green seemed to consider it for a moment. "Because they all want a cure? It doesn't seem like poor Tucker did. My source tells me he cries a lot when he thinks about who he used to be. That must have been something. That little ray of sunshine as a psycho. Makes me think of Mengele with a movie-star face. I don't know that he's going to fight for the doc here."

Now Owen shifted his focus. She knew the words he spoke were meant for Green, but his will was all directed at her. "He will. Tucker will come for her not because he wants a cure but because we're brothers and I love her. He'll save her because I would do the same for him. Because I would risk my life to save River and Ariel and Erin, even though she might not thank me for it. That's what I didn't understand before. We are a family no matter what, and we protect what each brother loves."

Levi stood in front of him and for a moment, Becca was terrified he would lash out. Then he sighed and stared down at Owen. "It must be nice to have a brother who cares about you, who acknowledges you. I suppose I'll have to be ready for it when they come for her then." He turned around, facing Becca again. "Now, Doctor Walsh, or should I call you Rebecca? After all, we're going to get close, you and I."

"I swear if you touch her, I'll kill you," Owen said.

"In a few hours you'll be on your way to Beijing. I don't think you'll do anything to me." Green dismissed him utterly. "Now we need to talk about where that package is because I might have something McDonald called the cure, but I'm going to need the rest of her research. I think you have it. If we're going to restart Project Tabula Rasa, I need the background materials."

Something tightened in Owen's eyes, like he was trying to tell her something. Like he was desperate for her to do something. Or not do something.

"I don't know where it is." She breathed a sigh of relief as that tightness eased. "We were talking about it when you decided to nearly murder us all."

"Again, apologies." Green gave her a courtly bow and offered her a hand up.

She stared at him like he was a snake ready to strike.

"Let him help you," Owen said. "He won't hurt you as long as you do what he wants. That's the deal we're making, Levi."

"You're not in any position to make a deal," Green replied. "But I'll take it because I was already planning on doing that. Dr. Walsh will find me a perfectly pleasant companion as long as she behaves. And as

315

long as she behaves, you'll be fine in my custody as well."

He would hurt Owen. Of course he would. He would use Owen to force her to comply. She put her hand in Green's and allowed him to help her up. She was unsteady on her feet for a moment.

This was really happening. She wasn't going to wake up and turn over in bed and tell Owen about the crazy dream she'd had. This was happening, and she was going to be taken and Owen was going to be taken.

"It's going to be okay, Rebecca," Owen said. "I want you to know that I love you. Survive. They'll come for you."

"You can believe that all you like." Green dropped her hand. "But I think after you realize what you can do, the difference you can make in the world, you won't want anyone to come for you. I'll take care of everything else and all you'll have to do is your research. Nothing will touch you. You can spend days and days in your lab, your every need met. You'll thank me one day, but I do need that package. It wasn't in your office or apartment. I need to know where you put it so we can begin again."

"You're not going to restart anything at all without me," Paul declared, his shoulders squaring.

He'd started all of this. There was one thing she was absolutely certain of. "I'm not working with him."

Paul's eyes narrowed. "I think I have some leverage here. I want her dead. I want you to kill her right now."

Levi Green turned. "You want her dead? Not a problem."

Becca's heart seized as Green pulled his gun.

* * * *

Owen tugged at the ties that held his hands. They'd bound his hands to the chair, pulling each behind him and zip-tying him to either side. They'd left his feet free, but his bloody feet weren't going to do him any good if Levi Green shot Becca.

Why? Why would he do that?

A heavy hand hit his shoulder and held him there. "Don't move."

Donnie Lennox stood over him. The CIA agent was a hulking mass of muscle, and Owen was trying to figure out how to take him out. He would have to if Green was going to hurt her.

Green flipped the gun around and offered it to Huisman.

"Becca, get behind me." That hand on his shoulder tightened, but Owen couldn't leave her out in the open like that. He couldn't watch her die. He'd been calm because he'd known Green wouldn't physically hurt her as long as she complied. He'd been willing to go with MSS calmly if it meant Becca lived and remained unhurt, but he would fight like hell now.

Nothing mattered. Nothing except her. She had to stay alive because his brothers would come for her. They wouldn't leave her behind, and Green was wrong about Big Tag. Big Tag might hate what he'd done, but MSS better get everything they wanted quickly because Big Tag wouldn't leave even a man he didn't like behind.

He did have a family. And he wasn't about to lose the newest member now.

Becca stood there, seemingly frozen in place.

"Get behind me." He would take that bullet first.

Becca looked to him, her eyes round with fear.

A hole opened inside him because he couldn't protect her. He couldn't fix this. She was about to die and he couldn't fix it.

"You want her dead?" Levi stalked to where Huisman stood, his skin having gone pale. "You do it. You want to work for me? Prove to me you can handle it."

Huisman reached out and took the gun with shaking hands.

A nasty smile spread across Levi's face. "Do it. All you have to do is pull the trigger and your enemy is dead. You're the man, right? You're better than she is. You deserve this. Think about it. You're her god right now. You decide if she lives or dies."

"Levi!" Owen shouted, his heart pounding in his chest. He could feel it. Pain ripped through him as he twisted his wrists, trying to get his hands free. "Don't do this."

Huisman shook his head. "I can't."

Becca took a visible breath of relief, her shoulders coming back down as she relaxed.

Levi nodded and took the gun back. "It's okay. The safety was on, Rebecca. I wasn't going to let him kill you, but I did want to see if he would try."

Levi stepped back and in one easy motion lifted the gun and fired one shot into Huisman's forehead.

A gasp went through the room as Huisman fell forward.

Becca rushed to Owen, avoiding Donnie's big hands as she threw herself into his lap and wrapped her arms around him.

"It's all right, love," he whispered.

"I'm sorry you had to see that, Rebecca," Levi was saying. "But he was going to be a problem, and I don't want anything to interrupt our work. This way the ties are neatly cut. Mo Chou didn't want to lose her position with his father anyway. Sometimes side deals are far more important than the main deal. You have nothing at all to fear from me. Nothing has changed." He glanced down at his watch. "Donnie, go and see what's taking Mo Chou so damn long. We need to move out. Rebecca's not going to give me any trouble."

Donnie nodded and strode to the hallway, stepping over the body.

Becca was shaking, her mouth against his ear. "These chairs are surprisingly delicate. If you can break it, would your hands come free?"

Shit. She was likely terrified, but she wasn't letting it hold her back. "You stay safe. You let me go, love."

She took a deep breath and slid off his lap, standing in front of Levi Green. "I'll do what you ask if you'll take Owen with us. I don't even understand why they want..." It seemed to hit her suddenly. "They want to experiment on him. They want to see if they can figure out what she did to erase his memory."

"Yes, I believe that's what they'll try to do," Levi replied evenly.

"But the only way they can do that is to study his brain," she replied.

A single brow rose over Levi's eyes. "Yes. Did I misjudge the situation? I thought once you figured out how he used you, you wouldn't be so emotional about him. He set you up every bit as much as Huisman did and I don't see you crying over him."

He had in so many ways. He didn't blame her if she saw it that way.

"I'll go quietly and I'll do all the work you want me to do if you let me keep Owen," she offered.

Relief flooded his system because she didn't hate him. There had to be something still between them if she was willing to fight to keep him alive. It wouldn't work. She was going to get herself in trouble. How long would Donnie be gone? MSS would be here soon and she would be on her way to god only knew where.

She'd said the chair was delicate. If he could get his hands free…

He needed enough force to break the chair and then enough time to get on his feet or he'd be the one taking the bullet this time.

Donnie strode in, turning under the balcony. "We should move out now. I can't find her, but there's a strange car in the driveway. I didn't get close enough to check it out, but I know it wasn't here before."

Levi frowned. "She's got to be here. It's a big house. It's probably her contact."

"Doesn't feel right," Donnie said.

Levi nodded, making his decision in seconds. "Then we move. I'll take Rebecca out to the car. You prepare our friend for transfer. Looks like you get your wish, Doc."

Oh, he was lying. Donnie's shoulders had gone tight and he'd nodded, his face cold as ice. They couldn't risk taking him along. He was trained. He was a variable Levi wouldn't want to deal with.

But he would want Becca compliant, and that meant not killing him until they were out of earshot.

Of course, he could always create a little chaos and see where things fell. He didn't have a thing to lose.

"You'll bring him with us?" Becca asked.

"He'll come along behind us. I'll have my team pick him up," Levi lied smoothly. "We'll talk about it on the plane."

She looked over at him and he could see the uncertainty there.

He gave her what he hoped was an encouraging smile. "I love you, Becca. Stay safe."

He would have said more but there was the crack of a gun going off and then blood bloomed across Donnie's chest. It took him a second to realize what had happened.

A sniper. There was a sniper inside the house. On the balcony above them.

"Stand down, Levi. Send Dr. Walsh and Owen out right now or I take you out, too."

That had not been the voice he'd expected to hear. For a mere second he'd thought somehow Ezra had found his way here. Or Dante and Sasha and Tucker. But they were radio silent for hours yet. Only two people knew they'd been taken.

That commanding voice had a crisp English accent and an unmistakably feminine tone.

Ariel was pissed.

Levi had Becca in his grasp, his gun lodged firmly in her side. "Dr. Adisa, I didn't think you had it in you. And you would have taken the shot if you had it. I salute you. You're willing to do what the boys aren't. You play hardball, sister. How about we make a deal? I leave Owen for you and you let me head out of here with Rebecca?"

Levi had shrunk back against the wall. He'd moved them under the balcony where Ari would have no shot. Levi looked to the hallway under the balcony as though trying to decide if it was a path that wouldn't get him killed.

Owen took the opportunity to stand up. It was awkward and he felt ungainly, but if there was even half a chance, he had to take it.

"After what you did to Robert, I think I'll pass," Ari yelled. "And we're done playing your games, Levi."

Levi's eyes turned to Owen. "Well, then I guess I can do what I like."

He was out of time. Levi raised the gun his way, and that was the moment Becca made her move. Her elbow came up and back. Owen threw his body to the ground, holding his head up. He felt heat graze his shoulder and then pain flared as he hit the ground and the chair came apart. Owen spread his arms and they came loose. He was still bound to the arms of the chair, but a few painful tugs and he was free. He rolled toward Donnie Lennox's body. He needed that gun.

Becca struggled as Levi fired again, throwing his aim off.

Owen cursed those bloody zip ties but managed to get that gun in his hand.

He forced his body to move and brought the gun straight up, and he found himself staring right at Becca.

"Your move, Owen," Levi said, his voice showing no sign of tremor. "I've got this to the back of her head. You might be able to make the shot, or you might hit that big gorgeous brain of hers."

Levi wasn't much taller than Becca. He was right. Taking the shot would be risky, and he wasn't as steady as he should be.

"Becca, do not move," he commanded. "Don't hurt her."

"We're at a standoff, you and I," Levi said. "I'm going to back out. I don't trust that Ariel is still in that perch of hers, so I need to get out of here now or she'll come in behind me. We can do this the nice way or I can go down in a blaze of glory. It's your choice."

There was no choice at all. "Just let her go." He struggled to get to his feet. "I'll take her place. I'll go with you and we can work something out."

He wouldn't. He would kill the fucker the first chance he got, but he would lie through his teeth if it meant Becca was standing at the end of this. And Levi was right. Ari was out there. Ari was coming down those stairs, and not for a therapy session.

"I think I'll skip the hostage-taking portion of the day, but I need a head start. Sorry about this." Levi pulled the trigger and Becca screamed.

Owen's shoulder lit up like it was on fire, but he stayed on his feet. Levi shoved Becca his way and she stumbled into him. He looked her over.

She shook her head. "I'm fine. Go. Get that asshole."

It was all he needed. Despite the fact that his left arm didn't seem to work anymore, he took off after Levi Green.

He caught a glimpse of the man running down the hall before he turned and disappeared. Owen slowed, not wanting to get caught in a trap. He eased around and saw the door closing.

He raced to the end of the hall and flung it open just in time to see Levi Green hit the street. Levi had dropped his weapon and he started down the street, seeming to revel in how many people were walking along the front of the house.

"Damn it," Ariel said, running up behind him. "You can't shoot him here and he knows it. Bastard."

Levi turned and tipped his head as though to say they were welcome to try again another day.

"We have to move out. He'll call the police in again." Owen forced himself to shut the door. "We have to call them in ourselves. Apparently there's a kid in this place somewhere."

"The police are going to have a field day with this one." Ariel held a semiautomatic in her hands, the same one he'd seen Robert pack during their flight from the cabin.

"Owen?" Becca walked in, her face pale. "Owen, are you okay?"

He was now. He strode to her, and despite the pain in his shoulder, he wrapped his arms around her. "I'm fine, but we have to move out and quickly."

"I'm parked behind the house. Rob is waiting for us. Well, he's passed out in the back, but he'll live. A couple of university students were renting a cabin not far from the accident site. They got us to hospital. After they patched Rob up, I hotwired a car and we left before we could be questioned."

"How did you find us?" He refused to let Becca go, taking her hand in his and following after Ariel.

"It was a hunch. Becca had said Levi must be working with Huisman. He couldn't take you to a hotel. Rob told me MSS was coming. They wouldn't make a move until they knew they had you, so that bought us some time. It was a good bet he would bring you here." Ariel moved to the rear of the house. "I parked in the back and snuck up."

"You're hurt." Becca hustled to keep up.

There was blood on his shirt. A lot of it. "I think the bullet's still in there."

"It's not a fatal wound. We'll deal with it after we get away." Ariel held open the door to what looked to be the garage. "Don't mind the body. I had to deal with the MSS agent."

Owen gaped at the woman on the ground. That was a lot of blood. It looked like Ari knew how to use a knife, too. He stared at her, wondering where his peace-loving shrink had gone.

Ari merely shrugged. "I wasn't always a therapist."

He took Becca's hand and walked out of the house to join his friend. He was in excruciating pain, but they had one more stop to make.

Ariel rushed to the car, a minivan. It was still running in the long drive that led back around the house and out to the street where Levi Green was likely trying to get the upper hand back by bringing in the police. "Take Owen to the back of the van with Robert and do what you can for them. I'll get us out of here."

She could hear the wail of sirens on their way. Her heart ached for Paul's son, but they had to go.

Becca opened the door and stepped inside. Owen followed as Ariel took off.

Sure enough, Robert was laid out on the bench seat. His eyes opened briefly. "Sorry, man. They wouldn't pull out the bullet without anesthesia. How did we get you back?"

"Ari is lethal, mate. You need to watch yourself with her." He sat back with a groan of pain. "And she's a terrible driver."

"Hush." Becca wasn't in her seat. She knelt down. "I'm going to have to pull the bullet out of you when we get somewhere safe. Try not to move it."

"Ariel saved you?" Robert still sounded out of it.

Ariel was a superhero. "Yep, and she took out the bad guys while she was doing it. She's a keeper, mate."

Robert's smile was slightly goofy. "I bet she's hot when she's assassinating people. Holy shit. Baby, tell me you murdered Levi Green. We could celebrate by having our first date. You want to go out with me, right?"

"It has to wait," Ari said. "Green's alive, and we have to get out of here. We're going back to London to lick our wounds."

Robert sighed. "That's not what I want to lick."

Before he could laugh, Becca was kneeling next to him. "Owen, are you all right? You went pale."

The world was going pale. Ariel took a corner and his shoulder hit the door. Pain exploded through his system and he felt himself falling down a deep hole.

He tried to hold on to her, sure that he would lose her this time.

Chapter Twenty-One

"**A**re you sure this is safe?" Owen asked, staring up at the building where he'd briefly found something akin to peace. Oh, it hadn't always been peaceful. Sometimes it had been crazy and emotional and chaotic and absolutely the best time of his brief life.

"I want to face him." Becca sat in the back of the van that would eventually take them to the small airport where he would board a plane to London.

He would board. There was no reason for her to go now. In the three days since he'd passed out from the bullet wound in his shoulder, McKay-Taggart had worked miracles. Phoebe Murdoch had managed to find the proof that was needed to exonerate Rebecca Walsh, and the Huisman Foundation was standing behind her. The story was Paul Huisman had been involved in a plot to help a Chinese agent steal medical research. Jean Claude Huisman had come out in the press vowing to better protect the foundation and denouncing his son, not bothering to mention that he'd been the one having the affair with an MSS agent. Owen rather thought the Agency was working some magic since in all the reports on the news, no one had mentioned the dead CIA employee or the MSS agent's corpse in the garage. According to the media, Paul Huisman had likely been murdered by one of his criminal cohorts.

"Are we worried this guy is dangerous?" Ezra sat in the driver's seat, Theo Taggart beside him.

Becca snorted. "Only if you're something that got mailed to me. The asshole picked up my mail from time to time. It's one of the reasons he had a key. Apparently he liked to look through it. Jerk."

Ezra sighed and put the car in park. "I'm sorry we didn't send someone out earlier, but until yesterday I worried it was too risky. According to my source at the Agency, they're backing off for now. It's why we can take the team back to London for a while."

Where they would have to figure out who the mole was. It was all too clear now that they had a traitor in their midst. Levi Green had been fucking with his head, yes, but he'd also been telling the truth. He had someone on the inside, and they would have to deal with it. One way or another.

And he would have to deal with the fact that she was going to stay here. There was no reason for her to leave her home now. She was high profile after all the press, and that would give her some cover. A bodyguard would keep her safe. It was all about who she wanted to watch over her.

It wouldn't be him.

"We're sure he has it?" Theo asked, turning slightly in his seat. His wife had gone home the day before, but not until she'd stopped by the small clinic that had been willing to give Owen and Robert a place to recuperate. Becca had stabilized him in the field, but they'd been separated when they'd driven hours out of Toronto and found a tiny backwater clinic that was willing to take a large donation in exchange for losing all record of their two patients suffering from gunshot wounds.

"Oh, I'm sure," Becca replied. "He's waiting to use it against me. I'm surprised he hasn't gone to the press with it."

"I think he's waiting until he can talk to you," Ezra said. "He's probably planning on using it as leverage. He's been leaving voice mails."

"Someone has my phone?" Becca asked.

"We tossed it out, but that doesn't mean Jax can't get into your account and see who's calling. Carter has been trying to talk to you for days," Ezra explained.

"That asshole is going to try to blackmail me," she said.

"He won't after I'm done with him." Owen wasn't giving up. He couldn't. This would be the first time he'd been alone with her since that day at Huisman's. He'd woken up laid out in a bed next to Robert's, and they'd proceeded to spend the next two days complaining about the food and missing their women. At least Ari had come to see Rob. They'd talked about having their first date.

It had made Owen cranky.

"Let's get this over with if you're going to do it." Ezra unlocked the doors. "Theo and I will stay out here in case we need a quick getaway, but remember we just managed to get off the police's radar. Try not to kill him."

"I'll try, but it's going to be hard." Becca got out of the van.

"I think he was talking to me." Owen followed her.

"Well, I'm the one who's pissed. That weasel." She strode into the building. "As for you, don't fight with him. You'll tear your stitches and then you'll be late for the plane." She stopped and looked around. "Wow, it's weird to be back here. I know it's only been a few days, but it seems like a lifetime."

"Becca, I want to talk. I can't leave for London without us talking." He wasn't sure he could leave for London at all.

"There will be plenty of time for that later." She sniffled a little and turned back to the hallway, moving to the lift. She passed the modern one, toward the one she'd sworn she would never use again. "I'm sure we'll need to talk about a lot of things. How long will you be in London?"

He hated this polite talk when all he wanted to do was to force her to look him in the eye. "I don't know that I'll be going to London at all."

The lift door opened and she walked inside. "You're going on the new mission? I heard Ezra talking about exploring what happened at Kronberg with Tucker. I'm going to put him in touch with a woman who worked there. I should have known you would go with your brothers."

How was he supposed to answer that? He would go if he had to. He owed those men. But he wanted to be with her. "I missed you. I wanted to see you the last couple of days."

That seemed to fluster her. "I wasn't avoiding you. There was a lot of stuff that had to be done. I made sure you were stable. The doctors at the clinic seemed knowledgeable. You weren't in any danger and neither was Robert."

How kind of her. "The doctors at the clinic were bribable."

The door opened and she strode out. She didn't seem to care that they'd been in the very lift where they'd first made love. Oh, she might have been having a good time, but now he knew that he'd been making love.

"Well, they wouldn't let me take you to a regular hospital." She stopped in the middle of the hallway. "Shouldn't we talk about how we're going to handle this thing? Am I going to distract him while you search for the package? Maybe you should distract him and I'll look for it."

Anger and frustration thrummed through his system, and he wanted to get this over with so they could have the fight they'd needed to have since the moment he'd screwed up. He'd been an arsehole, but he loved her. He'd told her he loved her. Now she thought she could pretend it never happened?

"Let me show you how this is going to go." He turned and strode down the hall toward the apartment Carter Adams occupied. He could feel Becca behind him, racing to keep up.

"Remember what I said about your stitches," she was saying.

He didn't give a damn about his stitches. All that mattered was getting rid of the last piece of this mission that existed between them. When he had that damn package in his hands, they could be done with all the stupid things that had come between them and maybe he could finally gain her forgiveness.

He slammed his fist against the door.

"Owen, maybe we should talk," she said, more tentative than she'd sounded before.

Before he could reply, the door opened and he was staring at Carter, who glared at him before turning his attention to Becca.

"Ah, Dr. Walsh," he said with a frown. "I knew you would be here after your brush with the law. You'll have to tell me how you managed to get out of that. You didn't have to bring your meathead boyfriend with you. I think we should discuss this situation alone, don't you?"

That was not happening. He needed to make a few things plain. If Carter thought he was some kind of a thug, he could play that role. He pulled back his right hand and smashed it into the fucker's face.

Carter's head snapped back and he heard Becca gasp.

"Owen, someone could call the police," she said.

He was sick of that argument. "Who? Carter's not going to be able to in a few moments, and the rest of the bloody floor is currently preparing to flee the country." He followed Carter inside and was satisfied when Becca closed the door behind them.

Carter was on the ground, desperately backing away while trying to ensure his nose stayed on his face. He looked like a three-legged crab, except far less coordinated. "Get out."

Not until he had what he'd come for. "Where is it?"

Becca seemed to have found something that interested her on his bar. "This is my mail. And my hair clips. Why do you have my hair clips?"

Owen could answer that one. "He's a pathetic pervert who can't understand why no one wants to sleep with him. But it's all right. I'm going to make it easy for him. I'm going to cut that prick right off you, Carter. Then you won't have to worry about it again."

Carter's eyes went wide. "It's in my desk. It's a letter that asks Becca to keep this for her. For old times' sake. It's a thumb drive. It's got a bunch of medical research and files on it. Tabula Rasa. I think it's illegal. She was testing on humans, and I think she was doing it against their will. Becca was involved. She was in on it."

"She had no idea and if you decide to tell anyone, the next time you see me will be right before I slit your throat," Owen promised. "Do I make myself clear? If you have other copies, tell me now because I won't take it kindly."

He shook his head. "None. That's the only one. I bribed the postal worker to let me take them to her. I looked through her mail so I would know her better. I was trying to find things we had in common."

"You have nothing in common." Owen found the desk and opened the top drawer. There was a box with Becca's name on it. It was posted from Malaysia. Dr. McDonald had reportedly held several of the men, including Tucker, there. Owen picked it up and made sure the thumb drive was there. The desk had nothing else of interest in it, though the man needed to lay off the mints. "If you come anywhere near her again, I'll kill you. If you talk about her, I'll kill you. Do you know what I'll do if I even find out you whisper her name again?"

"You'll kill me?" The question came out on a squeak.

"It's good that we understand each other." He turned to the door. "Let's go."

He was done here. It was time to deal with the real problem.

"I would take back my hair clips, but I don't know what you've done to them," Becca said. "And while I took a vow to do no harm, that doesn't mean I can't let him do you harm. Asshole."

Owen stalked down the hall to the lift. It was a fitting place to have this particular conversation.

"I can't believe he did that to me. I can't believe I didn't realize he was such a pervert. Cathy told me she didn't like him, but I was trying to be tolerant," she said as she hustled into the lift.

She hit the button for one and the doors closed, but he knew how to handle the lift.

He pressed the emergency stop button and turned on her, holding the package out. "This is yours."

She took it but stared at it like she wasn't sure what to do. "Ezra wants it."

"Then give it to him if you like, but if you don't then you keep it. You do what you need to with it whether or not that means giving it to my team. I'll fight to make sure it's your right." That was out of the way and he could get to his point. "If you think I'm letting you go without a fight, you don't know me at all. Maybe I don't know myself, but I do know this, I'm not quitting. I love you and I'm not going to stop saying it."

She frowned up at him. "I know you think you do, but I'm not going to hold you to it. It's guilt. I turned out to not be the crazy person you thought I might be, so now you feel bad about using me."

Was she daft? "I love you. I've never said that to anyone before."

"That you can remember."

"Don't you hold that against me. I know what love feels like. And I never thought you were crazy. I had a moment of weakness. Please don't let that ruin us."

"Ruin us?" She crossed her arms over her chest. She was in a deep red cardigan today that let him know she'd done some shopping while he'd been waiting for her. "What are you talking about? Owen, I think we should wait to talk about this."

"Wait? You think if you put me off this will go away?"

She leaned back against the lift wall. A soft smile curled up her lips. "Where would it go? Owen, I think your brothers are mean. Did they tell you I quit Huisman?"

No. No one had told him shite. When he'd asked, they'd all simply said he should talk to her. This was his first chance to do it. "Why would you quit?"

"Because I have a new job and it pays horribly and my lab apparently is going to consist of a couple of rooms in this club thing," she said. "I didn't stay away from you because I don't care. When Phoebe managed to get the charges dropped, I flew home for a day and a half to talk to my dad. I needed to explain things to him, and he agreed that I have to do this. I have to fix this. I'm going to London to work on reversing Dr. McDonald's work. I'm going to get Robert's memory back. And yours. But you might not want me when you remember. That's what I've been thinking about for days. Memory is a funny thing. It's a part of our personalities. It's the sum of the forces that shape us. You could wake up one morning and not want me anymore."

Not want her? "Never. I'll never not want you. I don't care what memories come back to me, you'll be the first thing I think of every morning and the only woman in my dreams at night. Becca, I love you. I think I've loved you from the moment I saw you. Oh, my love, if I get my memories back, the old ones can't erase the new ones. They can't erase what I feel for you."

"And I love you, but we have a lot to work out. Ariel thinks we should go into couples therapy. That's what I meant by having time, but if you're going on the new mission…"

He wasn't wasting another second. He'd almost lost her, almost lost everything. He moved into her space, shoving her back against the lift wall. "Ariel needs to stick to assassinations. She's damn good at them and I don't find it annoying. As for you, I'm never leaving you, love. If you're in London, that's my home. I might have to travel occasionally, and I definitely have to help my brothers, but you should know that I'll always come home to you."

Her hands came up and he could see the vulnerability stamped on her face. "Tell me this is real, Owen. I would rather we took a step back and worked through all of this if there's the slightest chance that you're going to wake up and realize that you don't love me."

He put his forehead on hers, rubbing against her and feeling better than he had in days. "Never. You're my everything, Rebecca. I'll go to any therapy you want to go to, but you should know it won't change how much I love you."

"I love you, too." Her face lifted to his. "I love you so much. It's killed me to be away from you, but I had to get everything ready. I had to be sure."

He kissed away whatever she was going to say next. He kissed her and felt as though the world opened up again.

This was what he'd been waiting for all his life. He didn't need his memories to know that.

His mum would have loved Becca. He simply knew that, too. His mum would be thrilled he'd found the love of his life.

"Will you come back to Scotland with me?" He whispered the question.

She nodded. "I'll go anywhere with you."

It wouldn't be that way, but he appreciated the words. She was the brilliant one. He would follow her. He would be the man who protected her so she could work. He would be the man who reminded her that she was loved for more than her brain. He would watch over her and give her everything she needed. It was his job in life.

And she would lift him up. She would make him whole.

"I want to go back with you. I think I might find something of them there if you're by my side. I might feel some connection."

Her whole face lit with an empathy that seemed to come so easily to her. "I want to try a couple of things with you. You're having flashes. I think we might be able to get some of your memory back. I want to try. I want to give them back to you."

She'd given him so much already. "All I need is you."

The sound of the phone ringing jarred him from his intent.

Becca's smile rocked his whole world. "You should probably answer that."

He didn't want to. He wanted to shove her right back against that wall and have his way with her.

The ringing continued. With a curse, he picked it up. "What?"

"Eh, someone's telling me the elevator's stopped again." Colin was back on the job. "Sorry, I'll get right on that. I mean not right on it because I'm walking my dog at the moment, but I'm sure he'll be done soon. Then I'll be right there."

331

He hung up the phone without saying another word. He turned back to his lady, lowered his head, and got back to business.

* * * *

Forty-eight hours later Robert McClellan sat in the conference room at The Garden and stared down at the report he'd been handed. It hadn't taken Jax long to break the encryption they'd found on the thumb drive Owen had taken from Carter Adams. Though it would take them a while to get through all the files and completely understand it. What they did know was that McDonald had sent Becca a large amount of data, and most importantly in Robert's mind, she'd sent their personal records. Though those were proving difficult.

"There's nothing about history in these records?" Damon glanced up from his seat at the head of the table. "And she doesn't actually name the subject? Is this some kind of code?"

Damon's wife, Penny, sat next to Ariel and set down her tea mug before addressing the crowded conference room where the whole team was gathered. "I've looked through it and there's no real code. I think this was her cheeky way of recording her experiments. She used Latin to name the project and Latin to describe each subject. We've figured out a few of them based on timing and medical records. We believe Theo Taggart's file is the one named *Interim Militem*."

"It's Latin for the perfect soldier," Becca explained. Her hair was up in a high ponytail and despite what he knew were long nights and little sleep, she looked bright and shiny in the way only a well-loved woman could look. "I'm fairly certain Robert's file is the one marked *Ex Novo*. That means built from nothing. I'm not sure why she named your file that, but you have a rare blood type and this file is the only one that matches."

"You can match us by blood type?" Dante asked, leaning in.

"Not always," she replied. "There are over seventy files in here. It's going to take some time to match them up. I'm afraid I think most of these test subjects are no longer with us."

Because they were dead. McDonald had been a monster and they had a lot of cleanup to do.

Starting with a new mission.

But first he was going to get through this very thorough debrief, and then he was finally going to do what he'd wanted to do since the moment he'd set foot in this place. He was going to take Ariel Adisa out on a date. Sure he would have to do it in a foreign city because they were hopping on another plane in a few hours, but that would make it all the more special.

Becca went on about the files, but Robert had more pleasant things to think of.

Ari. Gorgeous, smart, surprisingly mean Ari. He would never forget how she'd fought to get him the help he'd needed after that massive ass had shot him. Ari hadn't faltered. Not once. He'd pulled away from her initially because she'd been worried about their patient-therapist relationship. But he knew what he wanted, and he'd never wanted anything more than Ariel. Not even his freedom.

He'd separated himself from her professionally. Ari served as the therapist for the rest of the group, but Robert was seeing Kai Ferguson. He did it via phone calls and over the Internet, but it worked and it meant he was free to pursue the woman of his dreams.

Her eyes caught on his and they warmed, her sensual lips curling up. God, he loved it when she wore white. It made a stark contrast against her gorgeous skin. Her dark eyes practically ate him up.

He was going to get his hands on her tonight.

This was the right time. This was their time.

"Robert, are we boring you?" Damon's icy tone cut through his inner thoughts.

Ari grinned his way as though she'd known exactly what he was thinking. "He asked a question three times."

Yep, he was in trouble. "Sorry, boss. My mind was elsewhere."

Damon sighed. "Yes, that seems to be a problem these days. I asked if everything was set for the flight this afternoon?"

Everything was good to go including reservations at a very nice restaurant that Damon didn't need to know about. "The jet is ready. Tucker's finishing up his prep, which is why he isn't here. Everyone's got new passports and we've got the go from the McKay-Taggart team. They say Green is in DC and he seems to be hunkering down after the defeat we handed him."

"Or he's found someone new to work on this cure he claims to have," Owen said.

"Do we believe him?" Ariel sat back. "He's been known to lie."

"I'm looking through the material we found," Becca replied. "But there's a lot of it. Walter, Steph, and I are going through it down in the lab. Faith Smith is coming in next week and she's going to help us. So far I've seen nothing that makes me think she'd worked on a cure, but I've still got hundreds of files to go through."

Walt, Becca, and Brody's wife, Stephanie, had taken over the lab. It was now filled with white boards and computer equipment, and apparently they were getting some high-tech medical stuff that the docs would be playing with.

All so they could potentially get their memories back.

He wasn't sure he wanted to know, but he intended to cooperate. After all, he meant to help his brothers.

Except one of his brothers was a traitor.

"All right then." Damon nodded his way. "Let's break and we'll meet tomorrow morning for a regular weekly. Robert, could you stay behind? Ariel, we might need you."

Ariel's eyes flared briefly, and he knew she was surprised. But he wasn't. Tucker's mission to explore some of his past was one they'd all argued over. Going back to Kronberg was dangerous, but Tucker was insistent. He needed to know. Robert was likely going to have to advocate for his brother again.

"Get ready, Rob," Owen said, his hand tangled in Becca's as they moved to the door. "I promise I won't crash the plane. I can't promise I won't lose Tucker. You'll need to keep eyes on him. The boy needs a leash. He follows every shiny object he sees, and by object, I mean women."

Becca laughed and shook her head as she followed her boyfriend out of the conference room.

Boyfriend? Not for long. Owen was already talking about rings. He would be attending another wedding soon.

And then maybe he could start thinking about his own because Ari was the one. The only one for him. And he'd known Ari far longer than Owen had known Becca. Sure, they'd had their ups and downs, but starting tonight, they were going to be a couple, and it would be smooth sailing from here on out.

The conference room emptied and he was left with Damon, Penny, and Ari.

"Tucker is going to be fine. We won't let him do anything crazy."

Another thought hit him. "You can't possibly be worried about Owen. Or is it Tucker you're worried about?"

They had a mole. No one was talking about it, but Robert was sure Damon was working with the Dallas team to figure it out. He hated the thought that one of them wasn't what he seemed.

Or maybe there was another explanation. As Ari had pointed out, Levi Green lied. A lot.

"I'm not worried about Owen. Of all of you, Owen is the one I'm certain didn't have ties to Green or McDonald beforehand," Damon replied, his expression grim. "I've known Owen for years. Despite what happened with his mum and sister, I trust him implicitly. It's why he's still on my team. Big Tag and I are going to work with Ezra to try to figure out what's going on, but I'm worried about Tucker for different reasons."

Ari moved to his side. "I've given you my assessment, Damon."

Penny shook her head, blonde curls shaking. "No, it's not about who betrayed the team. We're worried Tucker could be volatile when it comes to his past."

Damon put a hand on his wife's shoulder. "He's not rational about this. He needs someone who can take charge in the field and make the call to pull him out if needs be."

That was what this was about? "Of course. I'll handle it all. You don't have to worry."

Damon frowned and sighed as though he didn't like what he was about to say. "Ariel, you're in charge of this operation. Do you understand me? Robert can have the final say when it comes to logistics, but on whether or not the op continues or gets shut down, that stops with you."

Embarrassment flashed though his system, but he tamped it down. Damon was worried about Tucker's state of mind. Ari was the shrink. Of course she should make the call in case Tucker was in mental trouble.

Not that it would ever come to that.

"Yes, sir," Ari said, but her eyes had trailed Robert's way.

He gave her a reassuring grin. "You're the boss."

And he firmly planned on getting it on with his boss.

"Excellent," Damon said. "Carry on then. Let me know when you land."

He took Ari's hand, not bothering to hide it from the Knights. Everything was going to be okay.

In a few hours they would be in Munich and his life would truly begin.

* * * *

Robert, Ariel, and the whole McKay-Taggart team will return in *Lost in You*, now available.

Author's Note

I'm often asked by generous readers how they can help get the word out about a book they enjoyed. There are so many ways to help an author you like. Leave a review. If your e-reader allows you to lend a book to a friend, please share it. Go to Goodreads and connect with others. Recommend the books you love because stories are meant to be shared. Thank you so much for reading this book and for supporting all the authors you love!

Lost in You

Masters and Mercenaries: The Forgotten, Book 3
By Lexi Blake
Now available.

Robert McClellan was forced to serve as a soldier in a war he didn't understand. Liberated by McKay-Taggart, he struggles every day to reclaim the life he lost and do right by the men he calls his brothers, The Lost Boys. Only one thing is more important – Ariel Adisa. The gorgeous psychologist has plagued his dreams since the day they met. Even as their mission pushes him to his limits, he can't stop thinking about taking his shot at finding a life beyond all this with her.

Ariel Adisa is a force to be reckoned with. Her performance in Toronto proved she's more than just a brilliant mind, but Robert still acts as if she is a wilting flower who needs his protection. Joining him on the mission to Munich should be the perfect opportunity to test their skills and cement their relationship. She and Robert are an excellent match. But when a stunning secret from Robert's past is revealed, their world is turned upside down and nothing will ever be the same again.

While they chase dark secrets across Europe, Robert and Ariel realize that the only thing worse than not knowing who you are could be discovering who you used to be...

Enchanted

A Masters and Mercenaries Novella
By Lexi Blake
Now available.

A snarky submissive princess

Sarah Steven's life is pretty sweet. By day, she's a dedicated trauma nurse and by night, a fun-loving club sub. She adores her job, has a group of friends who have her back, and is a member of the hottest club in Dallas. So why does it all feel hollow? Could it be because she fell for her dream man and can't forgive him for walking away from her? Nope. She's not going there again. No matter how much she wants to.

A prince of the silver screen

Jared Johns might be one of the most popular actors in Hollywood, but he lost more than a fan when he walked away from Sarah. He lost the only woman he's ever loved. He's been trying to get her back, but she won't return his calls. A trip to Dallas to visit his brother might be exactly what he needs to jump-start his quest to claim the woman who holds his heart.

A masquerade to remember

For Charlotte Taggart's birthday, Sanctum becomes a fantasyland of kinky fun and games. Every unattached sub gets a new Dom for the festivities. The twist? The Doms must conceal their identities until the stroke of midnight at the end of the party. It's exactly what Sarah needs to forget the fact that Jared is pursuing her. She can't give in to him, and the mysterious Master D is making her rethink her position when it comes to signing a contract. Jared knows he was born to play this role, dashing suitor by day and dirty Dom at night.

When the masks come off, will she be able to forgive the man who loves her, or will she leave him forever?

Discover Lexi Blake writing as Sophie Oak

Texas Sirens

Every girl dreams of her alpha cowboy, the one who sweeps her off her feet. In Texas Sirens, every girl gets two.

Set in both small Texas towns and cosmopolitan cities, Texas Sirens features beautifully broken heroes and heroines who discover that unconventional love is their best chance at happily ever after.

Small Town Siren
Siren in the City
Siren Enslaved
Siren Beloved
Siren in Waiting
Siren in Bloom
Siren Unleashed
Siren Reborn

* * * *

Nights in Bliss

Bliss, Colorado, is home to nudists, squatchers, alien hunters, a bunch of ex-military men, and a surprising number of women on the run. Bliss is a place where cowboys hang out with vegan protestors, quirky is normal, and love is perfectly unconventional. So grab a chair and settle in. If you can forgive the oddly high per capita murder rate—and the occasional alien sighting—you'll find that life is better in Bliss.

Each Bliss story is a standalone, though found family is important so expect the characters to stick around, playing a part in each novel.
Three to Ride
Two to Love
One to Keep

Lost in Bliss
Found in Bliss
Pure Bliss
Chasing Bliss
Once Upon a Time in Bliss
Back in Bliss
Sirens in Bliss
Happily Ever After in Bliss

About Lexi Blake

Lexi Blake lives in North Texas with her husband, three kids, and the laziest rescue dog in the world. She began writing at a young age, concentrating on plays and journalism. It wasn't until she started writing romance that she found success. She likes to find humor in the strangest places. Lexi believes in happy endings no matter how odd the couple, threesome or foursome may seem. She also writes contemporary Western ménage as Sophie Oak.

Connect with Lexi online:

Facebook: Lexi Blake
Twitter: authorlexiblake
Website: www.LexiBlake.net

Sign up for Lexi's free newsletter.

Printed in the USA
CPSIA information can be obtained
at www.ICGtesting.com
LVHW041319170923
758435LV00001B/139